ALL MY RAGE

ALSO BY SABAA TAHIR

AN EMBER IN THE ASHES QUARTET

An Ember in the Ashes

A Torch Against the Night

A Reaper at the Gates

A Sky Beyond the Storm

ALL MY RAGE

RAGE

SABAA TAHIR

RAZORBILL

RAZORBILL

An imprint of Penguin Random House LLC, New York

First published in the United States of America by Razorbill,
an imprint of Penguin Random House LLC, 2022

Copyright © 2022 by Sabaa Tahir

Visit us online at penguinrandomhouse.com.

LIBRARY OF CONGRESS CATALOGING-IN-PUBLICATION DATA
Names: Tahir, Sabaa, author.
Title: All my rage / Sabaa Tahir.
Description: New York : Razorbill, 2022. | Audience: Ages 14 and up.
Summary: A family extending from Pakistan to California,
deals with generations of young love, old regrets, and forgiveness.
Identifiers: LCCN 2021049700 | ISBN 9780593202340 (hardcover)
ISBN 9780593202364 (trade paperback) | ISBN 9780593202357 (ebook)
Subjects: CYAC: Pakistani Americans—Fiction. | Family life—Fiction.
Immigrants—Fiction. | Forgiveness—Fiction. | LCGFT: Novels.
Classification: LCC PZ7.1.T33 Al 2022 | DDC [Fic]—dc23
LC record available at https://lccn.loc.gov/2021049700

ISBN 9780593202340 (HARDCOVER)
1 3 5 7 9 10 8 6 4 2

ISBN 9780593524176 (INTERNATIONAL EDITION)
1 3 5 7 9 10 8 6 4 2

Book manufactured in Canada

FRI

Design by Rebecca Aidlin
Text set in Dante MT Pro

For those who survive.
For those who do not.

Dear Reader,

Please be aware that *All My Rage* contains content that may be triggering. For a list of content, please see the bottom of the next page.

PART I

The art of losing isn't hard to master;
so many things seem filled with the intent
to be lost that their loss is no disaster.

    —*Elizabeth Bishop,*
     "One Art"

CHAPTER 1

Misbah

June, then

LAHORE, PAKISTAN

The clouds over Lahore were purple as a gossip's tongue the day my mother told me I would wed.

After she delivered the news, I found my father on the veranda. He sipped a cup of tea and surveyed the storm looming above the kite-spattered skyline.

Change her mind! *I wanted to scream.* Tell her I'm not ready.

Instead, I stood at his side, a child again, waiting for him to take care of me. I did not have to speak. My father looked at me, and he knew.

"Come now, little butterfly." He turned his moth-brown eyes to mine and patted my shoulder. "You are strong like me. You will make the best of it. And at last, you'll be free of your mother." He smiled, only half joking.

The monsoon rain swept over Lahore a few minutes later, sending chickens and children squawking for cover, drenching the cement floor of our home. I bent my head to the ground in prayer regardless.

Let my future husband be gentle, *I thought, remembering the bruises on my cousin Amna, who married a light-haired English business-man against her parents' wishes.* Let him be a good man.

I was eighteen. Full of fear. I should have prayed instead for a man unbroken.

CHAPTER 2

Sal

It's 6:37 a.m. and my father doesn't want me to know how drunk he is.

"Sal? Are you listening?"

He calls me Sal instead of Salahudin so I don't hear the slur in his words. Hangs on to our Civic's steering wheel like it's going to steal his wallet and bolt.

In the ink-black morning, all I see of Abu's eyes are his glasses. The taillights of traffic going into school reflect off the thick square lenses. He's had them so long that they're hipster now. A Mojave Desert howler shakes the car—one of those three-day winds that rampage through your skin and colonize your ventricles. I hunch deep in my fleece, breath clouding.

"I will be there," Abu says. "Don't worry. Okay, Sal?"

My nickname on his lips is all wrong. It's like by saying it, he's trying to make me feel like he's a friend, instead of a mess masquerading as my father.

If Ama were here, she would clear her throat and enunciate "Sa-lah-ud-din," the precise pronunciation a gentle reminder that she

4

named me for the famous Muslim general, and I better not forget it.

"You said you'd go to the last appointment, too," I tell Abu.

"Dr. Rothman called last night to remind me," Abu says. "You don't have to come, if you have the—the writing club, or soccer."

"Soccer season's over. And I quit the newspaper last semester. I'll be at the appointment. Ama's not taking care of herself and someone needs to tell Dr. Rothman—preferably in a coherent sentence." I watch the words hit him, sharp little stones.

Abu guides the car to the curb in front of Juniper High. A bleached-blond head buried in a parka materializes from the shadows of C-hall. Ashlee. She saunters past the flagpole, through the crowds of students, and toward the Civic. The pale stretch of her legs is courageous for the twenty-degree weather.

Also distracting.

Ashlee is close enough to the car that I can see her purple nail polish. Abu hasn't spotted her. He and Ama never said I can't have a girlfriend. But in the same way that giraffes are born knowing how to run, I was born with the innate understanding that having a girlfriend while still living with my parents is verboten.

Abu digs his fingers into his eyes. His glasses have carved a shiny red dent on his nose. He slept in them last night on the recliner. Ama was too tired to notice.

Or she didn't want to notice.

"Putar—" *Son.*

Ashlee knocks on the window. Her parka is unzipped enough to show the insubstantial WELCOME TO TATOOINE shirt beneath. She must be freezing.

Two years ago Abu's eyebrows would have been in his hair. He'd have said *"Who is this, Putar?"* His silence feels more brutal, like glass shattering in my head.

"How will you get to the hospital?" Abu asks. "Should I pick you up?"

"Just get Ama there," I say. "I'll find a ride."

"Okay, but text me if—"

"My cell's not working." *Because you actually have to pay the phone company, Abu.* The one thing he's in charge of and still can't do. It's usually Ama hunched over stacks of bills, asking the electric company, the hospital, the cable company if we can pay in installments. Muttering "ullu de pathay"—*sons of owls*—when they say no.

I lean toward him, take a shallow sniff, and almost gag. It's like he took a bath in Old Crow and then threw on some more as aftershave.

"I'll see you at three," I say. "Take a shower before she wakes up. She'll smell it on you."

Neither of us says that it doesn't matter. That even if Ama smells the liquor, she would never say anything about it. Before Abu responds, I'm out, grabbing my tattered journal from where it fell out of my back pocket. Slamming the car door, eyes watering from the cold.

Ashlee tucks herself under my arm. *Breathe. Five seconds in. Seven seconds out.* If she feels my body tense up, she doesn't let on.

"Warm me up." Ashlee pulls me down for a kiss, and the ash of her morning cigarette fills my nostrils. *Five seconds in. Seven seconds out.* Cars honk. A door thuds nearby and for a moment, I think it is Abu. I think I will feel the weight of his disapproval.

Have some tamiz, Putar. I see it in my head. I wish for it.

But when I break from Ashlee, the Civic's blinker is on and he's pulling into traffic.

If Noor was here instead of Ashlee, she'd have side-eyed me and handed me her phone. *Not everyone has a dad, jerk. Call him and eat crow. Awk, awk.*

She's not here, though. Noor and I haven't spoken for months.

Ashlee steers me toward campus, and launches into a story about her two-year-old daughter, Kaya. Her words swim into each other, and there's a glassiness to her eyes that reminds me of Abu at the end of a long day.

I pull away. I met Ashlee junior year, after Ama got sick and I dropped most of my honors classes for regular curriculum. Last fall, after the Fight between Noor and me, I spent a lot of time alone. I could have hung out with the guys on my soccer team, but I hated how many of them threw around words like "raghead" and "bitch" and "Apu."

Ashlee had just broken up with her girlfriend and started coming to my games, waiting for me in her old black Mustang with its primered hood. We'd shoot the shit. One day, to my surprise, she asked me out.

I knew it would be a disaster. But at least it would be a disaster I chose.

She calls me her boyfriend, even though we've only been together two months. It took me three weeks to even work up the nerve to kiss her. But when she's not high, we laugh and talk about Star Wars or Saga or this show *Crown of Fates* we both love. I don't think about Ama so much. Or the motel. Or Noor.

"MR. MALIK." Principal Ernst, a bowling pin of a man with a nose like a bruised eggplant, appears through the herds of students heading to class.

Behind Ernst is Security Officer Derek Higgins, aka Darth Derek, so-called because he's an oppressive mouth-breather who sweeps around Juniper High like it's his personal Star Destroyer.

Ashlee escapes with a glare from Ernst, but this is the second time I've pissed him off in a week, so I get a skeletal finger digging into my chest. "You've been missing class. Not anymore. Detention if you're late. First and only warning."

Don't touch me, I want to say. But that would invite Darth Derek's intervention, and I don't feel like a billy club in the face.

Ernst moves on, and Ashlee reaches for me again. I stuff my hands in the pockets of my hoodie, the stiffness in my chest easing at the feel of cotton instead of skin. Later, I'll write about this. I try to imagine the crack of my journal opening, the steady, predictable percussion of my pen hitting paper.

"Don't look like that," Ashlee says.

"Like what?"

"Like you wish you were anywhere else."

A direct response would be a lie, so I hedge. "Hey—um, I have to go to the bathroom," I tell her. "I'll see you later."

"I'll wait for you."

"Nah, go on." I'm already walking away. "Don't want you to get in trouble with Ernst."

Juniper High is massive, but not in a shiny-TV-high-school kind of way. It's a bunch of long cinder block buildings with doors on each end and nothing but dirt between them. The gym looks like an airplane hangar. Everything is a dusty, sand-blasted white. The only green thing around here is our mascot—a hulking roadrunner painted near the front office—and the bathroom walls, which, according to Noor, are the precise color of goose shit.

The bathroom is empty, but I duck into a stall anyway. I wonder if every dude with a girlfriend finds himself hiding from her next to a toilet at some point.

If I'd been hanging out with Noor instead of Ashlee, I'd already be sitting in English class, because she insists on being on time to everything.

Boots scrape against the dirty tiles as someone else enters. Through the crack in the stall door, I make out Atticus, Jamie Jensen's boyfriend. He enjoys soccer, white rappers, and relaxed-fit racism.

"I need ten," Atticus says. "But I only have a hundred bucks."

A lanky figure comes into view: Art Britman, tall and pale like Atticus, but hollowed out by too much bad weed. He wears his typical red plaid and black work boots.

I've known Art since kindergarten. Even though he hangs out with the white-power kids, he gets along with everyone. Probably because he supplies most of Juniper High with narcotics.

"A hundred gets you five. Not ten." Art has a smile in his voice because he is truly the nicest drug dealer who's ever lived. "I give you what you can pay for, Atty!"

"Come on, Art—"

"I gotta eat too, bro!" Art digs in his pocket and holds a bag of small white pills just out of Atticus's reach. A hundred bucks? For that? No wonder Art's smiling all the time.

Atticus curses and hands over his cash. A few seconds later, he and the pills are gone.

Art looks over at my stall. "Who's in there? You got the shits or you spying?"

"It's me, Art. Sal."

For a guy who careens from one illegal activity to another, Art is uncannily oblivious. "Sal!" he shouts. "Hiding from Ashlee?" His laughter echoes and I wince. "She's gone, you can come out."

I consider silence. If a dude is dropping anchor in the bathroom, it's rude to have a conversation with him. Everyone knows that.

Apparently not Art. I grimace and step out to wash my hands.

"You doing okay, man?" Art adjusts his beanie in the mirror, blond hair poking out like the fingers of a wayward plant. "Ashlee told me your mom's up shit creek."

Ashlee and Art are cousins. And even though they're white—and I stupidly thought white people ignored their extended families—they're close. Closer than I am to my cousin, who lives in Los Angeles and insists all homeless people should "just get jobs." Usually while he drinks Pellegrino out of a ceramic tumbler he ordered because a Pixtagram ad told him it would save the dolphins.

"Yeah," I say to Art. "My mom's not feeling great."

"Cancer sucks, man."

She doesn't have cancer.

"When my nana Ethel was sick, it was miserable," Art says. "One day she was fine, the next she looked like a corpse. I thought she was a goner. She's fine now, though. And she got a painkiller prescription she never uses, so that's lucrative." Art's laugh echoes off the walls. "You good? Cuz I could give you an old friends' discount."

"I'm good." Not even tempted. One shit-faced person in the house is enough.

I hurry away just as the bell rings. The dirt quad empties out quicker than water down a drain. As I turn the corner to the English wing, Noor appears from the other side.

The sun hits the windows, painting her braided hair a dozen colors. I think of the pictures she has all over her room at her shithead uncle's house, taken by a massive space telescope she told me about once. That's what her hair is like, black and red and gold, the heart of space lit from within. Her head is down and she doesn't see me, instead intent on racing the bell.

We reach Mrs. Michaels's door at the same time. Noor's face looks different, and I realize after a second that she's wearing makeup. She pulls out her headphones, hidden in her hoodie, and a tinny song spills from them. I recognize it because Ama loves it. "The Wanderer." Johnny Cash and U2.

"Hey," I say.

She gives me a nod, the way you do when you've stopped seeing someone because you've got your own shit to worry about. Then she ducks into the classroom, a blur of beaded bracelets, dark jeans, and the cheap, astringent soap her uncle sells at his liquor shop.

For a second, the Fight hangs between us, specter versions of ourselves six months ago facing each other at a campground in Veil Meadows. Noor confessing that she was in love with me. Kissing me.

Me shoving her away, telling her I didn't feel the same. Spewing every hurtful thing I could think of, because her kiss was a blade tearing open something inside.

Noor staring at me like I'd transformed into an angry kraken.

She had a pine cone in her hands. I kept waiting for her to peg me with it.

The door slams behind her and I grab the handle to follow her. Then I stop. The bell rings. The hall clock behind me plods on, each tick a dumbbell slamming to the floor. A minute passes. I read and reread a sign on the door for a writing contest that Mrs. Michaels has been bugging me to enter.

But even though I've walked into AP English every day for five months, today I can't make myself do it. I can't sit across the room from Noor, knowing she'll never tease me about my llama socks again, or kick my ass in *Night Ops 4*, or come over on Saturday mornings and eat paratha with me and Ama.

I try to remember Ama's smile when she was well and would pick me up after class. The way she lit up and asked me about my life, like I had climbed Everest instead of merely survived another day at school.

"Mera putar, undar ja," she'd tell me now. *My son, go inside.* I sigh, and as I reach for the door, a bony hand grabs my arm.

"Mr. Malik—" The handle slips from my grip. Ernst's pale green eyes bore into me, daring me to snap, or wanting me to. "What did I say earlier?" he asks.

"Don't." I jerk away from him. *Shut up, Salahudin.* "Don't touch me."

I wait for him to paw at me again. Suspend me. Call Darth Derek. Instead he lets me go and shakes his head, a man sternly disappointed in a rebellious dog, giving the leash a little yank.

"Incorrect," Ernst says. "I said 'first and only warning.' Detention. My office. Three o'clock."

CHAPTER 3

Noor

My uncle loves theorems. He loves explaining them to other people. But the audience for his genius is limited. It's either me; his wife, Brooke; or the drunks who come into the liquor shop. He likes the drunks best because they always think he's brilliant.

Under the cash register next to his bat, he keeps a stack of graph paper and a mechanical pencil. He refills both every Sunday.

The door jangles and Mr. Collins walks in. He's an engineer on the military base just outside town, and he likes a little Jack in his coffee. Cold air follows him in. The sky outside is dark. I can't even see the mountains that ring Juniper. There's still time to do Fajr—the dawn prayer.

But I don't. Chachu wouldn't like it. *"God,"* he likes to rant, *"is a construct for the weak-minded."*

My head aches as I restock the candy aisle. According to the Pakistani passport and the US green card I keep in my backpack at all times, it's my eighteenth birthday.

My phone dings. I look up at Chachu, but his skinny form is turned away. His brown hair falls in his face as he scribbles on the graph paper spread across the counter between lighters and lotto tickets. I peek at my screen.

The message is from Misbah Auntie. She's not actually my aunt.

But she is Pakistani, and calling her Misbah would, as Salahudin likes to say, "piss off the ancestors."

Misbah Auntie: Happy 18th birthday, my dear Noor. ★ 🌹 ★ 🌹
You bring such light into my life. I hope you will come to see
me. I made your favorite. 😊 😊

Above that message is a string of others. From January. December. November. September.

Misbah Auntie: Are you angry at me too? 😨

Misbah Auntie: I miss you, my dhi. I'll make paratha
on Saturday for you. Please visit.

Misbah Auntie: Noor, it is raining! I am thinking of how
you love the rain. I miss you.

Misbah Auntie: Noor, talk to me.

Misbah Auntie: Noor, please. I know you are mad
at Salahudin. But can't you talk to him?

I've read that last message a dozen times. It still makes me mad. Salahudin is Misbah Auntie's son.

He's also my former best friend. My first love. My first heartbreak. So cliché and so, so stupid.

Misbah Auntie came into the store a couple of Sundays ago. I wanted to hug her. Tell her Sal had broken my heart and that I was lost. Talk to her the way I used to before the Fight, even if I was afraid that she'd reject me.

But I froze up when she spoke to me. I haven't seen her since.

"Noor." Chachu's voice makes me jump. I shove my phone back in my pocket, but he's not looking at me. "Finish stocking."

"Sorry, Chachu."

My uncle frowns. He hates that I call him Chachu. It's the Urdu title for *father's brother*. After a second, he turns back to Mr. Collins, with whom he's discussing Fermat's Last Theorem.

Mr. Collins nods as Chachu wraps up. The strains of Handel's "Hallelujah Chorus" fill my head as Mr. Collins's face lights up. A caveman discovering fire. I shouldn't be surprised. No matter how obscure the theorem, Chachu can explain it. It's his gift.

"You could be doing my job," Mr. Collins says. "Hell, you don't even have an accent like some of the guys working at the base. Why are you here selling liquor and groceries?"

"The vagaries of fate," Chachu says. My spine tingles. His voice has that edge.

Mr. Collins looks to where I'm restocking.

"Noor, is it?" Sometimes, Mr. Collins comes in Sunday mornings when I open the store. "You as smart as your uncle?"

I shrug. *Please shut up.*

Mr. Collins does not shut up. "Well, don't waste it," he says. "If you're anything like him, you'll get into any college you want."

"Ah." Chachu bags Mr. Collins's bottle and catches my eye. "Has Noor been talking about college?"

I'm glad I didn't eat breakfast. I feel sick and breathless.

"No," Mr. Collins says. I breathe again. "But she should be. You're a senior, right?"

At my shrug, Mr. Collins shakes his head. "My son was like you. Now he's a human billboard for an apartment building in Palmview."

Mr. Collins looks at me like I'll be joining his son any second. I want to throw a Snickers bar at him. Hit him right between the eyes.

But that would be a waste of good candy.

When he's gone, Chachu crumples up the graph paper. *Turn on the radio.* Our love for nineties music is the only thing we have in common, other than blood. We don't even look alike—my hair and skin are darker, my features smaller. *Turn it on. Distract yourself.*

Instead, he nods to the other end of the shop.

"There's something for you out back," he says.

I'm so surprised I stare at him until he waves me away. A birthday present? Chachu hasn't remembered my birthday in five years. The last gift he gave me was the dented laptop he left in my room a year and a half ago without explanation.

I pick my way through the storage room. Outside, the wind rips the back door's handle from me and I struggle to close it. The desert beyond the alley is a flat blue shadow and it takes me a second to see my gift leaning against the store's stucco wall. A battered silver bike.

As I run my hands along the steel frame, I hear the *snick* of Chachu's lighter and jump.

"After you graduate," he says between drags on his cigarette, "you'll be able to take over the day shift here while I'm in class. It'll make all our lives easier."

People love talking about the greatness of the human heart.

No bigger than a fist, pumps two thousand gallons of blood a day. Et cetera.

But the human heart is also stupid. At least mine is. No matter how many times I tell it not to hope that Chachu cares about me, it hopes anyway.

Back inside, Chachu flips on the classic rock station and turns it up when Nirvana's "Heart-Shaped Box" comes on. My head is splitting, and as I grab my backpack, I think about asking for a mini bottle of aspirin.

Don't push your luck. The thought makes me angry. Why can't I ask my own uncle for some aspirin? Why, when—

Stop, Noor. I can't be angry at Chachu. He is the only reason I'm standing here.

I was six when an earthquake hit my village in Pakistan. Chachu drove for two days from Karachi because the flights to northern Punjab were down. When he reached the village, he crawled over the rubble to my grandparents' house, where my parents lived, too. He tore at the rocks with his bare hands. The emergency workers told him it was useless.

His palms bled. His nails were ripped out. Everyone was dead. But Chachu kept digging. He heard me crying, trapped in a closet. He pulled me out. Got me to a hospital and didn't leave my side.

Chachu brought me to America, where he'd been in college. Left his engineering internship at the military base and put a down payment on a failing liquor store with the little cash he'd saved up. And that's where he's stayed for the past eleven years, just so we could afford to live.

He gave up everything for me. Now it's my turn.

Chachu clears his throat, his attention drifting to my braids, one over each shoulder, then to the green kerchief tied behind my bangs.

"You look like a FOB with those braids."

I don't respond. I had the braids in my passport picture, too. I like them. They remind me of who I was. Of the people who loved me.

"Your shift starts at three fifteen," Chachu says. "I have to be somewhere. Don't be late."

To Chachu, tardiness is illogical, and if there's one thing Chachu hates, it's the illogical.

Some days, I think of throwing Kurt Gödel's Incompleteness Theorem in his face. It's the idea that any logic system in existence is either inconsistent or incomplete.

Basically, Gödel is saying that most theorems are bullshit.

Which I hope is true. Because Chachu has a theorem about me, too. Chachu's Theorem of the Future, I call it. It's pretty simple:

Noor + College = Never going to happen.

My face is frozen by the time I lock my bike to the school rack and head to English. But I don't mind. The ride to school let me think. About Auntie Misbah and the hospital where I volunteer. About Salahudin and school. Right now, I'm thinking about numbers.

Seven applications sent.

One rejection.

Six schools left.

University of Virginia was my early-action school. I applied because they have a good bio program, and because I thought I'd get in. The rejection arrived yesterday.

My face gets hot with anger. I force it away. I'd have needed a scholarship to attend anyway. And it's one school. One out of seven is no big deal.

"Noor . . ." Mrs. Michaels clears her throat at the front of the class. I don't remember opening the door. I want to disappear, but I'm frozen at the threshold. Jamie Jensen turns to stare, ponytail swinging. Her blue eyes fix on me, so everyone else's do, too.

Sheep.

"The lights, Noor." Mrs. Michaels positions her wheelchair next to her laptop. I flip them off, and mouth *thank you* to her as everyone shifts their attention to the poem illuminated on the whiteboard. I sink into my seat in the back row, next to Jamie. Who is still watching me.

The Police's creeptastic "Every Breath You Take" plays in my head. Ten bucks says that one day Jamie makes a band perform it at her wedding.

"What'd you get?" She leans over. Nods to the downturned paper on my desk. Last week's essay. Mrs. Michaels must have handed them out before I got in. She wanted us to talk about the themes of a Dylan Thomas poem called "Light Breaks Where No Sun Shines." I gave it my best shot. But I know it was a crap essay.

Jamie stares. Waiting. When she realizes I'm not going to answer her, she settles back. Smiles her tight, fake smile.

"—work on your final papers, which will account for half your grade this semester," Mrs. Michaels is saying. "You'll need to pick a work by an American poet—"

I glance at a seat across the classroom. It's next to the red fire alarm. And it's empty. But it shouldn't be. Salahudin was behind me. I thought he followed me in.

"*Mr. Malik,*" a voice says in the hall. Principal Ernst, nailing Salahudin for being tardy again. Ernst says "Malik" like "Mlk" because vowels are beyond him.

I pull out my notebook. Salahudin is not my problem. I have bigger ones. Like the rejection from UVA. Like making sure I pass this class even though I suck at English without Salahudin to give me notes on my essays. Like Chachu's Theorem of the Future and what it means to defy it.

Jamie corners me in PE. She waits for Grace and Sophie, her eerily identical posse, to leave the little dirt patch outside the locker room before approaching.

"Hey—Noor!"

My name rhymes with "lure." Not too difficult. I don't even expect people to roll the *r* at the end, like Auntie Misbah does. But Jamie's always pronounced it "Nore" like "bore." I've known her since I moved to Juniper in first grade, and in all that time, she's refused to say my name right, even though I've asked.

For the first five or six years of my life here, Jamie mostly ignored my existence.

Then in seventh grade I got Student of the Month. I won a

speech contest. I took advanced classes. She didn't befriend me. Never that. But she did start keeping an eye on me.

"You look tired." Her eyes linger on my face. "The Calc problem set last night was brutal, huh?"

Jamie is innocent enough on the surface. Class president. Straight As. Big smile. A pleasantness that got her on homecoming court even if it didn't get her the crown.

And yet.

"Have you heard from any colleges?" She doesn't want to ask, but her competitive streak gnaws at her. "I know it's only February, but you did early action, right? My sister said I should have heard from Princeton by now—"

I don't remember telling Jamie I did early action. I haven't told anyone at school about applying to college. There's no one to tell. Until six months ago, Salahudin was the only friend I ever needed.

There's an awkward pause. After Jamie realizes I'm not going to say anything, she steps back. Her face goes hard. Like that time I scored in the top ten at the Golden State Engineering and Science Fair and she didn't place.

"Fine. Yeah. Fine. I get it. Okay. Sure." She sounds a little like a seal barking. Once the image is in my head, I can't get it out. Which means I smile. Which makes her madder, because she thinks I'm laughing at her.

A crowd of seniors passes, Grace and Sophie among them. They look at us curiously—they know we're not friends. Jamie jogs to them, her thousand-kilowatt smile pasted on. She'd make a great politician. Or serial killer.

As she disappears to the field, Salahudin comes out of the locker room, still pulling on his shirt. I catch a flash of rigid brown stomach muscle.

"What did that psycho want?"

The casual way he talks. Like we haven't been avoiding each other for the last six months, two weeks, and five days.

My brain refuses to formulate a response. After the Fight, I'd lie awake thinking of all the things I should have shot back at him when he told me he could never fall in love with me. When he said I'd ruined our friendship.

Now I can't remember a single one. I should ignore him. But the way he looks at me—careful and hopeful—it's a punch. And I fold.

"Re—remember when she told you to dress up as a terrorist for Halloween?"

"Sixth grade. Never trusted her again."

We glare at Jamie's retreating back. For a moment we're kids again. Unified against an invisible evil.

He lifts his arm, rubbing the back of his head, and I catch a flash of bicep. *Look away, Noor.*

"God, I wish she had a weakness." I glance accusingly at the sky, though God probably doesn't live there. "Insecurity. Jerk parents. Bad hair. Bad gas. *Something.*"

"She's got heinous taste in shoes. Look at those." He nods to Jamie's neon Nikes. "Like her feet got eaten by traffic cones."

Salahudin usually has dad humor, but that wasn't bad. I almost say so. He glances at my face. I want to hide. Or run away. He steps closer.

"Noor." He sees too much. I wish he didn't see so much.

"You should go." Ashlee watches us from the field. "Your girl-friend's waiting."

That word still makes me want to kick him in the teeth. *Girl-friend*. I'd glare at him, but I'd have to crane my neck. Last time I was this close to him, he was two inches shorter. With worse skin.

If the universe were just, he'd have shrunk. Grown questionable facial hair. A wart would be good. Maybe a personality transplant, too. A potbelly instead of a six-pack.

But the universe is not just.

"Right," Salahudin says. "Yeah— I wanted to ask you a favor."

I cross my arms. A short conversation is one thing. But we both know he shouldn't be asking for favors.

"Could you text my mom?" he says. "Tell her to push her doc-tor's appointment? Ernst gave me detention for being late and—" He lifts up his phone. "It's—not working."

"I have a charger."

"No, it's—" He fidgets, which is weird because Salahudin isn't a fidgeter. "There's a problem with our account. Some . . . billing thing. Ama's on a separate plan, though, so her phone's fine. Never mind. Forget I asked."

He turns away. The bunched cords of his neck tell me he's upset. As soon as I think it, I'm angry. I know him so well. I wish I didn't.

"Hey—" I reach for his arm, then quickly let him go when he jumps. I shouldn't have grabbed him. He hates being touched.

Though as soon as I do touch him I want to do it again. Because touching him makes him real. And that makes me remember how I used to feel about him.

How I still feel.

"I'll text Auntie," I say, thinking about her message to me this morning. About the food she made me. She loves me. I know that in my bones. Salahudin being an idiot isn't her fault. "And I'll stop by after I'm done at the hospital. How is she doing?"

A long pause. He could say a hundred things. But his shoulders harden. His brown eyes drift away.

"Not great."

"What do you mean?" I ask. "What happened?"

Salahudin gives me a sad half smile. I don't recognize it. *In Him we put our trust,* " he says.

One of Auntie's religious sayings. Salahudin would argue with her about it. *"What about our will?"* he'd say. *"What about what we want?"*

She'd answer in her don't-make-me-smack-you-with-my-chappal voice. *"What you want is what you want. What you do is what God wishes for you to do. Now ask for forgiveness, Putar. I don't want the gates of heaven closed to me because my son was disrespectful."*

Salahudin would grumble. Then he'd ask for forgiveness. Always. Auntie knew how to answer his questions. She knew what to say to him.

But I don't. He pulls away. I let him go.

CHAPTER 4

Misbah

November, then

Amid the brilliant silks of Anarkali Bazaar, the fortune teller was a sparrow. Her small feet tapped impatiently in cracked rubber sandals. "She's younger than you, Misbah," my cousin Fozia told me, "but she will ease your mind."

The fortune teller beckoned me to sit across a rickety wooden table and took my hands. The cross at her neck marked her as a Christian.

"You are to marry," the fortune teller said.

"I am not paying you one hundred rupees to tell me cows make milk." I lifted the Sahib's Bridals bag in my hand. The girl's laughter creaked out of her. Perhaps she was older than she looked.

"Your fiancé is a restless soul." She stroked the lines on my hands and poked at the calluses. "You will travel across the sea."

"My fiancé is the only son. He will not desert his parents."

"Nonetheless, you will leave Pakistan," she said. "You will have your children far from here. Three."

"Three!"

"A boy. A girl. And a third that is not she, nor he, nor of the third gender. You will fail them all."

"What do you mean I will fail them? How? Will—will they die? Will they be sick?"

The fortune teller met my eyes. Hers were small and long lashed, the crisp brown of fallen leaves.

"You will fail them all."

I offered her one hundred rupees to change the fortune. Then two hundred. But no matter what I offered, she said no more.

CHAPTER 5

Noor

Chachu wants me at the store by 3:15, but Auntie didn't respond to my text, which worries me.

I spend the last two periods of every school day in a volunteer program at Juniper Regional Hospital. Chachu doesn't like it, but it's during school hours, so he can't do much about it. When I finish my shift, I head to the motel. On my bike, it's only ten minutes away. I should have enough time to check on Auntie and get to the store.

The motel's quiet when I roll across the cracked concrete in the carport by the main apartment, where Sal's family lives. Auntie never locks the door, and when I enter, the warm smell of sugar-toasted semolina fills my nose. I call out, but there's no one inside. I walk behind the carport to the fenced-off pool and toolshed, but they're empty, too. "Cold Moon" by the Zolas plays in my earbuds. I shut it off as the chorus winds down.

The east wing of the motel is quiet, the parking lot empty. Business hasn't been great, I guess. None of the rooms on the west wing are open, either. But the bright blue door of the laundry room creaks in the wind.

I push it open to find Auntie leaning against the wall inside. She has a towel clutched to her chest.

She looks awful. Her brown skin is gray and sickly. She's breathing too fast. I see her pulse jumping. The knot of her pink hijab, which she usually wears pulled back and rolled into a bun at her nape, is coming undone.

"Auntie?" I get to her side in a second.

"Oh!" She jumps. "Asalaam-o-alaikum. Kithay rehndhi, meri dhi?" *Peace be upon you. Where have you been, my daughter?*

"Auntie, you need to sit down. Take my arm. Did you get my message? About Salahudin having detention?"

"Yes, I canceled the appointment." I try to give her my arm, but she waves me off. "And don't think because I'm speaking to you I've forgiven you. After all those parathas, you couldn't come and visit your old auntie?" She smiles. But I feel her sadness.

"Mafi dede, Auntie," I ask for mercy hastily. *Half of forgiveness is saying sorry,* she once told me. "I'm an idiot. Let's go in the apartment." She's so gray I'm surprised she's standing. I need to get her to a doctor. But she won't go unless I ease her into the idea— probably over tea.

"I didn't think you'd come." She squints in the bright winter sunshine. "But I made you halva and puri just in case."

Just thinking about the deep-fried, puffed bread makes my mouth water. "You didn't have to—"

"It's your birthday, na? Eighteen! Very—very important—" She stops to catch her breath, and I finally get her to take my arm. I could pick her up, she's so light.

Once inside, a bit of color returns to her face and she lets go of me. She makes her way through the dim living room, patting the wall of the apartment like it's an old friend. She loves this place. Even if it's sucked all the life out of her.

The kitchen is off to the side and shaped like an L. A big window faces the east wing. Three CorningWare dishes sit on the old butcher-block counter, next to a four-person dining table where I've eaten hundreds of meals.

I'm half reaching for the cholay—Auntie's turmeric and cumin chickpeas—when she turns on the stove to warm up the puri. Her hands tremble.

I nudge her into a chair. "Let me make you some tea. Then I'm calling the doctor, Auntie. Birthday halva can wait."

"I rescheduled for tomorrow, so stop worrying. We have time for tea."

As I pull out two mismatched mugs and PG Tips tea bags, I relax. The UVA rejection doesn't seem like such a big deal. The failed English paper doesn't, either. Something about Auntie makes me feel like I can face those things.

I want to tell her all this. *This is home. You and Salahudin are home. I'm sorry I was gone for so long.* I crack a few cardamom pods between my teeth, planning and abandoning a dozen apologies. It's like when I try to write. Only worse.

"It's okay," Auntie says, and I glance over at her. Her eyes are hazel, much lighter than Salahudin's. Right now, they are fixed on me. She puts a hand to her heart. "I know."

The knot that's lived in my chest for months loosens. We let a companionable silence fall as the halva crackles and the puris puff up. After I join her at the table, Auntie doesn't touch her food, but I'm halfway through mine before she takes a sip of tea.

"Wow." I finally take a breath. "You outdid yourself, Auntie."

"You haven't been eating enough." The crease between her eyes deepens. "I offered to teach Riaz to cook, you know." She's always called Chachu by his last name. "When he first brought you to Juniper."

I put my puri down. Chachu hates Pakistani food. He hates Pakistani everything. "He, um, he prefers sandwiches, I guess."

"Brooke wanted to learn," Auntie says. "Did you know?"

I shake my head. Technically, I should call Brooke "Chachee," since she's Chachu's wife. She thought it was cute when I first brought it up. Chachu shut that down quick. He only let me call him Chachu because at six, I couldn't say "Uncle" properly, and he hated mispronounced words more than Urdu ones.

"Anyway, your chachu heard about it. So she didn't come back." She takes a deep sip of tea.

"Auntie, why haven't you been going—"

"You know, Noor, now that you're eighteen—"

We both stop and she gestures for me to go on.

"You've been missing dialysis appointments, Auntie."

Her expression darkens. "Oh, those are rubbish anyway," she says. "They don't make me feel any better, but they cost an arm and a leg. I drink turmeric in milk—"

"Kidney disease is dangerous, Auntie," I say. "You can't cure it with turmeric. You have to get dialysis. What about insurance?"

"No insurance." She glances at her desk, littered with bills. "I have to get back to cleaning. Play me a song before I go, Noor Jehan."

She uses the nickname she gave me when I was little and she first realized I loved music. Noor Jehan, for the famous Pakistani playback singer.

"All right, you know how you love that Johnny Cash and U2 song?" I pull out the smartphone she gave me last year—one she said a tenant left behind but that I suspect she paid for herself. "Well, I have another Johnny Cash collaboration. It's called 'Bridge Over Troubled Water.' This time with Fiona Apple. You like her, too."

I find the song, and the first strains of Johnny's guitar strum out. Auntie closes her eyes. When the chorus hits with both him and Fiona singing, she reaches for my hand.

"That is you, Noor," she says. "My bridge over troubled water. And Salahudin's. But . . ."

She leans forward to look at me. Really look at me. I drop my head, letting my bangs fall into my face.

"Noor," she says. "I need to—I need to tell you . . ."

But she stops talking. Like she's too tired. "I don't feel well, Dhi," she whispers. I manage to get in front of her as she slumps forward, body suddenly limp.

"Auntie—oh no—okay—" I try to grab my phone without letting go of her. But it slips from the table and bounces off the linoleum and is too far to reach. The front door opens.

"Salahudin?" I call out. "Something's wrong with Auntie!"

But it's not Salahudin. It's his dad, and I can smell the liquor on him before he appears in the kitchen doorway.

"Noor?" he mumbles. Then he sees his wife and his voice breaks. "Misbah?"

"Call 911, Uncle Toufiq," I say. Auntie is collapsed against me, her heartbeat thudding strange against my shoulder. "Now!"

Juniper is small enough that the ambulance doesn't take long to get to the motel. Uncle Toufiq stares while the paramedics load

Auntie into the back, the terror of his wife's illness briefly sobering him up.

He tries to shove his car keys into my hand, but I shake my head. "I don't know how," I say, relieved that he isn't trying to drive. "Ride in the ambulance. I'll leave a note for Salahudin and bike over."

I grab a sheet of paper.

Hey, ASSHOLE, I write, but immediately cross it out.

*Your mom collapsed—*No. That's just going to freak him out.

Come to the hospital ASAP. Emergency room. Your mom is OK. But she had to be admitted.

My phone dings as I hop on the bike. A quick glance tells me it's Chachu. 3:17. I'm two minutes late.

The liquor store is five minutes away. But once I get there, Chachu's going to walk out. He won't care that Auntie is sick. He never even wanted me hanging around here.

I shove the phone into my pocket, grab my backpack, and follow the ambulance.

CHAPTER 6

Sal

By the time I reach the hospital, it's almost seven and I'm sweating so hard it looks like I ran through a car wash. I found Noor's note, but not the spare car key. When I called her from the motel phone, she didn't pick up. So I ran.

"Where the hell have you been?" Noor paces at the entrance to the ER. "She's in the ICU—come on."

As we hurry through Juniper Hospital, Noor catches me up. I flinch at her voice, a Gatling gun firing off fact after fact. *Your ama is weak. Hallucinating. The lack of dialysis took a huge toll. High levels of potassium in her blood—she's at risk of heart arrhythmia—*

A few nurses greet Noor as she passes, but she hardly notices. As she speaks, she brings her hands together and apart, twisting them like she's rubbing on soap. She's terrified.

Part of me wants to tell her: *"Stop. Look at me. Everything will be fine."* That's what Ama would say.

But I hate lying. I especially hate lying to Noor. Her fear catches, infecting me. By the time she stops at the door to the ICU, I'm sweating again, and not from the run.

"Give them your name when you go in. They'll only let in one visitor at a time, and they already kicked your dad out." Noor's voice softens at my expression. "He—got a little sick. I'll go check on him."

Ama is hooked up to a million machines. She's only forty-three. But she looks like she's aged twenty years. I tuck her hair under her hijab and straighten the gown they've put her in, pulling the blanket over her bare legs. Ama keeps her legs covered in public. The docs here know her. They know she prefers modest dress. They didn't even have the decency to cover her up properly? Assholes.

"Why didn't you get your dialysis?" I whisper to her. "Why didn't you listen to the doctors?"

"Putar." *Son.*

I grasp Ama's hand—the only person whose hands have always felt safe. She settles her gaze on me.

"How are you feeling, Ama?"

"Where's your abu?"

Embarrassing the hell out of himself by throwing up in the hallway.

"He's outside." I don't give her more than that, but she recoils at the venom in my voice.

"He's sick, Putar," she says softly. "He—"

He's not sick. He's never been sick. Weak, maybe. Pathetic. "He's drunk, Ama. Just like always." The hurt on her face makes me hate myself. But I don't apologize. This anger must have lurked within me for a long time, coiled like a hungry snake.

Ama squeezes my hand. "Your father . . . he—"

"Don't make excuses for him. He's outside decorating the ER with lunch while you're in here—" I shake my head. "But don't worry. Everything's under control—"

"Where is Noor?"

"She's in the waiting room." I can't talk about Noor with Ama. Not again.

"Putar, you must make up with her. She needs you. More than you know. And you need her."

"Ama—don't worry about me and Noor, okay?" I wish I could lose this edge in my voice. I'm trying. I'm trying to be calm but my body feels not like a body at all and instead like a dark cave of stress and uncertainty and fear, ejecting words that aren't words but hawks, with razors for wings and knives for beaks.

"Noor is fine," I say. "She's been fine without us for six months. You always—"

"You'll need to call my cousins in Pakistan," she whispers.

"Why—" My voice cracks and I imagine it as words on a page, nudged, molded, bent to my will. When I speak again, I sound normal. "You'll call them yourself, Ama."

"You'll have to pay the bills, Putar. Your father forgets," she says. "Water the flowers. Ask—ask Uncle Faisal for help—"

"Ama, when he visited in the summer, he gave me a trash bag of his son's old Brooks Brothers so I'd look 'less like a daku.'" A criminal. "I'm not asking him for anything."

"I miss—him." Ama's voice is faint, but she looks past me so intently that I glance over my shoulder.

"You miss Uncle Faisal?"

"No," Ama whispers. "My father. 'Little butterfly,' he called me. He'd play carrom board with Toufiq and his father. He loved Toufiq's jokes."

I nod even though the last time I remember Abu telling a joke, I was still in Hulk-themed underpants.

"Sir?"

A nurse enters, tall and dark-haired. "Your, ah—father. I think he might need you."

My father, I want to say, *is not the one who needs me right now.*

"I'm good." I turn back to Ama, but the nurse reaches out a hand as if to touch my shoulder. I pull away before she can make contact, and she raises her eyebrows.

"Honey, I'm sorry, but your dad can't be here. He's upsetting patients in the emergency room. Speaking some other language—"

"That's Punjabi," I say. "His native language."

"You need to deal with him. Or we'll have to call the police."

Noor enters, catching the tail end of the conversation.

"I got the keys from your dad," she says as the nurse leaves. "Imam Shafiq brought your car."

The young imam/engineer who leads Juniper's tiny mosque is Ama's friend. But I didn't call him. "How—"

"I called him earlier. He had to leave, but, um, your dad probably needs a way home." Noor shifts from foot to foot. I thought she didn't know how bad it's gotten between me and Abu. But I guess she's figured it out.

"I'd take him, but Auntie only gave me a couple of driving lessons before . . ."

Before I shouted horrible shit at Noor and she ran away like any sane person would.

"I'll take him," I say. Goddamn Abu. I need to be here with Ama. I need to make sure she's okay. But he's going to be a mess tonight, and I don't want Noor dealing with him—or him harming himself. "I'll be back, though. Just . . . stay with her. Please."

"I'll be fine," Ama speaks up. "Take your father. Give him water. Put him on his side. And don't be angry at him, Putar. Please, he—"

"Don't defend him, Ama." I walk out before I say something I'll regret.

Dr. Rothman is in the hallway, and I catch him. "Should I bring her anything?" I ask. "Medicine or—"

"She's not in pain," he says. "We'll be moving her to a room soon, so she can complete her dialysis comfortably. Pajamas, maybe. Toiletries. And—" He checks his clipboard. "I see we don't have an insurance card on file—"

Shouting drifts through the doors to the ICU. I recognize Abu's voice.

"I'm sorry." I'm unable to meet Dr. Rothman's eyes. "I—I should go."

The emergency room, down the hall from the ICU, is curiously silent. Other than my father, snarling at two cops watching him warily from the door.

"Sir—" One of them, a brown-haired woman, sounds tired. "Just step outside with us, okay? There's no need to—"

"*Haramzada kutta!*" *Dog of a bastard.* Abu's less of a wrathful drunk, and more of a sleepy one. I've never heard him curse in English, let alone Punjabi.

He sees me and stabs at the air like a sloshed Perry Mason. "That's my son. He'll tell you. My wife is inside. I need to go to her, but no one will let me—"

Even upset as he is, Abu's accent is the gentle swell of an ocean. I never noticed it until two years ago, when I put him on speakerphone at the grocery store. As he spoke, I stopped dead in the aisle, because he sounded suddenly unfamiliar. His *r*'s rolled and he lingered on *l*'s and *d*'s, making every word more poetic.

But these cops don't care about that. To them, he's a shit-faced foreigner who reeks of despair.

Everyone in the waiting room stares. Ailments and misery aside, watching someone even worse off is a relief. Or entertainment, at least.

My skin goes prickly and hot at those stares, and though I want to muzzle Abu, I feel weirdly protective of him, too. Hunched like he is, with his hands fisted, he looks so small.

"Abu." I put myself between him and the cops. "We need to get home. Ama wants us to go home." I turn to the cops. "I'm sorry— he's upset because my mom is sick."

"I know him." The cop with short blond hair and a mustache looks Abu over. His name tag says MARKS. I wish I knew what he was thinking. But maybe it's better that I don't. "We've had him in the tank before."

For a moment, I imagine Abu in an army tank wearing camouflage. The image is so bizarre that I laugh, a weird, shrill sound I've never made before. Then I realize what the officer means—a drunk tank. My laughter dies.

Marks's face changes from neutral to irritated.

"I'll just—I'll get him home," I say. "Abu, come on." I don't want to, but I take his hand. He's skin and bones, and I remember when he wasn't. When he could throw me up onto his shoulder like I was a feather pillow.

"No—" He jerks away, arms windmilling. When his hand smacks my face, I think at first that Marks has hit me—that's how unlikely it is that my father would ever lay a finger on me. Then I realize what's happened. It stings like hell and my eyes water— even as my panic rises. A cop seeing my dad hit me is not what we need right now.

It will be fine. I wipe my eyes. *In a few hours, you'll be writing about this in your journal because it will be the past instead of the now, and everything will be fine.*

"Oh—oh no. I am so sorry, Salahudin." My dad looks stricken, but it's not him I'm focused on right now.

Marks steps forward, his voice steel. "Sir, that's enough. Step back, son—"

"He didn't mean to," I say quickly, trying to keep this situation from spiraling. Something about how I'm talking reminds me of Ama and I cringe at the thought. "It was an accident. Please trust me—it's not who he is." Even Ama's whacked me with a spoon if she thinks I'm being disrespectful. But never Abu.

The other officer—Ortiz—puts a hand on her partner's arm. This time, when I grab Abu's hand, he doesn't fight me.

"We're going, okay?" I tug him out, and he follows, muttering.

"Sorry, sorry, Putar, I'm sorry."

Marks shakes his head. "Get him home," he says. He and Ortiz—and the rest of the emergency room—watch us as we walk out into the frigid desert night.

My ire rises again because I can taste their disgust. Their judgment. I want to turn around and scream at them. *This isn't who he is. This isn't who we are.*

We weren't always like this.

CHAPTER 7

Noor

Auntie closes her eyes after Salahudin leaves. Her fingers twitch as she sleeps. She moans, like she's in pain. An hour ticks by. Then another. I dig out earbuds. It took two months of extra hours at the store to pay for them. Chachu doesn't exactly believe in fair wages. But they were worth every penny.

Auntie can't hear, but I play the artists she loves. Reshma and Masuma Anwar. Mohammed Rafi, who was her father's favorite when he was little, and Abrar-ul-Haq, who was hers.

I check to see if Sal has called—but he hasn't and I immediately regret looking at my phone. I have twenty-five unread texts and ten missed calls. Every single one from Chachu.

Emergency at hospital, I finally text him. Had to stay late.

Auntie Misbah murmurs and blinks awake, so I turn off my music.

"Salaam, Auntie." I take her hands carefully—touch can be jarring to a patient when they wake up in the ICU.

"Pani," Auntie whispers. *Water.*

A cup sits on Auntie's bed tray. I bring the straw to her lips. She manages a sip, but her throat isn't working right.

"Tou—Toufiq."

"He's home safe," I say. "Salahudin will be here any minute."

My hands shake, but my fear will only upset Auntie, so I sit up and make myself smile.

"You look good, Misbah Auntie." I brush back the hair that's escaped her hijab and dab the sweat from her forehead with a tissue. "I wish you were home. I'd make you a cup of tea and we could catch up on *Dilan dey Soudeh*." It's her favorite drama. *Matters of the Heart*. "What happened in the last one?"

She responds so quietly, I have to lean forward to hear. "Akbar's sister told him that Saira's degree is fake," she says.

"*What?* That's garbage! Saira went to Oxford! And she still loved him after he lost everything!"

"I don't know what happened after," Auntie whispers. "No fun to watch without you."

"We'll have a proper party when you get home, okay?" I say. "Endless cups of chai with too much sugar. Did I tell you I took your advice and played all of *Nach Punjaban* at the store last Sunday?"

She smiles, and I'm relieved to see the color in her face. "I eat my words," I say. "Abrar-ul-Haq is not a hack. 'Wangan Chappan' made me cry. And 'Tere Rang Rang' is a classic. In fact—"

I clean my earbud with a wipe and tuck it into her ear. The strains of sitar and thudding of dholak come through and she closes her eyes. Down the hall, a machine screams out. Someone's vitals just went crazy.

"Code Blue," a cool voice sounds over the loudspeaker, drowning out Abrar-ul-Haq's singing. "ICU, Code Blue." A dozen people rush by. *Please let whoever just had a heart attack make it*, I pray.

"Noor." Auntie offers me the earbud and I turn off the music.

"You don't belong in Juniper, meri dhi," she says. *My daughter.*

She's called me that since I met her as a six-year-old, unable to speak or read English, mourning a family whose faces I no longer remember. Auntie Misbah didn't even know me, and she called me "dhi." It's just how she is. "You are better than this place. More than this place."

"I—I'm trying, Auntie," I say. "I applied to a bunch of colleges. I'm scared I won't get in. I feel kind of lost—"

It seems a stupid thing to say to someone in a hospital bed. But she just looks at me, her gaze intent.

"If we are lost, God is like water, finding the unknowable path when we cannot." She squeezes my hand, her own cold. The skin feels thin like an old person's, even though she's so young.

"I know you are angry at Salahudin," she says. "But you should be angry at—"

She works her mouth, unable to speak. Her eyes flutter. Her blood pressure machine beeps rapidly. Her number drops. Slowly, at first. Then faster.

"Nurse?" I release Auntie's hand for a quick second and step into the hall. "Nurse!"

But the station is empty. Juniper Hospital isn't well staffed, and the Code Blue will have most of the doctors tied up. *Shit.* I check my phone but Salahudin still hasn't called.

I type a message quickly.

WHERE ARE U, GET TO THE ICU NOW.

Another of Auntie's machines goes off.

"Noor." Auntie's eyes are sunken in. I get a sick feeling in my stomach. Something is happening. Something bad. Something beyond me. The air is full and angry.

"Noor." All she can say is my name, but there's so much in it.

"Auntie—you're going to be fine. Let me get the doc—"

Her vitals go crazy. Her blood pressure tanks. Her oxygen sensor blares. "Doctor," I call over my shoulder because I don't want to let her go. *"Doctor!"* I get up, still holding her hand, and holler out the door. "I need help!"

"Noor." It's a chant. "Noor."

"I'm here, Auntie Misbah." *Stay calm, Noor. Calm.* "You have to stay with me, okay?" I say. "Stay with me so you can show me more great Punjabi albums, and so we can get Salahudin to finally drink chai, and—"

I fumble for a prayer, one she taught me because Chachu refused to. I say it aloud, though I'm mangling it because I'm panicking. I'm not even halfway through when she squeezes my hand so hard that I think for a second everything will be fine. No one with that kind of grip could die.

I squeeze back, trying to give her strength. Trying to repay her for all that she's given me. *Take a few years for her, God. I don't need them.*

"Noor," she whispers. "For—forgive."

"Auntie Misbah? *Auntie.*"

Nurses and doctors pour into the room. They push me out. As I look back at her, her eyes stay fixed on my face.

But she doesn't see me anymore.

PART II

Lose something every day. Accept the fluster
of lost door keys, the hour badly spent.
The art of losing isn't hard to master.

—*Elizabeth Bishop*,
    "One Art"

CHAPTER **8**

Misbah

January, then

"What do you like to do?"

Toufiq's hands moved restlessly, clasping, unclasping, fiddling with his chai, pulling at his tie. He was handsome, long lashes framing midnight eyes, with the high cheekbones of his quiet father, a police officer and the only member of his family I had met so far. His beauty would have been intimidating, but his hands told the truth.

"I like to read," I told him, glancing out the door at my brother, Faisal, our escort for this little outing. Thankfully, Faisal was a terrible chaperone, more interested in his new Suzuki than his sister's izzat.

"I like collecting stories," I said. "I'd love to own a restaurant or an inn. To gather the stories of everyone who passes through. But . . . my mother prefers that I marry."

"Why not do both?" Toufiq tilted his head and smiled. "Gather stories and marry?"

His eyes turned up at the corners, but he was sad. I felt it. Perhaps if we married, the years together would reveal why. We would learn each other's secrets. A thrill went through me at the thought of him discovering me—the real me. The Misbah who dreamed and hoped and flew far in her imagination.

"What are you reading?" I nodded to the book poking out of his bag.

"The Yosemite. *It is by an American author named John Muir,"* Toufiq said. *"One of my engineering classmates in London brought it for me from California. I hope to visit there one day."*

I took the book, letting my wrist touch his shirtsleeve, and opened it to an underlined passage.

" 'The brow of El Capitan was decked with long snow-streamers like hair,' " I read. " 'Clouds' Rest was fairly enveloped in drifting gossamer films, and the Half Dome loomed up in the garish light like a majestic, living creature . . .' "

The words took me there. So often I shied away from English-medium books, though my father insisted I read them. English was like the broken shards of glass that lined the high walls in wealthy neighborhoods. Urdu was melodic. Like gossamer, as this John Muir said.

"Clouds' Rest," I said. "What a beautiful name."

"Yes. Beautiful." He glanced up at me and down again quickly, and my face warmed. I thought he would say more, but he only called for tea.

"Do you—" His hands moved again. "Do you want children?"

I was surprised. Even if women didn't want children, I always thought most men did. Enough that they'd never care to ask the question. I nodded. "You?"

He drummed his fingers on the table, and looked at the chaiwallah, still brewing our tea. He looked at the people at the other tables. He looked everywhere but at me.

"I love my father, but I am not close to my mother. I worry—I wonder— will I be more like him? Or like her?" Toufiq laughed, rueful and charming. "I am sorry. It is a stupid thing to say."

The chaiwallah brought sabz chai, Kashmiri-style. It was pink and milky, sprinkled with cardamom and brimming with crushed pistachios and almonds. A romantic tea, I always thought. Perhaps because I mostly enjoyed it at weddings.

I risked a quick glance over my shoulder at Faisal. He bragged to the chaiwallah about the Suzuki's boot, preening as the chaiwallah nodded dutifully.

"It's not stupid," I say. "Perhaps if it matters so much to you, it will be enough to make you a good parent."

Toufiq seemed embarrassed then, his hands as ceaseless as the tide. I reached forward to hold them, and for the first time since we took our seats, they were still.

CHAPTER 9

Sal

February, now

When Abu and I arrive at the cemetery in the Civic, it takes me ten minutes to find parking because the lot is full. *Sorry for being late to your funeral, Ama.*

Ha! I imagine her warm voice in my head. *If you were on time, then I would know you were dhokay baz.* An imposter.

For two days, I've tried to conjure Ama's voice. This morning, while putting on the shalwar-kameez she got me last Eid: *Wear jeans instead of shalwar, Putar,* she whispered. *Unless you want your ankles showing.*

And again when I was tempted not to shave: *Have you no tamiz? Don't you dare show up unshaven to my funeral!*

Funeral. The word hurts. Makes me feel like I'm on a disappearing shoreline, watching a wave roll toward me. One that's too high to avoid entirely, but so slow that for now, I can turn my back on it.

I know I'm being an ostrich. I know I need to look this shit in the face. But I also need to get through the day without complete internal collapse. I can write about the word *funeral* and what it means later. *Breathe. Five seconds in. Seven seconds out.*

Imam Shafiq meets me and Abu at the car, the freezing wind nearly blowing the topi from his head. He's Pakistani, too, in his

late twenties—but commanding in a nonobvious way. He came by
the motel just after dawn to pray Janāzah—the funeral prayer—
with Abu and me. Now he explains to Abu in quiet Urdu what will
happen next.

My father—sober, for now—looks to the gathering crowd. He
closes his eyes for a long time. I hate that when he opens them,
we'll all still be here.

At the same time, the sight of him makes me want to smash
a car window. He's the reason I wasn't at the hospital when Ama
died. Instead I was at home, dragging him into the house after he
passed out in the car. Getting him into bed. Changing his clothes
when he soiled them because he'd drunk himself insensate, and I
knew Ama would smack me with a slipper if I left him in a puddle
of his own urine.

"Asalaam-o-alaikum, Salahudin." Sister Khadija, Imam Shafiq's
wife, opens my door. Her deep brown skin is ashen against her
navy hijab. The grooves beneath her eyes tell me she slept about as
much as I did. "I'm so, so sorry." Her southern drawl is as gentle as
a hug. My eyes get hot.

Don't cry, Salahudin. Once you start, it's over. On Thursday, after
Noor couldn't reach me and called Imam Shafiq to the hospital, it
was Khadija who volunteered to wash Ama's body and prepare her
for burial. They met at the tiny Juniper mosque enough times that
Khadija knew the religious rules were important to Ama.

I almost ask Khadija if she's *sure* it was Ama's body she washed.
When I finally got to her hospital room, Ama's IV had been taken
out, the machines clustered around her like sentinels in mourning,
having failed in their mission to keep her alive. Ama lay beneath a

sheet, and though it said MISBAH MALIK on her hospital bracelet, this person didn't look like Ama at all. Too small. Too faded.

Too dead.

I look for Noor but don't see her. My throat tightens. She's the only person on the planet I could stand to be near right now. She was there for Ama, at the end.

Unlike me. A stab of self-hatred pricks me, and I dance with it. Better that than the wave licking at my heels.

The cemetery grass is yellow, broken up by graves and the occasional stunted tree. People approach to tell me how they knew Ama: A mechanic who haggled with her over tire prices. An old tenant who hid from her meth-head boyfriend with Ama's help.

My pediatrician, Dr. Ellis, and her wife, my elementary school principal, are there. Abu's AA sponsor, a no-nonsense woman named Janice, waves to me sadly. She hasn't been around in a while. But she adored Ama.

As Imam Shafiq coaxes my father toward the grave, Ashlee makes her way to me, black skirt dragging across the grass. I didn't want her to come. Ama didn't know I was dating Ashlee. I had an argument all planned for when Ama found out. *You can't be angry at me for kissing someone when you don't say shit about Abu being a drunk.*

"Hey." Ashlee falls into me. Her nose is cold against my neck and I remind myself she's touched me a hundred times. It's fine. I'm fine. As I try to focus more on her body than my own, I notice that her arms are heavy, her neck is loose, and she's leaning on me like I'm the only solid earth in this cemetery. Gingerly, I ease away and whisper into her ear.

"Ashlee—what did you take?"

"Nothing. I had a backache. My tailbone . . ."

It broke during labor and some days it hurts like hell. She's told me a hundred times.

Some of Ashlee's pain meds make her temperamental, and some mellow her out. If I let go of her, she might sag to the ground. Or she might get upset and make a scene. Not knowing which it will be makes my throat dry with anxiety.

Abu is like this sometimes. Unknowable—unpredictable. Maybe that's why I'm with Ashlee. She's familiar.

"Hey." Khadija taps Ashlee's shoulder gently. "We're about to start. Salahudin's father needs him. Will you stand with me?"

Before Ashlee can protest, Khadija's ushered her away with that smooth competence she must call on in courtrooms, when she's defending her clients. Imam Shafiq guides Abu to my left, and my father stares at his black shoes, unable to lift his gaze to the coffin.

Then the imam invokes the name of God, and the world tilts, because he speaks of Ama as someone who *was*, instead of someone who *is*.

The wave gets closer. I can't listen to this. If I listen, I'll shout. Or break. I'll drown.

There must be some way to get out of this gracefully. I could plug my ears. Hum to myself. Laughter singes my throat. A crazy, chittering laugh, like Gollum's at the end of the Lord of the Rings, right before he hurtles into the lava.

What is wrong with me? It's Ama's funeral. *Ama's funeral.* Worst pairing of words in history.

Then there's a rustle beside me, the warmth of another body, and I'm looking down into Noor's well-dark eyes. My relief nearly drops me to my knees.

She tucks something into my hand. A black earbud—wireless and hardly noticeable. The other is mostly hidden behind a curtain of hair.

I pretend to scratch my head and put the bud in my ear, letting my own hair fall over it. A bass guitar strums, joined shortly by a deep voice. Johnny Cash and U2 singing "The Wanderer."

Ama loved this song. Noor first played it for us when she and I were thirteen, sitting in the kitchen at the motel. We were pretending to do homework but actually stealing the chapli kabobs Ama was frying up.

He's a wanderer, Ama said. *Like me.* I teased her about what Johnny Cash would make of a hijab-wearing Punjabi woman singing along to a song about a preacher.

If you made him these kabobs, I bet he'd be fine with it, Noor said. I go back to that day, to the hot ghee popping off the pan, the tang of onions and bite of garlic, the wet-cotton cool of the air conditioner. I go back to Ama's laughter, and Noor's and mine.

I stare at the cold blue mountains in the distance as Noor plays the song once. Twice. I'd be happy if it just kept going. But Imam Shafiq finishes his speech and Noor shuts off the music. The silence is a monster on my chest, suffocating me slow. The coffin is lowered into the earth and the sound that comes out of my abu makes the hair on the back of my neck rise.

I don't know if I believe in hell, but if it had a sound, it would be the strangled howl of your father finally realizing that the love of his life is being put into the ground.

Noor's body shakes. My eyes are dry. The wave is waiting, but I won't face it. Not now. I'm not going to fucking weep.

It wouldn't cost me anything to reach out to Abu. To Noor. To hold their hands. Give them whatever strength I have.

But my arms don't move. Tears don't come. I stand still as a statue, freezing because I forgot my jacket, staring at the coffin. Wondering how someone who filled up a room could fit into a box so small.

By the time Uncle Faisal, Ama's only sibling, and his douchebag son, Arsalan, show up from Los Angeles to pay their respects, Abu is quietly hammered.

We've scraped up about eighteen Muslims from Juniper and a few nearby desert towns to do the sunset prayer. Imam Shafiq's voice soars when he delivers the call to prayer—and Abu remains impressively upright. But when everyone touches their foreheads to the scattered prayer mats, Abu closes his eyes for a little too long.

As he rises again, he sways. Sticks out his hand as if he's about to fall. Only he doesn't fall, so it just looks like he's performing some weird interpretive dance. Uncle Faisal and Arsalan exchange a surreptitious glance. Drinking alcohol is forbidden in Islam. Drinking while praying? I'm surprised the devil's not at the door.

I try not to hate Abu. He's in pain. I know that.

Noor, in a black shalwar-kameez and with her dupatta wrapped tight around her head and neck, weaves her way over and places a folding chair behind Abu. She nudges him into it and he stops swaying. Eighteen people breathe a collective sigh of relief and Imam Shafiq quickly completes the prayer.

After, I escape to the storage room off the kitchen, and stand there in the dark like a psychopath. If I turn on the lights, I know what I will see. Ama's perfect cursive, honed at a girls' school in Pakistan, faded against neat strips of masking tape attached to bins: Keys. Doorknobs. Tools. Yarn. She loved bringing order to her world. That's probably where I got it from.

I pull my journal from my back pocket. It's small enough to carry around and messy enough that I'm the only person who can read it. I haven't written in it since Ama died, because what's in my head would just come out as a scream. Not an *aaaaa* scream but every inch of every page blued out with pure ink.

Seems like a waste of paper.

Don't be weird. Go back inside. Ama taught me Pakistani hospitality long ago. Even in the middle of Podunk, California, there are rules. One is that you don't leave dozens of people in your house to fend for themselves, no matter what the occasion.

In the apartment, the stink of drooping flowers is inescapable. Everyone hovers in the living room, helping themselves to the platters of food that Imam Shafiq and Khadija have set out. I stare out the wide kitchen window, at the motel's east wing. A single room is lit up. Room 4, rented by Curtis Franklin, our only weekly tenant.

Right in the middle, between room 3 and room 4, a blue door glows under the fluorescent floodlights. The laundry room.

My stomach churns at the sight of it and I turn my attention to the weeds popping out of the cracks in the concrete. I'll have to take care of those. Ama hated weeds.

The phone rings, a shrill distraction, and I grab it quickly.

"Clouds' Rest Inn Motel, how can I help you?"

Most of the calls have been from Pakistan. Ama's cousins, her aunts and uncles—a blur of brown faces that I should remember better from a lone visit a decade ago. Some are in disbelief. Others say Ama's death is the work of the evil eye—nazar. All wish to talk to my father.

This call is different. "Misbah Malik?" a stern voice says. "I'm calling from Yona County Debt Collection—"

Before I hear any more, I hang up, heart juddering. Then I jump, because my cousin Arsalan has materialized next to me, horror movie–style.

"Dude, 'inn' and 'motel' are the same thing," he says. "So when you say 'Clouds' Rest Inn Motel,' it's—"

"I don't need grammar lessons at my mom's funeral."

"Apologies. I was being stupid," Arsalan says in a rare fit of self-awareness. "Sorry about Auntie. She was great. Such a nice lady."

Yes, Ama was very nice. Which is why she kept her comments to a minimum whenever Arsalan or his family came up. That was as close to shit-talking as Ama got about the brother who lived three hours away, but never visited, who could have donated a kidney to her, but refused even though they were a match.

"—a ton of great memories," Arsalan drones on. "Once, you guys visited for Eid—"

I remember. I burgled Hot Wheels from him. Stuffed them

down in my overnight backpack, wrapped them in my dirty pajamas because I knew no one would ever look there. I never felt guilty about those thefts. Not until I told Noor, anyway.

He has two playrooms and his own room. He didn't even notice, I'd defended myself to her after showing her the cars, irked that she wasn't impressed with my treasure.

But you know you stole them. Noor looked so perplexed at my perfidy that I started to squirm. The next time I went to Arsalan's house, I returned the damn cars.

I examine my cousin's shoes. They are these ugly loafers with TODS emblazoned on the side. He'd get along with Jamie. I crack a smile and look around for Noor. She's toying with the ends of her long hair and staring at a picture Ama put up a few months ago. It's one I took before the Fight, of the two of them drinking tea, rapt as they watched a Pakistani drama.

Arsalan smiles at her and I step into his line of sight.

"So, your senior year, huh?" He refocuses. "Picked a college yet?"

What I would give for a human mute button. "Ama's dead," I say. "My dad's a drunk. I'm not going to college, Arse-alan."

Mocking his name is a low blow. Ama would give me the stink eye if she heard me. Arsalan falls silent, mouth agape.

At that moment, the motel's bell sounds with a wrathful *BZZZZZ* like a drone missile shrieking down from the sky. I can't get away fast enough.

The door connecting the office to our apartment opens silently. Behind the high front counter, the young guy from room 11 taps his fingers impatiently. I rented him the room in a blur last night, and haven't seen him since.

"Can I get some towels, man? I've called like five times."

I stare. "Towels?" I say. A knot forms inside me, twisting tighter and tighter. The towels are in the laundry room.

"Shit, I thought you spoke English." Room 11 pulls his shirt away from his body and pretends to wipe his hands with it. "Tow-ells?" He raises his voice. "For clean-ing?"

"I got it." Noor must have followed me, though I didn't hear her. She's so close that I flinch. But she doesn't touch me. She reaches around me for the master key that hangs on a hook next to the phone switchboard, and disappears outside. Room 11 follows her and the knot in my stomach relaxes.

I lean against the office counter and think of everyone waiting in the apartment.

No way I go back in there. I'd rather be chained to the top of a mountain with an eagle pecking out my liver.

Since that's not an option, I grab my mom's Dockers jacket from the hook by the door and go outside.

The cold slaps my face. But it's a good slap—the kind you see in a black-and-white Western that knocks a gibbering idiot out of their hysteria.

I head for the pool behind the carport. Ama padlocked the chain-link gate months ago, worried some kid might wander through and fall inside. It rattles when I pull myself over it, the only sound in a quiet, freezing night. I drop to the concrete, dangle my legs off the deep end, and look down. With the floodlights off, it's like staring into a black hole.

We'll fill it next year, Ama said last summer. *I'll be better and your abu will be back at work. You can finally teach me to swim.*

When I was a kid, the pool was always full. It looked like a cheerful blue kidney bean, or a giant's footprint. We had parties every September for my birthday. Sometimes Noor was the only kid who came, but that just meant no one complained when we did cannonballs off the diving board. After we dried off, we'd gobble up the mango kulfi Ama churned in her old ice-cream maker.

Then a year and a half ago, a few months after Ama got sick, I came outside to find Abu muttering to himself and pissing in the pool. I thought he was someone else at first. It didn't occur to me that he was drunk because for as long as I could remember, Ama made it clear that I was never to touch alcohol.

Ama helped me get Abu inside. The way she soothed him, turned him on his side, and put a bucket next to the bed told me she'd done this before.

After that, we drained the pool. Ama wanted to fix it before refilling it. She wanted to sand the cracks and paint the whole thing periwinkle to match the sky.

The fence clinks behind me and Noor hops over. I get up to meet her.

"Imam Shafiq was looking for you," she says. "And I think I should get home."

The imam will have to wait. "I'll walk you."

Juniper's streets empty out around nine p.m., so we walk right up the middle of one, Noor on the right side of the white line, and me on the left. The wind's kicked up again, biting through our thin clothes, bringing with it the earthy scent of creosote. Noor's shivering, and I give her Ama's jacket and step closer. Our arms touch. Brief. Electric. I can't tell if it feels good or bad. I can't make sense of it at all. *You're all right,* I tell myself. *Five seconds in. Seven seconds out.*

Noor looks up, surprised at the touch. Maybe she's thinking about the way her fingertips brushed my jaw just before she kissed me months ago.

I wanted the kiss and I didn't want it and it terrified me. Instead of trying to explain, I shouted at her that she was ruining our friendship. I don't understand why I snapped like that except that I'm strange inside. And when she kissed me, it strummed that strangeness until it was a chord I couldn't bear.

"You know, I was really mad at you," she says when the motel is far behind us.

"I deserved it."

"Yeah, you did." She looks down at our hands, almost touching. I think about taking hers. An apology of sorts. I have a lot to be sorry for, when it comes to Noor. But she tucks her hand into Ama's coat, and it's too late. "Darpok!" Ama would call me. *Scaredy-cat.*

"Look—about the Fight—"

"Leave the Fight, Salahudin," she says. "Auntie wouldn't have wanted either of us thinking about it tonight."

"Okay—uh, how are college apps going?" It's a clumsy change in subject and Noor looks at me askance, smiling slightly.

"Didn't you shit on your cousin for talking about the same thing?"

"He deserved it."

"He is awful," she agrees. "He kept talking about his watch collection? Then he asked me for my number."

SABAA TAHIR

"Ugh," I groan. "What did you say?"

"I told him it was 968-273-3685."

At my confusion, she chuckles for both of us. "It spells 'you are foul.' Not that he'll ever figure it out."

A few seconds later, we slow as her uncle's house comes into view. It's in a housing tract next to a stretch of empty desert, low and pale like everything else in Juniper. A lamp in the front room casts a circle of light over a scraggly flower bed. I haven't been by in months, but the BEWARE OF DOG sign that Riaz hung up years ago as a burglar deterrent is still there. No dog yet.

"Thanks for everything today," I say. Noor glances at the front door, shoulders caving, like she can already hear her uncle's censure. Riaz is the opposite of Ama: cold and analytical and forever reminding Noor that she's going to work at the family business after high school. I've known him since I was a kid, but every time he sees me—or Ama or Abu—it's like he's smelled a rotting goat carcass.

Normally, Noor and I would walk around the block a few times. But the whole day presses against my brain, the wave too high now, too close.

"Call me or text if you need anything," Noor says. "Don't be alone in your head. I'm here and . . ." She picks at the sequins on her kameez. Her nails are painted black, which I hadn't noticed before. "All that stuff from last year is forgotten, okay?" She tries to smile, but doesn't quite stick the landing. "You don't have to worry about me saying or doing something that . . . makes you uncomfortable. I'm over you."

"Sure. Yeah." I say it too quickly, ignoring the disappointed flip

62

in my stomach. When I look down at her, she doesn't meet my eyes, but I don't mind. For a second, I think I'll hug her. But I am afraid of what that would feel like.

"For what it's worth," I say. "I'm really sorry."

It doesn't take me long to get back to my street, and when the motel comes into view, I stop. Because when I walk inside, it won't be home. Ama won't be waiting for me. There will be a mess from dinner. Sheets to clean up. My passed-out father.

Later when I can't sleep, when I get up at three a.m. to wander the house like a shade, I won't hear Ama puttering toward me, or see her face shining out of the dark.

Chai, beta? She was so courtly when she asked. *I'm making a cup and it's no fun to drink it alone. Come, I'll tell you the story of the woman with the silver-and-ruby heart who stole an entire room from under our noses!*

Ama, I hate tea.

I know, she'd say. *But I always hope.*

Hope didn't help her, though. She hoped Abu wouldn't be a drunk. She hoped that she'd get better. Hope was, in fact, a shit strategy.

I sit down in the middle of the road, and the wave slams into me, pouring out of my eyes so fast that I can't see. I thought I would eventually write about today. Order my thoughts, put my pain into words. Now I realize that I won't. I can't. Today is a poltergeist I'll chain to the back of my brain, one forever linked to freezing desert wind and dirty asphalt and a loneliness so deep that it shouldn't belong to this world.

In the last few months, as Ama got sicker, as it finally sank in,

I thought: *One day my ama will die. Everything that she ever was will die with her. The way she walked quickly, and flour in her hair when she made roti, the lines in her forehead when she yelled at me for doing something stupid. Her Saturday morning parathas and her smell, cardamom and Pine-Sol and lotion.*

I figured that such thoughts would prepare me for her death. They didn't.

I'll survive this. I'll live. But there's a hole in me, never to be filled. Maybe that's why people die of old age. Maybe we could live forever if we didn't love so completely. But we do. And by the time old age comes, we're filled with holes, so many that it's too hard to breathe. So many that our insides aren't even ours anymore. We're just one big empty space, waiting to be filled by the darkness. Waiting to be free.

CHAPTER **10**

Noor

When Salahudin and I were ten, we broke into Chachu's study in the back of the house. I knew better than to go in there. But Salahudin made me brave.

Or stupid.

He decided that Chachu had a stash of full-size Kit Kats. Said he had a dream about it. We didn't find candy. Just stacks of papers and envelopes where Chachu kept every piece of mail he'd ever gotten. On the bookshelf, next to the CDs of Depeche Mode and Pixies and Snoop Dogg, we found math textbooks. I opened one. The page was covered in meticulous notes and faded highlighter.

Being in there felt awful. Like I was a thief.

That same feeling came over me at Auntie Misbah's house. Pakistani cooking shouldn't exist if Auntie Misbah isn't scolding me for sampling it. Prayers don't feel real without her teasing me for wrapping my scarf too tight. *Like a gray-haired village granny worried about her virtue,* she used to say.

Being at the motel without her was wrong. Unnatural.

I don my headphones. I'll go inside to Chachu's house after I listen to a song. Just one song. I find Sigur Rós's "Untitled #8." It's nearly twelve minutes long.

Standing in the dark of the porch, I watch the stars and think of how I never saw my own parents die. I barely remember them.

Until I saw Auntie's coffin, I think some little kid part of me hoped my parents were alive. Sitting in a whitewashed brick house ten thousand miles away. Eating dinner in a courtyard, sighing when the power went out, sending a cousin to crank the generator. Waiting for me in a village that's forever lost.

But today—the funeral, the coffin—reminded me of what death is: final.

Auntie Misbah slow-cooked kofta for me when I aced a test. Taught me why ullu da patha—*son of an owl*—was her favorite Punjabi curse. Told me about hearing the legendary Noor Jehan when she was a girl. *Her voice was so powerful I thought it would split my soul. Maybe your parents named you after her. That's why you love music.*

Everything Chachu refused to do because it was too Pakistani? She did it *because* it was Pakistani.

But I didn't visit her when she needed me. All because of a stupid fight with Salahudin.

There are some things in life I'll never be able to take back. Avoiding the only person on this earth who loved me like I was her own child is one of them.

Snow Patrol's "Set the Fire to the Third Bar" comes on. A guitar strums. A piano joins in. A man and woman sing of distance and longing. I slip the key in the lock and open the door slowly. Brooke doesn't wake up easy, but Chachu is a light sleeper.

"Noor."

I jump. Scramble to switch my music off. Chachu sits in the living room. His brown hair pokes up over the back of the couch. The

TV is on low in the background. He turns, his features in profile. My father's face flashes in my head. I try to hold on to it.

My chest hurts. I miss . . . something. A place? A person? I don't remember much from before the earthquake. I don't want to. Those memories wake me up in the middle of the night. They trick me into thinking I'm trapped in that closet, back in the village.

But this memory isn't like that. It's warm. Sticky luddoo sweets at a wedding. The creak of a rope bed as I snuggled with my grand-mother. Chasing a skinny chicken through a courtyard. The mellow green of my grandfather's hookah. A littler voice. Brother? Sister? Cousin?

I don't know. Chachu won't tell me anything and there's no one left in Pakistan to ask. The village was leveled. The quake killed everyone but me.

The memory fades. I feel empty. It's that emptiness that drives me into the living room with Chachu. That need to look at another human who shares my blood. My uncle puts down the paper he's reading. Tom Petty's "Don't Come Around Here No More" plays in the background. The Heartbreakers' *Greatest Hits* album was the first one he played for me after I moved in with him. "It will help you learn English," he said. Maybe it did. But mostly it taught me that music can be more of a home than four walls and a roof.

"How was it?" Chachu's voice brings me back. He wants to know about the funeral.

"Sad. But a lot of people came."

"They weren't scared off by the chanting and bowing?"

I should have gone to my room. "They came to the burial," I say. "They didn't stay for the prayer."

"But you stayed." Chachu stands. Turns off the music, and drops the newspaper, unfolded.

I am quiet. Still.

"I don't understand why you believe in that trash." His accent is usually undetectable. When I hear it, it's best to disappear. Like now. But sometimes leaving makes things worse. So I stay. I try not to get mad. Before she died, Auntie Misbah told me to "forgive."

I try to forgive.

"Do you even understand what they're saying in Arabic?" Chachu asks. "It's backward and illogical, Noor." He shakes his head, disappointed. "'Religion is the sigh of the oppressed creature. It is the opium of the people.' Karl Marx. Misbah was stupid to encourage it."

"Faith isn't stupid," I say, because someone should stand up for Misbah Auntie. "Auntie knew prayer made me feel better. She knew it made me miss Pakistan less."

Chachu laughs. "If you'd grown up in Pakistan, you'd have wanted to leave. Our family lived in a hut. Your grandfather went to masjid every day, all five prayers, holiest man in the entire damn ilaqa—"

Ilaqa. *Neighborhood.*

"—white pagri on perfectly straight every day." Chachu goes on. "He even *looked* like a saint. What did it get him? A hovel that collapsed on him and killed everyone he loved."

Except me.

A door creaks from down the hall. Brooke, listening. Chachu doesn't notice.

"You know we found them together. The whole family. My

parents wrapped in each other's arms. Your father with a Qur'an in his hand. I could have told my brother that a book wouldn't hold up a jhompri built of hope and mud."

I try to remember what *jhompri* means. House? Hut? I don't ask. Chachu never talks about our family. No pictures. No videos. No stories. This is the most he's ever shared. It hurts, what he's saying. But I don't blink, because I want him to say more.

"He'd argue with me, your dad," Chachu says. "Because I wanted to do something with my life. He—"

Chachu is there now, in that moment, years and miles ago, with an older brother who disapproved of him. His fists close. Open. Close.

Open.

I breathe again.

"I need you to take a full morning shift." He turns to his room. "I have to enroll for summer classes tomorrow. I'll be in at noon."

Usually I only work until ten on Sundays. Which is why I have a phone interview with UPenn tomorrow at 11:45. I don't want to reschedule it. But I also don't want to imagine Chachu's face if he walks in on me in the middle of it.

"I promised, um, Jamie, that we'd go—go over an English essay tomorrow morning." The trick is to pick someone he's heard of, but who he won't run into.

He turns. Slowly.

"Misbah taught you so much, but not that lying is wrong?"

Down the hall, the door to Brooke and Chachu's room closes. I take a step back.

Chachu is the only reason I'm standing here.

I was six when an earthquake hit my village in Pakistan. Chachu drove for two days from Karachi because the flights to northern Punjab were down. When he reached the village, he crawled over the rubble to my grandparents' house, where my parents lived, too. He tore at the rocks with his bare hands. The emergency workers told him it was useless.

His palms bled. His nails were ripped out. Everyone was dead. But Chachu kept digging. He heard me crying, trapped in a closet. He pulled me out. Got me to a hospital and didn't leave my side.

Chachu studied math and engineering in college. He got an internship at the weapons center in Juniper—a coveted spot. He was a natural. But he gave it up when he was only twenty-one. Because he had to take care of me.

That's who Chachu is. He saved me.

The front door slams. He's gone now. Brooke emerges. She walks the way she did when she moved in years ago. Like she's avoiding broken glass.

She met Chachu at the store on a Saturday a few months after I got to America. Her then-boyfriend threw a bottle of Duggan's at her in the parking lot. I screamed when he did it. Chachu called the cops.

Brooke stumbled inside the store, taller than us both. Shoulders rounded from a part-time job at the DMV. Eyes blank from a string of shitty boyfriends.

Chachu wiped the blood off her face and sanitized the cut. She brought a plain cheesecake the following weekend to say thanks. A year later, they got married in the courthouse while I was at school.

Her eyes are still blank.

We've never been close. But sometimes, she'll leave me gifts, like the NYX lip gloss I found outside my door a couple weeks ago, or a bag of T-shirts from Goodwill. When Chachu heads to Los Angeles to buy stock for the store, Brooke and I will make popcorn and watch a movie. But she doesn't talk much. Never has.

She drifts past and silently folds up the newspaper. Straightens a tilted lampshade. Takes Chachu's plate with a half-eaten sandwich to the sink.

I go to my room. My arms ache. My head. I hear a step outside my door and tense up.

"It's me." Brooke. She closes the door behind her and leans against it, shifting from foot to foot.

"You get your letter a few days ago?"

The UVA rejection. We haven't spoken since the day Auntie died, I realize. "Yeah. Thanks for giving it to me."

"Did you open it?"

"I didn't get in, if that's what you're asking."

Brooke nods. She never pushes. Some days, I wish she did.

"Can you get the colleges to email you? I don't want your uncle seeing one of these."

"He hasn't checked the mail in about a decade."

"I know. But in case he does." When I don't respond, she takes a step forward. "Are you . . . "

Okay? Sad? Scared? Whatever the word is, she doesn't find it. She just gives her head a little shake and leaves. I lock the door behind her and take out the letter from UVA.

I imagine texting Auntie Misbah. *I got a rejection last week. I'm so sad.* I'd sneak out my window and walk the fifteen minutes to the motel. She'd be waiting, ice cream in hand. "Ben aur Jerry tay ter-reh chang-ay tay pehreh vakth tay prah vah," she'd say. *Ben and Jerry are your brothers, in good times and bad.*

But my "brothers" aren't here now. Neither is Auntie Misbah. My room—my posters of distant galaxies where I'd rather live, the bio books I know by heart—will have to be enough.

I tear the letter into tiny pieces and think of what Auntie Misbah said.

You are better than this place. More than this place.

I have to get out of here. For Auntie. For myself. I have to become something. I didn't survive an earthquake and learn English and lose everything and rebuild everything so I could rot in Juniper. There's something better for me. Auntie believed it. So I need to believe it, too.

I put my headphones on. I close my eyes as Ani DiFranco sings about her "Swan Dive." About how she just needs a shot—one little chance—at making something of herself.

You are better than this place. More than this place.

One school down. Six to go.

CHAPTER 11

Sal

The last time I cried like my soul was being ripped out was years ago, when Noor, Ama, and I all watched this movie Ama loved as a kid. *The NeverEnding Story*. There's a part where a horse named Artax sinks slowly in a swamp while his rider desperately tries to pull him out. It's brutal. I lost it.

I'd forgotten how crying hollows you out, drains away all the shit, and leaves everything clearer.

By the time I get home I'm not feeling better, exactly. Just less like I want a rogue tornado to snatch me up into the ether.

Though when I see Ashlee slouched against the office door, the wind pulling at her hair, I rethink that sentiment. She comes in for a hug, and I'm too exhausted to step away.

Though I shudder at her closeness, she holds me tight. When we first got together, Ashlee realized pretty quickly that I wasn't great at touch. I told her I had allodynia.

" 'A severe nerve-related condition' "—she'd looked it up on her phone—" 'in which the patient feels pain from stimuli that don't usually cause it.' "

I don't have allodynia. Saying I do is shitty since there are people who actually have it and suffer. But it's the only thing that gets people to back off. How else do I explain that Ama's hugs felt like home, but a stranger's tap feels like an attack? That when Noor touched my arm today, it fizzed electric in the best way, but a tussle on the soccer field can make me nauseous? That if I accidently touch another person, I'm fine, but if they do the same, I want to cannon them into the stratosphere?

It doesn't make any sense. Thus allodynia.

Finally, I can't take it and I pull away. "Where's Kaya?" I ask.

"At home with my mom." Ashlee's clear-eyed now that whatever shit she took this morning has worn off. "Are you okay, Sal?"

I step back. She must know the answer to that.

When I don't say anything, she reaches for me again, but I sidestep and sit on the wrought iron bench Ama placed outside the office. It's strangely fancy, incongruent against the whitewashed cinder blocks and winter-shriveled rosebushes on either side.

"Ashlee, did you tell Art my mom had cancer?"

"Yeah," she says. "I thought it was okay. He's my cousin—"

"She didn't have cancer," I say. "She had advanced kidney disease. Cancer is mercurial. Sometimes you can beat it and sometimes you can't. But Ama could have stayed healthy. She just had to rest and go to dialysis and she didn't."

"Why—why didn't she go?"

"Too much to do at the motel," I say. "Too expensive. We don't have health insurance. I should've made her go. Abu should have helped her with the motel. My asshole uncle should have donated a kidney. But none of us did what we should have done."

"Maybe it hurt," Ashlee says. "And she was afraid."

I don't know. I never will. I didn't talk to my ama enough. I didn't listen to her.

"Hey," she says. "Your—mom. She had a painkiller prescription, right?"

"Yeah," I say. "Why?"

"Do you—would you mind if I—"

Oh. *Oh.* It takes me a second, but then I understand.

"My prescription's out," she says at the look on my face. "And my back's really been—"

"What the hell, Ashlee?" I once read in a magazine that you're never supposed to break up or hook up after a major life event. But whoever wrote that probably didn't have a girlfriend ask them for their mom's painkillers the day of her funeral.

Anger sears my chest—at Ashlee, but it feels bigger than that. I'm angry at Abu, for the way he hunts for oblivion in a bottle. At Ama, for not listening to her doctors or her body. At myself, for not fixing her.

"We—I can't do this." The moment I say it, I feel calmer. In control. "I can't see you anymore."

Ashlee stares at me like I'm speaking another language. The office phone rings. And rings. Abu's probably passed out. If he's on his back, he could choke if he throws up. Abu might be depressed and he might be a drunk, but he's still my father and I don't want to lose him, too.

"I have to look after my dad," I fill the silence. "Help him run this place. A relationship, on top of all of that—"

"I could help you."

"You were high this morning."

"You were a jerk, Sal." She drops onto the bench, then gets up again, agitated. We haven't been together very long, so I didn't expect Ashlee to be this upset. "You didn't want me to stand with you. You didn't want your dad to see me."

Abu was so shattered I don't think he'd have noticed Ashlee if she was smashing a gong in his face.

"All I wanted was for you to not feel alone," she says. "You're punishing me for giving a shit."

The phone rings again. The Civic is in the driveway, but Abu might not be home. Maybe he got thrown into the drunk tank. Maybe he got hit by a car.

I miss Ama with a fierceness that makes my chest hurt. How did she not go crazy from the worrying? One day in, and I want to tear out my hair.

I've been quiet too long. "I have to go," I tell Ashlee. She looks so sad that my anger at her drains away. "Will you be able to get home?"

"Like you care." Ashlee grabs her phone off the bench and heads for her Mustang, a dull shadow on the street. When she reaches it, she turns around.

"I'm glad I didn't introduce you to Kaya," she says. "You didn't deserve to meet her."

She's right, but before I can say so she's slamming the door.

I wait for her to drive off and then unlock the office. A habit I picked up from Ama. *You do not re-enter your home until your guest is on the way to their own.*

Inside, our apartment is dark and silent, other than Abu's snores. I'm relieved to hear them. At least he's alive.

Imam Shafiq and Khadija cleaned up everything but the flowers. The fridge is stuffed with enough food to last weeks. But it's a reminder of today, and I know I won't eat any of it.

Sleep's not happening, so I flip on the light and make my way to Ama's desk, where a stack of bills has tipped over, half covering a stapler that only works if you sacrifice a box of staples to it first.

The fate of this place—of me and Abu—lies in that stack.

Maybe that shouldn't matter to me. If it wasn't for the Clouds' Rest, Ama wouldn't have worked herself to the bone. Abu would have been forced to clean up his act and get a job.

Now that she's gone, he's not going to run this place. He's not even going to try. And where does that leave us? I listened to Ama stressing over bills enough to know that we don't have savings. That we were barely hanging on every month.

I take the bills to the kitchen and set them down on the wood counter, soft from years of use. Outside, the east wing of the motel is dimly lit. Ama planted some kind of freakishly hardy plant in the window boxes of each room, and the floodlights turn their deep green leaves blue.

Water the flowers. A few hours from dying and that was what she was thinking. Because she adored the Clouds' Rest. When business was good, she loved talking to the people who came through: the scientists headed to the military base, or the hikers excited about Death Valley, or the artists hunting for inspiration. She fought for years to make the Clouds' Rest into something she was proud of.

I can't lose this place. Not after losing her. In the end, I didn't make Ama rest or drag her to dialysis. I didn't do shit to save her. I failed her. But I can save the Clouds' Rest. I can make sure the blood, sweat, and tears she put into this place weren't for nothing.

I find a butter knife and start ripping open the bills. As I add everything up on my phone, the room shrinks. In addition to being three months behind on our car payment, there's an electric bill, gas bill, water bill, hospital bills, cell phone bills, credit card bills.

But the one that makes me break out in a sweat is only a page long.

First Union Bank of the Desert
607 N. Sparfield Ave.
Juniper, CA 99999

Dear Mrs. Malik,

You are in arrears on your business loan payments. As of January 28, you are 60 days late on your payments. Failure to bring your account to current by paying the full amount of $5,346.29 by April 15 will result in fees and precipitate the loss of your business—the complete seizure of all assets associated with said business.

The letter goes on, but only two things matter: We owe more than five grand to the bank. And if we don't pay it in ten weeks, everything Ama worked for will be gone.

CHAPTER **12**

Noor

I like opening the store on Sundays. Six a.m. is too late for the night revelers. Too early for everyone else.

It's freezing inside because Chachu is too cheap to run the heater for the five hours the store is closed. I move quickly so my hands don't go numb. Shades opened. Fluorescent lights on. Register unlocked. Ice machine filled. Candy and sodas and groceries restocked.

I'm myself but not myself. Like I'm watching someone else from far away. Auntie Misbah died a little more than a week ago. Shock has faded into numbness. But grief is an animal I know. It's retreated for now. But it'll be back.

Chuck D raps in my ears, making the work go faster. By the time the sun's turned the desert outside a bluish gold, I'm warm. The ancient furnace blasts. I get behind the counter and break out my laptop. The UPenn interview—which I rescheduled after canceling it last week—is at 11:30 a.m. Less than six hours from now.

I glance over the prep questions. *What is a current project you are working on unrelated to your proposed field of study?*

Surviving senior year? Trying to fall out of love with my ex-best friend? Mourning the woman who was the closest thing I had to a mom?

My English paper, a fifteen-page monster due at the end of the year, will have to do.

Though I can't talk about the paper without writing some of it. Mrs. Michaels wants us to analyze a poem. I picked Elizabeth Bishop's "One Art" because I liked the first sentence.

Well. Sort of. Mostly I picked it because it's short.

But it's also weird. It's about misplacing stuff, like keys and houses. How the hell do you misplace a house? I'm reading the poem for the tenth time when the bell over the door dings.

I think it's Auntie Misbah for a second. Before the Fight, she came in every Sunday morning, chai in hand, ready to watch *Dilan dey Soudeh* and argue over Nusrat Fateh Ali Khan's music. (Verdict: I love him. She called him "the Wailer.")

"Slmnr, bta." It's Uncle Toufiq and it takes me a second to translate the mumble. *Salaam, Noor beta.* I pause Public Enemy and glance at the clock. Seven a.m.

He's starting early.

He finds eggs, milk, and bread. When he walks past the wines and bourbons, I relax. Until something catches his eye and he slows down.

Come on. Keep walking, Uncle.

He stops to add a bottle of Old Crow to his basket. I almost don't see it, he's so fast. Like if he grabs it quick, maybe he didn't really grab it. He piles everything on the counter, hiding the liquor in the middle.

I did the same thing a few weeks ago when I bought foundation at CVS. I guess I was hoping if I buried what I was ashamed of, no one would see it right under their nose.

The screen blinks when I slide his credit card. *Authorizing . . . authorizing . . . authorizing . . .*

"Sorry, Uncle," I say. "It's slow."

I busy myself by bagging everything up. Outside, a gust of sand scrapes against the glass door. Uncle Toufiq taps his fingers against the counters, then his pockets.

The credit card machine beeps. DECLINED flashes across the screen.

The groceries are eight bucks. The alcohol another eleven. I don't even want to sell him alcohol. Every time he drinks, life gets a little harder for Salahudin.

But shame is hard, too. Especially when you're already broken. I imagine Uncle walking out without the liquor. Heading to Ronnie D's and his card getting declined there, too. Getting desperate. Stealing the liquor.

"Is—there a problem?" Uncle Toufiq asks. "With the card?"

"No problem," I say. Chachu does inventory on Sunday nights, and he doesn't pay attention to much other than the liquor. I hate lying. I'm also bad at it. But I can text him after I leave—tell him I spilled a bottle of Old Crow when I was cleaning.

Uncle Toufiq mutters a salaam and leaves. I watch him until he disappears behind the low-rent apartments next door. There was always something sad about him. Even before he started drinking so much. As Salahudin might say, he's seen some shit.

I wonder what he's seen.

Less than five hours until my interview, but my concentration is broken. I stare at "One Art." Read it out loud even though it makes me feel stupid. As I'm finally making sense of it, the front doorbell chimes again.

This time, my stomach flutters. It's Salahudin, idiotically clad only in a T-shirt, jeans, and Chuck Taylors with cracks at the toe, despite the fact that it is eighteen degrees outside. His eyes are red. Shadowed, like they've been all week. I guess he's not sleeping, either.

"I didn't know brown people could turn blue." I reach for my coat, but it would fit one of his arms. So I throw him a shawl I've got stuffed in my backpack instead. "You looking for your dad?"

"Nah." Salahudin drapes the shawl over me. "I know Ama used to visit you on Sundays. Thought you might want company."

I pull off my headphones, where "Holler If Ya Hear Me" is blasting.

"I have 2Pac for company." God. What is wrong with me? "I'm glad you're here," I add quickly. We haven't talked much since the funeral. He only came back to school on Friday.

Salahudin cocks his head. He tries to smile. I want to tell him that he doesn't have to. That if he never wants to smile again, I get it, because I was six when my parents died and I still feel that ache.

"What are you working on?"

"That stupid poetry paper. You're probably already finished." English is the only class Salahudin even bothers putting effort into.

"Yeah," he admits. "But Mrs. Michaels wants me to enter some writing contest. A five-thousand-word story inspired by real life." He laughs without smiling. "Let me see what you got."

He comes around the counter. Leans over my shoulder. "'In

"One Art" by Elizabeth Bishop, loss is presented as—' Noor, that's passive voice."

I don't need your help. I almost say it. *You took it away and I was just fine.*

When I turn, his face is close to mine. Very close. Brown skin. Unfairly smooth. Dark curls falling into his eyes. Something warm unfurls inside. He hasn't been this close to me in ages. I miss it.

"I don't understand poetry," I say.

"Everything you listen to is poetry. Here. I need a distraction." He takes the laptop from me and types. Passive voice becomes active. He litters the page with notes, suggestions.

I used to love watching Salahudin write. He gets this focused look, like he's dancing a tango with the words in his head. It calms him. Helps him bring order to his world.

His big hands move over the keyboard and I think of how I won't hold those hands. They'll never caress my face or any other part of me, and that makes me sad.

But I don't look away. They are my favorite part of him.

He moves to the next paragraph and shakes his head. He looks . . . shocked, but that's not the right word. The word I'm looking for is an SAT word, a Salahudin word.

Aghast.

"Noor, how are you surviving this class?"

"How are you surviving Trig," I say, "without me explaining quadratic equations?"

"I drank unicorn blood." He taps through a couple of paragraphs, leaving more notes. "Worked, too. Unlike this sentence. Do we need to discuss commas again—"

"It worked because you're too smart to be in that class," I say. "Your ama—" I stop. Auntie Misbah's ghost hangs in the air. Salahudin looks suddenly exhausted.

"Come on, Noor." I can barely hear him. "What's the harm if my classes are easy? School's the last thing I can focus on."

"Oh, boo-freaking-hoo," I say. "My parents are dead, too. Both of them. Remember? You don't see me slacking off."

He shakes his head. There's that word again. Aghast. I cross my arms, unwilling to bend, and he fixes his dark eyes on me. His expression is warm but in a way I've never seen. My face feels hotter than it should.

He cracks a smile. "I missed you, Noor."

"I missed you, too." I stare down at the duct-taped toes of my Doc Martens. "Though I don't miss your nerd humor. Unicorn blood? Seriously?"

Salahudin sticks around for my interview, and I'm grateful because by 11:27, my palms sweat and my head aches. Chachu isn't due until 12:30, but I check outside every ten seconds to make sure he hasn't showed up early.

"If anyone comes in while I'm on the phone," I tell Salahudin, "just stall."

"I could scare them away," he says. "Or scream that there's a rat. No one likes rats."

"No—no, Salahudin, don't do that. Tell them stories. Tell them about how the Clouds' Rest got its name. And if Chachu gets here early—"

"Don't worry." Salahudin waves me off. "I got you. I'll text."

Five seconds later, at 11:30 exactly, my phone rings.

"Good luck," Salahudin calls as I run for the bathroom. I shove my headphones in my ears, slam the door shut, and answer.

"Is this Miss Noor Riaz?"

The UPenn interviewer sounds so calm. Almost bored.

I clear my throat. "She is me. I am her. I mean—" *Really, Noor?* "Hello. Yes. This is Noor Riaz."

"Miss Riaz. I'm glad we're finally getting a chance to connect. You're a hard woman to pin down." She chuckles. An "I am not amused" laugh. I wipe my palms on my jeans.

"I'm sorry," I say. "I work at the family business. The hours are unpredictable."

"What's the family business? I don't see it mentioned—" Papers rustle, a pen clicks.

"Um. I work at my uncle's liquor store."

The pause that follows is long enough that I think she's hung up. "H-hello?"

"Is it legal to work at a liquor store if you're not twenty-one?"

"Yes, ma'am." I'm yanking nervously on a braid and make myself stop. "The legal age is fifteen as long as it's not a tavern."

"I see. This is the same uncle who's listed as your guardian?"

"Yes, he's my guardian. Is that relevant?" I don't mean to snap. But why does she care who raised me? It's none of her business.

"I'm sorry." I make myself calm down. "I didn't mean—"

"I should think its relevance is clear, Ms. Riaz," the interviewer says. "Especially to someone seeking to become a doctor. Nature versus nurture? How you were raised and why you were raised that way impacts your personality. Your personality is one of the primary things I'm interrogating in this call."

"Of course." *Did she just say interrogating?*

"To be frank, Ms. Riaz, we were a bit baffled by your application. Many UPenn hopefuls are excellent at studying and regurgitating facts. Good grades. Good test scores. But we're looking for students who can contribute to the intellectual landscape of our school. We want the spark of creativity, of curiosity. Since writing helps us get a sense of that, the essay is the most important part of the application. But your essays were . . . vague. So. Back to your uncle . . . ?"

"My parents died when I was young." I hope she can't hear me grinding my teeth. "My uncle took me in."

"Well, your transcript shows the hard work your uncle put into you. Why don't you tell me about—"

"My uncle didn't put any work into me," I say. "He doesn't want me to go to college, even." Why am I telling her this? I should shut up.

But I don't know how. First she pried. Now she's making assumptions.

"Everything good on the transcript happened because I was disciplined." *Calm, Noor. Professional.* "Because I want the best future for myself. My uncle wants me to work at this liquor store for the rest of my life. He doesn't want me to become a doctor, or anything, really—"

"You mentioned your faith in your essay, Ms. Riaz. You are Muslim?"

Muzz-lem, she says. "I am," I say. "My uncle's not. Even if he was, Islam's not about oppression. Lots of Muslim women—"

YOUR UNCLE PULLED UP. ABORT MISSION.
ABORT MISSION.

I drop the phone when Salahudin's message flashes. *Shit!*

"Ms. Riaz, I would *never* make that assumption," the interviewer is saying. "In your personal statement, you mention faith as a key component of your life. I'm trying to get to know you better."

TOLD HIM U HAVE STOMACH ACHE. HE'S HEADED
FOR BATHROOM. HANG UP!

Frantically, I delete Salahudin's messages, my thumbs hitting every button but the trash can.

"Noor?" Chachu is at the bathroom door.

In my headphones, the interviewer calls my name, too. "Miss Riaz. Are you there?"

"What are you doing?" Chachu says. "Are you—"

I don't say anything to the interviewer. I don't explain. I just hang up and shove my headphones in my pocket.

The door handle is slippery under my fingers, and I open it to find that Salahudin has followed Chachu.

"I—I told you, she's sick," Salahudin says, the lie obvious to anyone who's spent time with him. Fortunately, Chachu hasn't.

"Sorry, Chachu," I say, and I don't have to fake illness. The interview was so bad that I want to sink to the floor. "I'm—not feeling good,"

Chachu squints at the phone. "Who were you talking to?"

"No one."

He grabs the phone. Opens up my recent calls. I don't dare look at Salahudin, and he knows Chachu well enough to stay quiet. Still, I feel the frustration rolling off him. He's never liked Chachu. The loathing is mutual.

"Who is this?" Chachu finds the interviewer's number. "You were talking to them a minute ago."

"A—a nurse," I say. "At Juniper Hospital. Thought she could diagnose me. It's her cell."

Chachu cocks his head. Calculating. He calls the number back, and puts it on speaker.

Don't pick it up. Don't pick it up. Please, God. Please. It's a clumsy, desperate prayer. The kind of thing I'd ignore if I were God.

The phone rings and rings. Finally, it goes to a generic voicemail.

I guess it's a good thing I'm not God.

Chachu hangs up, mystified, then puts the back of his hand against my forehead. A knot in my chest loosens. *He believes me.*

"I can . . . take her home," Salahudin speaks up, and Chachu gives him a hard look before nodding.

"Fine," he says. "No detours. Tell Brooke to make you some soup."

He disappears to the front of the store and I follow Salahudin out to his car. I just blew my chance with UPenn after that train wreck of an interview.

But I'm so relieved Chachu didn't catch me trying to get in that I can't bring myself to care.

CHAPTER 13

Sal

Two weeks after Ama's funeral, most of her creditors figure out the motel's phone number. They stop blowing up her cell—which I eventually turned off—and start calling the Clouds' Rest.

Over.

And over.

And over.

"Are you going to answer that?"

Noor drops her headphones onto her math book, the haunting sound of a girls' choir blasting through. Her hair is loose, but she massages the top of her head when she's doing problem sets, so it's tufted up into a little horn. I catch myself before I reach out to smooth it down.

She's been over every day after her shift at the liquor store. We stay in the front office because I don't want her to see the mess in the apartment. Or Abu reeking of liquor. Or the fact that he faced all Ama's pictures toward the wall.

I just want things to go back to how they were between Noor and me. I don't want to screw up so badly that she never speaks to me again.

"Salahudin." Noor taps the bottom of my sneaker with her foot. "Phone."

"Ignore it." I dig through the drawers beneath the counter. I have to replace about twenty burned-out bulbs that Ama never got to, but I can't find her stash amid the spare Ethernet wires, stacks of soap, and a macramé plant hanger.

The phone stops ringing. A second later, it flashes, which means someone new is calling and hearing Ama's automated greeting: "Thank you for calling the Clouds' Rest Inn Motel. For a tenant, please press the room number and the pound sign. For the front desk, please press two. For directions . . ."

The ringing starts again. My heart rate spikes.

"It's just robocalls," I tell Noor. "You don't—"

Noor's bracelets jangle as she reaches for the phone. The sun catches her cheekbone, painting it a deep golden brown. Noor hides her face, mostly. Or tries to. Keeps her bangs in her eyes and her head down. Keeps her smiles to herself or the few people lucky enough to see one.

I'm over you, she told me.

So stop staring at her, asshole.

It all passes through my head in an instant and then she's picking up the phone. "Clouds' Rest Inn Mo—"

The person on the other end starts speaking immediately. I catch the words "Malik," "late," and "legal action," before Noor hangs up. She finds the ringer and switches it off.

"Leave it on," I say. "Sometimes people call for prices."

"They can find that online." She sits back down, hand twisting the hair on her crown, observing me—a math problem she can't solve.

"How bad is it?" she finally asks.

"It's fine. I rented two rooms last night. Paid down our cell phone bill this morning."

"That creditor said you owe eight hundred dollars in past-due cable bills and they're about to shut off the Wi-Fi. And you haven't been turning on the heat. Maybe you and your dad should talk about selling—"

"I'm not selling the Clouds' Rest. Ama loved this place. The least I can do is try to keep it running. It was her dream."

"But what's your dream, Salahudin? What do you want?" At my expression she leans forward, dark eyes on mine, and I catch my breath, because there's an intensity to her regard. "If you could do anything? Be anything? What would you be?"

"I—I don't know," I sputter. When I was a kid, I wanted to be Lionel Messi. Then for a while a teacher. And then—nothing. I wanted normalcy. Order. Control. I wanted Ama to feel better. I wanted Abu to stop drinking.

"I like to write," I finally say. "But I can't do anything with that. All I do is journal."

"That doesn't mean you can't do anything with it," she says. "There's a prize for that writing contest Mrs. Michaels wants you to enter. It's not much, but—"

"I was thinking I could get a job."

"How are you going to run this place if you're working and going to school?"

"I'm looking for something after school," I say. "I applied at a few places. The girl at Java House said she had an opening."

While I filled out the application, Art Britman wandered over, eight-dollar drink in hand, new Jordans on his feet. *Broke, huh?*

I've been there, man. There are other ways to make money, though.

"Look, don't worry about it," I say. Noor gets what it's like to be broke. To marvel at the ways the rich kids in Juniper throw away money that would equal three months of internet or a dozen trips to Goodwill. Still, I'm embarrassed that she knows how bad off Ama left the motel. I hate the idea of Noor thinking I can't handle my own shit.

I grasp for something to change the subject, and notice a slight discoloration at her jaw—the line of her foundation.

"Hey," I say. "What's with the makeup?"

"I can't wear makeup?" She stiffens. "You didn't have a problem when Ashlee did it."

"No—it looks good. I'm not used to it, I guess."

"Well, it's not for your benefit, so I don't see why you care." Noor stands up and packs up her books. *Sal, you idiot.*

"I'm sorry," I say. "Don't go. Please. I didn't mean to upset you—"

"You didn't." She gives me a smile that's so fake I wince. "It's almost eight. I have to get home anyway. You know Chachu."

She throws a quick "salaamoalaikum" over her shoulder and then she's gone, the *tic-tic-tic* of her bike gears fading into the cold night.

"What's with the makeup?" I imitate myself as I flip on the outside lights. "Salahudin, you dumbass."

The office door opens and the bell shrieks. *Please, God, let it be a customer.*

I paste a smile on my face. "Welcome to the Clouds' Res—"

"Looking for Misbah Malik." An older guy with a gut and a mustache like a squirrel's tail stands at the counter. The door's open behind him and I hear the throbbing growl of a diesel truck.

"She—ah—she died."

The guy snorts. "Yeah, I've never heard that one before. Well, when she resurrects, you let her know that her car's been repo'd for nonpayment." He slaps a paper down. "If she wants it back, she can call the numb—"

"She's not gonna be resurrected." I dig my fingers into the counter so hard that I think my nails might pop off. "She's not going to call the number."

"Look, kid, I don't know if you don't understand English or—"

"Misbah's my mom. Was my mom." My voice shakes, and maybe that's why he doesn't tell me off or walk away. "She died a couple weeks ago. On February first. She—she was really sick at the end. I'm sorry she didn't pay but she was really, really sick."

His face changes and it hurts to watch. It makes what I'm saying so real. I don't want it to be real.

He looks around the office, taking in the fingerprint-smudged counter, the stack of dirty laundry behind me, the CALIFORNIA PARKS calendar that's stuck on January.

"You got a dad?"

"He's a drunk." It's the first time I've said it out loud.

"Well. Shit." The guy hikes up his pants. "Look, I've got to take the car. That's my job. I'll hitch her up quiet-like. Make sure we don't put a scratch on her. Best I can do. You got the key?"

After I hand it over, the repo guy moves quickly, hooking a couple of long cables to the Civic's chassis. To quell the panic building in my chest, I try to imagine his story. How many repos he's done. If he ever gets into fights. I haven't written since the funeral. Maybe I'll write about this.

He gives the car a pat when he's finished, nods at me curtly, and gets in the truck. But before he drives off, he rolls down the window.

"Kid." He stares at me for a moment. He's got blue eyes, and even though he looks like he probably eats nails for breakfast, something flashes across his craggy face that makes me think he treats the people he loves like gold.

Maybe he's going to offer me some pearl of wisdom. That's how it goes in the stories, right? The person you least expect is the one who has all the answers. And this guy's probably seen some shit. *How do I fix it all?* I want to ask him. *How do I bring her back and do it over?*

"If your dad picks up the car," the repo guy finally says, "tell him he's gotta show up sober. The guy who runs the lot is a dickhead. He'll call the cops over the tiniest shit."

I stare after him until his taillights fade. Above, the sky is murky from all the dust the wind's stirred up, and I search the haze for even a single star. But there's nothing, so I give up and go in to the father I don't know how to talk to and the pictures I don't know how to look at and the bills I don't know how to pay.

CHAPTER 14

Misbah

April, then

The Gold Mirage Banquet Hall was swathed in artful swoops of orange and red organza. The tables glowed with marigolds and rose petals, and the glistening, sumac-sprinkled kabobs and bubbling haleem beckoned from silver chafing dishes. My cousins milled about the stage, bright as cayenne on an ear of buttered corn. I could see all of it from the anteroom where I'd waited for half the day.

But the barat, the groom's wedding party, was late.

"Even for a Lahorite," my cousin Aisha fretted, "six hours is extreme."

"He has family arriving from Jeddah. Perhaps their flight was de-layed."

"Your makeup is melting off, na!" Aisha dabbed at my face. "You will be a puddle by the time he sees you."

I peeked in the mirror. Other than a bit of foundation that rubbed off on my red dupatta, I looked exactly as I had when I stepped out of the bridal salon. The lights flickered and a generator roared to life somewhere outside.

"Stop pacing," I said. "Everything will be fine."

Drums thundered in a familiar, joyful rhythm—the signal that the groom and his retinue had arrived. "See?"

"What a silly tradition." Aisha peered out the window. "He looks so

serious, riding in on that horse. Like his life depends on staying in the saddle!"

"He probably doesn't want to break his neck on his wedding day."

"Yes, that would get in the way of the wedding night."

Aisha grinned at me, but I shrugged. I was nervous. My mother wasn't forthcoming about the wedding night, but my married cousins were. Aisha, with her unrequited flirtations at university, saw fit to supply me a small box of "necessary items." I was dying to look inside.

Outside, a man shouted. Aisha's dark hair swung as she parted the window curtain. Her shoulders stiffened.

"I'll be right back," she said. "Sadaf," she called to her little sister, who was sulking in a corner over an Archie comic. "Bring Misbah Baji a 7UP."

Sadaf nodded dutifully. The moment Aisha disappeared, she ran to the window. I joined her, thankful that she was too young to know that I shouldn't be seen.

The shouting continued and I sought out Toufiq but instead found his father, dressed impeccably and pleading with his wife. Toufiq's mother gesticulated wildly to my brother. I thought my brother had offended her. It would not be the first time Faisal had put his foot in his mouth.

But for once, Faisal appeared blameless. Toufiq's mother grabbed my brother by his kurta, and my own mother appeared, along with my cousins. I saw them speaking quickly, attempting to calm Toufiq's mother. From his horse, Toufiq appeared stricken. But he did not dismount, or try to pull his mother from Faisal.

"Get away from there!" Aisha appeared at the door and yanked me from the window. "He isn't supposed to see you!"

"What is happening? Did Faisal say something stupid?"

Aisha shooed away Sadaf, who pretended to disappear into her book but was obviously eavesdropping.

"Toufiq's mother is . . . acting strange," Aisha whispered. "She is—we think she is inebriated. Faisal mentioned the lateness of the barat—and she exploded. I could smell it on her, Misbah."

Of all the things I expected, a drunken mother-in-law was the last. My family was not particularly conservative, but we did not gamble and we did not drink. I would not have even known where to buy alcohol in Lahore.

"Misbah." My father entered. His smile would have eased my heart, but for the topi wadded in his hands. My mother followed him, her round face pinched.

"There was a small delay, but it is nothing to be concerned with," my father said.

"Baba," I said. "Aisha said Toufiq's mother was drunk." Though I tried to control it, my voice shook, and Baba took my shoulders.

"Come now, little butterfly," he said. "Do not worry. Toufiq is a good boy. And an only son. Your new mother-in-law simply began to celebrate early. We cannot always help the foolishness of our families, na?" He put a big, warm hand on my head, offering comfort as he had since I was a little girl. "All will be well."

Behind him, my mother appeared less convinced.

"All must be well," she muttered under her breath. "The marriage papers are signed."

CHAPTER 15

Sal

March, now

There's a Shelob-sized spider lurking between the o and the v of our NO VACANCY sign. I'm trying to figure out how to capture the monster and get him out of the office when Curtis from room 4 clears his throat behind me.

"Hey, Sal." He's a big guy and the office is tiny. The counter rocks as he bumps into it, sending another pile of bills I'm too afraid to open to the floor.

"Sorry," he says of the bills. "I came to pay—Christ on a god-damn cracker." He recoils at the sight of the spider.

"Yeah," I say. "He deserves his own zip code."

A familiar silver flash zooms by the office window. A minute later, Noor opens the door.

"Hey, Salahudin. Hey, Curt—holy *shit*." She steps behind me, standing on her tiptoes to peek up over my shoulder at the spider. Something about her face and the way she's using me as a shield makes me want to take this eight-legged beast down, just for her.

"He's not that scary," I say.

"Then why are you standing six feet away with a broom?"

"You're braver than me, son." Curtis takes off his hat, revealing a thick head of salt-and-pepper hair. "Your mom was braver than both of us. She'd have caught it and put it outside."

"Yeah, she hated killing bugs."

"Sounds about right. She always made little animals out of the bathroom towels." He smiles. "I don't like foreigners usually, and the first time I come in here and see her wearing that thing on her head, I said to her, 'Why are you wearing that thing on your head—'"

"It's called a hijab—" I begin, but Curtis grabs the gold cross resting in his curly chest hair and shakes it at me.

"She said, 'Why do you wear that thing around your neck?' I said, 'Because Jesus Christ is my lord and savior,' and she said, 'Well, I have nothing against Jesus, he was a great man. I think he would like my scarf. His mama wore one.' Then she laughed, and hell, I started laughing, too. Maybe Jesus would have liked her scarf, at that." He clears his throat and digs his credit card out.

"Sorry it's late," he says.

"No worries," I say. "It's 250 dollars total. I can charge next week, too, if you like."

"Ah—well." He shifts from foot to foot, pulling at his Guns N' Roses shirt. "I'm not sure I'll be staying on after Friday."

Shit. *Shit.*

"The Wi-Fi is down. Has been for a few days. I need clean towels a bit more regular. Figured I should move on. Might be best if your old man tries to sell the place—"

"We're not selling it. But the Wi-Fi will be back up tomorrow—" *Now that you've paid me.* "Here—" I step out the door to the Coke machine in the carport and bring him back a cold can. "Talk to Noor about nineties music. She loves it, too. I'll be done with your room in a few minutes."

"I can help—" Noor offers, but I just shake my head. It's bad enough that she feels like she has to come over here every day.

Curtis's room looks—and smells—like a rabid bear has been living in it. I mouth-breathe, and try not to gag. After Ama first got sick, she never let me clean the rooms. It was only in the last few months, when things got bad, that I insisted on helping—though between school and soccer, it was never enough. Maybe if I'd done more, she wouldn't have worked herself to death.

Or maybe Ama could have gotten dialysis. My sudden wrath stops me in my tracks, and I have to sit, Pine-Sol-soaked rag in hand. *Maybe she could have made Uncle Faisal help her. Found a way. Maybe she could have tried to live, knowing that I'd be up shit creek if she didn't.*

I hate her in that moment and then I hate myself for hating a dead woman whose grave I haven't even bothered to visit.

Do the work, Sal. Just do the damn work.

I collect every can and bottle. Ama made an extra fifty bucks a week recycling everything. Once those are out of the way, I conquer the bathroom.

It's a horror show—streaks in the toilet, toothpaste congealed on the sink, and a trash can overflowing with five days' worth of takeout boxes. I squash a few ants, reminding myself to call the exterminator.

Though I don't know how I'll afford it. Abu's unemployment check took care of the electric bill. But everything else is too much to even think about. Now the hospital's started calling my phone. I deleted three messages from them without even listening.

When I finish Curtis's room, I realize I'm short a few towels. My stomach lurches. I've dropped Abu's and my laundry at the wash-and-fold, because the owner knew Ama and didn't charge me for all of February. We've had so few tenants since Ama died that I've been able to stick a hand into the laundry room and grab what I needed off a shelf without going in.

No longer.

The blue door of the laundry room taunts me. *You're eighteen years old,* I tell myself. *You can walk into a laundry room and throw some sheets in the washer.*

The door sticks, so I give it a solid shove. The scent of detergent and bleach overtakes me. Instantly I'm nauseous. Like I'm smelling rotted meat instead of something clean. I grit my teeth and shove the sheets into the washer—which isn't empty. There are towels that have been in there so long they've dried stiff.

One thing at a time.

I drop the new laundry onto the floor and turn the washer on. Measure out the Costco powdered detergent and a half cup of bleach. My head starts to spin. I'm going to sit on the floor, just for a moment. To get my balance.

No—nope, not going to sit on the floor. I'm going to be sick.

"Hey." A hand on my arm. I jump at the touch, but it's only Noor.

"Come on—come here, Salahudin."

She pulls at me but I can't stand and we stumble-walk from the laundry room. Outside, she hands me a mop bucket just in time for me to hurl my guts out. I'm so embarrassed she's seeing this. Not the upchucking, though it's not a great look since I don't want her to find me totally repulsive.

No, I hate that she sees the weakness. The lack of control. Me sweating. Barely able to walk.

"I'm sorry," I whisper.

"Stay here."

Her footsteps are light, and I hear the *click-click* of the washer switch turning, and the chug of water pouring into the drum. The dryer snicks open, and for a few minutes, there's nothing but the occasional swish of a sheet through the air.

I put my head between my legs and try to breathe, realizing I'd rather inhale this smell, of vomit and concrete and a nostril-freezing desert winter, than that of the laundry room. I wish I knew why I was like this. I wish I could make sense of it.

Do you, Salahudin? Do you really?

I avoid the thought the way I avoided doing the laundry. The way I've avoided visiting Ama's grave, even though I know she's probably lonely.

"Salahudin." My name is a song when Noor says it. I'm too humiliated to look at her. She takes away the bucket and returns a few minutes later with her backpack. A couple of wet wipes appear under my nose. Then a peeled banana.

"It'll settle your stomach."

I take a bite. My throat is raw and my voice is a rasp. "Did you learn that at the hospital?"

"I used to get motion sick in the car," she says. "Chachu isn't totally useless, I guess."

When I'm done, she stands and offers her hand. I take it gingerly, but there's nothing unpleasant in her touch. Just warmth and a slight tingle.

"I'll deal with the laundry," she says. "Let's get you inside."

In the apartment, Abu is sleeping on the couch, the remote loose in his hand. I put a blanket over him and turn him on his side.

I hate the fact that I have to do it. Hate that it's me taking care of him, instead of him making sure I'm all right.

Our dining table is hardly visible beneath unopened mail, plates, crumbs, and a foil-covered casserole dish that should have been thrown out a few days ago, judging by the smell.

"Sorry for the mess."

Noor hums a few notes of a song that I don't recognize. "'Mess Is Mine,'" she informs me. "Vance Joy singing what I'm thinking, which is that I don't mind your mess."

"Is that the one with the creepy polar bear video?"

She laughs. More than one person has commented on Noor's infectious laugh, though she gets embarrassed when they do. Right now, it's the only good thing in this apartment.

"I'll help you, Salahudin." She leans against the wall, her hands clasped in front of her. "But you have to let me."

"She'd have hated this," I whisper. "You seeing all this." The sink's gross. The fridge is empty. I haven't vacuumed. There's a plastic bag in the corner, an ancient thing spilling over with an unfinished sweater Ama had been making for the past decade. It was supposed to be for Abu—she'd poke at it once a year and then put it away until the mood struck her again. She'd joke that the day she finished it would be the day Abu retired.

Retirement came early. Abu's never been able to hold a job for long.

The silence between Noor and me lengthens—but it's not uncomfortable. Sometimes, when Ama and I were talking, if I didn't respond quickly enough she'd snap her fingers at me anxiously, like she thought I was going to get lost in my own brain.

But Noor lets me think.

"You asked how bad it is." I haven't wanted to think about this part, let alone say it aloud. "It's bad. There was an eviction notice on the front door this morning."

She inhales sharply and sits next to me.

"I need five grand by April fifteenth," I go on, "or the bank's taking the Clouds' Rest. The Civic didn't break down. It got repossessed. I told Abu, but . . ." I don't even know if he heard me. "His unemployment benefits are about to expire, and he won't stay sober long enough to renew them."

Noor chews on her lip. "Did you hear anything from the jobs you applied to?"

"They all need someone during school hours."

"What about Uncle Faisal?"

I want to erase the memory of that call. Of Uncle Faisal sighing like I was asking him for his immortal soul instead of for help. *There's no point in me giving you money, Salahudin. If I do, your father will never learn to stand on his own two feet. And neither will you.*

"He won't help. Why are rich dudes always so cheap?"

Noor raises an eyebrow. "How do you think rich people stay rich? By being nice?" She taps her chin. "I could rob his house. Sell your cousin's ugly-ass watch collection for a couple G's."

"Only Arsalan's arse enough to buy that kind of hideous shit."

Noor groans. "That joke will never be as funny as you think it is." She leans close enough that our heads almost touch. I close the distance and breathe her in until I'm calm again. Beneath the soap, she smells like mint and raat ki raani—a flower I only ever saw in Pakistan. I wonder why I never noticed it before.

"Look, we can't fix the money problem right now," Noor says. "But we can fix this." She waves at the mess. "Maybe cleaning will clear our heads, too. Help us come up with something. And"—she hands me an earbud—"it will give me an excuse to make you listen to this live Pink Floyd album."

I tackle the kitchen as Noor works her way through the dining room. Her off-key humming is a strangely soothing counterpoint to "Comfortably Numb" blasting in one ear. After a few minutes, I'm able to push First Union Bank from my mind.

Though I want to pour Abu's liquor down the drain, I resist. It won't change anything—he'll just burn through money buying more. So I water each bottle down a little and shove them in a corner. Then I wipe down counters, scrub dishes, change sheets, mop, vacuum. I clean the way that Ama used to clean. The way I wish Abu would.

"Hey." Noor calls me into Ama's bathroom and gestures at a dozen bottles of medicine. "Juniper Hospital has a drug disposal site. I can take these."

I stop cold, a duster in hand, considering. I hear Art Britman. *There are other ways to make money.*

"I'll take them myself later."

By the time we're done, just after dark, the place is almost as clean as Ama would have gotten it.

We drag a few trash bags out to the dumpster behind the motel, and Noor switches off her music. "Feel better?"

"I'm starving," I say. "Does that count?"

She rolls her eyes. "No."

"I'll be fine," I say. "I won't jump in front of a train or anything. I might come wail mournfully under your window at two a.m., though."

"Salahudin." She looks at me askance. "That is not comforting."

"I'm the one hurling into buckets, Noor. You're supposed to be comforting *me*."

"You're ridiculous. I'm here every day anyway, so the laundry's my job from now on, okay? At least until your dad . . . recovers."

"So for the next ten years. That might put a dent in your college plans."

"It won't be ten years if you talk to your abu about going back to AA."

Oh hell no. I'm already shaking my head. "How am I supposed to talk to him, Noor? He's basically the Punjabi Rip Van Winkle. If I managed to drag him to consciousness, I don't even know what he'll say. He's so . . ." *Unknowable. Unpredictable.*

"Salahudin, you can't control him. All you can do is try to help him." She doesn't let me retort. "If he sobers up, maybe he can figure out how to pay the bank."

"Maybe squirrels can fly, too."

"There is such thing as a flying squirrel, genius." She sighs at the look on my face. "What if he finds your mom's painkiller stash? Addicts come into the ER all the time." She shudders. "Half-dead from whatever evil stuff their shithead dealers sell them."

Noor starts packing up her bag. "April fifteenth is less than five weeks away," she says. "That time's going to disappear. You're out of options, Salahudin. Talk to him. Maybe get him to go to Auntie Misbah's grave with you."

"No way—" I stop myself. "I'd . . . rather not go to the grave yet. But I'll talk to him. Promise."

Not that it will do any good. Abu isn't going to get sober. He isn't going to solve my problems. Neither is Uncle Faisal.

I walk Noor home as usual, but she can tell I don't feel like talking, so halfway through the walk, we listen to a live version of "Shake It Out" by Florence and the Machine that makes my chest clench tight.

When we turn onto Noor's street, her uncle's dented blue car sits in the driveway.

"I'll walk from here. If he sees you, I won't hear the end of it." She pulls on her braid, the left one. It's always the left one.

As I watch her, I think of how, in freshman year, I busted my ankle in soccer practice and got benched. Three months later, I walked out to the field, each step a question mark until I reached the goal and realized my bones would still carry me.

That same warmth floods me now. I still know Noor's body. I know *her*. I guess I thought I didn't deserve to, anymore.

She turns, surprised when I weave my fingers between hers

and squeeze. A shy spark kindles between us, and Noor regards me quietly, the half-moon above twinning into pale boats that drift in the nadirs of her eyes. She squeezes back. Then she's gone.

As I walk to the motel, shivering because I've forgotten my jacket again, I pull out my phone and run through my contacts. Friends. Family. Acquaintances.

None of them can get First Union Bank off my back. None of them can make that eviction notice go away. *You're out of options,* Noor said.

I swipe through phone numbers until I find *Britman, Art.*

Can u talk?

I send the message before I can chicken out. It doesn't mean anything. He might not respond. He might be pissed that I broke up with his cousin. He might think I'm writing to him about Trig or—

Art: Sure thing. Stop by Saturday night.

And then, after a few seconds:

Art: Figured you'd come around. ☺

That damn happy face. It makes me sadder than the rest of the day put together.

CHAPTER 16

Noor

"We regret to inform you—"

"While your grades and scores were impressive, unfortunately—"

"After reviewing your application, we have made the difficult decision—"

The letters come hard and fast. Like the gunshots in M.I.A.'s "Paper Planes." *Bang. Bang. Bang.*

Yale. Columbia. Cornell.

Rejected. Rejected. Rejected.

Five rejections. Out of seven.

Meanwhile, Jamie's informed all of Juniper that she got into Princeton. And she won't stop asking me if I've heard anything yet.

Part of me just wants to tell her: *I got rejected from five schools. The two I haven't heard from are UCLA and Northwestern, so I'm screwed. You won. Congratulations.*

The only good thing about Chachu's obsession with theorems is that numbers make sense to me. So while Mrs. Michaels talks about metrical pattern in poetry, I go over the numbers again. I got a 1430 on my SATs. I have a 4.2 GPA. I've aced sixteen honors classes in four years, even managing an A- in dreaded English. I've volunteered at Juniper Hospital five times a week since I was a junior. I had three recommendations, all glowing.

It must have been the essays. *The essay is the most important part of the application,* the UPenn interviewer said. I used the Common App, but a lot of the schools had separate questions. There were so many. Every time, I had to write about something new:

A problem I solved. (Truth: heartbreak. What I wrote: a poor English grade.)

A life-altering experience. (Truth: my entire family dying and the smell of their bodies rotting around me. What I wrote: working at Juniper Hospital.)

My biggest life challenge. (Truth: they don't want to know. What I wrote: bullying in high school.)

For the admissions essay, I tried to write about the earthquake. About my parents and Chachu and the liquor shop. I shoved it into a drafts folder the next day. Wrote about volunteering at a traveling clinic instead, spell-checked, and sent it in to every school but UCLA. That application was a whole different disaster.

But there are still two schools left, I remind myself. Two isn't zero. Two is two. And it only takes one yes.

You are better than this place. More than this place.

"Hey—*Noor.*"

Jamie pokes me. The bell will ring in a few minutes and Mrs. Michaels is waving my homework at me—the first half of my year-end fifteen-pager. I go up to collect it, and notice that Salahudin is watching me from his seat beneath the fire alarm, two rows away. He raises an eyebrow. *What's wrong?* I shrug and smile. He has enough to deal with.

Jamie cranes her neck. "What did you get?"

"Why do you care?"

I don't mean to snap at her. Or maybe I do. Maybe I'm sick of her.

"Just curious." Jamie's mouth smiles even if the rest of her doesn't. "You don't have to be rude. I know you've been struggling." She looks down at her nails. Only I can hear her. "Without Sal to write your essays for you."

"What the hell is that supposed to mean?"

Mrs. Michaels glances up, surprised. Atticus, Jamie's boyfriend, gives me a dirty look and snatches my paper away. "Watch your mouth, Riaz."

I grab at it, but Atticus has gorilla arms and lifts it out of the way. Class is almost over, and everyone's talking as Mrs. Michaels hands out the rest of the papers.

"Stop, Atticus." Jamie's smirk says, *Good job, Atticus.* "Give it back to her—"

Salahudin leans over me then and grabs the paper back. "Don't be a dick, Atticus."

Atticus glares at him, but Salahudin looks right back, dark eyes cold. They're on the soccer team together, though they're not friends. Atticus stares him down for a second before shrugging and offering me a half smile.

"Just messing around," he says. "And hey—good job."

Salahudin gives me my paper—with an A on top. Jamie sees it. "Nice." She glances at him. "Guess you two are friends again."

"I wrote the paper myself."

"It's fine if you had help." She's quiet, but there's a weird heaviness to her voice. Like she's spitting, not speaking. "You don't always have to be the best at everything."

"I wrote the paper," I say slowly, "myself."

"Come on, Noor," she says. "I've seen your writing in group projects. You—well—you struggle. I get it. English isn't even your first language. You speak it really well—"

"Careful, Jamie." Salahudin is back in his seat. "Your inner Klansman is showing. After you've tried so hard to hide it."

"What the hell, Sal?" Jamie's head snaps toward him, face paling. "I'm not a racist. I was *trying* to give her a compliment. I don't have anything to hide." She glances at me, eyes roaming over my face. "Seems like Noor does, though."

My fingers go numb at the tips, and I tell myself to breathe. She thinks Salahudin's helping me cheat. Or somehow she's figured out I'm hiding all the college rejections.

Or maybe—maybe she knows something else.

My paper shakes. No—my hands. I ball them into fists and tuck them under my desk. Jamie stares at me, waiting for me to deny that I'm hiding anything.

But I don't deny it. Because she's right.

The second the bell rings, I'm out of there. The Who howls about teenage wastelands in my ears, so I don't know Salahudin is calling me until he's right next to me.

"What is going on?" he says. "I've been chasing you for like five minutes. Are you okay?"

I'm fine is on my lips, but I can't say the words.

"Jamie just—she got to me today."

"Why?"

"Because—"

He doesn't know about the rejections. He only knows I applied to UPenn because of that disastrous interview. We weren't talking last fall, when I was sending off transcripts and writing bad essays.

"Noor." He steps in front of me. "Talk to me."

I look up at him. Salahudin has brown eyes, along with four billion other people on the planet. You'd think songs about brown eyes would be common. But no. We've got "Hey Blue Eyes" and "Pale Blue Eyes," and "Green Eyes" and "Blue Eyes Crying in the Rain." We've got a thousand fantasy books with gray-eyed heroes. (Which is BS, because who *actually* has gray eyes, and is also handsome and can also swing a sword? No one.)

But if those singers or writers saw Salahudin's eyes, they'd change their tune. His eyes are the deep brown of a haveli door, with a ring of smoke around the edges. No one has eyes like his.

Don't look away, I think at him. *But also, please look away. Because this hurts.*

"I haven't gotten in anywhere," I finally whisper. "I applied to seven schools but I got rejected from five of them. There's only UCLA and Northwestern left."

"Shit, Noor, why didn't you say something? What about your safeties?"

I shake my head. "UVA was my safety. And not a very smart one. I only picked schools I really wanted. Didn't have enough money for more applications."

"Aren't there fee waivers or—"

"I'd have needed a counselor to complete it. And I was scared they'd call Chachu. I had to sneak into his office and dig around his taxes just so I could fill out the financial aid forms."

Brooke didn't go to college. Chachu doesn't want me to go. Juniper High has one guidance counselor who spends most of his time dealing with opioid addictions and teen pregnancies. Even figuring out how to apply for college took me hours of research.

"There's only two schools left. My essays were awful—"

"I bet they weren't as bad as you think. Send them to me."

I shake my head. "No point. Salahudin . . . what if I don't get in anywhere? I can't stay here—I can't—"

My eyes get hot. I pretend it's not happening. Clear my throat and cross my arms. But a fat tear drops right down onto Salahudin's boots. We stare at it together for a second before I look up at him. He takes a step back, his face weirdly dazed, before he shakes himself.

"Noor—"

"I'm not crying!"

"You're totally not." His voice is quiet. He steps forward and pulls me toward him. I'm so surprised, I don't understand what's happening and stumble. Then his arms come up around me and he tugs me into his body. His chin rests on top of my head. I feel the rise and fall of his chest against mine.

Salahudin Malik is hugging me.

It is a gift so strange and unexpected that I melt into him and let go, sobbing into his chest right there in an alcove behind C-hall with the entire school heading to class around us. I'm crying because I'm scared. Sad. I miss Auntie. I miss my parents. I miss things I can't put into words because they were taken before I knew how precious they were.

The bell rings. I'll be late to class. So will Salahudin. Maybe I should pull away. Salahudin doesn't like touch. It's selfish of me to hold on like this. But I realize as I cry into his shirt that I feel rootless. Pakistan isn't home anymore. Juniper never was.

But Salahudin—Salahudin feels like home.

So I stay.

CHAPTER 17

Sal

Hugging Noor is not easy.

For a brief, delusional moment, I think it will be. She looked up into my eyes, and I wished I could go to every school that rejected her to confront their admissions boards and tell them that they are fools and charlatans. But since that's not an option—a hug.

Then she starts crying. Her shoulders shake and some part of me knows that this isn't only about school, or leaving Juniper or even Ama. Something deeper is making her feel this way, and I can't fix it. I don't even know what it is.

But I can keep holding her. So I do, and it's fine—until suddenly it's not. This feeling comes over me, like I want to erupt from my own skin. *Breathe. Five seconds in, seven seconds out.*

It doesn't help and I hate myself so much. I make no sense. My body makes no sense. I trust Noor—I like her. More than "like," considering that I've found myself thinking about how funny she is and the way she looks when she's solving a math problem and the shape of her lips. And now, when I'm finally holding her, I can't even lose myself in it. All I can think is, *Get away.*

Once, I read a story about a guy in the Amazon rain forest who was the last to speak his language—after he died, it would never be heard again. People tried to learn it, but it was impossible. Sometimes, I feel like the language of my body is equally unfathomable. I'll die being the only person who ever knew how to speak it.

I break free and Noor drops her arms quickly.

"Are you—"

"Fine," I say. "Don't worry about me." She sniffles and digs in her overstuffed backpack for a tissue. When she can't find one, I offer her my arm.

"Arm hair," I say. "Works better than tissue, eight hundred thread count."

"Ew," she laughs. "I'm not using your arm hair to wipe my tears. You don't even have that much."

I grasp my heart. "What kind of Punjabi man doesn't have a nice, warm pelt of arm hair for his"—I was about to say *girl*, but change my mind at the last second—"for his friends to cry on?"

"First of all, I wasn't crying. I just had some lacrimal gland secretions, along with some mild dyspnea. Second, you can't call that a pelt. It's more like a dusting. Pretty sure Brooke has more hair on her arms than you do."

"Are you saying I'm not a man, Noor?"

"You're definitely a man, Salahudin Malik." She runs her eyes over me in a most un-Noor-like way. My heart, thudding along dutifully a second ago, loses its shit from sheer excitement. "If you weren't, my life would be much simpler."

"More *man*-ageable, perhaps?"

She groans. "How can someone so good with words make such awful jokes? Anyway, thanks. For the hug and for . . ." She gestures to my sodden shirt.

"Accepting your lacrimal gland secretions?"

"Yeah." She smiles at me, and it's a comet flashing across a sky. "That."

We part and head to class. For the first time in a while, I feel a lightness in my chest. Because even though I might lose my home and Abu's a drunk and Ama is never coming back and my body is weird, the girl I'm falling for flirted with me.

For the rest of the day, I can't stop smiling.

My descent into the criminal underworld of Juniper begins the next night in Legacy Village, one of those cookie-cutter subdivisions with a clubhouse and a fake waterfall and an overzealous gate guard. When I came here for Art's eighth birthday, I remember thinking my entire apartment could fit into his parents' kitchen.

"Come in, come in!" Art does a weird half bow as he opens the door. He must not have a lot of people over.

He leads me into a den with a TV so big that I sort of wish we were better friends so I could play *Bandit Brotherhood* on it. After a minute I change my mind. The room is beautiful but cold; no one has stirred a pot of steaming kheer over the stove while breathing in the scent of milk-and-saffron-soaked rice laced with rosewater. No one has played Ludo at this table while stuffing their faces with fresh, icy mangoes as *The Empire Strikes Back* blared in the background.

Art has set out two frosted glasses of beer—something I've only ever seen anyone do in a commercial.

"I'm good." I push the drink away. It smells like the alley behind the motel when Abu is at his worst.

Besides, I want this over with. Ama's pill bottles are like hot coals in my pocket, so I lay them out quick on the coffee table. As Art examines them, I look away.

You're saving the Clouds' Rest, I think. *Making sure you and Abu have food and a roof over your heads and running water. You're surviving.*

"All right, so I could sell these for you," Art says. "But things are bad, yeah? I mean, you wouldn't be trying to work at Java House if they weren't."

At my nod, Art considers. He reminds me sometimes of that lizard in the car insurance commercials. Friendly, thoughtful, and a little dense all at once.

"I think *you* should sell them. Not me. Hear me out." He grins at me like he's offered me a winning lottery ticket. "I'll take a cut, since you'll be working off my contacts. Thirty percent. But—if it goes well, we can expand."

Sudden fear constricts my chest. *Seven seconds in. Five seconds out.* Ama has a few bottles of pills but she'd need five times as much for me to make the money for First Union. Art's suggestion to sell for him makes sense.

It's just not something I ever thought I'd do.

"You'll start basic," Art says. "Painkillers, Adderall, Xanax—that kind of shit. You can get the kids in the honors classes. But no Molly yet, no meth, no heroin."

Molly? "Okay."

Art smiles. As he talks about burner phones and getting me my product, I feel like I'm watching him through a porthole. This is my life—but it's warped and distant and wrong. And I don't know how to change it back to what it was.

You can't change it.

Selling Ama's meds—and whatever else Art gives me—isn't forever. It's just until the motel starts doing better. I already have ideas for how to get rooms rented. I can make this work, make the Clouds' Rest what Ama hoped it would be.

I just need time.

Outside, the sky is heavy and close. I get a whiff of Mojave petrichor: that singular scent of rain falling on dry earth mixed with sweet creosote. Ama got grouchy when it rained, hating the snarled traffic, leaking motel roof, and flooded streets. But to me, rain in the desert felt miraculous. Abu and I would buy firewood and make s'mores. Abu never talked about his parents or family in Pakistan. When it rained, though, he'd tell me stories of his college years in London.

The last time I picked up my journal was before Ama's funeral. But maybe I should write Abu's stories down. Or ask him to tell me more. Maybe it will help him remember a better time.

When I get home, I see Ama's desk has been disturbed. The bills I organized are all over the place, and I recognize Abu's scrawl on a pad of paper, tallying up the numbers, as I did weeks ago. He must have gotten the same shock I did.

Except I didn't disappear into a bottle when I found out how bad off we were.

I find him asleep on the recliner, while a panel of talking heads snipes at each other about the opioid epidemic. No stories from

Abu tonight, I guess. Anger writhes in me at the sight of him. I want to shake him awake. *Help me, you selfish asshole,* I'd shout. *Help me the way you didn't help Ama.*

The room goes black when I turn the TV off, and Abu jerks awake.

"Misbah?"

Nothing kills anger faster than pity, and the hope in my father's voice shoots my rage dead. I've never wanted to lie to anyone more in my life than in that moment. *Yes, it's her, Abu. She's here.*

I kneel beside him. "It's me, Abu," I say. "Salahudin."

Silence. A sigh. "Ussi ki karanh, Putar? Ussi ki karanh?"

What do we do, my son? What do we do?

Once, he knew the answer to that question. He worked. We went to Yosemite and Disneyland. He taught me to bend a soccer ball. But between those moments were days of him waking up late, or disappearing into his room. He was lost. I just didn't see it.

"I'm here, Abu." I hold his cold, limp hands in mine. "Don't worry. I'm going to take care of everything."

PART III

Then practice losing farther, losing faster:
places, and names, and where it was you meant
to travel. None of these will bring disaster.

—*Elizabeth Bishop*,
"One Art"

CHAPTER 18

Misbah

December, then

We lived with Toufiq's parents for a month. One night, while Toufiq was in Islamabad for work, his mother, Nargis, arrived home from wherever she'd been all day, dull-eyed and smelling sharply of liquor. Her words fused and flowed into one another so completely that it was as if she spoke another language.

Toufiq's father, Junaid, tried to warn me away, gently suggesting I take a rickshaw to my parents for the night. I did not understand.

Until that day, Nargis had been polite enough, if a bit aloof. I could not reconcile the belligerent, drunken woman from the wedding with this taciturn individual. But late at night, I'd hear her arguing with her husband. Toufiq slept through it—but I'd stay up listening, repelled and mesmerized by the harsh chop of her speech.

On this day, she heard Junaid warn me off and stumbled into me, grasping my face hard. I held my breath. She smelled awful.

"Is my son's new wife too delicate to see such behavior?" she asked.

"Nargis, leave her," Junaid pleaded. "She is new—"

"Not new anymore," Nargis guffawed. "She's been plucked. I was plucked, too, long ago, though I was younger. Much, much younger—"

"Nargis!" Junaid tried to step between us, but she spun me away from him, thumb and forefinger pincering my chin.

"Junaid here saved me. And he saved Toufiq."

I tried to step away, but she wouldn't release me. "Your husband is a whore's son, did you know? But Junaid—Junaid is my hero." She spit the last word out, and then her husband was between us, breaking Nargis's grip, ushering me out of the house, apologizing, putting me in a rickshaw and giving the driver my parents' address.

He did not tell me Nargis was lying or that I shouldn't listen to her or that she was crazy. He only said: "Toufiq will come for you when he returns from Islamabad."

When I reached my parents' home, I expected shock when I told them what happened. But my father only sighed and waved me through the courtyard, into his room. We sat together on his charpoi, the rope creaking beneath our weight.

"Junaid is a good person," my father began. "As is Toufiq. As is Nargis."

"But what she said about Toufiq—"

"She has had a difficult life," my father said. "Junaid helped her escape that life. But it left its mark, little butterfly."

"She—she prays! How can she pray when she lives another life, drinking and doing God knows what else—"

"Yes." My father's tone grew sharp. "God knows. What she does or does not do is not for you to judge, Misbah."

Toufiq picked me up the next day, and we moved to a flat with a blue door and a street tandoor on the corner. It was near my own parents' home. My mother kept busy searching for a bride for my brother. But Baba visited regularly, as did Junaid, and evening often found them bent over a carrom board, laughing at Toufiq's quiet wit.

Toufiq's mother visited, too. But always late at night. Her Punjabi was slurred, her voice at turns pleading or booming. Whenever we heard her outside, Toufiq excused himself. Ten or thirty minutes later, he would return, acting as if nothing had happened. But if he slept those nights, he dreamed, and his dreams ended, always, in sweat and terror.

"I worry she will destroy herself," he once said upon waking. "I worry I cannot save her."

Junaid came almost daily, stopping by on his way home from work. He loved Toufiq with a quiet fierceness and, in time, we became friends. When Toufiq was traveling, Junaid brought me food and ate with me. When the monsoons came, he swept the water from the house and filled sandbags. Sometimes I asked him about his childhood in Sharaqpur, about his sister who used to live far away, in Karachi. He never answered.

"Tell me your tales," he would say. "They are more interesting than mine."

He was a kind voice, a steady hand. The four of us—Toufiq, Junaid, my father, and I—shared laughter and stories and endless pots of tea. Junaid never asked about children, though my own mother pestered me endlessly. He never criticized. He just appeared, a quiet old soul, content to be near us.

And then, one day, Junaid did not come.

CHAPTER 19

Sal

April, now

When Noor and I watched TV shows about criminals doing stupid shit to make money, I'd mock them.

Now I get it. The stupid shit is temptingly simple. And the pay-off is huge.

Though it doesn't make me less paranoid that I'll get caught. I worry that everything I'm trying to fix will fall apart. That Abu will find my stash and start using it. That Ernst will catch me and expel me. That the police will arrest me.

But worse than the fear that I'll get thrown in jail is imagining Noor's face if she knew what I was doing. The Fight 2.0. Not a silent, broken-hearted Noor, but an enraged one. *Shithead dealers,* she'd said. If she found out, she'd never speak to me again.

A few weeks after I start working for Art, he meets me behind the motel. "Saaaaal!" he shouts, holding out both hands like a mob boss greeting a loyal hit man.

He's irritatingly chummy, but I'm not about to complain. During my first week under his tutelage, I made enough to get the Civic back from the repo lot. A week after that, I paid the water bill, the trash bill, and the electric bill. Yesterday, I paid First Union eight hundred dollars and got them to extend their deadline to April 30.

The hospital keeps calling—but they're easy enough to ignore. I'll pay them, too, now that I'm finally getting a handle on things.

After I hand over Art's cut, he offers me my next week's supply, neatly packed in a Tupperware.

"My mom sent cookies." He grins at me, because he loves using these stupid codes. "You're not keeping your shit at home, right? Or in the car?"

I shake my head. It's one of the first things he taught me, and I've been using a paint can in a shed at the back of the motel. *The last thing you need is for anyone to rob you,* he'd said. When I asked if I should carry a weapon, he laughed at me and started calling me Walter White after the *Breaking Bad* character.

As I stuff the Tupperware in my backpack, Art digs around for a cigarette, cursing when the wind puts out his Zippo. "I saw Atticus being friendly with you. Remember—"

"Clients aren't friends." I repeat his words back to him, but I don't need the reminder. Though I've not been picked on much since middle school, I've never had a horde of buddies, either. Juniper is casually racist, and even though I have what Noor refers to as "male sportsball immunity," there's still the occasional snide comment or shove in the hall.

Though now, even the assholes who'd cough "camel jockey" when I passed are polite. They want their pills. I want their money.

"Why do you sell to Ashlee," I ask Art, "if we're not supposed to be friends with our clients?"

"Ashlee is family," Art says. "She'd never screw me over." He considers me. "You're doing well," he says. "I have stuff that's more lucrative than Addy and Oxy. Interested?"

That April 30 date looms in my head. "Yeah," I say. "That'd be great."

"Salahudin?"

Noor comes around the corner of the motel into the alley, backpack hanging off one shoulder. She stopped wearing makeup for a few weeks, but she has it on again today. Her eyes seem bigger, cheekbones sharper.

"I thought that was your voice," she says, and briefly, I panic, wondering how much she heard. "Hey, Art."

"Greetings, fair lady." I practically sprain my eyes trying not to roll them as Art looks between us with a knowing grin. "I will excuse myself. See you around, Sal."

"What was he doing here?" Noor walks back to the apartment with me, and the Tupperware in my backpack suddenly feels heavier than Abu when he's full-on passed out.

"Smoking a cigarette," I say, because it's not a lie.

Noor looks askance at me. Her boots crunch in the sand that dirties the parking lot. Ama used to sweep it clear every week, a cussed war she waged with the desert.

"But what were you talking about?" Noor says. "I didn't know you were friends."

"He mentioned Ashlee," I say after a pause. I am the king of assholes for bringing up my ex, but it does the trick. Noor's face closes up and she doesn't ask about Art again.

Before I started dealing, I would never have manipulated her like that. I hate that obscuring all this from her is habit now.

Maybe working for Art is changing me. I think of a book we had to read in eleventh grade English. *The Picture of Dorian Gray.*

How the main character's portrait becomes uglier and uglier as he does worse and worse shit. How every act of deception and vice makes the next one easier.

Once we're inside, Noor says salaam to Abu, who appears half-sentient for the first time in days, and is actually renting out a room.

I promised Noor I'd talk to him, but it went about as well as I could expect. He nodded the whole time, then walked off. Two hours later, he snuck a bottle of Old Crow into his room. When I called his sponsor, Janice, she sighed.

"We can't help him unless he wants to help himself, Sal."

Noor washes, then prays namaz in the front room as she does most afternoons. She hasn't commented the past few weeks when I've skipped namaz. But today she offers me the worn green prayer rug.

"It helps," she says quietly. "Trust me."

When I finish the prayer, I don't get up. Ama's favorite part of namaz was the end, when she'd ask God for everything she needed. Little things, like for the NO on the vacancy sign to get lit up. And bigger things, like patience or better health.

"*The more you ask for,*" she'd say, "*the better. Because it means you've put your faith in something greater than yourself.*"

I never did it, because it felt like I was ceding control. If I left everything to the almighty, then what the hell was I supposed to do?

Now that I'm sitting here, I figure I should ask for something. Does God listen to drug dealers? I'll pretend the answer is yes. *Please let Ama be at peace. Please let Noor get into college. Please let Abu stop drinking. Please let us keep the Clouds' Rest.*

After folding up the rug, I find Noor digging around in the fridge.

"Sorry, there isn't much," I say, because all the money I've made has gone to overdue bills. I did buy eggs, though. I go to grab them, and when I nudge her out of the way, she jumps about a mile.

"Whoa," I say. "You okay?"

"Sorry!" she squeaks at the same time. "The freezer door slammed on my arm at the store and it hurts like hell—"

"Hey, it's okay." She's acting weird, but I let it go. Not like I can judge. I pull out some eggs. "Aanda curry?"

She nods. "Make it chat-pati, though. None of that weak jalapeño you buy from Ronnie D's. Use the good stuff. Lal mirch."

"Lal mirch gives me a stomachache!"

"How are you even Pakistani, Salahudin?" She digs around the pantry and pulls out an old spaghetti sauce jar filled with cayenne. "You're so embarrassing."

"Rude. When you pour Tabasco on our fries, I don't get jalapeño face about—"

She groans and puts her fingers on my lips. "No vegetable puns—" I realize she's touching me at the same time she does.

"Sorry," she whispers, not squeaky now, but soft and buttery like the word is made of caramel. Neither of us moves. Her brown eyes make my head spin, that delicious vertigo of tipping your head back on a playground swing and watching the horizon crest and crash. I wonder how I could have been so stupid last fall, when she kissed me. I want to find that Salahudin and kick his ass.

I let the anger fade, and instead hold on to the perfection of this moment. The way Noor smells, minty and warm, and the way her body curves beneath her worn the Cure T-shirt, her delicate brown fingers, and the silver stud in her nose.

"Noor," I whisper. At that exact moment, when she's arching toward me and my skin is tingling in a good way for once, my accursed burner phone, on the counter behind Noor, dings.

I don't have names in the phone, but I recognize the number—Atticus. I can't ignore it. He's having a party this weekend. It's a chance to make a lot of money.

"Just—um—just one sec." I step away, and after I text him that I'll be there, I find Noor watching me.

"New phone?" she asks, and her gaze is so steady that I'm certain she knows exactly what I use it for.

"Ama had a separate cell for business," I say, which isn't a lie, even if it has nothing to do with me selling drugs. I turn to the eggs. "Hand me a bowl?"

Please don't ask more questions, I beg. *Please.*

One day soon, I'll have First Union paid off. I'll figure out how to make the Clouds' Rest profitable. I won't have to do illegal shit. Maybe then I'll tell Noor about all this. She can yell at me and be angry, but I can promise her that I'll never do it again.

She turns to her own phone, and the sound of an electric guitar hums through the air. "Who is this?" I ask.

"Echo and the Bunnymen," she says quietly. " 'The Killing Moon.' Salahudin—" She glances at my burner phone and I make myself breathe. *Five seconds in, seven seconds out.*

She shakes her head then. "Don't forget the lal mirch," she says, and hands me the jar.

CHAPTER 20

Noor

April, now

You can't sneak into the Juniper mosque. Because it's not exactly a mosque. It's a twelve-by-twelve room in the north wing of the All Faith Chapel on Juniper's military base. Hindus get the room on Thursdays. Muslims on Fridays. Jews on Saturdays. Protestants get it the rest of the week.

I haven't been here in months because it requires going through the gates of the military base. And that means I have to show my ID and answer questions like "Where are you going?" and "Why?" and "Wait, we have a mosque on base?" from soldiers holding giant guns.

Today, though, I have time. Oluchi, the hospital's volunteer co-ordinator, let me off early.

"Go have a life, Noor," she said. "Go to a party. Live a little. You're like a grizzled old sea dog in a teenager's body."

But I'm not in a partying mood. I'm in an "oh crap, I better pray" mood. Since my last rejection, I've gotten another. Northwestern doesn't want me.

Which only leaves UCLA.

This Friday afternoon, there are five other people at the

"mosque." Imam Shafiq, Khadija, an army guy in camo, and an older couple I don't recognize.

There's no sermon at this time—Imam Shafiq saves that for the noon namaz. Prayer's just started when I enter and Khadija beckons me to sit next to her.

I try to fall into the rhythm of Imam Shafiq's voice. Usually, the mosque calms me. No matter how low I feel, there's a sense of community here.

But today, all I can think is that if I don't get into UCLA, I'm stuck in Juniper, working at the liquor shop. I'd go to Juniper Community College. Transfer to a four-year later. But Chachu won't let me.

I don't get to have what he didn't.

Anger is something I have in common with Chachu. I guess that's why I hate it so much. It rises in me now. I try to smother it.

You are better than this place. More than this place. The hope Auntie left me battles my rage, trying to silence it, or at least tame it. Auntie believed in me. Even at the end, she believed.

The prayer concludes. It feels sudden, but I just wasn't paying attention. Khadija disappears outside, phone held to her ear. I'm still on the prayer mat when Imam Shafiq comes over.

"Noor, salaam—" He glances at my hands, curled into fists so tight it looks like I'm about to start boxing. I loosen them. My nails have imprinted angry half-moons in my palms.

"Glad you came. Help me clean up? I want to make sure the place is ready for our Jewish brothers and sisters tomorrow."

"All eight of them?"

"Twelve now." The imam smiles. "Rabbi Alperin said a new family just moved here from LA."

They don't know how bored they're about to be. I fold up the prayer mats while Imam Shafiq sweeps the floor.

"How are you holding up, Noor?" he asks after a few minutes. "You and Auntie Misbah were close."

"I miss her. Salahudin does, too."

"I'm glad you guys are talking. He needs a friend right now. You both do."

A friend. I relive that moment I had my finger on Salahudin's lips. The way he looked at me. I thought, *Finally. Finally.*

Since then, nothing. Yesterday, after I finished the laundry and Salahudin wrapped up the rooms, we wandered around in Swat and Karachi on Google Maps. Watched travel vlogs about the Badshahi Mosque and Lahore Fort. I must have visited both when I was little because when I look at them, I smell the earthy red sandstone. Feel the reverberations of the call to prayer in my bones and hear the crackle of live electric wires.

"I miss it," Salahudin said that day. *"Even though I only visited once."*

"What do you remember?"

"I remember Ama with all her cousins, gathered around this giant barrel of iced mangoes. They were cutting them open and juice was dripping and everyone was laughing. I remember missing you. Wishing you were there."

"Pakistan lives in the blood," I told him. *"If you ever visit, you better take me. Your Punjabi is passable but your Urdu is embarrassing."*

"I'd want you to come even if you didn't speak better Punjabi." He'd given me a look then, brief and dark. A look that set me on fire.

A look I definitely don't want to be thinking about when I'm talking to the imam.

"—was like a parent to you, I imagine," Imam Shafiq is saying.

"Do you think you and Sister Khadija will ever have kids, Imam Shafiq?" After I blurt out the question, I realize how personal it is. How rude for me to ask. "I'm sorry—"

"No, it's okay." The imam is surprised. "We're pretty young," he says. "Khadija wants her law practice established. But sure, eventually."

"What—what makes a good parent?"

"Good parents take care of you," Imam Shafiq says. "They shelter you, guide you, feed you. They respect and protect you."

When he looks up, his brows are furrowed. I feel like a spotlight's on me. But he goes back to sweeping. "That last thing— protection," he says. "That one's pretty important."

"What if a parent doesn't do that?" I say. "What if the parent's actions hurt their child?"

The broom goes still. *Stupid, Noor.* Why did I open my big mouth?

"Noor. If someone is hurting you, you can tell me. Or Khadija, if you'd rather."

"No, you misunderstand," I say. "I'm worried about Uncle Toufiq. Salahudin's dad." I say it fast. So fast that the words become true. *Uncle Toufiq. I'm talking about Uncle Toufiq.*

"Salahudin's been running the motel alone since Auntie Misbah died. Uncle Toufiq—he drinks all day. Every day. He doesn't hurt Salahudin physically. But . . ."

Imam Shafiq sighs. "I'd wondered. Misbah didn't speak of it."

"Uncle Toufiq won't go to meetings, or talk to his sponsor. Salahudin needs to graduate high school—have a life. Instead, he's trying to do everything Auntie Misbah did."

"We all have our struggles, Noor," Shafiq says. "Uncle Toufiq's is heavy. I should have visited him. There might not be many Muslims here in Juniper, but none of us should feel alone. Thank you for reminding me."

He ushers me out and locks up the room. Khadija steps out of their SUV.

"Hey, throw your bike in the back," she says. "Come have dinner."

"I'm going to make chicken biryani," Imam Shafiq says. "My nani's recipe. She taught me the last time I visited Lahore. Invite Salahudin; we could pick him up."

I wonder what it would be like to have dinner with Khadija and Shafiq. To hang out with them and Salahudin like we're a family. To sit with people who don't hate me for going to mosque.

And the food. My mouth waters at the thought of a steaming bowl of spiced rice. Little garam-masala-soaked chunks of chicken baked in. Fried onions on top.

I practically have to wipe the drool off my face.

"Thanks, but I'm good." My taste buds squeal in protest. *Sorry, taste buds.* If Chachu sees Imam Shafiq and Khadija dropping me off, I'll never hear the end of it. "Chachu is making keema-aloo tonight. Also um, paratha." Lying to the imam. I wonder where that falls on the scale of forgivable to hell-bound.

Khadija gives Shafiq a look, but I'm on my bike already. Imam Shafiq pats his stomach.

"More biryani for me. Door's always open, okay?"

When Auntie Misbah got jealous, she'd say: Minue theh aag laagi-hoi eh. *I am aflame.*

Right now, I burn. Imam Shafiq visits Pakistan every year. I've seen his Pixtagram. His Urdu is effortless. His sisters played dholki at his wedding in Lahore. His family leaned into each other in the videos he posted. Teased each other in the comments below.

He's been to Saiful Muluk, the lake in northern Pakistan where a prince fell for a fairy. Eaten cayenne-dusted, charred corn in Anarkali Bazaar, named after the courtesan who died for love. He's seen Hunza Valley and Hingol Park, and the Palace of Mirrors in Lahore.

Imam Shafiq was born in America. But he knows Pakistan the way I want to, down to the biryani.

I mutter a goodbye and ride off. The pedals are stiff from the cold. I should go home, but instead I ride around the base until it's dark out. My throat feels tight. Thoughts rise in my head.

Don't think it. Shut up. Shut up, Noor. Don't think it.

But I do think it: *I wish Imam Shafiq and Khadija were my family.*

I hate myself for it. Hate that I'm still that stupid FOB who came over from Pakistan. Hate that I wish for something that will never happen.

I'm angry again. A biting, cutting anger. I can't silence it.

I guess that's why I don't bother coming in softly when I get to Chachu's house. Why I walk into the living room, even though going straight to my room is smarter.

"Where were you?" Chachu flips off the TV. He hates keema-aloo. Hates paratha, too. Like he hates everything from Pakistan, including me. Especially me.

The rest of the house is quiet. Brooke is at the store Friday evenings.

"I was at—at the library," I say. "I have a bio project."

Chachu finishes his sandwich. Chews it slowly. Then he stands.

"Do you think I'm stupid, Noor?"

If I did, I wouldn't have broken out in a sweat. "No, Chachu."

"You think that because I work at a liquor shop, I'm an idiot. That because I have an accent—"

"You don't have an accent—"

"I know you went to the mosque."

"How did—how did you know?"

He goes into the kitchen. A cabinet slams when he chucks his trash. "I didn't," he says. "I passed you when you were heading to the base. That backward little prayer group is the only reason you ever go there. You just confirmed it."

Chachu returns to the living room. He paces back and forth. So many times that I lose count. He does that thing with his fists. Opening. Closing.

There's a song by Radiohead I found a few years ago. It's called "Street Spirit (Fade Out)." I wish I could live that song. I wish I could fade out of this moment, and this room. Fade out of this family. Fade out of this life.

I watch Chachu. Those fists opening. Closing.

Closed.

Chachu is the only reason I'm standing here.

I was six when an earthquake hit my village in Pakistan. Chachu drove for two days from Karachi because the flights to northern Punjab were down. When he reached the village, he crawled over the rubble to my grandparents' house, where my parents lived, too. He tore at the rocks with his bare hands. The emergency workers told him it was useless.

His palms bled. His nails were ripped out. Everyone was dead. But Chachu kept digging. He heard me crying, trapped in a closet. He pulled me out. Got me to a hospital and didn't leave my side.

That's who Chachu is. He saved me.

He saved me.

He saved me.

"I wish you'd listen to me," he says when I emerge from the memory. His voice drops. "You never listen. Why don't you listen, Noor? I'm not a fool. I had an education. But you think you're so much smarter, huh? Well, if you're so smart, figure out how you're going to get to school tomorrow without the bike. You can't be trusted with it, clearly."

I head to my room. The light stays off. My back hurts. My arms. I unbraid my hair. It's so heavy that if I had scissors nearby, I'd cut it all off.

Homework. Think about homework. The next part of my "One Art" paper is due. It's a Veruca Salt kind of night, so I put "Seether" on repeat, and for a while, I'm lost in Nina Gordon and Louise Post's rage, in their failed attempts to silence the girl inside as she screams and breaks things.

My phone dings.

Salahudin: Hey. What are you doing?

In bed.

Salahudin: Sorry! Sweet dreams.

Not sleeping.

Mrs. Michaels's essay. I don't get this poem.

Salahudin: One Art? You want help?

Yes, if you could transplant your brain
into mine, that would be great.

Salahudin: Sure I can. Not sure if you want to
be in my brain though ha ha

How come? Impure thoughts?

As soon as I type it, I want to take it back. Three dots blink for
the longest time and I make myself not say anything else because
I'll make things worse. *Please ignore it,* I think. *Please.*

Salahudin: Where are you stuck on the essay?

The first sentence. Ha ha ha. Kidding.

Not really.

Salahudin: OK, well everything you had about
Elizabeth Bishop's background was good. You
need to analyze the poem now.

How's this for analysis: Don't lose all
your shit, Lizzie.

Salahudin: 😊 It's about loss, yeah. She starts
with objects, right? Because they're easy to lose.
Think about all the shit I lose.

Bhondthar-eh-ah!

It's what Auntie Misbah called Salahudin when he forgot his jacket or phone or keys. It doesn't have a translation. But it's like saying, "Your head doesn't work!"

Salahudin: Ama wasn't wrong. Bishop's talking about grief.
About how when shit is bad for a long time, losing becomes a
habit. You could argue she's warning us. Telling us that once
you get used to losing, you start losing bigger things. Houses,
people. Etc. The more you lose, the higher the cost.

I reread the poem. I get what he means. But maybe Bishop's not giving us a warning. Maybe she wants us to practice losing. Because loss can be good. It can save you.

When Salahudin and I were in fourth grade, he came over to watch a movie. Chachu was yelling at Brooke in the kitchen. Salahudin kept looking at the kitchen door, and then at me. I hated him when he did that because he didn't understand. He didn't realize that even when the adults in your life were shouting, you could still watch a funny movie with talking rabbits. You could lose yourself in it, if you wanted to badly enough.

Elizabeth Bishop lost lots of things. Keys, and houses, her girlfriend. She saw the truth about loss. She learned that the more you lose, the better you get at it. The better you get, the less it hurts.

I slam my laptop shut. There's no need to write this essay. I won't get into UCLA. I won't escape Juniper.

Salahudin: Noor?

I'm trying to think of a response when he calls.

"You okay?" he says.

"Yeah, fine."

"Noor, are you crying? Do you want me to come over? What happened?"

I wipe my face. My voice shakes. Sometimes, I hate being human.

"Don't come over," I say. "I'm fine."

"Is it the essay? Mrs. Michaels loves you; I'm sure she'd—"

"I got rejected from six schools, Salahudin," I say because it's the easiest explanation. "I'm stuck in Juniper."

"Noor," he says after a long, quiet moment. "Why are you crying?"

Because I hurt, I want to say. *My back hurts. My head hurts. Because I'm scared.*

"I have to go," I say. "Out of battery."

I hang up. Turn off my phone. Turn off the light. For a while, I lie there in silence. But there's too much in my head. So I pull on my headphones, listen to the gunshots that ring out at the beginning of "My Life," and let the Game speak my pain for me.

CHAPTER 21

Sal

Trying to get Noor to talk about her feelings is about as successful as trying to shake down Uncle Faisal for cash.

"You hung up on me, Noor." The quad fills up around us and I lower my voice. I have five minutes between English and Trig to get her to talk—I won't see her again until after school. By then, she'll change the subject relentlessly until I want to backflip off a cliff.

"I told you," she says. "My battery ran out."

"You were crying. Why?"

"I don't want to go to community college." The dark shine of her eyes is almost lost in the purple shadows beneath them. Even with the makeup on, I can tell she hardly slept. "I'm a snob. And when Jamie finds out, she'll be horrible."

"You still haven't heard from UCLA. You never know—"

My burner phone buzzes—but I ignore it. Since I started selling for Art, I figured out why he was gung ho about me taking over his turf at school. It's a shit ton of work—and I do all of it while he collects his thirty percent.

"There's no way I get into UCLA," Noor says. "I had to write a whole different set of essays for that application, and by the time I got to them, I was dead tired. I barely looked at the questions. For one of them, I went on about the liquor shop and tea with Auntie Misbah and music. *Music,* Salahudin."

"Did you write about Chai-kovsky?"

"Did you just dad-joke me in the middle of my breakdown?"

"You walked right into it. Anyway, tea and music isn't so bad—"

"I'm applying to the bio department."

Shit. "Right, well, that's not great. But you can't take it *Bach,* so—"

"Stoooop." She swings her backpack at me and I jump out of the way.

"Okay, okay," I say. "Send me the UCLA essay. I mean it. I bet it's great."

My phone buzzes again, and Noor breaks away from me. "You should get that. Might be your dad. Oh, and can I get a ride after school? My bike's—busted."

"Yeah," I say, before realizing that she's cleverly dodged my questions.

"Noor—"

But she's gone, heading for gym, and even though I look stupid standing stock-still in the quad, trying to get one last glimpse of her, it's worth it when she smiles at me over her shoulder.

"Nice side hustle you've got, Sal." Jamie Jensen breaks away from her friends and falls into step with me. She's much shorter and I'm about to be late to Trig, so she's soon jogging to keep up. I find this oddly satisfying.

"Usually I do business with Art," she says. "But he says—"

"I'm not selling to you, Jamie."

She rears back as if I've slapped her. I'm thinking she doesn't hear "no" often.

"You want to make money, right? Mine's as good as anyone else's."

"It's really not."

"It is when I want a month's worth of stuff."

A month of Adderall will net me a few hundred bucks, even after Art takes his slice. I've socked away more than two grand. But First Union has been calling twice a day. They want their money and I'm still short.

Jamie senses me wavering. "I'll throw in an extra hundred dollars."

I do a quick calculation in my head. We got a new weekly tenant—one of Curtis's co-workers. I'm close. Jamie's money could put me over the top.

She's smiling. Satisfied. Like she can tell how much I need it. "Meet me—"

"Nah." I walk a little faster. "Get your fix somewhere else."

"What does your girlfriend think about this?" Jamie asks, and I think of that old movie *Jaws*, where, when the shark attacks, all I could see were fins and fangs. Jamie's teeth are nicer. But when she grins, the effect is the same.

"Should I tell her about your operation? Or wait—is she in it with you? Selling out of that little liquor store?"

A lifetime of putting up with motel guests who casually ask for condoms or five cans of Spam has given me a solid poker face. So Jamie attacks from another angle.

"Don't know why she's been so grumpy lately." Jamie gives me a cunning look. "She got into the schools she wanted."

I stifle a laugh. Noor says Jamie will make a good politician—

but I disagree. She's too artless to be truly manipulative.

"Piss off, Sherlock."

"Which college is Noor going to?" Jamie demands. Her petulance throws me off. Ama's funeral flashes in my mind, those moments when she was lowered to the earth, and my abu clutched at the coffin moaning, "Vapas dey dey." *Give her back.*

How can a moment like that exist in the same world as Jamie's pettiness? The gulf between them is so vast that it makes no sense.

"What's wrong with you?" I stop outside the Trig classroom and give Jamie all of my attention. "She's never done anything to you. Why do you hate her?"

"She deserves to know that you're a drug d—"

"Tell her what you want. It's not like she pays attention to you." I slam the classroom door in Jamie's face. I try to forget about her. But her threat gnaws at me.

By the time I meet Noor at my car after school, I have two dozen texts on my phone that tell me it's going to be a lucrative night. I've learned my lesson, though. I turn it off.

"You seem happy," Noor says as I start the car.

I want to tell her what a relief it was to pay my cell phone bill and buy a full cart of groceries with milk and apples and strawberries.

Plenty of kids at Juniper High have money issues. In this town, either your parents work at the military base and live well, like Art's or Jamie's, or they don't and you scrape by. There's some middle ground, but not much.

But no one talks about paying bills or buying eggs. In the end, most of the kids at school can count on having a roof over their heads.

Then again, that might just be how it seems. Maybe there are other kids like me, trying to make a legit dinner out of lal mirch and rice, knowing that if they talk about it, they'll feel more freakish.

"I'm happy because I'm with you," I say in response to Noor's comment. I figure it's better than *I'm happy because I can pay for gas, woo-hoo.*

But the awkward silence that fills the car makes me want to dissolve into the seat.

Noor looks startled—probably because she thinks I fed her a line. Not even a clever one.

Then again, she made that comment about impure thoughts last night. Which made me wonder if *she* had impure thoughts. About me.

"Salahudin?" She waves her hand in front of my face as I pull out of the school parking lot. "Penny for your thoughts—"

They are extremely, very, super impure and mostly about me kissing you. "Um—" My voice is strained and weird. I clear my throat. "You want me to drop you off at home?"

"The store." When she reaches for her seat belt, she gets a pained expression on her face. The color drains from her cheeks— something I've read about but never seen happen on a real human before.

"Noor?" I say. "You okay?"

"Seven schools. Six rejections." She fishes her phone from her backpack. "We've talked about this. Hey, let me play this song for you."

Noor lets me change the subject when I don't want to talk about something. Maybe I should let her do the same.

Or maybe that's the problem between us. Maybe when she'd said, "I'm in love with you," I'd have seen how terrified she was to bare her soul. And maybe when she tried to kiss me, she'd have felt how afraid I was to have someone so close.

Maybe we'd have understood each other.

"I know there's something wrong, and it's not just the college thing," I say.

She turns slowly to me. There's a plea in her eyes, but I don't know if she wants me to dig deeper or let it go.

I pull the car over, silent as the traffic passes us by. The wind shakes the Civic between its teeth.

"Noor." I take her hand in mine slowly, carefully. "Talk to me."

How can you know someone for years and still not know their inner currents? I want to sink into the swirls and eddies of her ocean. I want to understand her. But I can't unless she lets me.

She doesn't let me.

"It's the college thing." She pulls her hand away. "Really. Let's go." She says it in a voice that's not hers. It's Noor folded up and crumpled until she's nothing but tired creases.

I put the car into drive. After a minute, Noor plugs in her phone. The song that fills the car is old—older than both of us. "Shiver" by Coldplay, about a guy lamenting how invisible he is to someone he loves.

I glance at Noor, but she's looking out the window.

I do see you, I want to say. *I do. But not all of you.*

What don't I see, Noor?

What are you hiding?

After I drop Noor off, I pick up a bottle of pills, and some of the harder stuff Art gave me a few days ago.

Heroin, I think as I grab a dozen bags from the storage shed. *Call it what it is.*

The bags go into the pocket where I used to keep my journal—relegated to the bottom of my sock drawer. Once, I read that Teddy Roosevelt stopped journaling during the worst times in his life. Maybe he felt like I did—like writing down the worry and fear would make it sharper, honing the edges until it could cut like a knife.

I get to work, and nearly four hundred dollars later, I arrive home to find all the motel lights off. Abu must be passed out for the night.

Or maybe he's still drinking and doesn't give a damn. Either way, we've missed out on three hours of business because he couldn't bother to turn on our signs.

I throw the car into park and hurry to unlock the office. It's not until I've flipped all the lights on that I see the pale figure draped atop the bench in the front yard. Ashlee glances over her shoulder, waving through the office window.

When I get outside, she pats the seat next to her. I don't sit. "You walked right past," she murmurs.

"What are you doing here, Ashlee?"

"Business keeping you out late?" She lifts an eyebrow.

"You talked to Art?"

She gives me a reproving look. "I would have lent you money, Sal. Or my mom would have. I love Art, but he's an idiot."

"I wouldn't have taken your money."

"Why? You are—were—my boyfriend." I don't have a response to that. She shivers.

"Come on." I unlock the office door. She's not wearing a coat and the nights are still cold. "It's warmer inside."

The apartment is as silent as a mausoleum, and as empty of life. For a second, terror grips me. Images flood my head: Abu on the side of the road, hit by a car. Abu passed out for good.

"Your dad went for a walk," Ashlee says. "Left a few minutes after I got here." She sidles toward me. "Which might not be a bad thing for us . . ."

She takes my waist and I jerk away, as if a snake has dropped down on me unexpectedly.

Ashlee drops her hands, flushing. "Right."

"I'm sorry. It's not you—I'm just—"

Ashlee slumps onto the office seat, wincing when her tailbone hits the leather. "It's okay," she says. "I—my back's hurting all the time. And . . . I miss you. I texted you about the new Saga and you didn't even respond."

"There's this thing in my religion," I say. "After someone dies you mourn for three days. Then you're supposed to get on with life. After forty days, you read Qur'an for them. That's it. That's all the mourning you're supposed to do." I shrug. "Not sure why I'm telling you that."

"Because you wanted a clean break," she says. "I get it." Her phone lights up, and when she sees the text, she sighs.

"Kaya's not settling down for the night. I have to go." She takes out eighty dollars. "Help me out? My doctor has to call in a prescription, but she's on vacation."

"What would Lying Cat say to that?" I reference the Saga character, famous for calling out untruths.

Ashlee rolls her eyes and shoves her hands in my pockets, ignoring my flinch as she fishes for what she wants. She keeps two pills and gives the rest back.

"Ashlee—"

"I'm hurting, Sal," she says. "Don't be mean."

"Well, don't drink with this shit. Or mix it with anything else."

"Are you educating me about my drugs now?" Ashlee laughs. "A month ago, you thought Oxy was *moxie* spelled wrong." She hands me her money and blows me a kiss. "Let's hang out sometime," she says. "I promise I'll behave."

As her Mustang roars to life and she drives away, I feel sick. All of this—selling Ama's meds. Selling the shit Art gives me. It's wrong. Dealing to my ex-girlfriend, who has a child, is extra wrong. If something happens to her—if Kaya ends up an orphan because of me—

She'll be fine, I tell myself. I tuck the money into an envelope. I'm sixteen hundred dollars away from paying First Union. A few days more, if I'm lucky. A week, tops.

"And then I'm done." I say it out loud. As if by doing so, I'll make it true.

CHAPTER 22

Misbah

July, then

I waited until noon before phoning Junaid's home, but the line rang until it disconnected. Perhaps he got delayed at the market. Or he became ill.

The knock came at my door as I put on my shoes. A boy in dusty chappals waited outside.

"Baji, chethi ah—koi pehrei khabar eh!" Big sister, come quickly—something terrible has happened. *He went on, but too quickly for me to make anything out but one word:*

Bijli. Electricity.

As I ran down the stairs and into a rickshaw, my heart thundered like a wedding dhol. Many of the electric wires above our own apartment were live. I told Toufiq a thousand times to be careful when he sat up on the veranda with Baba and Junaid.

The street in front of Junaid's house was thronged with people and an ambulance. Even from thirty yards away, I smelled singed flesh.

A police inspector—one who worked with Junaid—found me. He told me what they had pieced together, that Nargis arrived home in the early-morning hours. She went to the veranda. Junaid tried to get her to come down, fearing she'd be electrocuted. She cursed him and stumbled into a live wire.

He grabbed on, trying to save her. The current took them both.

For hours, I debated how to tell Toufiq. Selfishly, I wished for my father so that he could deliver the news. But he was visiting friends in Rawalpindi.

In the end, I couldn't bring myself to tell Toufiq over the phone. I waited until he arrived home. He was always so calm. Quiet. Controlled. But when he heard, he put his head in his hands and wept.

"Not for me, you understand," he said after a long time. "But for her. For him. Because I couldn't save them."

We buried them later that day, in accordance with Islamic custom. That night was the first time I saw Toufiq lose himself in drink.

But not the last.

CHAPTER 23

Noor

April, now

Mrs. Michaels hands me the F silently. I expect her to be angry. To make a big deal out of it.

She doesn't. She calls out the next student to come get their paper. I walk back to my desk.

I've lived in America for twelve years. This is my first F. Maybe it will explode. Jump off the page and bite me. Burn a hole through the desk.

But it just sits there, ugly and red.

Jamie, sitting in front of me, glances at it, her pale eyebrows practically in her hair. She doesn't hide her smirk.

From across the room, Salahudin tries to catch my eye. I draw triangles in the margins of my paper. Things have been awkward since I hung up on him two weeks ago. No matter how many times I tell him I'm freaked out about college, he doesn't buy it.

Don't look at him. As soon as I think it, I glance over. My neck goes hot. His head is cocked a little, dark hair falling in his face. From here, his brown eyes are black. He's staring at me. Like he has something he wants to tell me. He flips a pen from finger to finger with a proficiency that is unfairly sexy. I snort at myself. *It's just a pen, Noor.* He's not smiling, but that only draws my attention to his mouth.

Which is not helpful.

I want to look away, but I can't. My fingers feel weird. Tingly. I imagine him watching me like this when we're alone somewhere. The pen falling, and his clever hands on my body instead. That mouth—

I let my hair fall over my face. *Stop.* I find his gaze again. What is he thinking?

Not what you want him to be thinking, Noor.

Jamie's noticed. "Get a room." She makes a gagging sound, and then, so only I can hear: "Maybe one at his little motel."

"Go to hell, Jamie." The room goes silent right as I say it.

Jamie gasps. "I cannot *believe*—"

"If you'd all turn to page 233 of your textbooks." Mrs. Michaels gives me a warning glance. "*Medea* by Euripides. A tragic masterpiece from the fifth century BCE. Adapted by the great American poet Robinson Jeffers. We'll read it aloud today—"

At the collective outcry, she lifts her hands. "Or you can turn in a three-page essay tomorrow about how Euripides represented gender roles via Medea's soliloquies. Show of hands?"

No one moves. Or speaks. Mrs. Michaels calls out the parts. *Don't give me one,* I think at her. *Don't do it, Mrs. Michaels.*

"Noor," she says. "You will play the part of the chorus."

She knows I hate performing. I have since grade school. I could barely sound out words back then. When the teacher made us read aloud, everyone in class would groan. *Anyone but her.*

This is for telling Jamie to go to hell. For failing the paper.

We launch into the play. It might be on the AP test and that test is half our grade. So I pay attention. Since the day I stepped into an American school, I have never stopped paying attention. I have never stopped doing my best.

But fear eats at me. A terror in my gut that it doesn't matter how well I do. I'll never escape Juniper.

"Noor?"

I scramble for my place in the play. "'Old and honored servant of a great house,'" I read. "'Do you think it is wise to leave your lady alone in there, except perhaps a few slaves, building that terrible acropolis of deadly thoughts? We Greeks believe that solitude is very dangerous, great passions grow—grow—'"

I stop. Maybe Mrs. Michaels assigned me this part on purpose. Maybe she knows something I don't want her to know.

Stop being paranoid, Noor.

Everyone stares, so I fake-cough and go on. "'Great passions grow into monsters in the dark of the mind; but if you share them with loving friends they remain human, they can be endured.'"

Forget enduring. I want to escape. I want out of Juniper. I'm the only one who can make that happen. And I'm so close to failing.

Screw Euripides. Screw Mrs. Michaels. Screw this stupid play and every school that's rejected me. I want to scream it. Flip a table. Break a chair.

You are better than this place. More than this place. I try to hold on to those words, but they dissolve into the dark like my family, like my past, like my future. All that's left is fear.

The world closes. Mrs. Michaels's voice goes distant. Everything shrinks to a point. The words on the page—words I should be reading—go blurry.

Some people want classmates to reminisce about them. I want to disappear from Juniper's memory. But I know these assholes. People still talk about how Billy Cunningham shat his pants in the fourth grade. If I don't pull it together, I'll be the orphaned brown girl who knocked herself out on the edge of a desk in senior year.

I need music. Something to bring me back. Karen O screaming out in her cover of "Immigrant Song." The melody winds through my head. I can't breathe. I try to whisper the lyrics. It's not enough.

Then the fire alarm blares out.

I swing my head toward Salahudin. The lever of the red alarm beside him is pulled down.

"Everybody line up!" Mrs. Michaels says. "Exit in an orderly fashion!"

She doesn't have to say it twice. The room clears out in seconds, and then a big, warm hand rubs my back.

"Hey. Deep breaths. Five seconds in, seven seconds out." Salahudin drops his voice. "Say you smelled natural gas. Okay? Otherwise, my ass is toast."

"Noor." Mrs. Michaels isn't in a rush to get out, and she's eyeing Salahudin suspiciously. "Are you all right? I know Euripides can be depressing, but . . ."

"I . . . smelled something—um, like natural gas?"

Mrs. Michaels purses her lips as she looks between Salahudin and me. "Why didn't you say anything before pulling it, Sal?"

"The smell was so powerful," Salahudin says, and I'm surprised at how easily he lies. "I thought it might knock us all out before we got the chance. I panicked."

He doesn't sound panicked. But then, he never does.

Mrs. Michaels sighs. "Pulling a fire alarm without cause is a misdemeanor—"

"I didn't pull it for shi—kicks and giggles, Mrs. Michaels," Salahudin says. "I smelled something weird and it was making me sick. Noor definitely looked sick. Maybe we should get out of here." The alarm still blares and the voices in the hall get louder.

Mrs. Michaels—in no hurry—gives us a level stare. "Sal," she says. "Have you written that story? For the contest?"

Salahudin sighs. "I'll start working on it right away."

"Good." Mrs. Michaels sniffs at the air. "Now that you mention it, I might smell gas, too. I'll tell Principal Ernst as much." She makes for the door. Not for nothing is she my favorite teacher.

My knees shake when I stand. Two seconds more and I'd have been fine. But Salahudin's arm comes up under me. The sides of our bodies touch. Our thighs. Hips. Up to my shoulder. I fit just under his arm.

He's warm, even though he's forgotten his jacket again. Mrs. Michaels tells us to hurry up. I don't want to move. This feels almost like the hug from a few weeks ago.

So I don't tell him I can walk fine.

M-hall is packed. No one seems worried about why there's an unplanned fire evacuation. When we're outside, Mrs. Michaels maneuvers her wheelchair around to face me.

"Salahudin," she says. "I need a moment with Noor, if you please."

I don't want him to let go of me. But he does, and waits against a wall a few feet away.

"Far be it from me to make assumptions," Mrs. Michaels says quietly. "But you weren't looking well in there. Does that have anything to do with the grade on your paper?"

"No, Mrs. Michaels."

Sirens blare from far away. Principal Ernst cuts through a group of students, bellowing.

"This is *not* an opportunity for you to skip school. I need everyone to the football field. The *football* field, Mr. Malik—"

"You can make it up," Mrs. Michaels says. We push through the crowd. "I don't submit final grades until after AP test results come back in the summer. If you pass the test, it's an automatic A from me. I know college is important to you. Have you . . . heard anything?"

The earth feels unsteady again. I make myself breathe.

"Nothing yet," I say.

"I see. Your uncle—is he supportive, Noor? Is your home life . . ." Her pink nails tap against the armrest of her wheelchair. "Is there anything you need to talk about?" She searches my face.

I shake my head. "Thanks for making me feel better about the paper."

She nods, and her shoulders relax. Relief, maybe. She moves away quickly after that. No backward glance. Like she's worried I'll change my mind. Like if she stays too long, I'll say something she doesn't want to hear.

CHAPTER 24

Sal

My stunt with the fire alarm means hours spent in Ernst's office, trying to convince him not to call the cops.

By the time he finally releases me, I've missed lunch. But it was worth it. My chest twinges when I think of how Noor's hands shook as she was reading. If pulling a stupid alarm broke her out of whatever mental hellspace she found herself in, so be it.

After school, I'm hurrying to my car when Art waylays me.

"Sal!" he shouts. "Hey, since we're business partners now, why don't we watch *Breaking Bad* together tonight? We could do a marathon." I nudge him with my backpack. Darth Derek is skulking nearby. Art lowers his voice not at all.

"We could get ideas," Art says, "for how to expand."

"Art, I'm working for you until the motel picks up. Then I'm done."

"All right," Art says. "But if you're waiting for your dad to figure out his shit, it won't happen. Whatever problem he has now, he'll still have in twenty years. Because if you aren't enough to make him change, then change ain't happening."

Art's occasional profundity always surprises me, especially considering how much of his own product he samples.

"You got plans with your lady?" Art waggles his eyebrows and nods to where Noor leans against the side of my car, her face shadowed within her hoodie.

Since her bike broke, I've been giving her rides to and from school and the hospital. The rest of the day always seems like a silent, sepia film compared to the vibrancy of those minutes with her, as she explains the lyrics of a London Grammar song, or argues about why the magic systems in my favorite shows make no sense.

Sometimes, I imagine telling her that I'm falling for her. But then I hear her saying, *"I'm over you."* At that thought, the earth shudders beneath me, and I feel like I'm being tipped out into space.

"She's not my lady," I say to Art, hoping he'll go away. Noor seeing me with him will just lead to more questions.

"Aw, come on." Art elbows me. "She's hot. In that shy-but-I-will-kick-your-ass-if-you-look-at-me-wrong kind of way. If you're not interested—maybe you could tell me what she's into—"

I give Art a death glare and he backs away, grinning.

"I knew you liked her," he crows. "Tell her. She's smart, right? She'll leave your ass when she goes to college. You might as well—"

"She's right there," I say between gritted teeth. "So if you could shut up?" Already, Noor looks between me and Art, her gaze narrowing. *Shit.* She knows there's no good reason for us to be walking together.

"Leave," I hiss, and Art slopes off, leering revoltingly.

"What was that about?" Noor eyes Art like he's a daku waiting to accost her.

"You don't want to know. I'm starving. No shift at the store today, right? Thurber's?"

"I could use some twisty fries." She slips into the passenger seat. "I'm buying, though," she adds. "I owe you. For today."

"You don't owe me anything," I say. "If it wasn't for you . . ." *I wouldn't have survived the past two and a half months.*

"You wouldn't have had to spend lunch convincing Ernst not to have you arrested." She shakes her head, but she's smiling. "I can't believe you did that."

"Just trying to live up to all those Pakistani drama heroes you and Ama are obsessed with."

She rolls her eyes. "Please. You could never live up to Saif Ilyaas in *Dilan dey Soudeh*—"

"Noooo." I clap my hands over my ears and drive with my knees. "Do *not* start in on Saif Ilyaas and his abs, *please*—"

Thurber's is packed, but I claim a table while Noor grabs the food, roast beef sliders for her and a vegetarian sandwich for me. Ama was strict about keeping halal and I feel guilty breaking the habit.

"Aah, cat meat," Noor moans ecstatically. "I have missed it." She glares and kicks my shoe violently under the table. "That's for keeping me away from Thurber's."

"I didn't stop you coming here."

"Did *you* come here after the Fight?"

"No," I admit. "Felt too weird."

My burner phone buzzes softly. I've ignored it all day, so when Noor gets up to refill her soda, I take a quick look. A bunch of numbers I don't recognize, and one I do. Ashlee.

She's been asking for painkillers again. I know it's bullshit to suddenly acquire morals when you are dealing people poison. But when she called, I wanted to hang up because I heard Kaya in the background. I heard Ashlee's mom calling them both.

At the same time, Ashlee's pain is real. And I need money. *She knows what she's doing,* I tell myself. *She'll be fine.*

Ashlee: Look up.

I'm snapped out of my thoughts. Ashlee is in a booth on the other side of Thurber's with Kaya and her mom, both of whom have their backs to me. When I meet her gaze, she smiles, and I'm struck by how gaunt she looks. Like she's lost ten pounds in the few days since I've seen her.

As her mom gathers up Kaya and throws out their trash, Ashlee gestures me over.

I look away—down—anywhere but at Ashlee. I sense her gaze flicking between Noor and me, and I glance up in time to see her stiffen. Then she follows her mom and Kaya out.

Noor stares thoughtfully after her. "Next time, maybe say hi."

"I thought you didn't like Ashlee," I say as Noor finishes her fries and starts poaching mine.

"You thought wrong," she says. "Hey, I got my first F today. On the 'One Art' draft essay."

I put down my sandwich. "Is that why you got so sick in class?"

"No." Just like that, Noor seems to lose her appetite. "Six rejections, Salahudin. Thank God Chachu never checks the mailbox. If he even knew where I was applying—" She shudders. "I haven't heard from UCLA. No email. No envelope. Every time I try to get into the stupid portal, it says there's an error. Probably because they kill the accounts of everyone they reject. To them, I no longer exist."

Her eyes go distant and I wonder if she's in the village where her family died, or with Ama at the hospital, or alone in Chachu's house.

"You can't just give up."

"*You're* telling me I can't give up? How's your contest entry coming, Salahudin?"

"I'm different," I say. "I have to deal with the motel. Anyway, I always knew I was going to Juniper Community. I'll transfer to a four-year eventually. But you need to get out of here, Noor."

"I only applied to seven schools, bro."

I smile to hide how much I hate that she just called me bro. "You haven't actually heard from UCLA. It only takes one yes."

"I'm low-key offended you're trying to get rid of me, Salahudin. Don't you want me to stick around?"

"Of course I want you to stay," I say. "But I love you too much to—ah—"

A flush creeps up her face.

"Oh my God," she whispers. "What is this weird hot feeling? Am I blushing? What is the point of being brown if you can blush? Not blushing is literally one of the only perks we get."

"I don't see anything." I look purposefully toward the ceiling, even though Noor blushing is one of the best things I've ever witnessed, and I'd give a month of my life to watch the whole thing again.

Noor covers her face with her fingers. "A gentleman," she says. "Sparing my dignity. It's okay." She drops her hands, composed once more. "I know you meant it as a friend."

"Untrue." I say it before I think. Because I'm an idiot.

Or because I'm done trying to control everything. The brave version of me, the one who pulled the fire alarm this morning, wants her to know how I feel.

Slowly, so she can pull away if she wants, I reach for her hand. When I take it, she squeezes and closes her eyes. She seems— sort of happy. Sort of not. But something about that look shoots straight to my lower belly.

Damn.

"You know I've got . . . some issues," I say.

"Yeah," she says. "You and me both."

"Tell me. The other night, you—"

"You tell me your secrets, Salahudin Malik." Noor opens her eyes. "And I'll tell you mine."

For a moment I skim a dark lake in my mind, like a bird dipping a claw into the water, only to flinch at the bone-chilling cold.

I go clammy, my skin prickling, and let go of her. We sit there, staring at each other. Food forgotten. Only a foot between us, but it feels like the whole universe.

CHAPTER 25

Noor

After Thurber's, we drive to the motel. A familiar gray SUV is parked in the driveway.

"Imam Shafiq." Salahudin rests his forehead against the steering wheel. He'll have to hide Uncle Toufiq's alcohol. Rush to clean the house. Pretend his father's not a drunk.

I fidget, imagining Salahudin's expression if Imam Shafiq mentions the conversation he and I had about Uncle Toufiq.

"I should get home." I hop out of the car and Salahudin's head jerks up.

"Don't leave," he whispers. Khadija's in the SUV, her window rolled down. "Come inside for five minutes? Distract the imam? While I hide Abu's . . . stuff."

Great passions grow into monsters in the dark of the mind; but if you share them with loving friends they remain human, they can be endured.

"Maybe you shouldn't clean up the house or hide your abu, Salahudin," I say. "Maybe Imam Shafiq needs to see that."

"No one needs to see that." Salahudin gets out of the car, grabbing my backpack from the back seat. "Abu would be so much easier to hate if he were meaner. If he got mad or broke things. If he used his fists, the way the drunks in movies do."

My body goes numb at those words. "Imam Shafiq ran mosques

in big cities," I make myself say. "He's dealt with worse than your dad."

"Asalaam-o-alaikum, guys." Khadija waves from the driver's seat. She has a giant file open in her lap.

"Hi," Salahudin says. "I mean, Walaikum Asalaam, Sister Khadija. Can I—do you need something?"

Khadija shakes her head. She looks between us and smiles. "Shafiq wanted to check on your dad. He meant to come by after the funeral, but he got wrapped up in work. He's waiting for you inside."

Salahudin runs his fingers through his hair. It sticks up crazily. I want to fix it. Put my palms on his shoulders. *Some things are out of our hands,* I want to say. *And maybe for good reason. Maybe you need to ask for help.* But I feel weird doing any of that in front of Khadija.

"The thing is," Salahudin says, "my dad's probably—ah—"

"We all have our struggles, Salahudin." Khadija says his name, but she looks at me. "Shafiq knows that. It's not his place to judge."

I can't look away. She's talking to Salahudin. So why is she staring at me?

Khadija's phone rings. "I should grab this." She turns away and Salahudin looks at me with puppy eyes.

"Noor—"

"Don't lie to Imam Shafiq. He's a good guy, Salahudin. And coming from me . . ." I don't like people, mostly. Salahudin knows it.

He hauls up my backpack and hands it to me. "If you feel shitty again or you hear from UCLA, call me," he says. "You told me not to get stuck in my own head. Take your own advice."

The walk home is too short. Chachu's car is out front. My

bike is still chained to the fence on the side of the house.

The sun's setting, the sky a color pink that deserves its own section in the dictionary. It's light enough to walk, so I circle the block, stopping near a Joshua tree in the empty desert nearby.

Izote de desierto, they're called. *Desert dagger.* There's a U2 album named after this tree. Chachu played it once when I was little and I loved it so much, I asked him to play it again. He refused. Hid the record. When I finally got my own phone, *The Joshua Tree* was the first album I bought.

I think about what Khadija said. *We all have our struggles.* My fists clench. Another habit I've picked up from Chachu. Anger fills me up so fast. It's like it's just waiting in my mind. The second I pay attention to it, it takes over.

Anger doesn't really cover what I feel, though. You get angry because someone almost runs you over in the bike lane. Angry because someone cuts in line at Walmart.

What's the word for when someone drinks so much, they are ruining your best friend's life? Or the word for a man so vengeful about his own past that he wants to destroy your future? What's the word for a woman who was sick for months, but refused to go to the doctor until it was too late? The word for the girl at school whose personal mission is to mess with your head?

Anger's not the right word.

Rage. That's what this feeling is, eating me up.

I scream into the cold night. Almost before the sound is born, I smother it, slapping my hands over my mouth. I was so loud that I freaked myself out.

My better sense kicks in. I bottle my rage. Shove it deep in my head. Anger won't help anything. I don't even know who I'm mad at. Chachu? Toufiq Uncle? Jamie? Misbah Auntie? God?

Myself?

Forgive, Misbah Auntie told me when she was dying. Her last attempt to guide me, to help me. *Forgive.*

But it makes no sense to me.

Who do I forgive, Auntie Misbah?

How do I forgive?

CHAPTER 26

Misbah

November, then

JUNIPER, CALIFORNIA

My father took a government posting in the city of Quetta when I was a year from matriculating. As our driver passed vividly painted trucks on the mountain roads of Balochistan province, Baba turned to me.

"Quetta is filled with so many apple orchards, little butterfly," he said, "that you can taste their sweetness in the air. It is a place in the clouds, five thousand feet above the sea. Did you know it was leveled completely in the 1935 earthquake?"

"And they rebuilt it? The whole thing?"

"Yes," Baba said. "It still stands, a testament to the strength of humanity."

Quetta was dry and dusty in the summer, but the mountains around it were draped in snow in the winter, a promise of something pure. We only lived there for two years, but I loved those mountains on sight.

I remembered Quetta here, in America, as Toufiq navigated our green Honda along a road that hugged the rocky blue Sierra Nevada. The car window was freezing. The night sky was like Quetta's, too, clear enough to see the thick cloud of the galaxy exploding across it, illuminating the snow-dipped peaks, giving them an unearthly feel.

Baba would love this place. He wept when I left, though my mother was stalwart. It pained me to know that we would rarely, if ever, look at the same stars at the same time.

"Will Ajeet be there?"

*Ajeet Singh had brokered the motel's sale. Toufiq knew him from uni-*versity. "It will give you a good income in case you have difficulty with your job," *Ajeet had told us.*

He knew Toufiq well.

"No, but he'll visit," *Toufiq said.* "I've heard there are a few Indian families. The base has people coming through all the time. Many stories for you, my heart. And Yosemite is not so far. We can visit. Though, I never thought—"

—that this would be how. With both of his parents dead. Uncles and aunts gone. His cousins scattered. He was a rare Pakistani with little family. No one to keep him tethered to a place that only brought him pain. When he got the engineering job at Juniper's military base, there was no decision to make. Pakistan was my home, but not his. And I wanted him to be happy.

We drove down a two-lane highway for so long that the dotted yellow line began to blur. After hours, Toufiq pointed to a vast, darkened valley in the east.

"There it is."

Lights twinkled in the distance, cheerful against the empty midnight desert surrounding them. As we turned off the highway and down a narrow connecting road, strange rock formations rose up around us. It felt as if we were in another world. My stomach jumped in excitement. This was the beginning of a new adventure, the kind I'd wanted to have as a girl.

The town appeared almost abandoned, other than a McDonald's where a lone car dawdled. A police vehicle roamed the main avenue, slowing down as we passed.

"There." I pointed to a battered green street sign beside a parking lot that said MCFINN'S FORD. "Yucca Avenue."

We parked beside a cluster of low structures. In front of them, a waist-high white wall formed a rectangle around three pale trees and a stretch of dead grass. The trees clacked in the wind.

Beyond the front yard, a squat building with a broad glass window had a single light glowing within. The rest of the motel was dark. A cat watched from the brick wall, unafraid.

When I emerged from the car, the wind was so strong that it nearly ripped my hijab off. A large, unlit sign moaned like a cranky old man. YUCAIPA INN MOTEL, it read.

"The first thing we must do," I told Toufiq, "is give this place a new name."

He removed our suitcases from the boot of the car and peered owlishly at the sign. "Why?"

"Yucaipa comes at the end of the alphabet," I told him. "Bad for business. And we need something melodic. Something that makes our guests feel welcome."

Toufiq wrestled with the stiff lock, and we flipped on the inner lights to find a small, sparse office and a freezing apartment. An envelope from the last owner sat on a rickety desk. The place smelled like dust and soap. The bed, in the larger of two back rooms, was stripped bare and had a suspicious stain.

I pulled out a sheet from one of the suitcases. As soon as the sheet settled, Toufiq collapsed onto it. He was asleep in moments.

I did not understand how he could be tired. My excitement was so great *my feet did not even touch the floor. I ran my fingers along the fat-bricked chimney that echoed with the howls of a wild wind. I passed through a small bedroom with a window that would spill sun onto a crib, should we be so blessed. The L-shaped kitchen had gleaming linoleum floors, and a wooden counter so old I could carve my initials into it with a fingernail. There were crackers in the cabinets, and I nibbled at one, then slathered it with dark honey from my mother's bees in Lahore.*

The ceiling crackled rhythmically beneath the soft paws of an animal traversing it. Beneath it, I paced my new home, considering.

A name could make a person. It could make a place, too. I thought of hotel names I'd seen. The Avari. The Pearl Continental. The Park Lane. None of those names seemed right.

It came to me in the middle of the night, deep in dreams. I shook Toufiq awake.

"The Clouds' Rest," I whispered to him. "We'll call it the Clouds' Rest Inn Motel."

CHAPTER 27

Sal

Inside the apartment, Abu is at the dining table. Imam Shafiq sits across from him, and I'm relieved that I cleaned the kitchen this morning. The smell of Pine-Sol almost masks the sweat-and-liquor reek rolling off Abu.

At least his bottles are out of sight. And he's upright.

Imam Shafiq nods in greeting. "Sit down, Salahudin. I was chatting with your dad about how I'd love to see him at the masjid. I'm there Friday mornings, too, if you want to come when it's less crowded."

As I can count the number of Muslims in Juniper on two hands, I don't think *crowded* is a word that applies to our one-room mosque.

"Definitely." I nod anyway. "Thank you."

My father fidgets like a surly kindergartner. It's embarrassing and I practically tear holes in my palms, my fists are curled so tight. Just for one night, I wish he'd behave like a damn adult.

"Do you want something to eat, Imam Shafiq, or—" I blurt it out. The habits of generations of Pakistani hosts die hard.

"I brought karahi over," Shafiq says, out-Pakistani-ing me. "Khadija made the rotis so they're . . . country-shaped, instead of round? But they taste good. Let me see if she wants to join."

"How much have you had?" I ask Abu when Shafiq is gone. "Can you sit through a meal?"

"I don't want to."

"Abu, he made dinner." *Which is more than your drunk ass can manage.* I don't say it, but he flinches at the way my voice bites. "The least you can do is eat it."

"I didn't invite him." Abu almost whispers the words. He's not belligerent. Just confused.

"Go shower," I say. His hands shake, and I steel myself and take them. His head jerks up. I've probably touched him twice in the weeks since Ama died, and once was to wake him up when I couldn't find the car keys.

"Please, Abu—can you just try? He and Khadija were Ama's friends."

Maybe it's that I'm touching him. Maybe it's that I mention Ama. Probably it's that he hasn't had a chance to get deep into the bottle. His shoulders straighten. He looks into my face and my eyes get hot, because I can't remember the last time he did that.

Abu? I want to say, as if the man who'd shuffled through the house for the last two years were a stranger and I could finally kick him out and welcome back my real dad.

Abu squeezes my hands. "Okay." He stands and I think about how Noor kept telling me to talk to him. I should have tried again after it went wrong the first time. "You two get started. I will join you."

By the time the shower is running, Shafiq is back with a tureen of food but no Khadija.

"Prosecutor's office is trying to pull a fast one," he says. Khadija's a criminal defense attorney. "She'll come pick me up in a bit."

I take the tureen from him—it's still warm and it smells so good I want to abscond with it. Pour the entire thing down my throat while snarling at anyone who gets close.

Shafiq glances at where Abu was sitting. "Did I scare off your dad?"

"Nothing scares him." I take the roti from Shafiq and toss it on a pan to warm it up. "Not even dying of cirrhosis."

There. I've said it. To my surprise, I feel better.

Shafiq might be disgusted by Abu, or think we're rubbish Muslims. But he's here. He's sitting down. He's eating with me.

I butter the rotis the way Ama used to, and we dig in. It's a lamb karahi, soft chunks of meat falling off the bone into a cumin-scented sauce of tomatoes, onions, and garlic. It's my first proper Pakistani meal since before the funeral. When I tell Shafiq, he smiles and gives me a second helping.

"I couldn't tell. So—Salahudin—"

I sense he's about to start asking me things responsible adults ask irresponsible kids. *How's school? Can you bring your abu to the masjid? Can you get him help?*

I head him off. "You're an engineer, right?"

"A structural engineer," he says. "My dad worked double shifts driving a taxi my whole life, and it's what he wanted. Fortunately, I enjoy it. But one day I'd like to just be an imam. I did that for a while when we lived in Los Angeles, and loved it."

"And Sister Khadija's a lawyer," I say. "Couldn't you guys live anywhere? Why come to this shi—um, Juniper?"

"The military offered me a job here. The pay is good. We

both grew up in big cities with huge Muslim communities. DC's Pakistani community for me. Atlanta's Black Muslim community for Khadija." When he laughs, I'm reminded how young he is. "We both wanted to try something different—quieter. I don't think we'll stay forever. But we're not planning on leaving soon. What about you? Your ama told me you loved to write."

"Not much anymore." My journal lurks untouched in the recesses of my sock drawer. "Pretty busy with—with other stuff."

"I guess it would be hard to leave Juniper, in any case. Your ama's grave is here."

Guilt quashes my appetite. I should go to Ama's grave. Pray there. She'd have wanted me to.

But every time I start driving toward the cemetery, I turn around. I don't want to see her name on that stone. I don't want to see the inscription. Noor picked it after Imam Shafiq asked her—I don't even know what it says.

"Gotta get this place running again," I say. "But I don't mind. Noor's the one who wants out."

"Is she . . . all right?" Shafiq mops up the last of his karahi. "She came to masjid last week."

If he doesn't know about the colleges, I'm not about to tell him.

"AP tests are coming up. And Noor's an overachiever."

"Do you know her uncle at all?"

"Riaz is an asshole. Shit—I didn't mean—" Shafiq raises his eyebrows. Double shit. *He's an imam, Salahudin!*

"He's uh . . . not nice," I say. "He's hates that Noor is religious. He makes her work at the liquor store, even though she barely has time to do homework. He doesn't want her to go to college. He wants her to take over at the store so *he* can go to college."

"Do you know if Riaz has ever hit Noor?"

For a long second I stare at him. I do not understand the question. "Hit—like—"

"Struck." Shafiq looks me straight in the eyes. He's young, but if he's run mosques before, people in the community must have come to him with their problems all the time. "Your ama was worried about Noor."

"If Riaz was hurting her, she'd have told me," I say. "Noor—"

Jumped when I touched her shoulder—out of pain, not surprise. Cried on the phone and wouldn't tell me why.

Has been wearing makeup in an inexplicable way off and on for the past couple months, even though she's told me she hates makeup.

Clammed up when I made a comment about Abu using his fists on me. *Wow, Salahudin, you dumbass.*

"Goddamn Riaz—" That piece of shit. Someone should kick his face. Me. I'm the someone. I'm half out of my seat when Imam Shafiq raises a hand.

"Sit down, Sal," he says. "More violence isn't going to help Noor. We're not even sure if that's what's really going on."

"Should I—should I ask her about it?" I try to be practical, to tamp down my wrath. "Should we call the police? I don't want to freak her out. She gets nervous around cops."

Shafiq considers. "We might need to get the police involved at some point. But right now, she should feel safe. Supported."

"Maybe the next time I talk to her, I can . . . let her know I'm worried," I offer. "No accusations. No questions. I'll see what she says."

"I'll talk to Khadija in the meantime," Shafiq says. "If you think

Noor's in any danger, get her away from Riaz. Then call me or Khadija—no matter what time of day."

His phone buzzes. "Khadija's outside," he says. "I'm sorry I missed your dad. I'll come by over the weekend. See if I can't get him to take a walk with me."

The shower is off, and something thumps in Abu's room.

"He wasn't always like this." I feel the need to explain. "He was a good dad. It's just been hard for him. For—for us."

"This life is jihad—struggle," Shafiq says. "Sometimes the struggle is more than any sane person can bear. I won't judge your father for his jihad, Salahudin. How dare I, when I couldn't begin to understand it?"

When he's gone, I obsess over what he said about Noor. *Your ama was worried about Noor.* But if Ama suspected Noor wasn't safe, she would have done something.

I open my texts.

> Hey—I need to talk to you—

No. This has to be an in-person conversation. And it has to be about her—not me.

> You missed some really great karahi. Shafiq left it
> if you want some.

Nothing close to what I want to say. But I send it anyway. Noor doesn't respond.

Another thump comes from Abu's room, and as I'm about to investigate, his door opens. He's clear-eyed, and when I ladle him a bowl of karahi, he actually sits down to eat it.

"Shafiq said he'd come by on the weekend."

"He doesn't need to," Abu says.

Just a few minutes ago, I'd have been so angry at his words that I'd have walked away. But I think of Riaz and Noor. Abu might be a drunk—but he'd never hit me.

"Maybe it will be good for you to have someone to talk to, Abu."

As he eats, with me as stubborn company, the light in the house changes, turning a fiery tangerine as a Juniper sunset blazes over the distant mountains and through the front window. Ama's bag of knitting still sits in a corner, her cookie tin sewing kit shoved atop it.

"When I was a boy," Abu speaks suddenly, "I went to live with my phopo." His father's sister. "She had a half dozen children of her own. But my own mother was a drunk and my father was trying to get her help."

I start. Abu's never talked about his parents. As far as I knew, his life began when he was eighteen and moved to England to attend school.

"My phopo loved me so much. Like I was her son. She and her husband were good people. But they were poor. Even with my father helping them, they struggled. My youngest cousin was my age. Samir." Abu runs a hand through his thick hair, streaked now with white. "He was so chalak, Salahudin. He'd trick the bottle-wallah into giving us free RC Colas. Flatter the older girls who lived across the street so they'd buy him candy. I never laughed more than I did with him.

"But after I lived with Phopo for a year, Samir was climbing a fence and he scraped his leg on a nail. He got tetanus. My father sent money but the doctor did not come on time. I stayed with him. It—it is a very bad way to die."

He looks down at his hands. "I couldn't do anything," he says. "Phopo stopped eating. I couldn't save her, either. I went back to my parents. To my mother. But she wasn't any better than when I left."

There's an entire life in the silence that follows. One I'll never know. I imagine my father as a boy. A thousand lonely, terrifying moments.

Maybe if I hold his hands, he won't feel alone. Maybe he won't drink again tonight. Tomorrow I can call Janice, and persuade him to go to a meeting. Calm comes over me as I think through the plan. I reach my fingers out, open my mouth to tell him. But he stands so fast he tips back his chair.

His plate clatters in the sink. A cupboard opens. A glass clinks. I smell it, that sharp stink I'll never get used to, and his sigh of relief, as his memories slide away, a quiet, merciful forgetting.

PART IV

I lost my mother's watch. And look! my last, or
next-to-last, of three loved houses went.
The art of losing isn't hard to master.

—*Elizabeth Bishop,*
"One Art"

CHAPTER 28

Misbah

October, then

From the kitchen window, the rain blurred the motel. The screaming fluorescent lights seemed quieter. The brassy room numbers became small orange fish, midswim.

The rain was clean and sweet. It brought the smell of parched earth rising and drinking and dancing. I smelled the hope, the possibility.

Also potato pakoras, stuffed with skinny green chilies and fresh from the fryer. Pakoras and green chutney were made for the rain.

I popped one in my mouth just as the bell rang. The sound was a screech, but I was used to it. It reminded me of a monkey one of my uncles kept as a pet, displaying his displeasure to anyone who didn't feed him swiftly enough.

I unlocked the office door, grunting as I yanked it open.

A small figure waited in the downpour, an even smaller one strapped across her chest. Her pale, thin hair clumped on her head like sad dead birds. A silver heart nestled at the hollow of her throat, a tiny red stone at the center of it.

"I'm sorry," she whispered. "To bother you late." She wiped her nose and eyes on her baby's blanket. "I hope you don't have kids."

"Not yet," I said.

"I need your help. I got this sick baby and eleven dollars to my name. I

don't got credit cards or ID cause my wallet got stolen. Please, ma'am—
my husband died and I'm living with his mama. She threw me out and the
shelter is closed and—"

"Your child's grandmother threw you out?"

The woman nodded, and I thought of my own grandmother, Bari
Dadi, gnarled and smelling of garlic and pomegranate with a large, soft
belly I would ram my head into.

She raised a dozen grandchildren—all my many cousins. She changed
nappies, calmed tantrums, even climbed trees.

Grandmothers who threw their grandchildren out. What a strange
country America was.

I considered the woman. You chose to kick at that moment, Salahudin.
Ama, you seemed to say, help her.

Even then, you were trusting.

I gave her the room we'd just renovated. We'd taken out the sagging
bed and ripped furniture and replaced them with a comfortable mattress
and freshly upholstered orange chairs. Toufiq fixed the broken TV. I found
a yellowing National Geographic about Yosemite and framed the pictures
from it to hang above the bed. The door was newly painted. It was a room
I was proud of.

"Here." Our keys were old-fashioned, brass with oval number tags, but
I thought they were charming. "Room one. To the right."

The woman looked up at me and her eyes filled. I patted her shoulder
and she flinched.

"Sorry." The woman looked down. "I'm sorry."

That night, beside my sleeping husband, I prayed. I prayed that the
woman's baby felt better and that she slept well and that she wasn't up
all night.

In the morning, when I went to clean the room, I knocked first. No answer. I took out the master key and entered.

At first, I did not understand. I stepped back to check the room number. It was the correct room.

But the room was empty. No repaired television. No fresh bedspreads. No reupholstered chairs, no new Formica table, no firm mattress. Everything was gone, stripped bare.

On the floor, I saw a scrap of the side table Bible ripped out. I read the words at the top. Ecclesiastes. The handwriting in the margins was messy.

"I'm sorry he made me do it."

I called Toufiq from the apartment. "Oh God, Toufiq," I whispered. "So much money we put in. What will we do now? I am a fool!"

"Kindness is not foolish, my heart." He put his arm around me. "Anyway. At least they didn't steal the pictures."

CHAPTER 29

Noor

April, now

Jamie Jensen announces she got into UCLA at the end of April. She's the only other student at Juniper High who applied—that I know of, anyway. Decisions were late this year, but if she's heard from them, then I should have as well.

But I haven't.

"I'm going to Princeton, of course," she says to Atticus, Grace, and Sophie at the end of Calculus. "But it's nice to know I have an acceptable backup."

She looks at me when she says this. So do her friends. My face gets hot, and I focus on shoving my binder in my backpack. But I'm not careful, and a pile of my things falls out: a change of clothes, granola bars, my passport, my wallet, my phone.

"Are you homeless or something?" Jamie laughs. "Why do you have all this shit in your backpack?"

As I'm grabbing my phone, she picks up my passport. When she flips it open, my old green card shakes loose.

"Awww, guys." Jamie holds both up to her friends. "Look at baby Noor!" She's smiling but her eyes are dead. "Why *do* you keep this stuff on you? So you don't get deported or whatever?"

I grab the passport, but she pulls the green card away. "Hang on a second." She narrows her eyes. "This card has expired."

"Ms. Jensen," Mr. Stevenson calls from the front of the class. "Enough."

"Mr. Stevenson." Jamie holds up the card. "Noor's green card has expired. She's illegal."

"I am not." I can barely get the words out. I'm so angry. "My uncle has my current green card." I managed to sneak my old one out of his file, because I needed the number on it for my college applications. I don't know why I kept it. I guess it made me feel safer. I grab for the card, but Jamie yanks it out of reach.

"Give it back," I say.

"I think we should probably keep it for ICE, don't you—"

"Knock it off, Jamie," Atticus says to her, strangely quiet. I vaguely remember a family report he did in eighth grade about a Cuban grandmother who was an asylum seeker. After glaring at Atticus, Jamie hands me my card.

The bell rings, and I bolt. But even if I'm done with Jamie, she's not done with me.

"What game are you playing, Noor?" She runs to catch up. When I keep walking, she jumps in front of me like a horror movie jack-in-the-box. "Why don't you ever talk? You know it's illegal to apply to colleges if you don't have a green card."

"Jamie." I keep walking. "Get out of my face. I have to go to Econ."

"No," she says. "This is wrong, Noor. Look, I know you've had it hard, but you can't just come into a country—"

"I'm not here illegally," I hiss at her. She takes a step back. "Even if I was, it wouldn't be a crime to apply to college. There are plenty of programs for undocumented kids—"

"The only way you'd know that," she says, "is if you're undoc-umented."

"Why do you care?" I'm so tired. "High school is almost over. We'll go our separate ways. You'll never have to see me again."

"I care because I'm an actual citizen of this country and my parents pay taxes to keep people like you out."

"Who's our congressional rep, Jamie?" At her silence, I answer. "It's Abigail Wen. That's a question on the citizenship test, by the way. You love this country. Shouldn't you know the answer?"

"You think you're so much better than everyone, don't you?"

There's a craziness to her. A hunger. I don't believe in people who say they can see the future. Now is now, and the only thing we know is that we don't know shit. But for a second, I see Jamie as an adult. Icy and thin-lipped. Bony wrists and a booming voice. Persuading gullible people that the wrong path is the right one.

She gets so close to me that I can see her pores. I can smell the bacon she had for breakfast.

"Say something, bitch!"

"I have nothing to say to you." I don't raise my voice. "Never have."

When I moved to Juniper I didn't speak a word of English. My parents didn't know I would need it. Chachu was too high-and-mighty to speak Urdu or Punjabi. I'd listen to him at the liquor shop, then go into the bathroom and practice in the mirror.

Hello, my name is Noor.

I'm sorry, can you say that again?

I'm sorry, I don't understand.

School sucked. Kids can be shitty. Salahudin was the only one who never made fun of me. Of course everyone else did. My accent. My clothes. My hair, which stuck out everywhere. I didn't understand why they were so mean. But now I get it. It's a tired old tale. I looked different. Talked different. It was easier to gang up on me than find flaws in themselves.

"I know your little secret," Jamie says suddenly. "Your *other* secret. And wherever you do end up going to college, Noor? I'm going to make sure they know, too."

"You—what do you mean?"

She stares at me, triumphant. The weirdest feeling comes over me. Not fear, like before. Not anger.

Relief.

Finally. Someone knows. *Your other secret.*

"Your essays," she says. "You got Salahudin to write them for you."

At my expression—which must be a combination of shock and sadness, Jamie practically crows. She says something else. I don't hear her.

When she said *I know,* I thought she *actually* knew. Knew the thing I am most afraid of anyone knowing.

The thing I wish someone *did* know.

But no one sees. No one knows. Not even the girl who's been watching me like a hawk since the first moment she decided I was a threat.

In the middle of her rant, I walk away. Like she's a dog barking at me instead of a human talking. I don't want to listen. I don't want to hear what she has to say. I don't care.

Because, I finally realize, no one will ever see.

There are people around us now. People watching. I try to ignore them.

"Hey!" she snarls, and her face is bright red, like all the hate she's stored up for me is exploding beneath her skin. "Answer me, you fence-jumping camel jo—"

She grabs my arm. I rip away from her and swing. My fist meets her face with a dense thump I know too well. She falls back, screams, grabs her nose.

Suddenly, something rams into my side, knocking the wind from my lungs. Darth Derek twists my arms behind me and presses my face into the dirt.

"Get off me, you motherf—"

"Stop resisting!" he roars like the cops on TV. "Stop moving!"

But I can't. All my rage seethes inside me and there's no place for it to go. I thrash. I scream. I snarl and bite. I let it course through me. I let it take me.

Nearby, Jamie sobs bloody murder.

CHAPTER 30

Sal

Grace says Noor threatened to kill Jamie. Atticus says Jamie said something terrible to Noor and she lost it. No one knows who called the cops, but a patrol car shows up fast, and I see an officer hanging around on campus through lunch.

Meanwhile, Darth Derek has gone full stormtrooper and is checking lockers and backpacks—even though that has nothing to do with the actual fight.

Are you OK?

Noor—what happened?

You want me to key Jamie's car?

She doesn't respond, and now I'm worried. If Riaz finds out what happened, he might get mad at her. Ever since Imam Shafiq told me his suspicions last night, I've been scraping my brain trying to figure out how to get Noor to talk about Riaz. But everything I think up sounds too obvious. I went back through our old texts and emails, trying to see if there was something I missed. I even read her UCLA essay, thinking maybe she hinted at it somehow.

It's not until lunch that I finally escape campus to see if Noor is at home. But as I get to my car, Art calls out to me. He's not smiling.

"Tell me you didn't sell to Ashlee." He's close—too close—in my face, his hands shoving me back into the door of my car. I throw him off violently enough that a few kids nearby stop to watch, sniffing a fight.

Art sees them too, and for once in his life, he lowers his voice.

"She just called me. Said she was in her car by the Ronnie D's. She could barely talk. I heard Kaya in the back. What did you sell her?"

"What you gave me," I say. "She wanted painkillers for her back. She asked for a patch, but I only gave her two pills—"

She paid me one hundred dollars. I put everything into the bank this morning, and finally paid off First Union. It should have been a victory. Instead I wondered how I was going to find next month's payment.

"Fuuuuuuuck." Art pulls his hair until he looks like a possessed hedgehog. "I sold her a patch, Sal. I thought she was only buying from me. I wouldn't have done it if I knew you'd given her anything."

"She took *both*?" Panic shoots through me. "We need to find her."

"We can't, man," he says as I unlock my car. "It's not safe."

"Are you serious right now?"

"What if the cops show up?" Art grabs my shoulders. "They could search us—"

"Don't touch me," I say, low and quiet. My hands are fists—and he sees. He retreats, wary, and I get in my car. I call Ashlee the second I'm driving, but she doesn't pick up.

Juniper's small enough that getting to the Ronnie D's takes a few minutes. But I don't see Ashlee's Mustang. I circle the lot and am about to head to her house when the ambulance screams past.

Then a cop car.

Then another ambulance.

Then a fire engine.

Before I follow them to the back of the Ronnie D's, before I hear Kaya screaming, before I see Ashlee's Mustang, I know. I know something awful has happened. I know it's my fault.

The cops haven't had time to put up any tape yet, and after I park, I run toward Ashlee's car.

"Hey." An officer steps in front of me. "You can't be here, kid."

"She's—she's my friend." The officer, an older white man with a thick mustache, looks at me like I might try to steal his sidearm.

"Is she okay? Is—" I am about to ask if Kaya is okay, but an ear-shattering wail tells me the answer. An officer tries to coax Kaya from the car. But she's not having it.

"Momma!" she screams. "I want Momma!"

Two of the paramedics pull Ashlee out while the other two get a stretcher. Workers from the Ronnie D's spill out of the back door, watching.

"BP is sixty-seven over forty-three and dropping. Oxygen is ninety-four."

"She's got a patch—"

"Here's the Narcan—"

The words splinter and break and then go silent as I catch sight of Ashlee. Her mouth is slack, her glazed eyes half-open with mascara running down the outer corners. When the paramedics move her, she oozes like all her bones have turned to water. Vomit's spattered across her clothes.

She doesn't look like a high schooler. She looks like she's survived a war.

"She's not breathing," one of the paramedics says, and I don't understand how he can be so calm.

They start to pump her chest. *You did that,* a voice in my head screams. *This is on you.*

A voice at my ear. The mustached officer. "This isn't a sideshow," he says. "Get out of here."

The paramedics load Ashlee into the ambulance.

You. You. You. This is because of you. I knew this could happen. I knew it and I sold Ashlee those pills anyway.

If Ama could see me now, she'd be sick at the sight of me. When I was little, she'd ask me what I wanted to be when I grew up. *What about writing, Putar? Take all these stories and put them in a book.* She expected so much more of me than what I've become.

And Noor. If Noor knew, she'd never speak to me again.

She asked me yesterday if I'd finished my essay yet. The prompt floats through my head now. *Tell a fictional story based on a real experience. You can use your own or someone else's, but it should be heavily inspired by real life.*

Now I know what I'd write about: a boy, and how stupid he was to think that a building, a home, was worth more than a human life. I'd write about his selfishness and his regret, and how it ate away at his insides until his body was just a rotten shell for a spirit he didn't recognize anymore.

CHAPTER 31

Noor

The secretary at the front office asks me who to call. I give him Brooke's number, and twenty minutes later, she arrives.

"I'm sorry you had to leave work." We enter Ernst's office, and my voice doesn't rise above a whisper. If I speak any louder, I'll start shouting. And I won't stop.

The office is organized chaos. Ernst has a dusty old COURAGE poster, with an eagle diving. Beneath it, an I LOVE MY 45 bumper sticker. There's a laptop on his desk, and a stack of books. As I wait for him to speak, I read the titles. The bright yellow one is called *Dear America: Notes of an Undocumented Citizen*. Atop that, a book called *The Sun Is Also a Star*.

He sees me looking. "My daughter's an immigration lawyer," he says. "Insists on trying to educate me."

"Has it worked?" I ask. To my surprise, Ernst smiles. He looks human for a second.

"A little. Ms. Riaz." He looks at Brooke. "Will your husband be joining us?"

Brooke tucks her blond hair behind her ears, puts a hand on my shoulder, and sits.

"He's not reachable right now," she lies. "I'll speak to him at home."

"This is a very serious infraction," Ernst says. "Ms. Riaz could have severely damaged Ms. Jensen's face. We're looking at possible assault charges. I've got a police officer here—"

"Are you going to have me arrested?" I fail to keep the panic out of my voice. Before Ernst can answer, the door opens and an officer pokes his head in. He's young and Black and his eyes, which settle on me for the briefest instant, are the only kind thing in this room.

"Mr. Ernst, I'm about to speak with Ms. Jensen's parents," he says. "Fine with you?"

Ernst nods and the officer ducks out. "Officer Dixon is here to take a statement, not arrest anyone. But—"

"Did Jamie tell you what she said to me?" I say. "She—"

"Ms. Jensen mentioned there were heated words exchanged." Ernst holds up a hand. "But physical violence isn't the answer to an insult, no matter its nature."

"She called me a fence-jumping camel jockey. She's been awful since grade school."

"If you felt that Ms. Jensen was bullying you, we have a pro-tocol—"

I laugh. "You wouldn't have done anything. And I don't know what she told you, but I'm *not* here illegally, not that that should matter—"

"Ms. Riaz, I know exactly who our undocumented students are. I know you are not one of them. And indeed, it should not matter and it does not matter."

He sighs, looking between me and Brooke.

"Noor . . ." Maybe Ernst thinks switching to my first name will soften me up. "You are one of Juniper High's top students. Mr. Stevenson vouched for you. He said Ms. Jensen goaded you in class. So, this will not be written up *if* you write Ms. Jensen an apology letter, and *if* you—"

I'm half out of my seat before Brooke pulls me back. "I'm not apologizing."

"Then you face a two-day off-campus suspension. It will go on your permanent record and be reported to colleges in your year-end transcripts."

"Fine," I say. "Are we done?"

"Noor—" Brooke's voice is so soft I almost don't hear it. "Maybe—"

"I implore you to reconsider, Ms. Riaz. This could have a detrimental effect on your chances of—"

"No way in hell I'm apologizing to Jamie Jensen." I can't leash my anger now. I don't want to. "As far as I'm concerned, I didn't punch her hard enough."

I stand up and walk out. I wonder if Officer Dixon will stop me, but he's on the other side of the office with Jamie and her mom, a tired-looking brunette. His arms are crossed and he looks unimpressed as Jamie rages, nose bloody.

"You need to *arrest* her," she's saying. "She assaulted me *and* she's an illegal. Do you even understand what—"

"Ms. Jensen, you'll speak to me with respect or we're done here—"

I don't hear the rest. Seconds later, I'm outside the office and heading for the parking lot. Brooke's soft footsteps sound behind me.

"Noor."

"Please don't tell Chachu."

She falls into step with me. "I won't. You know I won't."

"Do I?"

"You would," she says. "If you ever talked to me."

"If *I* ever talked to *you*?" I stop. "You never ask me anything. You don't have two words to say to me most days. And when—"

Chachu is the only reason I'm standing here. Not Brooke.

She doesn't respond and we're silent the whole way home. When we finally pull into the driveway, she looks over at me. "We'll say you came home sick. You'll stay sick, until the suspension is over."

It's a rare moment of solidarity. One I'm thankful for. I nod.

"We'll keep this between us," she says. "Okay?"

We do keep it between us. For a day.

And then everything goes wrong.

CHAPTER 32

Sal

Ashlee's mom paces the ER waiting room. When she spots me, she pulls me into a full-bodied mom hug so fast that all I can do is wait for it to be over.

"Mrs. McCann—"

"Ms. McCann, please." Ashlee's mom releases me. "McCann's my name and not my thieving ex-husband's. Haven't seen that bastard in seventeen years and I thank the Lord for it."

"I'm so sorry about Ashlee—"

"Oh, don't go apologizing, honey." Ms. McCann hustles me to a seat next to her. "I know you two broke up, and I understand. I told her, I said, 'Ashlee, that poor boy's momma just died, don't you go making it about you.' But teenage girls, my goodness, they think everything is life and d—" She presses her lips together and shakes her head.

"Did the doctor come out and say anything? How is she?"

"I've been asking," Ms. McCann says. "They keep telling me to wait."

"Where's Kaya? Is—is she okay?" I expected to see Ashlee's daughter here, crying still, like she was when the cops pulled her out.

"She's with my pastor and his wife."

Ms. McCann's voice shakes and I think she's about to cry, so I find her a box of Kleenex and look for coffee. It's so burned it singes my nose, but Ms. McCann drinks it without comment.

"Ashlee must have had a funny reaction to something," she says to me when I sit back down. "We got food from Jimmy's Grill last night. Ashlee looked green but I thought a good night's sleep would help." She grabs her necklace, a little silver heart with a red jewel in the center. "By God, if my baby girl doesn't make it, I won't rest until Jimmy is in jail, and if he isn't in jail, he'll damn well wish he was."

She either has no idea that Ashlee overdosed or she doesn't want to admit it.

The way her eyes never settle in one place, the way she grabs her necklace, makes me think it's probably the latter.

"Excuse me?" I recognize the gray-haired, pale-skinned doctor with fat half-moons sagging below her eyes. Dr. Ellis. My pediatrician. She gestures to Ms. McCann from the doors that lead to the hospital's main wing.

"Is she all right? Oh please, Lord—"

"Your daughter is stable. But it would be better for you to speak with her attending doctor—"

"No, Dr. Ellis. You've been taking care of her since she was a little bitty thing. I trust you."

Dr. Ellis notices me for the first time. She appears taken aback. "Salahudin—why—"

"He's family," Ms. McCann says. "Can we see her?"

"Not quite yet." Dr. Ellis is nonplussed, but guides us into the main wing and toward an ugly meeting room where nothing pleasant has probably ever been discussed.

When we sit down, Dr. Ellis peers at me again. But puzzled this time. Like she can't quite figure out what I'm doing here.

"I'll be discussing sensitive medical information with you, Ms. McCann. Are you comfortable—"

"He's not the same color as me, so he's not family? How many times do I have to say it?"

I expect Dr. Ellis to get flustered, but she shakes her head. "I asked because I'm supposed to, Ms. McCann."

"I can leave," I mutter. When I stand, Ms. McCann gestures for me to sit back down.

Dr. Ellis opens the folder on the table. "According to the attending doctor, Ashlee had a high dose of carfentanyl in her system. It's an extremely dangerous synthetic form of the painkiller fentanyl. She also had OxyContin—"

My stomach plummets. Oxy. The shit I sold her.

"Both are opioids. There have been quite a few overdoses in Juniper—"

"Overdose?" Ms. McCann holds on to her necklace. "My daughter's not a druggie."

"This is what the labs found in her system—"

"She might have took those meds because she wasn't feeling good. She's got back troubles after having her baby, but she's a mother, for crying out loud. She's not going to—to—shoot up heroin with her daughter in the car like some junkie—"

"It wasn't heroin," Dr. Ellis corrects her gently. "It was an opioid. The amount found in her body suggests she took too much at once. Ms. McCann—I know it's hard to hear. Sometimes we don't know why people do terrible things—"

Dr. Ellis glances at me then. But her face isn't accusatory. It's— something else.

Ms. McCann isn't having it. "Ashlee's not an addict, goddamn it."

The doctor takes out Ashlee's charts. Her test results. She goes through them calmly and quietly. She's a pediatrician, not an ER doctor, and I wonder if she's had this conversation before.

Ms. McCann keeps shaking her head. It seems crazy that she would deny what's right in front of her.

But then I think of how Ama would react if I overdosed. Of what she did when faced with Abu's alcoholism. I think of the way denial can weave its way through a family, whisper gentle lies, and make itself at home.

Ama asked Abu to go to Alcoholics Anonymous. To go to re-hab. She asked, but she never demanded. She cleaned up after his messes, but she didn't leave him when she realized he would never change. She hid his addiction from me until it was in my face. Even then, I never heard the word "alcoholic" leave her lips.

She never told anyone in Pakistan. She never asked for help. Not when Abu kept missing work and got fired from job after job. Not when money got tight. Maybe she didn't think there was anyone to help her. Maybe she thought God would help her.

I think of how Ama was with me, too. Memories sigh and shift, ancient creatures long slumbering. Strange memories—things I haven't thought of for a long time: Wishing for Ama when I was surrounded by other kids. Telling a teacher I needed to go home.

Saying it, then shouting it, then screaming it. Anger filling me, panic, a need for control, and none of it making sense.

Ama with a gentle hand on my chest. "Bas, Putar, bas." *Enough, Son, enough.*

Nightmares. A dark room. A blue door.

I realize I've made some sort of sound, because the room is silent and both Dr. Ellis and Ms. McCann are looking at me.

"Ms. McCann," I say. "My dad . . . has a problem." I try to pretend the doctor isn't sitting there, judging me. "He drinks. A lot." Now I know why Noor talks in short sentences. Sometimes it's the only way to get through a conversation. "He should stop but he doesn't. He's not a dad anymore to me."

It's the first time I've admitted that fact out loud. Even to myself.

"Maybe it doesn't have to be that way for Ashlee."

Ms. McCann stands up quickly. "I'll—I'll go find the attending doctor." She turns to me. "Thank you for coming, honey. You're just like your mom."

I can't imagine when Ama's path crossed with Ms. McCann's— but then I think of all the people I never met who showed up to Ama's funeral. "You knew her?"

"Yeah." She looks sadder than before, even. "She didn't know me. But I knew her."

A nurse escorts Ms. McCann away and I'm left staring at Dr. Ellis.

"Salahudin," she says quietly. "I've been calling you."

"You have?" For a brief, paranoid second, I think she's seen me dealing. But then I remember all the missed calls from the hospital. The pile of unpaid bills.

"There's something I wanted to discuss with you. It's a bit sensitive."

I stand. "I'm getting the money together to pay the hospital," I say. "You—you don't need to call me about it."

It's weird that she called me. She wasn't even Ama's doctor—she's mine. I open the door, because I want to get the hell out of there, but Dr. Ellis follows me into the ER.

"Sal, I wasn't calling about the bills," she says, and the wrinkles around her eyes deepen. "Did—did your mother ever speak to you about your medical records?"

"My medical records? Why would she talk to me about that?" I stop walking, alarmed. "Is there something wrong with me? Do I have a—a disease or something—"

"No! Nothing like that." Dr. Ellis looks around at the ER, waving half-heartedly when a nurse calls out a greeting. "I'd just like to discuss your records with you. I'll call you. Here—"

She digs out her cell phone, takes my number, and sends me a message. "Now you'll know it's me," she says. "And Sal?" She shifts from foot to foot. "When I call, please pick up. It's important."

Outside the hospital, I run into Art, skulking in the shadows.

"If you're here to see your cousin, go see her," I say. "But if you're here to talk to me, piss off."

Art looks around. For cops probably. "The police impounded her Mustang. Did you say anything—"

"'How's my cousin, Sal?'" I mimic his loud voice. "'What did the doctor say?'" Art has the decency to at least look chagrined. "Thanks for asking, asshole," I say in my own voice. "Tox test showed that she mixed Oxy with some horrible shit called carfentanyl—that patch you sold her. She's lucky to be alive."

Art breathes a sigh of relief because I guess he's not a complete monster.

"I'm done with this," I say. "I'm not selling anymore."

"Sal, don't be such a bitch—"

I walk away from him quickly, and it feels like walking through quicksand. Because I'm not really walking away from Art. Or the drugs. Or dealing. I'm walking away from the motel. From hope.

I'm walking away from Ama's dream.

It's afternoon when I get home, and I can't find Abu anywhere. He doesn't usually go out at this hour. Four p.m. is peak oblivion time.

The house has been cleaned. Not as well as when Noor and I did it, but a definite improvement over its usual state.

I walk out to the front yard, beneath the three trees Ama said represented our family. Despite how cold it still is in the morning, the trees shoot new leaves, and the wind has a touch of the zephyr in it.

A hinge moans; the laundry room door swings open. "Abu?" I loiter outside the door, unwilling to enter.

"You don't need to come in, Salahudin," my father says. "I'm nearly done."

I'm so used to hearing him slurred and sloppy that I'm confused. As I watch him, I realize he's sober. His hands shake and he's sweating. But he's clear-eyed as he peers at me through his thick glasses.

We'll see how long this lasts.

"I can help you fold," I say.

"You have homework? Or . . ." He is ginger with his words, afraid of how I will respond. Maybe I shouldn't doubt him. Ama would want me to support him. She always did.

"Yeah, I have some homework," I say. "A couple of tests next week."

"Ah. Go then," he says. "There's Kiri cheese and saltines in the fridge." I'm surprised he remembers my favorite snack. "I— won't be home tonight. I have a—a meeting with Janice—do you remember—"

"Your sponsor." A tendril of hope pokes its head out from the desert in my head. "I remember."

I could be angry at him. Tell him he waited too long to stop drinking. That Ama and I deserved better. Right now, it might actually sink in.

But I think of Shafiq. *This life is jihad—struggle. Sometimes the struggle is more than any sane person can bear.*

"I'm proud of you, Abu. I know it's not easy."

"It hasn't been easy for you," Abu says. "It's been very easy for me. But now—I am changing. Your mother." His voice dips. "She would have been ashamed of me." Abu takes a deep breath. "The fortieth day after her death has passed, Putar. We should have read Qur'an at her graveside. We didn't. But we could now. It would bring her comfort. We—we—"

Abu bows his head—mourning as the truth of his own words breaks over him. Until now, Ama's absence felt temporary. Like she was traveling. A trip to Pakistan, maybe. A few weeks visiting Uncle Faisal. She'd be back. Of course she'd be back.

The fortieth day is so permanent. We didn't even mark it.

I go to him, but as soon as I enter the laundry room, the smell of detergent and bleach hits me and I want to vomit. Once, I asked Ama why the smell made me so sick.

"It's like how Noor hates small spaces. It's just how you are."

Abu's face is strained as he watches me.

"I'm fine." I lurch back out. "Sorry. I'm fine."

"You—" His face ripples, collapses, and all the strength that made him Abu again for a few minutes is gone. He slides down the side of the washer, heaving great, silent sobs.

I breathe through my mouth and walk in because I don't know what else to do. I hold him in my arms. He's so much smaller than me. Sometime in the last year, I became taller than my father, bigger than my father, stronger than my father, and I hate the unfairness of it.

He sobs, this fearless man who buried his parents and crossed oceans, who fell in love with a woman he barely knew and built a life with her in a desolate place.

"I miss her," Abu whispers. "She knew all my secrets."

I whisper a prayer and hug Abu the way Ama used to hug me. Like hope lived in her skin and if she held me long enough, it would live in mine, too.

"You can tell me your secrets, Abu," I say. "I'll hold them for you."

"I couldn't keep anyone safe. Not my cousin or Phopo. Not my parents. Not your ama. Not you."

"What do you mean, 'not you'?"

But Abu pulls away and turns his back like he can't stand the sight of me. I hear that Elizabeth Bishop poem. *The art of losing isn't hard to master.*

She was right. I already lost my mother. Now I'm losing my father, too.

CHAPTER 33

Misbah

November, then

When you were born, my son, you were gentle-eyed like your father, and wild-haired like me. So quiet as you looked up, as we beheld you that first time.

Your father whispered the call to prayer in your ear. You listened and it was just the three of us in a perfect moment. You ate well. You slept like a dream. You woke up every morning with a smile. Chubby and happy and sweet. The motel guests loved you. They always said you should be in baby food commercials. Your grandparents adored you from afar. Baba paraded your picture to the whole ilaqa.

Your father—my God, you were his pride and joy. He came home from work to feed you every lunchtime, even if it meant he barely got a chance to eat his own meal. He rocked you to sleep at night. He clipped your tiny nails so carefully that you laughed when he did it. I could not believe he ever thought he would be a bad parent.

You were my world. But to you father, Salahudin? You were the solar system. Bigger. The universe itself. "He will be a neurosurgeon," your father said. "He will be a writer. He will be an architect."

Such plans he had for you. Such dreams. But is that not the case for all of us? We plan. We dream. We hope.

In America, on some days the dream feels so close you can taste it. And children, my putar? Children are the greatest dream of all. A dream manifest—walking, talking, venturing into the wide world. Open to success and joy and greatness. Open to wild, spectacular possibility.

But open to destruction, also.

CHAPTER 34

Noor

May, now

"You're not going to school. Are you sick?"

It's only been a day since I punched Jamie. Chachu is at my bedroom door. I'm curled up in bed, pretending to be nauseous. I'm even clutching a trash can to my chest.

Chachu's not buying it.

"Do you have a fever?"

"My body hurts." At least that's not a lie. I'm still bruised from Darth Derek's tackle.

My uncle's eyes narrow. "What is your illness?" he asks. "Symptoms?"

"Headache and fever," Brooke says from the door. Turns out she's a better liar than I knew. "And she threw up last night."

Chachu lays a hand against my forehead. I try not to cringe.

"You are not throwing up, you have no fever, and you apparently have all of your cognitive functions." He drops his arm. "Therefore, if you will not attend school, you will help me at the shop. It's going to be busy."

"Shaukat—" Brooke says right when I say "Chachu—"

"Get up. An idle mind breeds mischief."

He leaves. Brooke leans against my doorframe and meets my

eyes. *Be careful*, she seems to be saying. Easy enough. I can keep my mouth shut if she does.

Chachu's right about being busy. The Megaball is at nine hundred million, so there's already a line when we open up at six a.m. A few of the regulars tease Chachu, asking if he has a theorem about their chances of winning.

But he keeps the graph paper hidden. Even Chachu knows it's stupid to explain statistical impossibilities to lotto customers.

After an hour, the stream of people slows. When the last one leaves, Chachu launches into an explanation of statistical probability—or improbability, in the case of the lottery.

"In short . . ." He digs out a Pall Mall and lights it. "Everyone who buys a ticket is an imbecile."

"What would you do if you won?" The question is out of my mouth before I can think.

"You weren't listening." Chachu blows smoke at me. "As usual. First I'd have to buy a lottery ticket, Noor. Which I would never do. Because it's futile."

I turn back to the slushie machine I'm cleaning. Chachu says hope is for half-wits. But someone out there will win this prize.

Am I stupid for hoping that UCLA will let me in? That their letter got lost, and the admissions portal is glitching? It's a long shot. A statistical improbability, Chachu would say.

But I still imagine myself walking that brick-and-limestone campus. Taking classes and studying in the library and going to shows at clubs I've only ever read about.

The door jangles. "Hey, Noor. Hey, Mr. Riaz."

Jamie Jensen. "Seven Devils" by Florence and the Machine plays in my head. Jamie is all seven.

In my head, I tackle her. Throw a bag of slushie mix at her head. A rift opens in the crust of the earth and swallows her whole.

In real life, I stare. Chachu nods a greeting. He knows her vaguely.

"I'm glad to see you're feeling better, Noor." Jamie's nose looks fine. A little red. Either she has an incredible plastic surgeon or Ernst was full of it when he said I "severely damaged" her face.

She grabs a Luna bar and a Smartwater, and offers Chachu cash. "Are you heading to school today, Noor?"

I don't trust my voice, so I shake my head.

"Oh, right." Jamie makes a fake sad face. "You got suspended. I hope it doesn't affect college admissions."

She is jealous, Auntie Misbah said once when I complained about Jamie. *She wishes to be the biggest fish in a small pond. It bothers her that you wish to find a bigger, more interesting pond.*

Is that why Jamie hates me so much? Salahudin wondered about it. *Maybe her parents didn't hug her as a kid.* But Chachu didn't hug me either, and I'm not a monster. Maybe it's not because of parents or childhood. Maybe some people are awful and there's no rhyme or reason to it.

"College?" Chachu's voice is level. He doesn't look at me.

"Chachu," I say. "I didn't—"

"You worked so hard on those applications." Her eyes glint, and I think of her accusation—that Salahudin wrote my essays for me. "Immigrants, they get the job done, right? See you later!"

She walks out as Robert, a regular who talks too much, enters.

I've never been so happy to see him. Chachu doesn't seem upset. Another customer arrives, and another. Chachu rings them up without looking at me.

A roar outside. The Coors truck pulls up. "Restock the freezer," Chachu says to me. No clip to his words. His hands are loose. Shoulders are relaxed.

Maybe he didn't believe Jamie.

I finish with the Coors delivery. Then I mop, restock the candy, sweep the front sidewalk, and dust. By the time Brooke walks in at noon, I'm loitering in the back. If Chachu doesn't see me for a bit, maybe he'll forget I exist.

"Noor," he calls. "Come on. Let's go home."

"I can—uh—stay and help Brooke."

"You should rest," he says flatly. "So you don't re-sicken yourself."

He jerks his head to the door. Brooke glances up from the magazine she's picked up. Uncertain. Chachu glares at her. I try to catch her eyes, but she won't look at me.

Everyone has a lizard instinct. That voice that says *don't touch that poisonous snake,* or *step away from the train tracks, idiot.* The instinct that keeps you alive.

I've lost most of what happened before the earthquake. But I know that on that morning, the dogs were acting weird. Yipping and snarling. Even our German shepherd nipped at me when I tried to give her breakfast. It unsettled me. I was her favorite.

I don't remember my family's faces well. Or their voices. I don't remember our dog's name. But I remember the sound of the earth groaning. Like our dog's growl. Deeper, though. Older.

People began yelling. I ran to my parents' room. To the closet. I didn't think. Instinct pulled me there. Forced me to open the door. To fold myself inside that tiny space. To make myself small and silent as my whole world bled and broke and died slow.

Instinct kept me alive that day. It's screaming now. Raging at me. *Don't go, Noor.*

"Get in the car, Noor." Almost before he finishes saying my name, I'm walking to the car. Opening the door.

Some things are stronger than instinct.

Fear. Habit. Despair.

I get in the car.

CHAPTER 35

Sal

The morning after Jamie's fight with Noor, I swing by Noor's house, but no one answers the door. I've texted her about fifty times—to no avail. I go to school because I hope she'll be in class. But she's not. So I ditch.

On my way home, Ms. McCann texts.

Ms. McCann: Discharge this afternoon! Ash is tired but in good spirits. She'll be back to school Monday. I'll be looking into next steps then. She'd love to see you.

I send a smiley face. Then I find my burner and text Art.

Dropping off homework at your house. I'll leave it behind your garden hose.

As soon as the message is sent, I crush the phone's SIM card, bash it with a hammer a few times, and toss it in a dumpster. Then I dig out the paint can where I keep my stash: bottles and bottles of pills stuffed with cotton so they don't make noise, along with a few bags of heroin.

I shove it all into my pockets. It feels heavier than it actually is. The wind, warmer now that summer approaches, hisses through the branches of the pomegranate tree Ama planted near the shed.

I know what you have, the leaves seem to whisper. *I know what you've done.*

Back in the apartment, Abu paces the kitchen. He doesn't ask why I'm not in school. I'm not sure he realizes I should be. His battle with his need is carved into his face, grooves that make him look like he's always grimacing.

"Putar," he says. "Will you sit for a moment?"

It's past eleven a.m. I want to get to Art's house and then go by the liquor store to see if Noor is there.

But Abu rarely asks for anything. So I sit, noticing that the side table where Abu sets down a cup of tea is dusted and clean. He's placed a picture of Ama there. She's holding four-year-old me, the desert sun shining on her neat part, her brow furrowed as she regards me. I wonder where Abu found it.

"Salahudin, we need to sell the motel."

The hell we do. *Five seconds in. Seven seconds out.* I try to breathe, but my chest is too tight.

"We don't need to sell it. I have everything under control, Abu. The utility bills are paid through the end of May—"

He twists his hands together. "It's not about the money, Putar. I—this place—" He shakes his head. "Woh harh jagah mojood heh. Iss ghar keh dar-o-diwar bhee rotay-henh."

He speaks Urdu, not Punjabi. But still, I understand. *She is everywhere. The walls of this house weep.*

"Your mother and I talked about selling this place anyway. She wanted to put the money aside for your education and Noor's. She wanted—"

"We can't sell it." I grip the table tight, staring down at my hands, which are the same shape and color as Abu's. "Ama loved this place. You're ruining everything she wanted to hold on to." My voice rises. "All because you can't keep your shit together—"

"Salahudin—"

"No!" Suddenly I'm looming over him, fists balled. "You can't just check out for years—*years*—and then make decisions for both of us. You don't have that right."

"I am still your fath—"

"Bullshit. Fathers take care of their kids. Fathers don't act like toddlers because they're sad. I'm sad, too, but I'm still holding it together—" My voice breaks, and I turn my back on him so he doesn't see my eyes watering. "Ama was my mother and my father," I say. "You? You're nothing. It should have been you in that hospital bed. Not her."

He doesn't get up when I walk out the door. My hands shake as I turn on the car, but I make myself recite a prayer Ama drilled into me—the one she always said before she drove anywhere.

Which I should be thankful for. Because it's the only thing that keeps me from reversing the car too quickly and running over the person standing stock-still in the middle of the driveway behind me.

CHAPTER 36

Noor

Chachu is silent in the car, but his fingers tap. Thick knuckles bobbing up and down. This is worse than anything, this waiting. I wish he'd yell at me already.

When we get home, I make for my room. His voice stops me.

"The living room, Noor," he says.

I sit at the edge of the couch, and for a minute he doesn't say anything. Sixty seconds are endless when spent in silence with a dangerous animal. When Chachu does finally speak, he's curt. Like a teacher asking a math question.

"How many colleges did you apply to?"

"Seven," I whisper.

"How much was each application?"

"Some—some were forty. A few were eighty."

He stares down at the old, monochrome floor rugs. His eyes are hooded. I can't tell how angry he is.

"Did you steal the money from the store?"

I shake my head. "I saved it. From whenever you paid me. And—and from Eid—"

"Eid?" He swings his head up at mention of the religious holiday. I used to change into Eid clothes at Salahudin's house. Auntie

Misbah would call in sick for me—no one at any of my schools ever questioned it.

"Who was giving you money on—" Then he understands. "That woman is lucky she is dead," he says. "Or I would have taught her a lesson for interfering with you, teaching you all that religious garbage—"

"Don't talk about her!" I shout at him. My rage comes out of nowhere. I went straight from *be calm, Noor* to *shut the hell up, Chachu*. My face is hot. My head vibrates, like it's filled with bees.

"She was a mother to me. She cared about me. She loved me. She did more for me than you ever did, and *she* wanted me to go to college—"

Chachu is the only reason I'm standing here.

I was six when an earthquake hit my village in Pakistan. Chachu drove for two days from Karachi because the flights to northern Punjab were—

Down comes his fist right into my stomach and I can't breathe.

When he reached the village, he crawled over the rubble to my grandparents' house, where my parents lived, too. He tore at the rocks with his bare—

Hands tearing at my face. Chachu shouts. Screams. In rage. In grief. I can't understand him.

The emergency workers told him it was—

"Useless! You're useless, you ungrateful bitch," Chachu roars. "I gave up everything to take care of you!" He shoves me and I hit the wall so hard my teeth rattle. But it's fine. It's okay if it's on the inside. I'll only have issues if he hits my face. If it shows. *Go back in it, Noor. Go back.*

His palms—

Blood everywhere—it's pouring from my nose, my eye, and this is bad because I can't hide this. They'll know—at school, they'll know. I taste blood—

His nails were ripped out. My parents, cousins, grandparents— everyone was gone. But Chachu, he dug anyway until he heard me—

"I'm sorry, Chachu." I'm not shouting now, I'm sobbing. I just want it to stop. "I'm sorry—"

He pulled me out. Got me to a hospital and didn't leave—

My side is on fire. I'm on the ground and he kicks me, snarling something I don't understand. It's like twelve years of how he's really felt is exploding all at once. I curl up and wait for it to be over. The memory fades. Dissolves into nothing but what is happening here. Now.

Yes, Chachu saved me. He took me to the hospital. He didn't leave me.

He ranted about how he couldn't take care of me. How he was in the middle of school and he didn't have the time. Eventually, the doctors ordered him to sit outside until he could calm down. It is my first clear memory of him.

He called relative after relative. But everyone was dead. As if his family had never existed. He cried. Mourned. Then he raged. Screamed. Shouted at God.

"Why her?" Chachu would mutter about me to no one in particular. He asked it in the hospital and later, in a hostel where we stayed while he arranged my ticket and visa. He asked it on the plane to California. He probably thought I wouldn't remember. Or maybe he didn't care if I did.

"There must be someone who can take her," he'd say to himself.

But there was no one. We were—we are—the last two.

"How dare you!" he screams at me now, but he's crying, too. Maybe at what he's lost. Or at what he's doing. "How dare you!"

How dare I defy him.

How dare I survive.

His tennis shoe slams into my ribs. *Don't break. Don't break.*

Oh God. Help me. Someone help me. *Help me.*

Brooke? But even if she was here, Brooke's too afraid to stop him. She spent too many years dodging the rage of men. Even when she sees, she looks away and looks away and looks away.

One Sunday when Auntie Misbah and I were between dramas, I turned on a nature show to a lion chasing a wildebeest calf. The calf was weak and small. But it wanted to live. Desperately. So it ran and dodged, even when it looked like the lion had it. It took every chance it had, every tiny advantage. It leaped over rocks and up hills and eventually, it escaped.

That is what I have to do.

I open my eyes and his back is turned. He's muttering like he did when I was a child. Trapped, maybe, in those moments from long ago, when he first realized he was alone in the world.

I grab the closest thing to me, a heavy brass sculpture of an eagle that Brooke bought at a flea market. I scramble up. Chachu turns when he hears me. I hurl it at him and he screams something—my name, or a curse.

Then I stagger away. I grab my backpack, still sitting by the door, and I run and run and run.

CHAPTER 37

Misbah

August, then

Salahudin loved to wander around the motel from the moment he could walk. His favorite place was the laundry room. He'd seek it out on sturdy little legs when I was changing the sheets or sweeping the parking lot. I'd pretend I had no idea where he'd gone, then flip on the lights and sweep him up from his small nest beneath the towels.

One day, I lay down on the bed in room 6 for a moment. It was evening—and it was my last room. Salahudin had been playing with his toy vacuum near me. I smiled, listening to his small voom-voom sounds.

I closed my eyes. I fell asleep.

When I opened them, the universe had changed.

Toufiq found our son in the laundry room.

I did not understand, at first, what happened. Toufiq told me.

We took Salahudin to the emergency room. We called the police. But the tenant who hurt our son gave us a fake name. He paid in cash. He disappeared.

"Salahudin won't remember the assault." The doctor who told us this was young, with kind, sad eyes. Her name tag said ELLEN ELLIS. *I would call her many times in the years that followed. And she would always be kind. "Keep an eye on him. Watch for aggression, nightmares, bed-wetting—"*

I nodded but I did not wish to nod. I wished to scream. To find the man and make a pulp of him. To kill him slowly. To hurt him the way he hurt my boy. To break him the way he broke us.

When we returned home in the morning, Salahudin slept in my arms, still sedated. I was happy he was sedated. Happy he wouldn't remember anything.

Toufiq did not speak once.

No matter. I breathed in the scent of my son's hair, as sweet as it was the day before. I held him close and whispered a hundred prayers. And though I didn't want to lay him down, I did. Then I laid my prayer rug beside his crib.

Do not let him remember, *I prayed.* Punish he who did this. Punish him with pain, God. Punish him as only you can.

When I finished, I found Toufiq watching me. Silent.

"Say something," I pleaded. "Anything." For whom else could I share this grief with? Not my mother nor my brother, certainly. Not even my baba, who implored me always to return to Pakistan. "Please, little butterfly. Come home."

There was nowhere to turn but my husband.

But Toufiq did not speak. Instead, he went to the cabinet where we kept everything our tenants left behind. He took out a glass and filled it with an amber liquid so potent that my eyes stung to look at it. He drank it down, the way he had only once before, when his parents died.

But this time, he did not stop.

CHAPTER 38

Sal

May, now

Noor's arms are like armor holding her bones together. When I get out of the car, she meets my eyes. There's a cut on her forehead, and blood trickling down her face. Her overfull backpack is at her feet. Her two braids are a mess, the blue kerchief lopsided. I gape in horror, frozen because this must be a nightmare.

"Salahudin—"

She tries to say my name but no sound comes from her mouth. I rush to her, and she falls into me, limp and silent.

"Noor," I say. "I have to get you to the hospital." *And then I'm going to call the police and get your shitbag uncle arrested.*

"No," she whispers. "Nothing broken. I checked."

"We need a doctor—"

"Please," she whispers. "Let's just drive somewhere."

I pull away from her carefully and stoop to find her eyes.

"Noor, no. You're really hurt."

"I'm getting in the car." She looks up at me, shaking with a fury I've never seen before, unleashed and wild. I step back. "If you start driving to the hospital, I will jump out. I mean it. And if you call the cops—it—it will just make things harder for me. So don't."

"Let me call Imam Shafiq—or Khadija. Noor—"

She opens the passenger door of the Civic and sits. All her energy drains out of her.

"Just drive," she says. "Please. Please listen to me. Someone listen to me."

I grab her backpack and it spills open. It's always full, but for the first time, I understand why. Her passport is in there, and a change of clothes in a ziplock bag. Gleaming black prayer beads Ama gave her. Another ziplock of cheap granola bars, nuts, and a bottle of water.

She was always ready to run. Every day, she came to school wondering if this would be the day she had to get out. The realization makes me sick with shame. I should have seen. *Done* something.

"Drive, Salahudin," Noor says.

So I drive. We leave Juniper, and when the town is a distant speck behind us, Noor finally relaxes. The sun won't set for hours, so I head to Veil Meadows, deep in the mountains an hour north. Abu took us camping there sometimes when Ama was still feeling all right.

I clear my throat. "I haven't come here since . . ."

The Fight.

"If I ever get out of Juniper," Noor whispers, "I want to go somewhere green. Somewhere with no dirt and no tumbleweeds and no dust."

"*When* you get out," I say. "It's not a question. It's going to happen."

I lift a hand from the steering wheel and reach out to her before I lose my nerve. I don't know if she wants to be touched right now. Maybe after what Riaz did, she just wants everyone to stay away.

But she takes my hand and holds it so tightly that it aches with all the things she can't say.

We pull off the highway and onto a winding road leading up into the meadows. Scrub softens to forest and Noor puts thin fingers against the window, like she wants to grab on to the trees flitting past. The only sound is the gravel crunching under the tires, and the wind kicking up as we climb higher.

"Do you want music?"

She shakes her head, holding my hand more tightly. "Do you still have that kite in the back?" she asks. "The one we flew last time?"

"Gandalf?" The kite is a wizard with arms outstretched. The name was a foregone conclusion. I'm surprised Noor remembered its existence, though. "I don't think I ever took him out of the trunk."

We stop at the general store right outside the meadows. Noor waits in the car while I buy sandwiches, sodas, chips, and way more chocolate than either of us can conceivably eat.

When I get back to the car, she's resting her head in the crook of her arm. The cut over her eyebrow has scabbed over, and her cheek is red. The bruises at her throat darken, too, and rage consumes me so fast I feel dizzy with it. Riaz is smaller than me. Has a shorter reach, too. I could make him pay.

"Hey." Noor waves a hand in front of me.

"Sorry," I say. "Please let me take you to the hosp—"

"No."

"Noor, you are messing with my unnatural need to fix things. At the very least I'm cleaning the cut on your head."

"Fine." She nods. "You can clean the cut."

As I pull out the first aid kit, I rack my brain for some way to persuade her to let me take her to the hospital.

This is the type of shit they don't teach at school but that we need to know. What do you do when your best friend is bruised and bleeding, and she refuses to go to the hospital? What do you do when you want to help, but she won't let you?

Noor leans against the car door. She puts her hands in her pockets and tilts back. It's chillier in the mountains, and her St. Vincent T-shirt isn't warm enough. I shrug out of my sweatshirt.

"For once, you brought your jacket." She sniffs it as she puts it on. "Smells good."

"I think you threw it in the wash a couple weeks ago. I found it at the back of my closet today. It would reek of stinky boy if it wasn't for you."

Noor smiles, a flash that makes my heart thud faster. "Stinky boys aren't so bad."

Her eyes are on me, smoky and brown. She undoes her braids and pulls her hair out of the way. I dip a Q-tip into antibacterial gel and swab it on her cut, wishing a lifetime of ocular paper cuts upon Riaz with every dab.

"Noor," I say. "Please let me call Khadija. Or Imam Shafiq."

"I will," she whispers. "I promise. But not yet. I need—I need—" Her breathing is shallow and her brown skin turns blotchy.

"Breathe," I say. "Five seconds in. Seven seconds out. Like this." I show her. I've done this for years now. I wonder, suddenly, when I learned it. The memory loiters at the edge of my brain, coy and sinuous, before dancing away.

I shake it off. What matters is that she's gulping in those deep breaths, that she's with me—and that I've taken her hands in mine and it feels right.

When the color is back in her skin and the first aid kit is put away, I find the kite buried beneath canvas shopping bags, a floral sheet, and a rusty steering wheel lock.

Veil Meadows is the opposite of Juniper. It's this perfect, silent emerald in the Sierra Nevada. The grass is tall and soft, cut through with dozens of thick-banked streams that are a deep, video game blue. Not many people come here, because Yosemite is only two hours away, and who wants an emerald when you can have a diamond?

We follow an old deer path down to a stretch of meadow where the grass is shorter. The floral sheet is plenty big enough for us to spread out our bounty of alluringly trashy snacks. Noor ignores the food and goes for Gandalf.

"I'll run it," I say, and she's about to protest because she's better at launching kites than I am, but she's already hurting and in case something inside *is* broken, I don't want her to make it worse. "I'm taller," I say. "Closer to the updrafts."

She rolls her eyes, but takes the spool and unwinds the line. I barely have to launch it. The mountain wind grabs the kite, yanking it so hard that Noor seems to lift up off the ground, insubstantial as paper.

Fear seizes me at the sight. I'm convinced she'll disappear, like Ama. But then she steadies herself and we drop to the sheet. Slowly she loosens the line, until Gandalf is a rippling white mote against the vast blue sky.

Noor holds the spool in one hand and my fingers in the other. I marvel at the feel of her. Skin. Heat. As good as what a hug is supposed to feel like. I marvel that it doesn't hurt.

"Secret power," I say. "Invisibility, flight, or transfiguration?"

"Transfiguration into a dragon," she says. "So I could fly. And I'd have a blue stomach so I could disappear into the sky."

"No, no, no," I say. "You have to pick *one* power—"

I'm two paragraphs deep into why her answer doesn't qualify when I realize that her head is turned toward me.

Speaking is suddenly a complex endeavor that requires too much coordination between my mouth and my brain.

"Hey." She lifts her hand, and it hovers close to my face. I can feel her warmth.

"Hi," I say, and then lean into her hand for a few seconds. I pull away before it starts to feel bad. She doesn't seem upset. We reel in Gandalf, and make bulrush boats to race across the stream.

"Three stones each," Noor says. "Whoever sinks the other gets the last piece of chocolate."

I win, because her aim is shit, but give her the chocolate anyway. We argue over dumb celebrity feuds and listen to a dozen songs she hadn't yet introduced me to.

"You've been holding out on me," I accuse her. "You know I can't find this shit on my own."

"I was saving them," she says. "For a day like this."

I glance at her phone. Something called "I See You" plays, by Kygo. When I see the album title—*Kids in Love*—I think I'll float away. The old floral sheet becomes an island without time. I don't hate Ama and Abu for their choices. Riaz isn't a monster; Noor's not in pain.

It's like last year's ill-fated trip to Veil Meadows—but done right. Noor's warmth mingles with mine, and the fear that's hung on her like a pall since this morning starts to dissipate.

When night falls, we lie back and marvel at the stars. Noor points out Orion's Belt, and flutters her eyelashes.

"He's my celestial boyfriend," she says. "So noble with his bow."

I glare up at the constellation, feeling a surge of hatred for it. "Screw him, then."

"Jealous?"

"Of a stupid bunch of stars?" I snort, then consider. "Yes. Yes, I am."

She shivers in my sweatshirt, because it's colder than a penguin's armpits up here at night. The meadows are officially closed, but there's no one to bother us. When Noor taps my legs, I pull up my knee, confused, and she nudges my legs apart, settling herself between them, so her back is against my chest.

Too many synapses are firing. Too much of her is touching too much of me. My whole body prickles.

She goes still. But not in a bad way. In an I'm-trying-to-learn-your-language way. After I relax a little, she leans back. Uncertain, I hold out my hands like I'm balancing on a tightrope; then she skims her palms along my forearms and folds my fingers into hers. I feel the heat of her along my legs, my stomach, my arms, my chest. She's everywhere.

I hold her carefully, worried my arms are too heavy on the parts of her that hurt. She pulls me closer. The long curve of her neck begs to be kissed, so I bend my head, breathe her in, and bring my lips to her skin. She makes a funny sound, between a gasp and a moan.

Which makes me feel things that I'm very concerned she will also feel, so I pull my body back a little.

"Are you okay?" she whispers, and even that sends tingles through me, because her voice is low and sort of raspy, and I'm stupidly, spectacularly turned on by it.

"Yes," I try to say. "Ynnghh" is what comes out.

"Salahudin," she says. "I owe you an apology."

I'm bewildered. "You do?"

"When we were little, I heard Auntie say a million times, 'I'm going to hug you, okay, Putar?' And back in the fall, during the Fight, I still threw myself at you. I didn't—I didn't give you a choice."

"I don't know why I'm . . ." *Like this,* I was going to say. But I find it hard to talk at all.

She flips around fully and I find I miss her warmth.

"You're perfect," she whispers. "Okay?" I look up into her eyes glimmering darkly and put my hands lightly on her waist. Then I run one thumb along the soft skin above her hips. Her whole body trembles, but when I stop, she growls at me. *More.*

Her hands are on my forearms, my biceps, my shoulder. She runs her fingers through my hair, watching my face all the while. When she rakes her nails lightly across my scalp, with torturous slowness, I hold her closer. Something inside me coils in tight, and every part of me tingles, awake in the best possible way.

She pushes me onto my back. Her hair comes down on either side of my face, stars twinkling between like she's made of them. Her eyes drop to my mouth.

"Are—um—are you sure?" I ask. "You're hurt."

"I want to feel something else," she whispers. "Just for a little while. I want to not hurt. I want to forget. Help me forget, Salah-udin."

When our lips touch I'm sure I'll transform into a living cur-rent. Suddenly, I need her, all of her. I need her to be close to me. I sling an arm around her waist and pull her against me.

Everything falls away. There are no shadows between us. We're bound together, her lips on mine, the flare of her waist underneath my fingers. I explore her mouth deeper and she sighs into me, her hands light on my arms, my chest.

She pulls away, gasping for breath. The grass around us ripples and sings an ode to Noor, the moon lights her hair blue. Her big brown eyes are happy and hot on mine. *Remember this*, I think, al-most frantic. *Remember*.

"Whoa." She smiles; my heart clenches and I want to kiss her again, but I don't, because then we might do things that we're not ready for and I refuse to mess this up, since it's the best thing that's happened in my entire life.

"Noor," I whisper. "We should stop. If we don't, we might, um—"

She rolls away from me. "We're not supposed to do this," she says. "You know. Religiously. Not unless we're . . ." She looks away, embarrassed.

I grin at her. "Are you asking me to marry you?"

"Oh my God, no!" I don't have to see her to know she's blushing.

"I'm teasing," I say. "Anyway, there are probably other things God gets more upset about than two people kissing," I say. "Wars. Bombings. Murders."

"Monsters," Noor whispers. With that one word, reality slams into both of us like a meteor. These past few hours, this sheet, this meadow—it was all a distraction from the terrible shit that has happened to her. That has happened to us both.

"Noor," I say, and she turns away from me. "Will you—will you tell me what happened?"

"Nothing—I—" Her voice is choked, her demeanor as panicked as it was when I first picked her up. "Chachu is the only reason I'm standing here. He—he drove—"

She stops herself.

"I can't talk about it," she mumbles. "I just want to forget. I'm sorry."

We gather up the sheet and walk along a moonlit path that traces the curves of the river. I wish I could beam her to a hospital in the blink of an eye. I wish I could beam Riaz off the planet. Into the vacuum of space, where he could suffocate. Or to Mordor, where the orcs could eat him.

I need Noor to tell me what happened. Because I'm afraid that if she doesn't, she'll convince herself to go back to Riaz's house. To go on as before.

"Memory is weird," I say. Maybe to feel safe talking about scary shit, she needs me to take the leap first. Maybe to open the door to her secret, she needs to hear someone else's. "I say I don't know why touch makes me uncomfortable. But I wonder—I wonder if something happened to make me feel that way."

I trip over the words that I've never let myself think, let alone say.

"I—I know something bad happened," I whisper. "My body knows it. I think that—that's why control is so important to me. But I don't remember this bad thing. Not remembering makes it feel like it didn't happen. And if it didn't happen, then I don't know why I'm broken."

"You're not broken."

"A part of me *is* broken," I say. "Saying I'm not erases the fact that someone did something horrible to me. It erases that I've survived. Because yeah, maybe I'm broken, but I'm strong, too."

I turn inward, the way I've never let myself. To a strange space inside, an empty space that is pure white, the white of a funeral shroud, the white of a morgue floor, the white of an asylum wall. That space is the hurt. That space is the thing that happened. I want to find the moments that fill that space, but I don't want to find them. I want to understand it, but I want to run away from it.

I wonder if it will be like this when I am twenty-eight and thirty-eight and one hundred and eight. If I will one day die with that white space still open and gaping inside me, sharp-toothed and forever unknown.

"I'm just saying," I go on, "that there are some things we shouldn't forget, because if we do, then bad people get away with bad shit. And we keep getting hurt."

"He gets so angry," Noor says. "He tries not to. He'll pace or smoke. Talk to himself. But nothing I can say is right. Nothing I do is right. And then he loses it. It's like there's a monster inside him."

"It's him," I say. "He's the monster."

"Whenever he—he gets angry, I go into my head because it's easier than thinking that this is all there will ever be. Except he's this geyser of hatred and I'm the black hole where he pours it and sometimes it's too much. But I messed up his whole life. Is it any wonder he's mad?"

"It's not your fault." I stop walking. "It's *not*. Noor, stay at my place. I won't bother you. Neither will my dad. He probably won't even notice. I'll sleep on the couch. Please."

"I can't. You have enough to worry about," Noor says. "Did you ever figure things out with First Union?"

"I paid them but forget that—"

"How?"

She asks the question quickly enough that I do a double take.

"I . . . heard some stuff," she says. "About you and Art. I heard that you were . . . into some shit."

Maybe I should come clean. I've absorbed enough of Ama's dramas to know that keeping secrets always has a cost. But Noor has a lot on her mind. We only just became okay. Telling her will ruin this beautiful, fragile thing between us.

"A brown dude hangs out with Art," I scoff. "Of course people are going to talk shit. Nothing's going on."

Her face is in shadow and she hums something familiar, something slow that she's played before.

"'Terrible Love,'" she says quietly. "By the National."

We walk the rest of the way in silence.

CHAPTER 39

Noor

How can the worst day of your life also be the best?

Salahudin and I pack our stuff into the car and sit inside, fingers interlaced. We howl along to Jimi Hendrix singing "All Along the Watchtower." I tell him about decking Jamie. He tells me what happened with his abu in the laundry room.

I ask him if he's been to Auntie Misbah's grave yet. He doesn't answer and I tell him a little about the hours before she died—though I don't tell him everything.

I'd stay forever in his car if I could. My music playing. His voice low and warm. But when it's past midnight, he starts the engine.

"My abu, Noor," he says. "We got into it earlier. He'll be worried. And . . ." His eyes sweep over my face. "I'm taking you to the hospital," he says. "Please don't threaten to jump out of the car. When we get there, I'll call Imam Shafiq. He can help us figure out what to do about telling the police."

One time, when I was eight, someone heard me crying. The neighbors, maybe. The police showed up at the house. Chachu welcomed them in, brought me out. I smiled because he told me what would happen if I didn't. They asked him a few questions. He knew just how to answer. They left.

After that when things got bad, I'd stare at myself in the mirror.

Tell someone, I'd think. *Just tell someone.* But who would I tell? The cops wouldn't believe me. Teachers at school would call CPS and I'd be put in foster care. Chachu was family. My only family. If I lost him, I'd have no one. I didn't want to get Auntie Misbah involved. What if he hurt her, too?

I had so many excuses, each one born of fear. I was afraid I wouldn't be believed. I'd be screaming *"He's hurting me"* out into the world and the world would keep on going.

I close my eyes and lean my head back. The road is smooth beneath the wheels, the window cool against the bruise on my cheek. Anna Leone sings "Once" about what it means to move on from the past.

"Sometimes, Salahudin," I say, "it feels like too much. I think about the shit we've read in school. Those books all about one problem. A kid who's bullied. A kid who's beaten. A kid who's poor. And I think of us and how we've won the shit-luck lottery. We have all the problems."

"Nazar seh bachau." He utters Auntie Misbah's oath against the evil eye so fervently that I laugh.

Famine comes when you lament the flood, I hear Auntie Misbah say in my head. *It could always be worse.*

"Do you think our adulthood will make up for everything we've had to deal with as kids?" I ask him.

"Like we get out of here and you go to med school and I become a writer and our lives will be amazing?"

"They don't have to be amazing. Just not . . ." My face throbs. "Not this."

"You're going to escape this place, Noor." He looks over at me.

"You're going to become a doctor. Your adulthood is going to make up for all of it."

Hope kindles in my chest as he says it. He sounds as sure as Ama did when she talked about God. Sure enough to make me believe.

Salahudin takes the turnoff into Juniper, and seeing those tiny lights draw near makes me shudder. I don't want to go back. I don't want to face what comes next.

"What about you?" I distract myself. "You still have that writing contest to enter. And college classes to sign up for."

"Abu wants to sell the motel."

I wondered how long it would take Uncle Toufiq to come to that conclusion. "You could move to a bigger town," I say. "I could go with you guys. Go to community college. Get away from Chachu. Your abu could get help."

"No way." Salahudin's hands are tight on the steering wheel. "The Clouds' Rest mattered too much to Ama for me to let it go."

"Remember that song your ama loved? 'The Wanderer'?" I ask, and he nods. "The entire thing is based on a Bible passage about how you shouldn't put value in things. In places. All of that is meaningless and it will just make you feel empty. Your ama knew that, Salahudin. She'd understand if you guys sold the Clouds' Rest."

He's shaking his head. "You're like the narrator in 'One Art,'" he says. "Telling me that it's okay to lose things. But I can't. Ama would be so disappointed. Trust me. I knew her the way you didn't."

No you didn't, I want to say. Instead, I keep quiet. We're in Juniper now. The streets are mostly empty. I want to forget about the hospital, to keep driving like this forever. But when we get to the main road, Salahudin takes a left toward the giant red cross in the distance and speeds up.

My stomach twists.

I don't want to do this. I just want to sleep. I'm about to say it when lights flash behind us. A siren blares.

"What the hell?" Salahudin is instantly tense, which is weird. As a rule, he keeps his emotions leashed tight.

"Driving while brown," I say. "How dare you?"

Salahudin doesn't laugh.

"I must have been speeding," he says. "Shit. *Shit.*"

The car door slams behind us. The trim figure of a cop gets larger in the rearview. Salahudin takes a deep breath.

"Hey. It's fine." I touch Salahudin's wrist. He jerks away, like my skin burns him. "Salahudin, it's going to be fine."

My face twinges. The bruises—the cuts. If the cop sees me, he's going to think Salahudin did this to me. No wonder my friend is nervous.

As the cop reaches Salahudin's window, I pull up my hood, and lean my head against the window. Maybe if I pretend I'm sleeping, he won't look closely at me.

"You two are out pretty late." The cop shines his flashlight in Salahudin's face, letting it linger, before flashing it over me in a cursory fashion. He sounds bored as he asks for license and registration.

"Speed limit is twenty-five," he says as Salahudin hands them over. "You were at forty-five, easy."

"I'm sorry, officer." Salahudin's voice shakes. He drums his fingers on the steering wheel, and I want to take them just so he'll stop. "I'll slow down."

"Where were you headed?"

"The hospital. My friend's—not feeling well."

The officer turns his flashlight on me and I hold a hand up.

"Please put down your hand, miss, and look at me."

Shit. I do, and the flashlight stays way longer on me than I want it to. I feel the cop taking in every bruise. Every scratch. I can't see his face very well, but I spot his name tag. MARKS.

"Wait here." Marks's tone is hard. Cold. He disappears to his car. His radio crackles.

"Shit," Salahudin says. "I know this guy. He almost arrested Abu at the hospital the day Ama died." He glances over his shoulder. Then he lunges for the glove compartment. He grabs something from it. A paper bag.

He scans the back seat and finally hides the bag beneath a floor mat, then shoves my backpack on top.

"Salahudin, what—"

"It's fine," Salahudin says, but I can tell he's talking to himself. Not me. "Everything is fine."

Officer Marks is still in his car. Someone passes slowly—another cop, and pulls in ahead of us.

Salahudin's breath hitches. He grabs at his cargo pants. Whatever he tears out shines dully. He hands the objects to me. Both plastic. One solid, one slippery—a pill bottle, a baggie.

"What is this?" I whisper. "Salahudin?"

"Shove them under your seat," he hisses. "Hurry!"

I don't think. I just do what he says, right as Officer Marks re-appears.

"Mr. Malik." He has a hand resting on his belt. Not quite on his gun. But not far. "Please step out of the vehicle."

"Hey," I say. "He didn't do this." I gesture to my face. "It wasn't him—"

"Miss, stay where you are. Mr. Malik, I need you to get out of the car. Now."

"Sure," Salahudin says. "No problem."

Salahudin moves like he's new to his body. His skin is blue in the squad car's spotlight. A gust of wind blows a tumbleweed past and dust swirls. Across the street a truck slows down to rubberneck. The desert outside the car feels so big. Like it goes on forever. Like there's nothing else but us, this car, and the emptiness beyond.

My panic rises. It has no outlet. "Why are you getting him out of the car?" I blurt. "Just write him a ticket so we can go."

"Miss." Marks speaks slowly, as if to a little kid. "We're just going to talk real quick."

Everything will be fine. Nothing awful will happen because life has been shitty for too long and neither of us deserves for it to get worse.

We'll tell this story years from now. We'll laugh about it.

Marks has Salahudin against the car.

"Why do you need to talk if he was speeding?" I call out the window. The question comes out angrier than I mean it to.

Calm down, Noor. Hold it in.

But I always hold it in. I always hide what I feel. It hasn't done me any good.

"This is bullshit!" I yell it now, too enraged to be afraid.

Officer Marks radios for backup. There are already two cop cars and three officers here. They all have guns. We have snacks and a wizard kite.

I reach for the door handle. Then I think of the time Chachu called the police when a customer started breaking bottles. The guy was mad because Brooke carded him. The cops arrested Chachu instead. That's how it goes in small towns. Juniper's no different.

If I get out, I might make things worse. So I sit back. I seethe.

Salahudin's door hangs open. His window, too. The officer pats him down and I can't see his face, but I can imagine him grimacing.

Then Salahudin curses. I lean over his seat, trying to figure out what is going on.

The officer has pulled something out of Salahudin's pockets. He keeps searching—and finds other items that are too small to see.

A flash of silver. Salahudin turns, putting his hands behind his back. His jaw is tight—but that's all I can make out of his face. I don't understand what's happening.

And then I do.

The officer is cuffing him.

He's arresting Salahudin.

"No—*hey!*" I start to get out of the car. But another officer stands by my door, her hand out. I didn't even notice her walk up.

"Miss," she says. "Stay in the vehicle."

"He's arresting my friend. We didn't *do* anything—"

"Miss." Her voice snaps and I jump. "Stay in the car. Hands on the dash, where I can see them."

I do as she asks. "I don't understand why you're doing this," I say. "Just give him a ticket and let us go. He didn't do anything. We didn't do anything."

The cop exchanges a few words with Marks, and when she turns back to me, her voice is quieter.

"I need you to get out of the car slowly—and walk with me over here, to the curb. I'm going to open the door now."

I do as she asks. When we get to the curb, she tells me to put my arms over my head.

"I'm going to pat you down. Are you hurt anywhere else, other than your face?"

"My ribs," I say, and when she pats me down, her touch is gentle. I see her looking at my cheek, a furrow between her brows. Salahudin is also on the curb, but on the other side of the street. Two officers stand over him. I can't hear what they're saying.

"Why are you arresting him?"

"Your boyfriend knows why we're arresting him."

"He's not my boyfriend—and he didn't do anything."

The officer—whose name tag says ORTIZ—sighs. "Does he get mad a lot?"

"He never gets mad," I say. "Ever."

"Who did this to your face? And don't tell me you tripped and fell."

"None of your goddamn business."

Ortiz clucks. "You kiss your mama with that mouth?"

"My mom died when I was six."

It's not a sentence I say often. I don't have to. Everyone at school knows I live with my uncle and aunt. Everyone who comes into the store knows it, too. And that's pretty much my world. If anyone has ever been curious about my parents, they've never asked.

I can't see Ortiz's reaction. It's too dark, and she has a flashlight on me. But a few seconds go by, and she clears her throat.

"Does your friend make you sell drugs?"

"No!"

"Do you make *him* sell drugs?"

"No," I say. "And I'm done talking to you."

I practically spit in her face. People always see the wrong things. Jamie looked at me and saw a cheater. Ortiz looks at Salahudin and sees an abuser. But they'll look at Jamie and see a popular girl instead of a racist asshole. They'll look at Riaz and see a savior who took in his orphaned niece instead of a monster.

"Look," Ortiz says. "I can't help you unless you help me. Your boyfr—your friend—is in cuffs. He can't hurt you."

"He didn't hit me."

"Let's set that aside for now. You think we'll find anything when we're searching the car?"

I glance at the Civic. The trunk is open. Gandalf is on the ground, half under the boot of one of the cops. Two more officers search the front seat. Tires crunch as another squad car pulls up.

Salahudin talks—I hear his voice but not what he's saying. *Don't tell them anything,* I want to shout at him. *The more you tell them, the more they can screw you.*

"Tell me where you guys hid your stash," Ortiz says. "Maybe we'll go easier on you. You're young. And whether you want to admit it or not, it's obvious he's hurting you."

That stuff I shoved under my seat—*pills.* But Salahudin must

have an explanation for them. Because he told me he wasn't dealing. And he doesn't lie to me.

"Well, shit," one of the officers searching the front seat of the
car says. Suddenly, everyone is tense and silent.

"Marks." The officer breaks the quiet. "You need to come take
a look at this."

CHAPTER 40

Sal

It took me a long time to fit in when I was little. Before I knew what was wrong with me, the other kids seemed to. They sensed it in the way I kept my eyes down, and the way I didn't seem to hear the teacher, and the way I did everything a second too late. They never talked to me more than they had to. They never sat next to me. They listened to that part of themselves that whispered: *Different. Other.*

It made me sad. Because they didn't know things I did. Because they could have been kind, but they didn't know how to be.

Maybe that sadness would have transformed into something worse. Bitterness. A lifetime of rage. But it was held up, robbed of its potency a month into first grade by a girl who showed up late and entered alone, no parent to fuss over her.

Her clothes hung on her and her hair was pulled into two uneven braids. She didn't speak English.

A kind person would have looked at her and seen a six-year-old girl who needed love. The teacher, Mrs. Bridlow, looked at her and saw a pain in the ass. *"This is Nora,"* Mrs. Bridlow said. *"She's from Pack-ee-stan. Like Sal!"* She put the girl in the only empty seat, next to me, in the back of the class.

The other children talked and laughed and played. The girl and

I stared at each other like two surly dogs, brown eyes locking, broken meeting broken-hearted, Salahudin meeting Noor.

I didn't know then what role those eyes would play in my life, how often I'd look into them, how often I'd look away. We didn't say anything. We just stared. Neither of us seemed to find this strange.

"What's that?" I pointed to something purple and green on her arm.

She covered it up with a hand, but didn't speak.

"Ghoray varga lagadha heh." *It looks like a horse,* I said, since she was from Pakistan, and I wasn't old enough to realize that she might not speak Punjabi.

She peered down at it, as if she'd never considered that pain could take the shape of a farm animal. The teacher called us for story time; Noor followed me to the mat and sat next to me when the story began. She laughed when I laughed, which wasn't when all the other kids laughed. At one point, she pointed to a spider making its way up the shelf of toys beside us. We watched it together.

Suddenly, I understood why my ama told me, with that anxious look in her eyes, to make friends. Why all these kids clustered together. Because it felt good to have a friend.

It was the first time I'd called someone that, in my head. And all other friends would never live up to the feeling I got that day from thinking that word, because there has never, ever been anyone quite like Noor.

I think about that day now, as the cops pull the drugs from the car. As they put cuffs on her. As they push me into the hard plastic back seat of the police cruiser. As she turns to look at me through the glass, jaw clenched, eyes full. As she comes face-to-face with the extent of my lies and deceit and stupidity.

As she realizes her life will never be the same.

I watch, and I wonder at the horrific symmetry of it all. Outcasts always from then to now. From the moment that she saved me as a child to the moment that I've damned her as an adult.

I wish she'd sat anywhere else that day, long ago. I wish I'd been horrible to her. I wish she'd been horrible to me. I'd trade every adventure we've ever had if it meant that she wouldn't have to face what's coming.

But I can't. Her life will forever be divided into the moment before we got pulled over and the moment after.

And it is my fault.

PART V

I lost two cities, lovely ones. And, vaster,
some realms I owned, two rivers, a continent.
I miss them, but it wasn't a disaster.

—*Elizabeth Bishop*,
"One Art"

CHAPTER 41

Misbah

January, then

I have never been a violent woman, but your first grade teacher, Roberta Bridlow, was so horrible that my fingers itched to give her a thappad across the back of her head, the way my nani did to anyone impertinent.

Mrs. Bridlow had a small helmet of yellow-gray hair and lips that looked like she had eaten too much sour achar.

"Salahudin." Sall—ee—you—dinn. Her butchering of your beautiful name made me wonder how she became a teacher if she didn't know how to read simple letters. "He's unmotivated, Mrs. Malik."

"He's six years old."

"He won't write. He won't read."

I crossed my arms. "He loves stories," I said. "He will learn."

"Look," she said. "I don't know how it is where you come from, but here in America, parents have to be active participants in the school life of their children. I have thirty-two children in that class and I can't help all of them."

"Just the white ones, then?"

She opened and closed her mouth like a particularly stupid fish. "This—this has nothing to do with that. Sal—we call him Sal in class— isn't thriving, Mrs. Malik. Does he speak English at home?"

"He speaks perfect English. Punjabi, too."

"*The multiple languages must be confusing him—*"

"*Or perhaps you aren't doing your job.*"

She swallowed so loudly I thought she'd choke on the sound. Then she cleared her throat. "Perhaps homeschooling—"

"*You want me to homeschool him because you cannot do your job.*"

"*There are social issues, too, Mrs. Malik. He doesn't fit in. He gets upset if the other children touch him. Is he—safe? At home? Are you? I knew a girl once who was married to a Muslim man and they can be—*"

I stood so fast the child's chair I'd been sitting in landed on its back with a thunk. "I will be speaking with the principal about this conversation, Mrs. Bridlow."

I left. I did not speak to the principal. I spoke to her then-partner, Dr. Ellis.

Your teacher did not bring up homeschooling again.

But she was right that you struggled to fit in. I took you to a doctor—a therapist. She wanted to keep seeing you, but I was worried it would make you remember what happened. Make you relive it.

It broke my heart, the way you had changed. Little things. Silence where there was once laughter. Reticence where once you would run to me. You didn't seem to understand it yourself. Deep in the night, you would wake up and cry out. But worse was when you were quiet. Unreachable.

I didn't know what to do. Your father couldn't help me, no matter what I said to him. Maybe I should have let you keep seeing the therapist. Maybe she would have helped you understand yourself.

But I was young and foolish. I did not return to her. Instead I thought: Who my child becomes is not the sum of what happened to him. *I would not let anyone break you. If a hug gave you no comfort, then perhaps a story would. If conversation alarmed you, perhaps kindness would* soothe you. *If the other children didn't understand you, then I would speak to you of God, who understands us all, mind, heart, and soul.*

I tried, my son. I tried to give you back what that monster took. I hope it worked. Because now, as time escapes me, I realize the greatest thing he could have stolen from you was not your innocence, but your hope.

CHAPTER 42

Noor

May, now

FRIARSFIELD, CALIFORNIA

The booking area of the county lockup is packed. It sounds—and smells—like Juniper High's girls' locker room. The officer I've ridden with—I don't see his name—hands me off to a stocky blond cop who uncuffs me and scans my fingerprints. She escorts me to a blank white wall. I don't understand that she's taking my mug shot until she says, "Look here," and points to a tiny laptop camera.

I wonder if Salahudin was brought to the county jail in Friarsfield, too. My chest hurts, thinking of him. I knew something weird was going on. But I didn't want to believe it. And he didn't think I was worth the truth.

Twelve years of friendship, of him being the gravity that kept me from spinning into nothingness. And now I am cut loose.

Why why why, Salahudin?

No, he's not Salahudin anymore. He's the Liar.

The officer finds a small metal desk, sets me down, and gets the basics. Name. Date of birth. Citizenship.

"I need your green card."

"It's—it's in my things. But I know the number."

She notes it down. "Where were you born?"

"Kot Inayat, Pakistan."

"Kot-a-who?"

"Kot—In—ay—at." I say it slowly. She makes me spell it.

"Pakistan, huh? That's near Afghanistan, right?" Her "Afghanistan" rhymes with "a span of man." At my nod, she whistles. "A lot of terrorist types up there."

She says this like I might know them personally. Like maybe there are a few in my family.

"Yeah, a ton. They're all over the place."

If she catches my sarcasm, she doesn't show it. Instead, she goes through the rest of the questions: Address. Occupation. Social security number.

"Let's step into the hall for your phone call."

I shake my head. There are only two people I'd call in this situation. One is dead and the other is a liar.

The officer shrugs and takes me down a cinder block hallway to a plain white door. I know it's a county jail and not the state pen. I know I'll be in here for a few days, maybe. Not years.

Still, I think of "Prisoner 1 & 2" by Lupe Fiasco. The collect call at the beginning. The cell doors clanking open and closed. That song taught me more about jail than anything on TV or in a book. When I first heard it, I was surprised that it wasn't about fear.

It was about anger. About despair.

Songs help me process life. They help me feel. But right now, I don't want to do either. I push the music from my head.

Another officer opens the white door, and a wave of noise hits me. I step into a cell that's twenty feet long and twenty feet wide. It's full. Some of the women stare as I enter. One hisses.

There's a cot on the corner of the cell. An older lady with white hair lies on it while another—her daughter, it looks like—stands guard, arms crossed. I have to pee, but there's no wall to hide the toilet and there's no paper either.

Most of the women stand or sit along the wall. A few are white, a few brown, a few Black. I find an empty corner and lean against it, letting my hair fall into my face to hide my injuries. An officer calls out a woman's name and she rises as he unlocks the cell.

No one is coming for me. No one even knows I'm here, other than the Liar.

Stop, Noor. Think. I'll be fine. The drugs weren't mine. I've never dealt before. Mrs. Michaels will say so. Mr. Stevenson will say so. Oluchi at the hospital will say so. My phone records will say so.

I repeat this to myself for an hour. Then it starts to run together. It gets tangled in my head. The sun rises—I can see it through the slit of a window at the top of the cell.

I close my eyes, and feel the Liar's hands on me, so careful. I think of how his body felt like home. How so much of him close to so much of me almost let me forget why we were in Veil Meadows in the first place.

And his face when I asked him about Art. That shadow in his eyes. The lie. He was dealing. Of course he was—how else has he been paying everything off at the motel?

It wasn't worth it. The Liar screwed himself. And he's screwed me, too.

When I ran from Chachu's house, I wanted a sign from the universe. Something good. I wanted to know that even if I didn't get into college, there would be more to my life than an angry uncle, a liquor shop, a tiny desert town.

I thought the Liar was that sign.

Maybe I should have died in that earthquake. Maybe God has been giving me signs that I'm on borrowed time—I've just been too stupid to see them.

"Noor Riaz?"

An officer opens the door, a hand on his sidearm, in case any of the tired women in here try to attack an armed dude twice their size.

I stand up, but don't say anything. He cuffs me. His fingers squeeze my arm right over a bruise.

The room I'm led to is small and close, with a table with a chair on either side. There's a clock on the wall that tells me it's nearly noon. I'm left alone for long enough that my vague need to pee turns into an actual problem. By the time a strangely orange man with the name tag BREWER shows up, I'm ready to squat on the floor.

"Noor Riaz." Brewer settles on the chair with a thin file. His uniform is bulky—he has a vest with a million pockets. I wonder if he is supposed to go raid a drug den after this.

He stares at the file—my file—for a long time. Long enough that I know he's not reading it. He's just trying to make a point.

Well, I can make a point, too. I sit back and count the cinder blocks.

"Noor, Noor, Noor," he finally says. "Pretty name. What's it mean?"

"I have to use the restroom," I tell him.

"Sure," he says. "After we're done."

Just four words. But it's immediately clear that he's nothing like the officer who booked me. Or like Ortiz and her light questioning last night.

"Ms. Riaz, I'm going to ask questions. You're going to answer them." He doesn't wait for a response. "The officers who pulled you over found drug paraphernalia as well as a bottle of OxyContin and twelve grams of heroin under your seat. How long have you been selling drugs?"

"That stuff isn't mine."

"They also found a bottle of hydrocodone in the back seat, under your backpack. Can you produce your prescription for the hydrocodone?"

"Isn't that a painkiller?"

"You know your opioids."

I shrug. He looks pointedly at the bruises on my throat. My arms. "Did your boyfriend do that to you?"

"I don't have a boyfriend."

Brewer taps his pen on my file. I can't tell what color his eyes are. Blue, maybe. Or green. Something cold. Reptilian.

He's already made a decision about me.

"If Salahudin Malik was coercing you into selling, then we can nab him on domestic abuse charges, transportation charges, and possession charges. I checked out your school record." Brewer pauses. I wonder if, somewhere in the interrogation handbook, there's a section on how silence can make perps squirm.

"Your grades are good. Surprisingly good. You're planning on college, your principal said. But you've had a few disciplinary issues."

"One disciplinary issue."

"Says here your dad is Shaukat Riaz—that he owns a liquor store—"

"He's my uncle," I say.

Brewer raises an eyebrow. "You ever work in that liquor store?"

I fidget. I feel like I have to answer him. But I don't know what he plans to do with whatever I say.

"Yes." The truth is simplest. "I work there."

"Good place to sell your pills. Good cover. Your uncle get you into this?"

Shit. Brewer waits for a response. I don't give him one. Instead I think of Chachu. About how he'd shout at the TV when he'd watch *Law & Order*. *Don't tell them anything, you idiot.*

"I'd like to speak to a lawyer, please."

"Sure." He smiles without teeth. "But Noor? A bit of advice. Plead guilty. Don't drag your family into a mess."

"A few seconds ago, you were asking if my family got me into this."

"Did they?"

I shake my head and say it slower this time. "I'd like to talk to a lawyer."

"Of course." Brewer stands, but he stops at the door. "You know, I look at a kid like you," he says, "and I just don't get it. You're smart. You're pretty. You have a family. You got everything going for you. And you throw it away."

In this moment, I wish I were a poet. Not to speak beauty. But to speak pain.

I'd find a way to explain that this isn't my fault. That I didn't throw away my future—it was taken. Taken by the one person I thought I could trust.

I don't speak. There's no point. Brewer has decided he knows who I am. He's not going to change his mind. And I'm not going to waste my time trying to make him.

People see what they want to. I'm sick of hoping that they'll see me.

CHAPTER 43

Sal

Abu picks up on the third ring, and at the sound of his voice, the words I'd practiced—*Can you please come get Noor out of Friarsfield County Jail?*—leave my head. When he speaks, I hear Ama. Not her presence, but her absence: the weight of sadness that presses like a fist into Abu's heart; the rough timbre in his voice that tells of his loneliness.

"Abu." The horrible things I shouted at him earlier ring through my head. "Ama would be so ashamed of me. I messed up. I really messed up."

"Where are you, Putar?" His voice is clear—he hasn't been drinking. He's silent when I tell him. Silent when I finish.

"Don't worry about me," I say. "But can you please get Noor out? She can't call Riaz, he—"

Before I say more, I stop myself. Noor didn't tell the cops about Riaz. And they're probably listening to this call.

"Please, Abu," I say. "Get Noor. Then we can deal with me."

"I'll be there soon. We will sort this out. Okay?"

"Okay, Abu."

Ama taught me that saying thank you to your own parents is unnecessary. Akin to thanking your lungs for breathing. The times I tried, she looked at me like I'd rejected Saturday-morning paratha.

But I hope he hears it in my voice. I hope he knows.

The guy behind me tells me to hurry the hell up, and I hang up quickly. When I turn to glare at him, he steps back. Noor once lamented that I had RKF—Resting Killer Face. So I do not smile as two officers lead me to a holding cell. It's not hard—their hands on my arms feel like vises left in a fire for too long.

I'm six feet tall, throw a mean punch, and I've got my RKF on. But I'm still scared as hell when I enter the Friarsfield County Jail holding cell.

Just don't piss anyone off. And don't get your ass kicked.

There are only a few guys in here. Some ignore me, but one, a white dude with a shaved head and a swastika tattoo, gives me the once-over. I make myself meet his glare, and fear for a long moment that it is the last coherent decision I'll be making for a while.

But he looks away.

I imagine telling Noor that for once, my RKF was helpful. If she ever speaks to me again, that is.

She will. Abu will get her out, the police will realize she had nothing to do with my stupidity. She'll yell at me, but eventually she'll forgive me.

I shift under the gaze of a kid who looks younger than me, and who has parked himself on a dirty cot. His light brown hair is buzzed short, almost bald in places, like he did it himself. He could be looking at me for a million reasons. Because he's freaked out. Because he thinks I'm trustworthy. Because he likes my YOU SHALL NOT PASS T-shirt.

Eventually, he shuffles over. "Hey. Hey. Hey." The kid's' eyes are red-rimmed, and up close, he's got that twitchy, sweaty tension that plagues addicts when they need a fix. "What'd you do?"

I've read enough Elmore Leonard books to know you don't say shit to anyone in jail. But the guy takes my silence as an invitation to talk.

"My girlfriend called the cops on me for hitting her." He yanks up his sleeve, where there are four deep gouges that look like scratches. One of them is starting to scab over. I just stare at his red, red knuckles.

"That bitch hit *me*. She thinks I'm messing with her meth-head sister." He looks at me to gauge my response and when I say nothing, he leans closer. "Hey—you got anything on you? I've got money."

"The kid doesn't have drugs up his ass, tweaker." A heavyset man with skin a shade lighter than mine walks over. The tweaker scuttles away like a roach in sunlight.

"Ignore him," the man says to me. "He's been asking everyone. Wish they'd put him in his own cell already."

There's a tattoo on the guy's arm. *Ecclesiastes 1:14.*

"I'm Santiago," he says. "First time in here, huh?" When I don't respond, he laughs. "You got that look. All good, man. No one in the holding cell is gonna do shit to you with the cops watching. Not even White Power over there."

The skinhead looks up from his perch near the cot, eyes burning. He cracks his knuckles. Santiago stares back, bored.

"It's real prison you want to avoid. You talk to the cops yet?"

I shake my head.

"Good," Santiago says. "Don't. Wish someone had told me that the first time I got thrown in here. Those pendejos mean it when they say anything you say or do will be used against you."

My gaze falls to his arm again.

"What's your tattoo mean?" I ask him.

"It's a verse," Santiago says. "From the—"

The door clanks open, and an officer calls my name. At first, I think Abu must have arrived. But it's only been an hour and it would take him twice that long just to drive here from Juniper. And anyway, he's supposed to get Noor out first.

The cop cuffs me and takes me to an interrogation chamber that smells like a dumpster full of dead skunks. A few minutes later, a guy with a tangerine spray-tan and a black vest over a uniform walks in. His name tag says BREWER.

He stares at my file for a long time. I fidget.

"Salahudin, Salahudin, Salahudin." He butchers it, of course. "Cool name. What's it mean?"

"It means 'righteous of faith,'" I say.

"Hmm." Brewer nods. "You religious?"

"I believe in God."

He smiles. "Nice to see a young person who believes in something. So. Sal—can I call you Sal? I'm Officer Brewer. And I'm just here to chat."

He drones on for a while about my clean record. Tells me if I tell the DA who my supplier is, they'll go easy on me.

"I just want my friend to be okay," I say. "Is she okay?"

"Did your friend sell drugs with you?"

"No," I say. "She's—not like that."

The cop grimaces—or maybe it's a smile. He has a fat brown mustache, like in the old-school seventies cop shows that Abu watches until he falls asleep.

"The drugs were yours, then?"

"If I tell you the drugs were mine, will you let Noor go?"

"Let's focus on you for a minute instead of Noor." Brewer observes me with his chin in his hand. "Arresting officer said your parents run the Clouds' Rest over in Juniper. Your mom died and your dad's been in the tank a couple of times. I guess he took it badly."

I shrug and Brewer taps his pen on my file.

"My old man hit the bottle hard, too," he says. "Used to hit me while he was at it."

"My dad doesn't hit me."

Brewer hems. "He didn't smack you in a hospital a couple months back?"

Of course Officer Marks would have shared that.

"That was an—Look, my mom died that night—"

"Right," Brewer says. "So walk me through this. Your mom dies. Your dad's not being a dad. That leaves you to run things. A kid who's trying to get through high school. Seems a little unfair."

Putting it that way, it does seem unfair. I can't tell if he is being sincere. It seems like he is. I wish I'd watched all those *Law & Order*s that Riaz was obsessed with. My encyclopedic knowledge of fantasy nerd trivia is useless right now.

"My parents didn't want it to be this way," I say.

"Course not. So. You need money. You start dealing. This is small potatoes, kid. You're probably not going to get much time. Your friend, though . . ."

"Noor's not a drug dealer." I grip the table. "She works in a hospital. She's going to be a doctor. She *helps* people—"

"The hospital? Interesting. Plenty of loose meds lying around, I'm sure."

"No, wait—that's not—"

"For someone who's been there a while, it might not be too difficult to swipe a few, right? Did you threaten her? Did someone else?"

"No—"

"Look. We had a young lady in your town overdose the other day. She survived—barely. The shit you and your friend are selling is evil. It hurts families. Destroys lives. You don't look like the kind of kid who wants to be a murderer. So why don't you reverse some of the harm you've done? Who's your supplier? Where are you and Noor getting the shit you sell?"

I'm not about to turn Art in. I hate him right now, but he gets most of his product off the dark web and I don't know who else I'd be pissing off if I snitched on him.

"I want a lawyer," I say.

For the first time, Brewer looks irritated. He gets up, and as he opens the door, a cop pokes his head in.

"I gotta walk him to the courthouse for his arraignment."

"Get him a lawyer." Brewer turns back to me. "I like you, Sal. You remind me of me, when I was a kid. Think about your old man when it comes time to plead," he says. "A girl is just a girl. But your father's your blood, even if he drinks. If you end up in jail right after your mom died, that's going to impact him worse than anything. I wouldn't be surprised if your old man drinks himself to death before you're out of prison."

The courtroom for my arraignment smells and feels like a mothy trunk, the walls so close that I can hear the rattle of the bailiff's breath. The fluorescent light above makes everyone look like an extra from *The Walking Dead*.

The chair I'm led to is rickety and metal. It reminds me of the seats Ama would drag from the carport whenever we had company.

"Try to look harmless, Salahudin," my lawyer, an obscenely handsome guy named Martin Chan, warns me. He fits into this courtroom like a mullah at a topless beach. "We'll be here for a while."

"Okay." I feel compelled to whisper, worried that if I speak up the roof will cave in.

The judge, a gray-haired woman with a severe mouth, makes quick work of most of the people ahead of me. I listen to the quiet conversation between lawyers and their clients, startled to realize that there are criminals who have been here so many times they know which judges are in which rooms and which bailiffs are assholes.

Finally, my name is called out and the judge lists the charges. "Possession of heroin for sale."

She is talking about me. Not some drug dealer on TV.

"Transportation of heroin for sale. Possession of OxyContin for sale."

Not a stranger in a news report. Or a character in a book.

"Transportation of OxyContin for sale. Possession of fentanyl for sale."

Me.

I am the criminal here. The perp. The bad guy. This fact did not hit me when I was arrested. Or in the interrogation room with Officer Brewer.

Now it penetrates, with each charge the judge delivers in that flat, perfunctory voice.

Brewer's words come back to me. *I wouldn't be surprised if your old man drinks himself to death before you're out of prison.*

He was bullshitting me when he described what I did as "small potatoes." These charges—and there are so many of them—they're serious. They're felonies. If I'm convicted of them, I'll end up in prison. Abu will spiral. He might not sell the motel—he might just lose it to the bank. End up homeless. Or dead.

Martin enters my not-guilty plea and then argues for my bail. He speaks of Abu and the motel, of my school attendance, and my English and history grades.

It's embarrassing to listen to, the way he's scraping at the edges of my life for something good to say. Eventually, the judge nods. "Bond is set at twenty-five thousand dollars."

"Martin," I hiss after he thanks the judge. "There's no way in hell my dad comes up with that much money!"

"He only needs to come up with ten percent. And he's already in touch with a bondsman. You should be out of here in a few hours."

"What about Noor?" I ask Martin. "Did you hear—"

Martin sighs and speaks quietly. "Salahudin, you seem like a good kid. Really. But you're in some deep water. If you don't want to drown, you've got to start thinking about yourself. And about how we're going to beat these charges."

"I get that," I say. "I'm just worried about—"

"Your friend. I know. But you might be expelled from school. And you're looking at nearly eight years in prison."

Eight years. Eight *years*?

"Keep your head down," Martin says. "Stay clean. And stay away from Noor Riaz. For your sake. And hers."

CHAPTER 44

Noor

The next few hours are miserable. And educational. I learn how jailhouse medics can judge you without saying a word. I learn how uncomfortable courthouse chairs are. How a judge can discuss your entire future without looking you in the eye once. How hot a courtroom can get when you're the one the judge is talking about. I learn that "released on your own recognizance" means I don't have to wear handcuffs or have a cop following me.

"You're free to go." The lawyer assigned to me is a small, neat woman, with thick glasses and a head of curly brown hair streaked with gray. "Your pretrial hearing—"

"Ms. Bradley, right?" a smooth voice cuts in. "I'll take it from here. Asalaam-o-alaikum, Noor."

Khadija's wearing a pantsuit. Her hijab is a sober black. To anyone else, she'd look like a slightly annoyed lawyer.

To me she's every hero the Liar ever gushed about. Ms. Marvel. Okoye. Princess Leia.

"What—what are you—"

Khadija waves off my public defender—who looks relieved—and walks me swiftly toward the courthouse exit.

"Toufiq called," she said. "He's trying to get Salahudin out, but he didn't want your uncle coming around." Khadija's glance flits to my face before she looks away. "I'll be defending you now. We are going to figure this out. But—"

She stops just before the doors. They whoosh as they turn, an endless churn of people entering and leaving.

"Noor." She reaches out and touches the bruise on my face. "You're going to have to tell me everything."

I want the drive back to Juniper to be quiet. But Khadija has a dozen questions. And after that, a dozen more. She's kind—and persistent. She doesn't let me drift away.

Maybe she's right not to.

Night falls as we drive. She stops at an In-N-Out and orders me a burger and a chocolate shake. I haven't eaten since yesterday. Still, I barely eat half.

Because I told her about Riaz.

"You'll stay with us." It's not a request. "We have an extra room. Toufiq said you could stay with him and Salahudin, but—"

"I don't—" The Liar's hands in mine. His beautiful face. His betrayal. "I don't want to talk about him. Please."

"Will you be okay to see him in school?" she says.

I forget that somewhere in Juniper, my classmates are thinking about homework and prom and AP tests. Jamie Jensen is picking out the clothes she'll wear on her first day at Princeton.

"I can't stay with you," I say. "The jail didn't return my backpack—I don't have clothes—"

"I've already talked to Brooke. She's going to bring by some things for you. And you're going back to school. You have to take your AP tests. Graduate. You have a future, Noor. I won't let the court take it from you."

"Why help me?" I say. "I can't pay you, Sister Khadija."

"Don't offend me, Noor." For the first time since she picked me up, Khadija sounds mad. "You think I'm doing this to get paid?" She shakes her head. "Do you know what sadaqa is, Noor?"

"Good actions?" Auntie Misbah taught me that.

"Yes. And that's part of giving, which is essential to being Muslim. It doesn't matter that you're not blood, or that I'm Black and you're Pakistani. I'm doing this because my deen is strong." Deen. *Faith.* "Besides, you *will* pay me back, Noor. By doing the same for someone else one day, when you're a doctor."

She sounds so much like Auntie Misbah that my eyes fill up. I look out the window at the stars, bright out here in all this darkness, and press my forehead to the cool glass.

"Does Chachu know? About what happened?"

"Not yet, we don't think."

Small blessings. "My job at the hospital is gone, I guess."

"For now," Khadija says. "But I might need your boss or a co-worker as a character witness. Or at the very least, to rule out the idea that you might have stolen the pills from the hospital."

I'm friendly with a lot of the nurses at the hospital. Oluchi even wrote me a recommendation letter.

"Could—could I go there? Explain to them what happened?"

"Best not to," Khadija says gently. "I'll talk to your boss."

Khadija pulls into her street slowly. She scans the darkness. Examines the cars parked along the sidewalks.

She's looking for trouble, I realize. For Chachu.

The lights are on at her house. When we walk in, Imam Shafiq glances up from the couch. He pauses *Crown of Fates*, a show that the Liar used to sneak-watch so Auntie Misbah wouldn't yell at him about all the body parts showing.

"Isn't that a little racy for an imam?"

"I forward past the bad bits." He shrugs, and Khadija kisses him, then smacks him on the arm.

"You know he made me miss the NBA playoffs for this crap?" she says. "The *playoffs*, Noor. I was so ashamed. My brothers are texting me the score: it's game seven and it's in OT and this idiot is hiding the remote because King What's-His-Name is freaking out about who his father is."

"Oh, come on." Shafiq pointedly doesn't meet her glare. "It was a *big* reveal."

Khadija drops her purse and rolls her eyes. "Nerd." But she says it with love, and when he swoops in to kiss her, she lets him. I look away.

"You didn't eat." Khadija shakes the limp In-N-Out bag. "Let Shafiq fix you up something while I find you clothes." She disappears into the hallway, unpinning her hijab as she goes.

"She loves *Crown of Fates*," Shafiq says. "She just pretends not to because her brothers make fun of her."

I follow him into the kitchen, where he makes me a plate of kadu gosht—lamb and baby pumpkin. The quiet is a relief.

"I'm sorry for this," I say. "For coming into your house—"

"I'm sorry we didn't see sooner," he says. "We should have. I should have."

He puts the plate in front of me and then gets one for himself.

"Only so you have company while you eat, of course."

The kadu smells amazing. As good as Auntie Misbah's. I thought I wasn't hungry but I destroy the plate.

"Auntie Misbah used to say that God only gives us what we can handle," I say. "Do you think that's true?"

Shafiq considers. "She was a wise woman," he says. "She talked to me about you. She loved you. She really did. I think if she saw you now, she'd be in jail—for assaulting your uncle. However . . ." He takes a bite and mulls some more. "I don't agree that we only get what we can handle. Think of Uncle Toufiq. He *cannot* handle what has happened—so he turns to drink. Think of the refugees coming out of Syria. The people who lose everything in the floods in Pakistan every few years. Think of the war survivors who die trying to cross the sea. They all bear too much."

"Why does God do it?" I say. "Why should we pray? Why believe at all?"

"Because what religion—many religions, really—offers is comfort when it's all too much. A reason for the pain. A hand in the darkness if we reach for it."

"What if it's not real?" I say. "The hand? What if you reach for it, and it disappears?"

"I'm not going to tell you what's real and what isn't," Shafiq says. "That's for you to decide. But I do think that the hand is what we need it to be. Not what we want it to be."

It doesn't make any sense. The weight of today, of yesterday, is too much. I want a different life. One where my worries are things like math class. High school sports. A life where college is just a stop on the journey, instead of a lifeline.

But that life will never belong to me. Instead I get Jamie Jensen. Chachu's bitterness. Auntie Misbah's sickness. I get the earthquake and the rotting bodies. I get joy for a few hours and then an arrest and a drug charge.

I get a best friend who betrayed me so badly that my life might never recover.

I get the stupid brain that still thinks about him, that still wants him, that's still in love with him, even when I know better.

CHAPTER 45

Misbah

September, then

The first time Shaukat Riaz brought Noor to our motel, she looked terrified.

"Thanks for taking her, Misbah." It rankled me that I was older than him and yet he would not refer to me as Baji.

I met him a few weeks earlier, when he'd come by to introduce himself as the owner of the liquor store on Juniper's main street. When I'd greeted him with "Asalaam-o-alaikum," he'd drawn back, like I'd thrown spiders at him.

"I'm not Muslim."

He'd pronounced it "Moozlim," like the people on the news. I shrugged, because I didn't care either way. There are many Pakistanis who are not Muslims. Christians. Atheists. Sikhs. Hindus. They still say salaam. And they still have respect.

"The only true faith is mathematics," Riaz said to me that first day. "We should discuss your head covering one day, Misbah, and why you feel the need to wear it."

By now he knew better than to mention my hijab.

"Please don't speak Urdu or Punjabi with her," Riaz called over his shoulder, ignoring his niece entirely. "And no Pakistani food—I prefer American dishes and I want her to get used to them."

"Of course," I murmured. *When his car disappeared down the road, I turned to the child.*

"Asalaam-o-alaikum," I said to her. *"Thinu pookh lagi heh?"* Peace be upon you. Are you hungry?

She looked back at me with big eyes, and then out at the road, to where her uncle had disappeared.

"Hanh-jee, Auntie." Yes, Auntie. *I barely heard her whisper.*

So I smiled and tugged one of her braids. "Hai, tou bholdhi kidda sona-inh." How sweetly you speak.

I took her to the kitchen, sat her down, and made her a paratha. Salahudin smelled it cooking and came racing out of his room.

"Hi, Noor," he said, until I gave him a look and he ducked his head. *"Salaam,"* he said quickly.

"Walaikum Asalaam. Um—hello." She was hesitant, though they'd been in school together for a few weeks already.

"Want to play LEGOs?"

He spoke in Punjabi, having realized she couldn't understand English. They ran off. Salahudin did not act with her like he acted with the other children—so careful and quiet. With Noor, Salahudin was eager, joyful.

I watched them through the doorway of his room. They built a tower together. When part of it fell with a crash, Noor jumped and folded into a ball, her knees in her chest, her head down between them.

"I'm sorry," Salahudin said.

When I lived in Lahore, my parents' courtyard echoed with the joy of their nieces and nephews—my many cousins. I was the oldest girl, so I looked after them. Children are like kittens during play. They touch hands and tussle. They laugh and sit shoulder to shoulder and share dirt and air. They grapple for the same toy.

But Salahudin and Noor played with care. When she hid her face, he adjusted his blocks quietly, until her jumpiness receded. When he flinched at her touch, she was careful to sit across from him.

They were not kittens, these two. They were small, careful birds, chirping in a language only they knew. A language of pain and memory.

But they were speaking nonetheless. Speaking when I thought Salahudin might always be silent.

I looked at the girl. At the way her black bangs fell over her eyes. I listened to her laugh, the only part of her that wasn't careful. I remembered the fortune teller who told me I would have three children.

"A boy. A girl. And a third that is not she, nor he, nor of the third gender."

The boy was Salahudin. The "third," the motel.

And this was the girl. My last child.

CHAPTER 46

Sal

May, now

FRIARSFIELD, CALIFORNIA

Abu makes it to Friarsfield after borrowing Imam Shafiq's car.

He bails me out.

He tells me Noor is safe and with Shafiq and Khadija.

He walks me to the car.

Then he hands me the keys and gets in the passenger seat. Before I've even closed my door, Abu's pulled out his flask and taken a long sip.

Well. We're a couple of winners.

It's crazy how quickly you can get used to the thing you want. Abu was sober for a day and even though I knew it wouldn't last, even though he's fallen off the wagon over and over, deep down, I still thought: *This is it—he's better.*

Now, seeing him drink again, the disappointment is a knife easing slow into my body while its wielder kisses my forehead. Not just a broken promise, but a betrayal.

"Where—um—where did you get the money for bail, Abu?"

He doesn't answer. We drive the rest of the way in silence.

Around midnight a day later, the motel bell screams me awake. The raps at the door quickly morph into full-fist thumps. Someone's pissed.

My bedroom door is open and I see Abu shuffle to the office. I pull my blanket over my head. I spent all of yesterday cleaning rooms, trying not to text Noor, and waiting to see if Ernst managed to get me expelled.

Whatever is going on right now—not enough towels, not enough toilet paper, no hot water, Wi-Fi's out—I don't want to know. But then, I hear—

"—at that damn mullah's house?"

In a second, I'm on my feet. That's Riaz's voice.

The door slams, but before I can get outside, Abu is in front of me, a hand hovering over my chest. It shakes. He's sober again.

"Just leave it, Putar."

"Did you tell him where she is?"

Abu looks insulted. "Of course not."

"We need to call Shafiq and Khadija," I say. "Let them know he's looking for her."

"I will call them," he says. "Look—" He finds his cell phone and dials as I pace in front of him. A few seconds later, he leaves a message.

"What if they don't hear it? What if they're asleep and he does something?"

"Salahudin—he doesn't want to go to jail. The police have already been to his liquor shop asking him about the drugs. They searched it because Noor worked there. He has some painkillers and now he is worried they will say he was dealing drugs, too. Go to bed now, okay? Go on, Putar."

I go—but not to bed. I can't just let Riaz hunt Noor down. I have to do *something*.

I quietly pull on my hoodie and shoes. I wait until Abu's bedroom door closes. The cops haven't given our car back yet—which is just as well. With my luck, Juniper's police will be having another slow night.

Shafiq and Khadija's house is only a mile or so away. *Faster,* I think with each jolt of my feet hitting the pavement. *Don't let him hurt her. She's been hurt enough.* By the time I reach the end of their street, I'm so out of breath that I could keel over. And Riaz is already at the door.

Khadija stands beside Shafiq on the porch. Noor stays behind them, her arms crossed, appearing to listen as her uncle speaks oh-so-reasonably to her.

But her face is frozen. Her arms coil tighter around her body. When we were kids she got like this sometimes, if the classroom was too loud. If someone on the playground was too rough. Her face changed and she'd disappear into her head, where it was safe.

"Hey!" I move toward the house. A lifetime of Ama imploring me to respect my elders is at war with a rabid need to get Riaz away from Noor. "You leave her alone—"

"Ah, here he is." Riaz appears calm, but I see his anger hanging back, a wolf in the shadows behind his eyes. "The little felon. Haven't had enough of ruining my niece's life?"

"Yeah, I messed up." It would be so satisfying to scream at him, punch him so he goes flying like a punted football. It would also make everything worse for Noor. "But you hit her. And you're never going to hit her again, as long as I'm alive and breathing—"

"No one hit Noor. Noor fell—"

"You hit her." My gaze drops to Riaz's hands. "How else do you explain those knuckles?"

He balls his reddened hands into fists and turns away from me.

"Noor," he says. "Come home. There's no need for theatrics. This is not one of your little dramas. Brooke and I will sort out your arrest."

"You won't do shit," I say, my face hot with fury. If some neighbor sees and calls the cops, I'm in for it. But I don't care. "You're going to leave now."

Shafiq has a hand on my shoulder. "Salahudin—step back, man. Step away. It's not worth it."

"It *is* worth it," I say. "Why did you open your door to him? Can't you see what it must feel like for her?"

But maybe they can't. Even I don't understand. Noor lives the nightmare every day. She can't wake up. And she can't escape.

"Be reasonable." Riaz moves toward Noor. "We can figure this out. What choice do you have? You're not going to UVA or UCLA or any other—"

He's a cobra flaring its hood, trying to fill the vision of his prey. I step in front of him.

Khadija holds up her phone. "I don't want to call the cops. You both need to leave."

"Not until he's gone." I glare at Riaz.

"Just go." Noor's dropped her arms. Her hands are fisted and she looks between Riaz and me. "Both of you," she says. "I don't want to see you again, Chachu. Ever—"

"Noor, I *raised* you. I saved you. I'm the only reason you're standing—"

"I know, Chachu," she says. "And I've paid for it. I've paid. Leave."

He stands there a moment longer, scrambling for any way to exert control over Noor. Then he shrugs.

"Don't come looking for your things," he says. "You earn your own way now. See how easy it is."

When he's slammed his car door and driven off, I hear a light step behind me. I turn to face Noor.

"Noor," I say. "Could I talk to you? Just for a minute—"

Sorry, I was going to say. But her face is closed, eyes blazing in rage.

"You're worse than him." Her whisper feels like a shout. "I knew what he was. But you—"

My heart cracks, slow internal tectonics that grind my hope into nothingness. She's not going to forgive me, I realize then. Ever.

"Noor—I'm an idiot and I didn't mean for it to be this way. I—I understand if you can't forgive me. But can—can I call you?" I can fix this. I have to. "Or text—"

"You can go to hell."

For a second she meets my eyes and I flinch back. Beneath her rage, there's something even worse. Pain.

And betrayal.

CHAPTER 47

Noor

The first song I fell in love with in America was called "Bullet with Butterfly Wings" by the Smashing Pumpkins. I'd listened to a lot of music by then. But "Bullet" spoke to my soul from the first bass riff to the last. Billy Corgan was so angry. So thwarted. His rage had no place to go. He was trapped with it.

Just like me.

That song helped me when I was angry. It helped me calm down. I wish I could hear it now.

But the cops took my phone and my computer and I don't have my music anymore. I'm not going to school, which means I can't listen to it on the library computers. So in the days after my arrest, my anger doesn't cool. I'm not sure I want it to.

A few days after I get to Imam Shafiq's house, on a Wednesday, I have an unexpected visitor. Ashlee McCann.

She's holding a stack of papers in her hands. "Sal asked me to— oh *shit*."

I'd opened the door without thinking. Too late I remember the bruise on my face. It's faded. But not enough.

Ashlee looks green. "Your uncle?"

I try to say yes. My mouth won't make the word.

"You're the only one who didn't think it was Salahudin," I finally say.

She comes up the porch steps. Ashlee always seemed tall to me. But now she's different. Despite the perfect makeup and glittering silver nails, she feels smaller. Faded.

"Sal would never." She hands me the papers. "He's been collecting your homework. He asked me to drop it off. Hope that's okay."

I don't want to take the packet. I don't want to touch something he's touched.

"I heard about the arrest." Ashlee drops her arm when I don't grab the homework. "My aunt works down at the police station. You planning on coming back to school?"

School sounds about as appealing as the county jail. Khadija thinks I should go back. But even thinking about it makes me sick to my stomach.

"I don't know. Maybe."

We stand together without speaking. I don't know Ashlee at all, so it should be weird, but it's not. I wonder if she's thinking what I am—that it's a shame I didn't know her before. That I could have used a friend.

"I'm . . . afraid to go back," I say. "Afraid of people knowing what happened and . . . I don't know. Saying things."

"Yeah, they will." Ashlee takes out a cigarette and lights up. "But they don't know what happened. And if they do, you don't have to confirm it." She takes a long drag, and gives me an appraising look. "I overdosed the day before you got arrested."

I hear the synth beats of "Never Let Me Down Again" by

Depeche Mode popping in my head. Almost a decade after that song came out, Dave Gahan barely survived an overdose.

"Doc said I only recovered because the paramedics got Narcan into me so quick," Ashlee says. "I was all ready to get a few days off school. But my mom told me I was going back come Monday morning. Said that if I didn't graduate, what would I be teaching Kaya?"

"Did you go?"

"Yeah. I'm glad I did. My daughter—she's two, right? My mom watches her. Insists that she get up at the same time every day, eat at the same time, and nap at the same time. At first, I thought my mom was a tyrant." Ashlee smiles. "But routine helps me, too. Especially when withdrawal hits." She shoves the homework at me again. This time, I take it.

"Come back," she says. "It'll be a distraction. If you're worried about the bruise, I'll teach you how to cover it up really well."

"Your makeup's always beautiful."

"It's armor." Ashlee shrugs as she walks away. "Makes the world and all its bullshit feel farther away."

A few mornings later, over the weekend, Brooke drops off my clothes. She doesn't stop to talk. Khadija opens the door and finds the shitty blue suitcase Chachu got for two dollars at the Juniper swap meet and a Budweiser box full of random things from my room.

It's clear from what's in there—an eleventh grade science book, a bracelet I've never worn, a pair of low heels that don't fit—that Brooke was in a hurry. And that she knows me about as well as she knows the president.

But there's a cheap new phone, along with my old wired headphones. *Music,* I think. *Finally.*

Khadija drags the suitcase in. "Good thing she didn't knock," she says. "Or I'd have given her a—"

"Anger is a sin," Imam Shafiq calls from the kitchen.

"Then God shouldn't have put so much of it inside me," Khadija retorts. Shafiq laughs.

There's such understanding between them that I have to look away. I wonder what it's like to be with someone who can love you through your rage.

Though I suppose I do know what it's like. Or I did. For a few hours.

I take my stuff to my room and stick it in a corner with the growing pile of unfinished schoolwork. When I come back out, Khadija touches my shoulder.

"Come have breakfast," she says. "There's something we need to discuss."

Imam Shafiq sets out a bunch of mismatched Corelle plates that can be found in pretty much every South Asian household in America. He's made waffles. But not Ronnie D's box waffles, which are the only kind I've ever had. These are fluffy. Golden. Crispy, too. They have bits of pecan in them.

They're bribery waffles. As soon as I take a bite, I know whatever Khadija has to say, I'm not going to like it. I head her off.

"I was thinking that since I'm not going back to school," I say, "I could get my GED."

Khadija puts another waffle on my plate and exchanges a glance with Imam Shafiq.

"I was thinking it might be time for you to go back to school on Monday," she says. "Your face is nearly healed up. And there's only five weeks until graduation."

I shrug. My grades don't mean shit. "I'd rather get my GED," I say. "I'm stuck in Juniper anyway."

"Noor." Shafiq puts down his fork. "You've worked so hard. We talked to Principal Ernst. He wants you back. But—"

"There's no point." I'm not hungry anymore. "I didn't get into any of the colleges I applied to. Even if I had—they're not going to let me in with a felony on my record."

"AP tests start week after next," Khadija says. "Those classes count as college credit—you could finish coursework at Juniper Community within a year and transfer."

"You've only been out of school a week," Shafiq adds. "I spoke to your teachers. Most of them said it was just a review week."

"Will—will Salahudin—"

"He won't bother you. I spoke to him." Shafiq's voice is curiously neutral. Which is close as he'll get to anger, I guess. It's strangely comforting.

"He won't talk to you," Khadija says. "But you should get used to seeing him, Noor. You guys have pretrial, a preliminary hearing, another arraignment, and a trial to get through."

"Does he have a lawyer? Is he—"

"Let Sal worry about Sal. You worry about you."

So easy to say. I wish I could extract him. Rip him out from my heart like a weed.

Instead, I think about him in prison. About his kindness. His awful puns. The poetry of his body. How will he survive in there?

Let Sal worry about Sal.

"Going back to school will make an impact on the judge if you graduate with good grades," Khadija says. "That kind of thing might make them think twice about the felony charge, Noor."

I can't just say no to them. Khadija's representing me. They're letting me live in their spare bedroom. Shafiq has prayed with me at two a.m., when I can't sleep because I feel like the world is crushing me the way it tried to in the earthquake.

But going back to school means facing stares and gossip and whispers when the only thing I ever wanted was to fly under the radar and then get the hell out of Juniper High.

I wish it didn't bother me so much. I wish I could explain why it does. But, as ever, I can't find the words.

CHAPTER 48

Misbah

Then

For years, I did not understand why my father hid his illness from me.

As I stared at a sheet of paper that made no sense in a cold doctor's office, I understood. My father did not have the words. They stuck in his throat the way mine did, as if I'd eaten too much naan and couldn't find water.

Baba never even went to the doctor. He died with startling swiftness when Salahudin was only ten. No more wisdom given over too-short phone calls. No more entreaties to return home. No more "little butterfly." He left me. As did my mother soon after.

Doctors didn't help them. Or me. I had my blood work done. Waited anxiously to see why I could not get enough breath into this body. Why, at only forty-one and with a son of sixteen, I felt as if my bones were lined with lead and fire.

"Chronic kidney disease," the doctor said. "Quite advanced, Mrs. Malik. Stage four. You have to make significant changes to your lifestyle. It is something we can control; however, I'd like to discuss transplant options—"

"No." I shook my head. My English always fled me in moments like that. All language did. "No transplant." I left, even as the doctor called out behind me. We had no insurance. We could not afford a transplant.

Toufiq was sober, making a small salary as a contractor at Juniper's base. He had not had a drink for two years by then, but it was a tenuous hold on sobriety. God knew what he would do if he learned how ill I was.

My baba was right all those years ago, when he said I was strong. Between Toufiq and me, I carried the lion's share of the courage.

But Toufiq was often preoccupied with work. If I did not wish him to see, he wouldn't. Nor would Salahudin, busy with his books and writing and soccer and Noor. He had built order into his life. Structure. He didn't often see much outside that.

But Noor was different. Noor saw.

"Auntie Misbah." She had come over a few months after that first appointment to see Salahudin, but she wandered into the kitchen and started helping me make dinner.

"Maybe you should go to the doctor." Her voice was quiet and she reminded me of the redwoods in Yosemite. Strong and stoic, demanding little, offering much. "I've been researching. I talked to a nephrologist at the hospital. He said that sometimes when a person is tired the way you are, there is something wrong."

I met Noor's gaze as she observed me. Her eyes imparted calm like a river at a gentle ebb.

But I knew her.

The quickness of her hands when she tipped the onions into the pan—the way she jumped at the steam that curled up, the curve of her shoulders—they all spoke of her fear for me.

In my eyes, she was still six. Looking at a stack of crisp, flaky paratha I made just for her with hopeful, hungry eyes, her hair in messy braids.

Whispering in Punjabi to me, because Riaz had made her too afraid to speak any louder.

She was not of my body or my blood, this child. But she was of my soul.

And she had enough fear in her life. I gave her the smile my son inherited, and a kiss on the cheek.

"Do not worry about me, Dhi. I'm fine."

CHAPTER 49

Sal

May, now

Everything is shit. I don't want to go to school, but Martin saved me from expulsion, and he insists.

"Head down, mouth shut," he says. "Don't miss a single class."

So two days after I get home, I drag myself back to Juniper High. Before my ass can warm the seat, Principal Ernst pulls me out of English and into his office, glaring at me like I'm one Molotov cocktail away from burning down the place.

After a twenty-minute speech that ranges from "How could you throw away your future?" to "If you carry out any illegal activity on campus, you will be instantly expelled," I'm ejected back to Mrs. Michaels's class.

Where I can't pay attention. Mostly because everyone is whispering behind my back like we're in some dank high school movie.

But school is better than being at home. Abu has descended again, so swiftly that it's as if the few sober days he had were a dream.

Can't you just be my father? I want to ask. *Can't you stop drinking for me? Don't you love me enough?*

God, I'm pathetic. I read up on all of this after the pool incident, when Ama finally told me Abu had a drinking problem. I *know* addiction isn't logical. Abu loves me. But right now, his need for oblivion is greater than that love. Until he can change himself, that's how it's going to stay.

Intellectually, I get it. Emotionally, I'm a sullen third grader.

And Noor—I miss her so much. I can't sleep, wondering if she'll come back to school. If she's safe from Riaz. I try to write down all of it, to get the guilt and fear and worry out of me, but when I open my journal, the words skitter out of reach.

The cops took our phones, and I think of all the music she had on hers. Weird bootlegs she got from old CDs and live concert recordings. I wonder how she's listening to music now.

The pretrial is the first I see of Noor after the incident with Riaz. Martin and I are already seated when she enters, Khadija by her side. My friend moves even more carefully in the world than she did before. When she sees me, the muscles in her jaw jump, but Khadija whispers something and she relaxes.

"Salaam, Salahudin," Khadija says. Her voice is soft, and she brushes her hand lightly against my shoulder. "Could you switch seats with Martin, please?"

So Noor can be as far away from me as possible. Words aren't quite working for me. I nod and move so that Khadija and Martin are between us.

"Don't look at her," Martin murmurs. "Try not to think about her. Your future is on the line. The prosecutor there is Mike Mahoney. He might look like a kindly grandpa who carves toys for orphans, but he's watching every move you make."

The judge enters, and while Khadija and Martin discuss motions and timetables, I try not to stare at Noor. Or wonder what she's thinking. But every shift in her body crackles through me like lightning. The way she clenches her fists when Mr. Mahoney refers to her as Ms. Riaz—she's always hated her uncle's name. The play of emotions on her face, the frustration rippling through her limbs. I am a ship in her sea, tossed in the storm of her mind, her ever-shifting body. Broken apart, drowned, resurrected, and destroyed a dozen times over in the space of a few minutes.

After the hearing, Martin sits on a bench with me outside the courthouse.

"The DA's offered a plea deal," he says. "And you need to take it. It means implicating Noor, but if you don't take it, you're looking at years behind bars. We *could* argue that you were using and the judge might be more lenient—but I'd rather not risk it."

"I'm not screwing Noor over."

"The amount found under her seat—under her backpack—it's not looking good for her. But that might help you out. The quantities the cops found on you were much smaller. If you'd just—"

I give him a death glare. "We do *not* pin this on her."

"Salahudin." Martin rubs his eyes, and despite his youth, he looks suddenly tired. "My job is to defend you. Even if it hurts your friend. Because you can still have a life, Salahudin. But short of drastic intervention? Noor Riaz is going to prison. The DA's decided she's guilty. The faster you accept that, the better your chances are of saving yourself."

I don't have Noor's number or a car, so it's easy enough to stay away from her. A couple of times, I bike past Riaz's house. Once, he's out checking the mail. I hate his face, but seeing him makes me feel better. Because it means he's far away from her.

A week after the hearing, I'm sitting outside school before class starts, watching students pour in. Even though it's seven a.m., most are in tank tops and shorts, because the desert went from cold and miserable to hot and miserable in the space of seven days.

I spot Art lurking between the shadows of two buildings, talking to Atticus. Bags exchange hands and I wonder how long before Art ends up in front of a judge, too.

Probably never. He's got rich-boy luck.

"He's lucky you're not a snitch." Ashlee appears and sits next to me. "My mom told him she'd break his kneecaps if he came around again. I didn't tell her I bought from you." My ex looks me dead in the eyes. "I figure prison is punishment enough."

Ashlee's hands twitch for a cigarette, and as she grabs one, Jamie passes, with Grace, Sophie, and Atticus trailing her.

"—should be expelled," Jamie is saying. "I mean she practically tried to kill me. I read about how Muslim names have violent meanings like 'warrior' or 'sword' or—"

"She's getting real brave with her bullshit," Ashlee observes after they pass.

"Prepping for politics."

Ashlee watches Jamie with narrowed eyes. The bell rings and she puts out her cigarette. "Noor's back," she says casually, as if the news isn't a firework going off in my brain.

"Really? Oh. Wait, really?" I stammer like a dumbass, and Ashlee smiles tolerantly.

"Figured you might faint if you saw her in class."

"Right—sorry." I fidget. "This is awkward."

"Please," she snorts. "I'm over you. I'm dating a girl who knows more about Star Wars than you ever did. Might even introduce her to Kaya one day." She gives me a pointed look. "You gonna do right by Noor?"

"What do you mean?"

Ashlee blows smoke out the side of her mouth, pinning me with her pale eyes. "I mean, are you going to make sure she doesn't go to jail?"

"I'm going to try—"

" 'Do. Or do not.' " Ashlee quotes Yoda. *The Empire Strikes Back* always was her favorite. " 'There is no try.' "

Her words stick with me as I walk to class, and when I step into English my throat is so dry that even if Noor had been there, I probably would have just croaked at her.

But her desk is empty.

When I approach Mrs. Michaels after class, she sighs. "I don't know where she is. From what Principal Ernst told me, it might be best for you to keep your distance and focus on graduating." Mrs. Michaels crosses her arms. "Did you ever write the contest essay?"

"I want to, Mrs. Michaels," I say. "But—I don't know what to write." Before the arrest, I'd sat down to get a draft done and stared at the prompt for two hours. *Tell a fictional story based on a real experience.* When nothing emerged, I made myself take out my journal, hoping old words might inspire new ones. But I was thinking about all the dealing and only wrote down one sentence. *I'm a monster.*

"The good stories never come easy," Mrs. Michaels says. "You'll miss the contest deadline. But promise me when the story does come to you, you'll write it. Even if it's just for you."

I nod and leave, still hoping to find Noor. It's not until lunch that, while looking over my shoulder for her, I run straight into her. Figures.

She jumps away quickly. My heart thuds faster when I see her T-shirt because it's one I gave her. It says I LISTEN TO BANDS THAT DON'T EXIST YET.

That's a good sign, right? That she's wearing something I gave her? Unless she doesn't remember I gave it to her. Which is totally possible.

"Hi," I say before she can walk off. "You weren't in English."

She takes off her headphones, but no sound comes out. Noor doesn't really listen to music quietly. Which means she's probably walking around without music. It's so unlike her that I think about asking her a super-personal question to make sure she hasn't been body-snatched.

"Yeah," she says to my comment, voice flat. "I didn't see the point. Excuse me."

She tries to go around me, but I do a weird, praying-mantis sidestep, desperate to stop her.

"AP tests are next week," I gabble. "Mrs. Michaels gave us review questions." I dig around in my backpack. This is so weird and horrible. Talking to her like she's a stranger. I find the question sheet and hold it out to her.

She doesn't take it.

"You haven't heard from UCLA, right?" I say. "Your essay was really good. You might get in."

"It wouldn't matter if I got in." She snatches the paper from me and crumples it up. A few people stop to stare.

"Today's May tenth. The deadline to accept admission was a week ago. And I'm going to prison, Salahudin."

"Did you ever check the UCLA portal again?" I say. "Maybe—"

"I'm taking the plea deal." She spits the words at me. "Khadija's going to call the DA tonight after she gets home from work. She— she wanted me and Shafiq to be there."

"No. Noor, don't do that—"

"What else am I supposed to do?" The words explode out of her in a sudden, earsplitting shout. The students around us go silent. "Wait for the trial and get sentenced to eight years instead, you asshole?" Her voice gets louder. "If I don't take the deal, they'll throw the book at me."

"I'll explain that it was mine. I'll tell them the truth."

"God, you're stupid. You told them the truth, Salahudin. So did I. How did that go for us?"

More people gather to watch, Ashlee among them. A few students have their phones out, like they're waiting for us to maul each other.

"Your drugs were under *my* seat," Noor says. "Under *my* backpack. In the glove compartment inches from *my* hands. My fingerprints were on the bottles because, like an idiot, I took them from you. I'm going to prison no matter what."

"Martin says we can argue that we were using. The judge could—"

"Go to hell, *Sal*."

I grimace at her use of my nickname. It sounds as weird from her mouth as it does from Abu. "Noor—please. I didn't mean for it to happen. Can't you just forgive—"

She steps close enough to kiss me, or punch me.

"Don't you dare tell me to forgive you," she says. "Don't you put that burden on me."

"Fine, don't forgive me," I say. "But go to class. Don't give up. Think about—about Ama, Noor. She'd tell you that you're more than this."

Noor laughs, but it's all wrong. "Maybe I was more than this. Before you."

"Oh, look, the brown Bonnie and Clyde." Jamie saunters through the crowd. Atticus is with her, looking a bit hangdog. I guess it's easier to have a racist girlfriend when she's not so public about it.

"Bonnie and Clyde were bank thieves and murderers," I snap at her. "So that's a shit comparison."

"Still perps. Still destined for failure and an early death. Just like you." She leers at Noor, and as I seethe, Ashlee shoves through the throng.

"You're deranged, Jamie," she says. "Why don't you—"

"Don't talk to me, white trash," Jamie says. "You fucked this shit-skin, right? Of course you'd defend him."

A low mutter rolls through the crowd, and Atticus steps away from Jamie, though she doesn't notice.

Many of Juniper's denizens are proudly racist. We've had people spray-paint Nazi symbols and "Go back" and "White Power" in our rooms before. Abu told me that after 9/11, he and Ama had to replace the front picture window when someone threw a brick through it.

I didn't expect that kind of bald hatred from Jamie, though. She'd masked it under snobbery.

Noor speaks up, hands tucked beneath the straps of her backpack, like she's worried about what they'll do if she lets them loose.

"Go away, Jamie," she says.

"I will," Jamie says. "Right to Princeton. While you'll be rotting in jail, where you belong."

Noor shrugs. "You won," she says. "That's what you want to hear, right? You're going to college and I'm not. You're valedictorian and I'm second place. You're also a monster. I'm pretty sure your own parents don't like you. I know your friends don't."

Jamie laughs and turns to look at Atticus—who's disappeared. The rest of the crowd watches, silent.

She flushes red. "Insult me all you want," she says. "Your own life is your punishment. And it's what you deserve. I don't care what your excuses are, Noor. You're illegal. A criminal. You should be shipped back to the shithole country you came from, to get married to a guy fifty years older than you or a goat or whatever the hell it is you people do."

I get in Jamie's face now, vicious words on my lips, but Ashlee pulls me back and I don't even feel her hands, I'm so angry.

"Not worth it, Sal," Ashlee says. A few feet away, Noor gives me a quick, searing glance, filled with contempt.

Then she walks away.

I don't follow.

The conversation with Noor rattles around my head as I walk home, shaking its chains and rustling its bones. Not the worst bit of it—I've already put all that in my "shit to relive when you hate yourself" memory box.

No. I'm thinking about UCLA. About how Noor never heard from them.

Horrible as it is, I get why she didn't get in to the other schools. Her essays were shit. Noor said she choked during the interviews. But I read her essay for UCLA. And other than a couple misplaced commas and the word "memory" inexplicably spelled with two *r*'s, that essay was incredible. And she had everything else she needed to impress the admissions board.

Noor said she couldn't get into the UCLA portal. *Probably because they kill the accounts of everyone they reject. To them, I no longer exist.* But that doesn't seem right. And I know Noor; sometimes her fear is so loud that it's all she can hear.

She also said she didn't get a letter from UCLA. But maybe she did. Maybe she just didn't see it.

Thank God Chachu never checks the mailbox. He does, though. I saw him do it a couple of days ago.

If he even knew where I was applying . . .

Noor never told Riaz. But he knew—the other night at Khadija and Shafiq's house. *You're not going to UVA or UCLA.*

Noor only needs one yes. One victory. Something that will give her a reason to fight. To not take the plea deal.

From what I remember when Noor and I snuck in years ago,

Riaz kept every other damn piece of paper he got. Why not her acceptance letter?

Leaps of logic, Salahudin. Maybe Brooke told him about UVA and UCLA. Or maybe he got a letter but it was a rejection.

Ama used to say "hadiyan sach bolti hain." *Bones speak the truth.* Mine tell me that something is up with UCLA.

I stop in the middle of the sidewalk, my brain exploding with a sudden, brilliant idea. One that could get her the future she deserves.

One that could get her to forgive me.

CHAPTER 50

Noor

No one stops me as I walk off campus in the middle of a class period. No one cares.

The words I screamed at Salahudin pound in my ears. I'm so angry I think I'll break into pieces.

My headphones are in. I downloaded as much of my old music as I could find. But there's no song I want to hear. No playlist can fix this feeling that nothing good will ever happen to me again.

The only music I have room for in my head is broken guitars and short-circuiting amps. A cello plunged into flames, a piano dropped from a skyscraper, drums with the skins ripped out.

I'm angry that Salahudin lied about dealing, that he pulled me into his bullshit, that I'm going to do prison time, that my future is destroyed.

But the thing that gnaws at me the most is that the one person I trusted in this shit world hurt me the worst. He gave me what I wanted more than anything—love, safety.

Then he took it away. He can never fix that.

I think of the Verve singing "Love Is Noise." Florence and the Machine and the thundering drums in "Cosmic Love." Rihanna's consuming pain in "Love on the Brain." Masuma Anwar mourning her fate in "Tainu Ghul Gayaan."

They all mix in my head. A jangle of notes that don't make sense. Cutting through it, Auntie Misbah's voice. *"If we are lost, God is like water, finding the unknowable path when we cannot."*

But I'm not lost. I know exactly where I am. Trapped. Stuck in that closet again, with the world dying around me.

"Noor!"

A glimmer of dark hair. Mrs. Michaels waves at me and makes her way across the parking lot.

"I saw you from the staff room," she says. "Why weren't you in cla—"

"Because there's no point," I say, wondering if I should tattoo the words on my head so people stop asking.

"Well—here." Her leather bag is strapped across the side of her wheelchair, and she sifts through it before pulling out a paper. My final "One Art" essay. I worked on it at Khadija's insistence, and turned it in after reading more about Elizabeth Bishop's life.

Which, to be honest, kind of sucked. Something I pointed out in the conclusion of the essay.

One of Bishop's early titles for "One Art" was "The Gift of Losing Things." Maybe because of all the loss in her life—family, friends, homes, people—Bishop had to see loss as a gift. It surrounded her. In order to keep from drowning in it, she couldn't view loss as the universe's way of saying "I hate you." She had to make her peace with the loss, accept that it was part of her life, and find meaning in it. She had to learn that despite the loss, she would keep going.

"It was just wonderful," Mrs. Michaels says. "My favorite essay this year." She puts the paper in my hands. "Noor. You have so much to offer. I know what it is to go through hard times. Truly, I do. But I believe things will get better. And I'm asking you, please—don't give up."

She turns to head back to school, and as I watch her disappear between the buildings, I think of Auntie Misbah.

"If we are lost, God is like water, finding the unknowable path when we cannot."

For a moment, as I stare at the A+ on top of the paper, I believe it.

CHAPTER 51

Misbah

March, then

Two months after the doctor told me I was sick, Toufiq learned of my illness. I only knew because he started drinking again.

He tried to conceal it. But then he made a mess in the pool and Salahudin discovered him.

After I cleaned Toufiq up, I found Salahudin waiting in the kitchen, shaken. I dug out the PG Tips, cream, cardamom, and sugar.

"Chai, Putar?" I took out a second cup for him, in case. But he shook his head.

"Do I ever say yes, Ama?"

"No," I sighed. "But I always hope."

"Ama . . . What's wrong with Abu? Why did he smell like . . ."

Like the drunks that sometimes break bottles outside the motel, or fight in the alley behind the pool.

"Your father is an—" I almost said the word. Alcoholic. *But I couldn't bring myself to. "Your father has a problem, Putar. A problem with drinking."*

"But Abu prays," Salahudin burst out. "I don't understand."

"Your father prays for guidance. He is often lost. Adults get lost, too, you know."

"You never do."

"That is God's will," I said. "And no doing of my own."

"Ama," he said. *"Why did he start drinking when I was little?"*

"Your father couldn't be strong," I said. *"He's not like me, Putar. Or like you."*

Salahudin snorted. *"I'm not strong."*

I took his hand and he winced in surprise. I squeezed it too hard, trying to hold on to him. He must understand this, *I thought.* He must know that he can survive anything.

"I see so much promise in you, my son. You are what you wish to be," I told him. *"Wish for strength and God will make you strong. Tell me you understand."*

He gently pulled his hand from mine. *"I understand,"* he said. *"Um—I'm pretty tired, Ama."*

"Go." I gave him a kiss on the hair and watched his narrow back as he disappeared into his room.

He did not understand. I knew this. But he would. I would make sure he did, before I left this world. I pushed the tea away, and prayed.

Please, please. *I pressed my hands together so tightly that they tingled.* Give me more time.

CHAPTER 52

Sal

May, now

When it's nearly dark, Art finally returns to his house in his shiny Camaro. His parents aren't around and as he approaches the front door, I step out from a pillar near his porch.

"Sal, holy shit!" He jumps about a mile. "What—"

"Shut up." I don't touch him. I don't have to. He can tell it's taking all my self-control not to punch his stupid face. "You're gonna help me with something. Or I'm going to tell the cops who supplied me, asshole."

I explain my plan to him in the car, making him drive past the liquor shop, where we see Riaz's old blue Nissan parked in the back lot. A few minutes later we pull up in front of his house. Brooke's car is gone.

I point out Riaz's study window, which faces a neighbor's house, and the hedge next to it.

"That's our hiding spot," I say. "And we have to move quick." We need to be out of here before Khadija calls the DA.

"Even if she got into UCLA"—Art side-eyes the hedge—"she's going to prison. That letter is about as useful to her as a bag of broken dic—"

"Shut *up*, Art."

"I know you love her," Art presses. "But maybe you're not facing reality."

"*I'm* not facing reality?" I say. "What about you? Your own cousin overdosed. And you're still dealing."

Art fumbles at the radio and turns it to KRDK, a Top 40 station that I only ever put on when I am trying to annoy Noor. I slam it off.

"I'm still talking," I say. "Think of everyone you've sold to. What if one of them overdoses? Dies? That will be on you."

"You were in the game, too, Sal."

"And I'll regret it until I'm dead," I say. "My dad's an alcoholic; I get how insidious addiction is. I enabled that in other people. I destroyed my own life and probably my best friend's. But you can still get out, asshole."

Art shakes his head, knuckles white around the steering wheel. "Yeah," he says quietly, the most subdued I've ever heard him. "Maybe you're right."

He turns off his car and we approach Riaz's house in silence. It's easy enough to get to the study window. When I try to pry it open, it won't move.

"That's it, man." Art edges away. "Can't open it without breaking it."

I snatch his keys from him, wedge one below the window and jimmy it beneath the pane. After a tense minute, during which Art's breathing so loud they can probably hear him in Alaska, the window squeals open.

"All right," I say. "Get in there."

Art sighs and wiggles his skinny frame through the window, his feet sticking out ridiculously for a moment.

"Look for a big envelope," I say. "Probably white. It'll have a blue stamp—"

"I know what a college acceptance envelope looks like, Sal."

I hear rustling. A thump and a curse.

"Damn, this guy keeps everything," Art mutters.

I check the time and glance up and down the street. Brooke gets home before eight, usually, and it's already 7:50.

"I can't see anything," Art says. "I'm closing the curtains so I can turn on the light."

"Use your phone, dumbass!"

He grumbles something unintelligible, and a dim blue light flares.

"For a dude who drives a Nissan, this guy is super obsessed with BMWs. He has like thirty pamphlets—"

Car headlights shine at the end of the street. I squint. But it's too dusty to make out if it's Brooke's gray Ford. It looks too big to be her car. And it's not gray. It's blue.

"Shit—" I call through the window. "Get out, Art. Riaz just rolled up."

"No, I found something—"

"Out, dude. *Now.*"

Riaz pulls his car into the drive. I hear the whining guitar of a Soundgarden song that Noor's played for me a million times. "Black Hole Sun." The engine cuts.

The silence is . . . ominous. It's a word I understand conceptually because I've read it in a million books. But actually ominousness feels as thick and choking as mud.

Run, Sal. Get out of here.

"Hello?"

Shit. Riaz heard Art. I dive behind the hedge as quietly as I can and hope Art has the sense to turn off his flashlight. Dirt crunches as Riaz walks closer.

Don't come nearer. Please, God, give me a break.

He stands there for a long moment, and I wonder what it's like for someone like him, someone who lords over those he thinks of as weaker. I wonder how the hell he looks at himself in the mirror every morning.

Tackling him would be so easy. My future is four walls with about eight feet between them no matter what. I'd just be stuck there for a bit longer.

But he turns around and leaves. His keys jangle, and the front door creaks open. The study is down the hall from the front door. Far enough where Art can get out if he doesn't dawdle.

"Art," I whisper. "Hurry up, man, he's—"

"Hello?" This time, Riaz is calling from inside the house. Too late, I realize that the inside door to the study is open.

There's a flurry of movement. Riaz cries out.

"Hey!"

Art dives out the window, something white clutched against his chest.

I grab him, pull him up, and we run like hell.

CHAPTER 53

Noor

Imam Shafiq comes home at seven, after Maghrib prayer. I flip off the *Crown of Fates* reruns I've been watching since getting home from school. But not before he sees. He laughs so hard I think he's going to drop the takeout.

"I can't *wait* to tell Khadija," he says. "I caught her doing the same thing a couple of weeks ago. We can all watch the new episode together on Sunday. Just embrace it, Noor. Embrace your inner Dunlinian."

Khadija comes in from the garage. "Do *not* embrace your inner . . . thingy—"

"Dun-lin-i-an," Shafiq says. "Don't pretend like you don't know what it means, Khadija."

They bicker back and forth, and listening helps me ignore the fact that I have to make a decision about the plea deal tonight. I've already discussed it with Khadija so much that the decision should be made.

But I keep thinking of Salahudin. His hope. I shake my head. The plea deal is the best hope I have.

"I want to take it," I say, cutting Shafiq off midsentence. "Sorry." I feel bad about interrupting him. "I think it's the best thing to do."

Khadija takes a deep breath. "I'm going to talk to Mike Mahoney again," she says. "See if maybe we can't get the probationary time decreased, the felony charge dropped. With good behavior, Noor, you could be out in eighteen months, easy."

The doorbell rings. Instantly, Khadija's grabbing her phone. Shafiq pulls a kitchen knife—which I can't actually imagine him using.

"Noor," he says. "Head for the back door, please. If anything happens, run to Mrs. Michaels's house, okay? She—" Shafiq peers through the peephole. "Oh."

He opens the door. Even in the dim porch light and through the screen door, I recognize the tall form, the broad shoulders, the curling dark hair. Salahudin.

"Can I—talk—to—Noor?" His chest heaves as he tries to catch his breath. He's sweating, even though it's nice out, May being the one time of year that Juniper's weather isn't garbage. I move to the door, but Khadija is already there.

"Absolutely not," she says. "You *cannot* be here."

"Hey." Shafiq has a hand on Salahudin's shoulder. "Let's walk. Come o—"

"You got in!" Salahudin shakes a large white envelope. "Noor— UCLA. *You got in.*"

I push past Khadija. Art Britman lurks down the street in his black Camaro, pretending not to watch.

"Noor," Khadija says. "I don't think—"

"Two minutes," Salahudin says. "I know you're mad. I know you hate me. But just give me two minutes. Then I'm gone. I'll never so much as say your name."

"It's fine," I say to Shafiq, who finally drops his hand. Khadija gives me a look of *if he so much as makes you frown, he's dead.*

320

"Door stays open." She closes the screen, but doesn't fully retreat.

Salahudin holds the envelope out to me. It's white. A little creased. The stamp in the corner says UCLA in big, bold letters.

"I'm sorry I opened it," he says. "I figured it was a yes because the envelope was so big. But I wanted to make sure."

Dear Noor,

Congratulations! We are—

I don't read the rest. I just set the paper down on the porch railing. Quickly. It's fake. It has to be.

You are better than this place. More than this place.

"But I couldn't get into the online portal. I tried so many times."

"Not because they rejected you," Salahudin says. "Your uncle must have done something. Changed your username or your password."

Or canceled my account entirely. It's exactly the type of thing Chachu would do.

"But how did you know?" I say. "And how did you get this?"

"Don't worry about that," Salahudin says. "Listen, Noor. Don't take the plea deal. Look what you did. You got into one of the best schools in the country. In the world. If you take the plea deal, you'll be throwing that away."

"Even if I had the money to go—"

"There's a financial aid package in there," he says. "Grants and work study. You can go, Noor. But not if you're a felon."

"The deadline to accept—"

"Screw the deadline!" he says. "Call them! Have Khadija call them. Tell them the truth. You will figure something out. Noor, these kids—" He grabs the offer letter and points to a photo of a group of students laughing on a green lawn in front of a tower that, strangely, makes me think of the Badshahi Mosque. "You should be one of them."

The rage noise in my head goes quiet. Salahudin believed in me. He's always believed in me. He's giving me a reason to fight.

But if it wasn't for him, I'd never have needed that reason to begin with.

I want to close the distance between us. To look into his eyes, the safest place I've ever been. To feel his fingers on my waist. His body against mine.

He is suddenly uncertain, those graceful hands fiddling with the letter. He can feel it between us, I know. That spark. That want.

He steps forward, hopeful. We teeter on the edge of for-giveness.

But at the light in his eyes, I remember how much we have to lose. Especially now that I have a future to fight for. I realize how unlikely it is that I'll see that future.

My anger surges back. Stronger than before, like it's been work-ing out, building muscle, waiting to deliver a knock-out punch. I'm Fiona Apple dripping poison in "Get Gone." Julian Casablancas and the Voidz shredding guitars in "Where No Eagles Fly."

"This doesn't fix anything," I say. "You know that, right? I could still get years in prison."

His face falls. "I know," he says. "I thought—"

"I told you a lot of what your ama said the night she died," I say.

"But I didn't tell you the last thing she said." The memory is fresh and painful. Salahudin goes quiet.

"She said 'Forgive.' I guess she knew you were a shit friend who'd need forgiveness. But you don't deserve it. You weren't there for her. *I* held her hand as she died. *I* knew she was sick when you didn't notice. *I* told her to go to the doctor. You said I didn't know her, but I did. And she deserved better than you. You can't even do fucking laundry, Salahudin. You can't even handle this."

I shove him. He flinches, and my face is hot, like I've just been slapped—even though I'm the one who pushed him.

My hand burns. *Stop, Noor. This is wrong.* But I can't control myself.

"You better get used to that." Now my eyes stream. My voice shakes. "Because you're going to prison, and in there, no one will care what hurts you."

I turn my back on him. I try not to see the shock on Khadija's and Shafiq's faces.

Forgive, Auntie Misbah told me. *Forgive.*

But I guess I'm not the forgiving type.

CHAPTER 54

Misbah

January, then

The days slipped away, water through my fingers. Until one Sunday, Noor texted me, asking me not to come to the liquor store for chai and Dilan dey Soudeh, saying she had too much homework.

Then she began ignoring my messages.

When I asked Salahudin about it, he shrugged and sloped off into his room. He had been quieter of late. Silent at dinner or gone for hours after school, returning long after soccer practice was over.

"He argued with Noor." Toufiq had sobered up for a few days, after a bout of exhaustion left me bedridden. "A month ago, when we went to the mountains."

"What did they argue about?" And how could I have missed it?

But I might as well have asked Toufiq how Salahudin did at his last soccer match.

What to do? I loved Noor like she was mine, but I had no claim over her. If she was a niece of my blood, I could have visited her house, spoken to her uncle.

But in eleven years, Shaukat Riaz never stopped judging me. After realizing that I spoke Punjabi with Noor and fed her Pakistani food, he stopped leaving her with me. He hated my presence in her life. Going to her home would have only created trouble for her.

Weeks passed. I texted Noor. She never responded. I could not stop thinking about her. I pestered Salahudin so much that even his patience, which was more like his father's than mine, ran out.

"She's fine, Ama, okay?" he snapped. "She's mad at me over something stupid."

So I went to see her the following Sunday, about fifteen minutes after she opened the store. I said my salaam, found bread and milk, and placed it on the counter.

"I don't know what happened with Salahudin, Dhi," I said to her in Punjabi, "but I need to watch Dilan dey Soudeh. *Either you watch it with me or I do it alone, but I'm not waiting anymore."*

Another customer entered and I moved aside.

"I'm sorry, Auntie. You should watch it without me." Noor sounded so subdued. Not at all like the girl who argued with me about Nusrat Fateh Ali Khan. She reached overhead to the cigarette rack when the customer asked for Marlboro 100s.

Which is when I saw the bruise. Yellow and purple on her brown skin.

"Noor," I said when the customer had left. "What happened to your arm, meri dhi?"

She flinched and I knew. I knew it in my bones.

Riaz played the urbane mathematician to his customers. The enlightened immigrant cruelly destined to run a liquor shop though his mind was meant for something greater.

But he disdained women. Worse, he had a bitterness seething within. A rage-toothed tiger, caged and rabid.

"Auntie Misbah? Are you okay?"

Noor called to me and I wondered how long I'd been staring off. I glanced at her arm, but the bruise was hidden now.

I didn't know what to say, because I needed to think. Once before, I'd suspected that something was wrong and called the police. They did nothing.

But Noor was older now. Perhaps the police would believe her if she told them Riaz was hurting her. She would be eighteen in two weeks. She could leave Riaz. Come live with me and Salahudin and Toufiq.

I needed to talk to Dr. Ellis. She had been such a gift over the years. She understood young people. Perhaps she would know what was best.

"I—I must go." I shuffled away quickly. "I'm not—not feeling well."

"Should I—"

"I'm okay," I called out so she wouldn't follow. I forgot the milk. The bread. No matter. I made my way to the car and navigated home.

But in the driveway of the motel, my luck ran out. I sat in the Civic, my muscles so heavy that I felt as if I were melting into the hot fabric of the seat. My bones wouldn't work. I couldn't lift my arms. I couldn't even turn off the car.

"Ama?"

Salahudin stood at the window. His brow furrowed, the dent in his forehead just like my mother's.

"Did you know," I said to my son, "that it rained the day your grandmother told me I'd be married? Buckets and buckets of rain. I saw a fortune teller after—"

"Ama." I heard Salahudin's fear as he helped me into the house. "Do you need your medicine?"

"Time," I whispered. "I need time, Putar."

But he could not give me time. No one could.

CHAPTER 55

Noor

June, now

We reject the plea deal. Khadija wants me to testify.

"If you get up on the witness stand and tell the courtroom what really happened, it will be a powerful image for the jury." Khadija makes the same argument nightly, pacing her living room as Shafiq and I listen. "You'd show that you're prepared to fight for your future."

But I don't want to fight. I'm too afraid to lose.

The night before graduation, Khadija finally throws her hands up at the dinner table. "I can't make you testify," she says. "If you don't want to be up there, the prosecutor will figure it out and he'll hammer you. But do one thing for me, at least?"

I eye her suspiciously. Beside her, Shafiq tries to hide a smile.

"Go to graduation." Khadija disappears to her room and returns with a dark green cap and gown, which I distinctly do not remember ordering. "You'll regret it if you don't."

When I take them from her, she claps.

Now, out on the football field and surrounded by my classmates, I'm happy I came. I worked hard for this. Since the arrest, I've hated every minute of school. But Ashlee was right when she said the routine would help. And all the way up to the last day, Khadija was on my case about doing my best on every assignment.

"I didn't spend an entire week tracking down UCLA's dean of admissions so you could slack off," she'd said.

I find myself glancing around—wondering if Salahudin came. After he told me about UCLA, he stopped trying to talk to me. He graduated—his name is on the program. But he's not here.

"He was probably worried that he'd ruin it for you if he came." Ashlee ignores Principal Ernst's alphabetical seating arrangement and sits next to me, her girlfriend, Bonnie, on her other side.

"Did he say that?"

Ashlee shrugs. "Ask him yourself next time you see him."

You mean at court in a few weeks? I keep quiet. I don't want to ruin the mood.

As the school band plays an off-key version of "Pomp and Circumstance," the stupidest graduation song ever, there's a small commotion near the stage.

"Hey, look," Ashlee says, and a teacher I don't recognize scurries toward Principal Ernst, handing him a phone.

The students near him whisper, a *khoosr-khoosr* sound that spreads quickly, eventually reaching Ashlee and me.

"He just watched a video on someone's social," Bonnie whispers. "*The* video. And now he's reading the article."

"What video?" I turn to Ashlee, and Bonnie grins. "What article?"

"Oh, didn't I tell you?" Ashlee smiles and takes out her phone. "I took a video of Jamie's little speech the other day. Sent it to Princeton's dean of admissions. When I didn't hear back, I figured I should send it elsewhere." She hands me her phone, open to an article on Feedbait:

RACIST RANT COSTS CALIFORNIA
HIGH SCHOOLER HER FUTURE

Jamie Jensen, 18, landed in hot water this week when a classmate recorded her unleashing a racist tirade at another student.

"It's lasted all year," one Juniper High senior, who wished to remain anonymous, told Feedbait. "She's racist. She tried to hide it, but it finally came out."

California prosecutor James Atkins said that while Jensen's words were repugnant, strictly speaking, no crime was committed.

Meanwhile, Princeton's dean of admissions, Nicola Watson, released a statement: "We take the integrity of this institution very seriously, and that integrity is reflected in our students. Words and their intent matter, and are an indication of a student's ability to contribute to the overall culture of Princeton. As Ms. Jensen's behavior is in direct violation of our code of conduct—we have rescinded her offer of admission."

Other schools that offered Ms. Jensen admission are expected to follow suit. Ms. Jensen could not be reached for comment.

Principal Ernst strides to Jamie, who's obliviously mouthing her valedictorian speech to herself. Her face goes bright red when Ernst crouches and whispers something.

Moments later, he takes the stage and begins calling all the A's, skipping over Jamie's speech entirely.

"Guess she's not going to Princeton after all," Ashlee says with a grin, then nudges me with her shoulder. "And you, I hear, are going to UCLA."

I almost tell her no. But then I think of Auntie Misbah.

God is like water, finding the unknowable path when we cannot.

"Maybe," I say.

We throw our caps in the air, Bonnie and Ashlee kiss and whoop, and families flood the field. Khadija and Shafiq find me, jumping and cheering as if I'm their kid.

"Do you really think I could win the case?" I don't know how Khadija hears me. Everyone is so loud. But she does.

She reaches up to hold my face in her hands. She's so strong in that moment that I find myself standing taller. "I think there's always hope."

I close my eyes and hear Auntie Misbah. *Forgive.*

I'm sorry, Misbah Auntie, I think. *I'm not ready to forgive yet.*

But I am ready to fight.

CHAPTER 56

Sal

After I find Abu sobbing and fully clothed under a shower that's gone cold, a bottle of whiskey broken on the tiles, I call Imam Shafiq.

"Don't hang up, it's not about Noor. It's Abu, he—he—" Fear makes me talk too fast. "He needs help. We need help."

Imam Shafiq arrives so fast that I wonder if he has superhero powers he hasn't mentioned. I almost tell him to never mind, it's not worth it. But he's left work to be here. *There isn't anything to be ashamed of,* I tell myself. *Imam Shafiq gets it.*

"Get—get away," Abu says to us when we walk into the bathroom. His feet are bleeding everywhere. "I don't need your help."

I shut off the water. "Abu—please—"

"What's the point?" he slurs. "What's—"

"I *am* the point," I snap at him. "Ama was the point. She deserved better than this. I deserve better, too."

My father slumps and rubs his hands across his face. He's going to speak, but I don't let him. Because if I do, and if he tells me that he misses her or he's broken without her, then I won't have the heart to finish what I need to say. What he needs to hear.

"You've left me alone for months, Abu. Now I might go to prison, and yeah, it's my fault. But it's also because I didn't know what to do and you weren't here to ask." Abu looks up now, irritated. *Good,* I think. *Be annoyed. Angry. Anything but empty.*

"I own my mistakes, but you're the one who stopped being a father to me. I never stopped being your son. You can't just give up because you're in pain. You need to do better for *me*. We're it, Abu. You and me. She's not coming back."

Abu is silent for what feels like forever. Shafiq steps forward and holds out a hand. I hold out another. We pull Abu standing.

After we clean him up and I bandage his feet, Shafiq and I clear the house of every drop of liquor. It won't be the last time I do this. I know that. But it still feels good.

The next morning at nine a.m., Shafiq shows up with Janice, Abu's sponsor.

"I can't promise you anything, Sal," she says after I tell her about Abu's relapse. "He's got to want to stay sober. But if he gets himself to the meetings—if he holds himself accountable—then I'll be here to help him along."

When the real estate agent arrives to look at the motel a week later, Abu is sober. Seven days. His longest stretch in more than a year. Abu asks me to sit with them—and when the agent suggests a price for the motel, Abu asks me what I think.

A sign goes out front. Our agent, Mr. Singh, puts ads in Indian newspapers and Pakistani newspapers and Chinese newspapers and Korean newspapers.

"Fastest way to get a buyer," he says. "Let's hope someone bites."

In the end, the offer comes from a hipsterish Indian couple in their thirties, hoping to start a bed-and-breakfast. Their eyes shine when they walk through the place. They look past the peeling paint, the sagging roof, the cracked parking lot.

"I love the name," one of them says. "Clouds' Rest. It's perfect."

They see the place the way Ama did. For what it could be. Their excitement twists like a knife. But it gives me hope, too, and one of Noor's old songs—"Bittersweet Symphony"—winds through my brain.

"I won't sell it if you don't want me to." Abu and I sit down to dinner after Mr. Singh calls to tell us the offer. There's too much salt in the karahi tonight. But I don't give a shit because my abu made it for me.

"That couple is perfect," I say before I change my mind. "Take the offer. The trial starts next week anyway. You can't run this place alone."

"Your mother did," Abu says.

"Ama was Ama," I say. "You're you." We're quiet for a long time before I speak again.

"Tell me about her, Abu," I say. "Tell me the things I don't know."

And to my surprise, he sits back and smiles. "The first time I met her," he says, "was at a tea shop. Her brother was chaperoning her. I was so bloody nervous . . ."

As he speaks, I think of everything my mother taught me: How to love someone unconditionally. That joy can be found in small victories. That forgiveness is a gift to the person who grants it *and* to the person who receives it.

But then the anger that seems permanently lodged in my brain reminds me of everything Ama didn't teach me. That unconditional love isn't always the best for us. That small victories aren't always enough.

That some things can't be forgiven.

When Abu finishes his story, I ask him for another, and another. Until it's late and he finally stands. "We should go visit Ama. Let her know we're letting the place go."

The next day, with flowers and a Qur'an, and wearing a shalwar-kameez Ama always loved, Abu goes to Ama's grave.

I don't go with him. Staying away is a habit. And I'm ashamed. I didn't become what she'd hoped. I failed her. I failed Abu. I failed Noor. I failed myself.

I don't go to her grave because I don't want her to know this about me. And because a part of me hopes that somehow I can still make things right.

CHAPTER 57

Sal

On the day Martin makes his opening statement, the Friarsfield courtroom is sweltering. Which I should have expected, as Noor, Khadija, Martin, and I have all been here for the last two days for jury selection.

Still, it's worse than yesterday. The court reporter, the court clerk, the little plant sitting on Judge Manuel Ortega's bench all seem wilted.

Even in crime shows where everything is supposed to be gritty, courtrooms have that movie patina. But this one is gritty in a mundane, everyday sort of way. Unglamorous and kind of sad.

Judge Ortega himself is unaffected. He's a big man, and the fluorescent lights shine dully on his brown, bald head. When he walks into the chambers, everyone goes quiet, and when he's about to speak, everyone holds their breath.

Which just makes me more antsy. The judge's bench is only two steps higher than where Martin and I sit. But from down here he's like some sort of demigod, prepared to mete out merciless justice.

I sit, itching miserably in this suit, staring at the huge gold seal of California on the back wall, trying to look calm and responsible as the prosecutor, Mr. Mahoney, lays out the case against Noor and me in scathing, humiliating detail. Mahoney always walks into court wearing a trench coat over a rumpled suit, no matter what the weather is, and today is no different. It makes him look harmless and scatterbrained. He's anything but.

Abu sits behind me in the gallery. I've never been happier not to be able to see his face.

Sister Khadija's opening argument—which is mostly about how I'm an unrepentant perp who screwed Noor over—passes in a blur.

Then Martin stands up and talks about my history, Ama's death, my friendship with Noor. The jury watches Martin as attentively as they did Khadija and Mr. Mahoney. I try not to stare at them. If I were up there deciding someone's future, I wouldn't want that person making me sweat.

"My client has a drug problem." Martin's black suit and dark blue tie make him look almost somber as he speaks. "For which he should receive treatment. But the bulk of the drugs found in his vehicle were under Ms. Riaz's seat. Beneath Ms. Riaz's backpack."

What the hell?

Noor's back stiffens. Khadija puts a calming hand on her wrist, but she stares straight ahead, expressionless.

"The state will make the case that my client confessed to his alleged crimes while speaking to the police," Martin says to the jury. "But I submit that Ms. Riaz took advantage of her long years of friendship in an attempt to get Salahudin Malik to take the blame. That she manipulated a boy who had just lost his mother into being part of her money-making scheme."

Noor turns to me and her anger is pure and white-hot.

"Martin," I hiss at him. "You said you wouldn't pin it on her—"

"My job is to defend you, Salahudin," he whispers as the judge riffles through a stack of papers. "Even if that means defending you from yourself. Let me do my job."

Ortega says something to Mr. Mahoney now, and I've watched enough *Judge Judy* to know that causing a ruckus while the judge is speaking is a stupid idea.

I glance at Noor, swallowing at the sight of the fury in her eyes.

I don't look away. *You think I can't fix this,* I think, *but I can. I will. I swear it.*

The day after opening arguments, evidence is presented and witnesses are called. It goes on forever, it feels like, because Mr. Mahoney, Khadija, and Martin all have a billion questions.

Oluchi, Noor's boss at the hospital, appears as a character witness. Mr. Mahoney tries to get her to say that it's possible Noor could have stolen medicine without anyone the wiser. Oluchi doesn't fall for it, though.

"How many times do I have to tell you 'no'?" she finally says. "Noor Riaz had no access to any pharmaceuticals. She is a great hospital aide. One day, she'll make a great doctor."

Officer Ortiz, who searched Noor, testifies, along with Officer Marks. Ortiz is pretty straightforward, but Marks gets on my—and Khadija's—last nerve.

"How would you describe Ms. Riaz when you first pulled her out of the car?" Mahoney asks Marks.

"Evasive," Marks says. The microphone whines unpleasantly as he speaks. "She was definitely hiding something."

Khadija sighs, and even Martin rolls his eyes.

"Objection, Your Honor," Khadija says. "Speculation—"

"Sustained. The facts, officer."

Soon enough, the only two people left to testify are Noor and me—and she's first. I didn't expect her to take the witness stand. She likes public speaking as much as I like the laundry room.

But Noor is calm when the judge calls her up. She looks comfortable in the black suit jacket she's wearing over a pale pink shirt. Through Khadija's questions about school, grades, and her home life, Noor is beautifully composed.

"How long have you known Salahudin Malik?"

"Since I was six," Noor says. "We met in first grade. I didn't speak any English and he was the only kid who didn't seem to mind."

"Would you say you were best friends?"

"Your Honor." Mr. Mahoney stands—probably because he hasn't said anything in at least thirty seconds and misses the sound of his own voice. "Relevance of this line of questioning?"

"I'm establishing the relationship between my client and the defendant, Your Honor," Khadija says smoothly.

"I'll allow it," Ortega says.

"We were best friends." Noor goes on to tell the story of the arrest from her point of view. Mahoney picks at her—asking about the bruises and cuts on her face the night of the arrest. Asking if I was abusive. Asking who her abuser is.

Noor says again that it wasn't me who hurt her. But she doesn't elaborate. Judge Ortega doesn't make her. It's the only time during the questioning that she's visibly nervous.

It makes me hate Riaz all over again.

When Noor finally sits down, she exhales, long and slow.

"You were perfect," Khadija murmurs.

Noor's attention drifts to me, a car slipping over the double line to a place it shouldn't go. She faces front again quickly, but not before I see her eyes.

I didn't spot it when she was up there. But I do now. Her rage, her defiance—it isn't chained anymore. Now it's free and channeled into pure intention. She's angry. And she's not going down without fighting.

If I had any right, I'd be proud of her.

"You're up, Salahudin," Martin whispers. "Are you ready?"

I don't look him in the eye when I nod. If he knew what I was going to do, he'd never let me testify.

But he said it himself: *Short of drastic intervention? Noor Riaz is going to prison.* This is my drastic intervention.

Be brave. I find my courage in the memory of Noor raging at me, spilling her anger like venom. I deserved it. And it doesn't change that I love her. Nothing she could do would change that.

What has changed is that I don't expect forgiveness. Not anymore.

The judge calls my name. It sounds like it's coming through a tunnel. I take deep breaths. *Five seconds in. Seven seconds out.* A memory ambles to the forefront of my mind: A white room with stickers of orange fish on the walls, the crunch of paper on the chair beneath me. Dr. Ellis on a stool, and Ama with one warm hand on my chest, the other on my back.

"Like this?" she asked Dr. Ellis, who nodded.

"*Okay, Putar.*" Ama smiled at me so that I knew something was right with the world, even if everything in my head was a mess.

"*Breathe. Five seconds in, Salahudin. Seven seconds out.*"

The little boy in me wonders about her as I make my way up to the witness stand. Wonders if she's watching from somewhere. If she's with me. Or if I'm alone.

"Do you swear under penalty of perjury that the evidence you give shall be the truth, the whole truth, and nothing but the truth?"

They don't say "so help you God" like I think they will. But I say it in my head, for Ama.

"I do."

The judge nods. "Then let's begin."

CHAPTER 58

Noor

Sister Khadija was confident the whole trial. Shoulders straight. Voice clear. But where she seemed to wear her mood most obviously was with her hijabs.

"Dark red for when it's time to fight," she told me this morning on the way to court. "Purple for when I need to command. And red, white, and blue—"

"For 'Murica?"

"For victory," Khadija said.

She wears it today. The colors melt into each other, the blue matching her dark eyeliner.

But when Salahudin gets up to the witness stand, Khadija doesn't look victorious. She looks worried. Shafiq, behind us in the gallery, reaches forward. A touch on her shoulder, as if to say *I'm here.*

As Salahudin states his basic information, I think about my family. I make up things about them in my head: My father had kind eyes that were round like mine. He sang me old Punjabi songs when I couldn't sleep. My mother had long hair that hung down to her waist in a thick braid. She taught me how to play Ludo, and Snakes and Ladders.

Just stories. Made-up memories. I don't know anything about my parents. What were their hopes for me? What did they dream?

Not this. My face gets hot. Maybe they're watching from some-where. Looking down and wondering what happened.

I leave the past behind so I can listen to Salahudin. He tells the court how long he's known me in that deep, sure voice that only now seems to fit his tall frame.

"I have a statement I'd—I'd like to read. If that's okay."

Salahudin swallows. His lawyer, Martin, raises his eyebrows.

"Mr. Malik, we can get to that," Martin says. "Let's talk about the night in quest—"

"I'd really like to read the statement." Salahudin pulls out a folded piece of paper from his suit pocket. "It will save a lot of time. Everyone's time."

Salahudin looks pointedly at the clock. It's 4:15 p.m. Court is usually over by four. It's been a long day.

"Mr. Malik," Judge Ortega says. "Answer the question your lawyer is asking."

"Please—will you just listen?" Salahudin pushes. His voice isn't so steady now.

Judge Ortega sighs. "Mr. Chan," he says, "do you need a moment with your client?"

"I started selling drugs a few weeks after my mother passed away." Salahudin opens his paper and starts reading. "After—"

"Objection," Martin says. "Perhaps my client doesn't realize—"

Ortega shakes his head. "Now he's got my interest. Let him make his statement, counsel," he says. "Go on, Mr. Malik."

"After Ama died, I realized we were going to lose the motel she'd poured her whole life into. I felt awful. I didn't save her from her illness. So I thought I could at least save the motel. That's why I started selling drugs. But it was a bad reason. I should have accepted that sometimes in life you lose things. Parents. Places." He stops. "Friends," he says after a long pause. "The night I was arrested, I had all of my stash on me. None of that belonged to Noor Riaz. It all belonged to me.

"I didn't tell Noor I was selling drugs. She didn't know I was selling drugs. I panicked because I knew if I was taken out of the car and searched, I'd be in trouble. I handed her whatever was in my pockets, and told her to shove it under her seat. Even then, she didn't know what I was handing her. There's no way she could tell. It wasn't until—" He sighs. "Until the officers searched my car that she finally realized what had happened. What—what I did."

His hair falls into his eyes as he looks down at his paper. His hands tremble. I look down and find that mine do, too.

"I chose to sell drugs," he says. "That was my decision and my mistake. The night we were arrested, Noor Riaz made a mistake, too." He glances at the jury. "It wasn't selling drugs. Her mistake was trusting a friend she'd known since childhood. Her mistake was—was thinking that she knew me. Believing the best of me. Caring about me. She was wrong—she shouldn't have trusted me. She shouldn't have thought the best of me. But that's not a mistake she should go to prison for."

He clears his throat loudly, almost angrily. "That's it. That's the statement. Thanks for—for listening."

The courtroom is quiet. Then, Martin, Mr. Mahoney, and Khadija are all talking at once, each one trying to speak over the others.

Judge Ortega stares at Salahudin for a second. Almost surprised. Then he taps his gavel.

"Counsel," Ortega says. "My chambers."

Salahudin stays in the witness stand, unsure of what to do. He folds and unfolds his paper until the bailiff tells him he can sit. *Without our lawyers between us, I could reach out if I wanted to. Touch him.*

But I'm too stunned. I'm angry at him, but also grateful. I don't know what to think. What to feel. For the first time in weeks, I just want him to look at me. But he doesn't.

The chamber doors open. Martin's face is pale. Mr. Mahoney looks grumpy. And Khadija—I can't tell what she's thinking.

"In light of Ms. Riaz's testimony," Judge Ortega says when he's back on the bench, "as well as Mr. Malik's statement, the DA has decided to drop the charges against Noor Riaz. Closing statements in the case of the People of the State of California versus Salahudin Malik will go on in the morning as planned. Adjourned."

He bangs his gavel and I stare at Khadija.

"What does—does that mean?"

She grabs me in a hug. That's when I realize that she's crying. Which confuses me, because if she's crying, then this probably isn't good.

"What does it mean, Khadija?"

"It means," she says, "that you're getting the hell out of Juniper and becoming a doctor, Noor Riaz."

She turns to Shafiq, and Salahudin and I lock eyes. He looks lost. Scared. I still don't know what to think or say. So I let Auntie speak for me.

"If we are lost, God is like water," I whisper, "finding the unknowable path when we cannot."

Something flickers across his eyes. But I don't have time to interpret it. Khadija is ushering me out of the room and into the hallway, and I look back at Salahudin just in time for the courtroom doors to swing shut.

PART VI

—Even losing you (the joking voice, a gesture
I love) I shan't have lied. It's evident
the art of losing's not too hard to master
though it may look like (*Write* it!) like disaster.

—*Elizabeth Bishop,*
"One Art"

CHAPTER 59

Misbah

February, then

How quickly a body can betray you. It will carry you your whole life and suddenly—finished. It will carry your soul no longer.

Did the soul grow too weary for the body? Did the body grow too weary for the soul? Was it a betrayal of organs and tissues, sinews and cells?

Or was the betrayal that I did not care for my body the way I should have? That when I knew my body was screaming for aid, I ignored it, in service of what the soul wanted, which was the comfort of routine and familiarity.

Who was the traitor, truly? The body? Or the soul?

I was not in Pakistan for my baba's death, or my mother's. I never saw their graves. I regretted it, for how could I expect my son to read prayers at my grave and offer my soul comfort if I did not do the same for my parents?

Where was Toufiq?

These were matters he would understand. Where was he?

I remembered my baba, then. Oh, Baba—I wish I could see your face once more. I am afraid, Baba.

Where was my body?

Where was my soul?

"Auntie Misbah."

I opened my eyes to see my child, my girl. I needed to speak with her. I needed to tell her she deserved better than that villain she called Chachu.

"Pani." I asked for water so I could speak clearly. There was so much to say: That I loved her. That I should have done more for her. That I wanted to be a mother to her and a father. A grandfather and a grandmother. A sister. A brother. I wanted to be everything that she had lost, and I tried, but this body . . . This damn body.

Noor said Salahudin was coming. My son. I wished I could tell her how he looked at me when he was born. I had never been closer to heaven than I was then, when the fabric between this world and the next was breached for one ineffable moment as I gazed into my child's eyes for the first time.

A strange sound filled my head, loud and unrelenting. Like a flood, like the rushing wings of a flock of starlings. They landed near the canals by my baba's house sometimes.

"Das pathar thoreingeh. Ake pathar katcha. Hiran ka bacha. Hiran gaya pani meh . . ."

An old nursery rhyme.

Ten rocks we shall break

One rock soft and raw

Child of a deer!

She escaped into the water.

Escape, Noor. Escape like the deer.

"You don't belong in Juniper, meri dhi," I whispered.

Her hands were strong, warm. I thought: She'll make a good doctor one day, my girl will. But she has to get out, first. She has to know her worth.

"Noor," I whispered. I must tell her. I must. "Noor."

It meant "light," her name. Had I ever told her that? How could I ever make up for all the things I should have done but would never do now?

Baba. Help me. Baba, I am afraid.

"Noor. Noor." You are light. You are goodness. You are better than what you've been given. I should have done more for you. I should have done more. Oh, forgive me, my child. Here as I go finally to God. Please—please—please—

"Forgive—"

Me.

CHAPTER 60

Sal

July, now

The day after the charges against Noor are dropped, I'm found guilty on all counts.

The verdict is delivered in a perfunctory way. Neither the bailiff, the judge, nor any member of the jury looks at me.

I knew it was coming. But my stomach drops out anyway. Part of me still hoped the jury would go easy on me.

At least Noor is all right. Free. Away from Riaz and on her way to the life she should have.

Judge Ortega sentences me right after the verdict, at Martin's request. My lawyer switched gears as fast as I did, focused now on getting me as little time as possible.

As the judge peers down at his laptop, I wonder if he's saved any lives. I wonder if he's taken any.

Behind me, Abu coughs. Imam Shafiq is at his side.

"I've been a judge for twenty-five years, Mr. Malik," Judge Ortega says. "I've seen people lie to me, lie to themselves, lie to their counsel—all to get out of getting jail time. It's rare—exceedingly rare—to witness such a clear admission of guilt as I heard from you. The fact that you did so even though denying the charges could have saved you from prison makes your case even more interesting. Altruism isn't something I see often, in or out of the courtroom."

He steeples his hands, and his jaw hardens—just a touch. Enough to make me fear whatever's coming.

From the moment Noor and I got arrested, I felt simultaneously angry at Ama for dying and relieved that she couldn't see any of this. Now I wish she was here, somewhere. Standing with Abu, or even back at the motel, waiting to hear word. Just to know that she was in the world, listening, hoping, praying for me—it would be a comfort in this moment in which I feel so alone, like a kid lost in the dark.

"The charges against you are very serious," Judge Ortega says. "The DA is recommending you serve the maximum sentence of seven years and eight months behind bars. However . . ." He considers. "I see great promise in you, Mr. Malik."

His words hit me like lightning. Ama said almost the exactly same thing to me months ago. Is it a coincidence? Maybe.

Or maybe not.

"With regard to the possession of fentanyl for sale, the court suspends your sentence," Judge Ortega says. "With regard to the transportation and sale of fentanyl, the court suspends your sentence. With regard to the possession of OxyContin for sale, the court suspends your sentence. With regard to the transportation and sale of OxyContin, the court suspends your sentence. With regard to the possession of heroin for sale, the court suspends your sentence."

Martin is nodding beside me, thoughtful. Then he glances up.

"With regard to the transportation and sale of heroin." Judge

Ortega looks at me now, gaze hard. "The court sentences you to a minimum of five years, three years served in state prison, and two in mandatory supervision."

Moments later, the judge has vacated the courtroom. Martin speaks.

"—datory supervision is like probation. The three years will mean eighteen months served as long as you keep your head down. You're going to be fine, Salahudin."

It could have been almost eight years, I tell myself. *Eight damn years. And you'll be out in as little as eighteen months.*

"Salahudin, are you okay? I know it seems like a long time."

Martin thinks I'm not speaking because I'm worried or scared or angry.

But I'm none of those things. I'm thankful. And for the first time since the arrest, I'm at peace.

CHAPTER 61

Noor

September, now

LOS ANGELES, CALIFORNIA

This is what I know about my roommate.

    1. Her name is Neelum.

    2. She is half Indian and half Korean.

    3. She brought a microwave.

When I walk into my dorm room at UCLA, she's there alone. Which is weird. Everyone else is here with their parents and an SUV-load of stuff. Comforters, bikes, skateboards. One guy helps his daughter carry in a set of turntables.

I have one suitcase and a Target gift card that Khadija gave me at the Friarsfield bus station.

"Just order everything you need," she said. "You don't need to be lugging ten tons of stuff with you on the bus." She gave me the longest hug. I held her tight, trying to put all my gratitude into it. *Thank you for talking to the dean for me. Thank you for helping me get work study. Thank you for loving me. Thank you for guiding me.*

The dorm room is split evenly. Each side has a raised bed, a desk, a closet, and a giant window. Neelum has claimed her side with a *Crown of Fates* poster and some tour posters. The National. Kendrick Lamar. BTS. Little May.

As I walk in, she's filling her desk shelf with books. I've seen many of them before. In Salahudin's backpack, or on his desk at the Clouds' Rest. His were library books, but the titles are the same. *This Is How You Lose the Time War* and *War Girls*. *Legend* and *They Both Die at the End* and *The Beautiful*.

Neelum turns. Takes in my lone suitcase as I notice her R2-D2 socks. Eyes the electric tape around my Docs as I admire the blue in her short, dark hair.

Her gaze lands on my shirt, black, with what looks like black paint dripping down it.

"Jónsi?" she says. "The *Go* album is legendary."

I nod and switch off my music.

"What are you listening to?" she asks almost hesitantly.

"Um . . . it's called 'Broadripple Is Burning' by—"

"Margo & the Nuclear So and So's," she says, almost reverently. "Can I see?"

I hold out my phone to her and she thumbs through my playlist, muttering to herself. "Aqualung . . . Hozier . . . 2Pac . . . Kendrick . . . Tori Amos . . ."

Neelum glances up. "I realize we've just met and this might cement me in your brain as a loser for the rest of the year," she says. "But I have two tickets to the Los Angeles Philharmonic performing all the music from *Crown of Fates*. Only it's tonight and *technically* we have our dorm mixer thing—"

"Is that a serious question?" I say. "*Crown of Fates*. All the way."

Neelum grabs me by the shoulders. "I have been waiting for

you," she says. "My whole life. Tell me you're an English major."

I laugh. "Molecular bio."

"Do you read, at least?" She looks worried now, like she knew I was too good to be true and I'm about to sprout a second head that will yell science facts at her all day long.

"Not really," I say. "But . . ." I glance over her shoulder at her books. "Maybe I can start. Could you recommend something? Something that's . . . an escape?"

She scans her books and pulls out one with a black cover. "*The Bird King*," she says. "By G. Willow Wilson. Total escape."

I read the inside flap of the book. It makes me think of Salahudin. I almost put it down. But I make myself smile at Neelum, who watches me anxiously.

"Perfect," I say, and nod at Neelum's *Crown of Fates* poster. "So who's gonna die in the last season, do you think?"

CHAPTER 62

Sal

October, now

FRIARSFIELD, CALIFORNIA

The casual way in which people touch is the worst part of prison. A guard grabbing me to direct me into a different line. A rando brushing past me to get to the cafeteria faster. A cellmate shoving me if he feels like I'm in the way.

But the language I've always hated about myself has its uses. When two guys try to steal my mattress pad while my back is turned, I feel them behind me and clock one of them. The next day, when the guy I didn't punch tries to ambush me in the bathroom, I turn on him before he can make a fist.

I didn't want to hit either of them. But after that, the other guys in the group cell leave me be. It's unsettling how violence, too, is a language. One that Riaz spoke. One that I speak now.

Abu makes sure there's money in my commissary account, but I don't call him and he doesn't visit. I don't want him to see the razor wire, the guard towers, the words CALIFORNIA DEPARTMENT OF CORRECTIONS emblazoned on my shirt. Imam Shafiq said on the phone that Abu got an apartment and has been attending his meetings. But that it's tough going. This place would be too much for him.

Sometimes it's too much for me. Control—choice—they're a distant dream here. Occasionally, I find them in small rituals. Working out. Praying. Walking circles in the yard, missing the smell of the Mojave wind and the way the Sierra Nevada transformed every sunset into a poem.

Mostly, I count the hours until I'll get out.

Three weeks into my sentence, I get a visitor. I assume it will be Imam Shafiq, as he's the only one who sees me regularly. But when I get to the visiting booth, I'm so surprised to see the gray-haired woman waiting for me that it takes me a moment to place her.

"Dr. Ellis," I say over the phone to my childhood pediatrician. "Hi?"

"Salahudin," she says. "Thank you for meeting with me."

"Not much else to do in here, Dr. Ellis. How are you? How's your wife?"

"I called you after we spoke at the hospital." She ignores my questions.

But the very next day I got arrested and my phone was taken by the police.

"I'm afraid I wasn't very clear with you when I saw you that day, Salahudin. I apologize for that. It's been bothering me. I wanted to come and explain." She falls silent, but not the kind that invites a response, so I wait.

"Before your mother passed away," Dr. Ellis says, "she asked me for some advice about someone she was worried about, and in the course of that conversation, you came up. I asked if your mother planned to share your unique medical history with you.

She said she did not. That concerned me, because your mother indicated you'd had some issues with touch over the years. But you've never seen a therapist regularly. Salahudin, when you were very young—"

"Stop."

She does so immediately, like I've pressed a mute button.

"My mom wasn't always right," I say, trying to keep the bitterness from my voice. "She messed up a lot. More than I ever realized when she was alive. But I think she was right about not sharing . . . whatever it is you want to share."

"Remembering can be the first step to healing."

The smell of the laundry floods my brain, and for a second I'm light-headed. Then I pull it together and look her in the eyes.

"My body remembers that something bad happened, Dr. Ellis," I say quietly. "My mind doesn't need to."

The words open a door in my head, and the blank room that's squatted there for so long starts to crumble away, giving up its space to other, more important things. Like forgiveness for my ama. And forgiveness for myself.

"Of course." Dr. Ellis glances away. "If you don't wish to discuss it, you shouldn't have to. You can seek somatic therapy, perhaps. Or do breath work or meditation. Because you're right. The body remembers." Her kind eyes seek mine. "But the body heals, too, Salahudin. Promise me you'll give yours that chance."

I don't know if I will. If I can. But she looks like Ama in that moment. Hopeful. So I nod.

"I promise."

A month in, and I'm still in the group cell. Any day, I'm supposed to get my permanent cell assignment, but I want to crawl up the walls out of boredom, and to escape the peculiar despair of being around so many people for so long without a moment alone.

That's when the first book arrives.

It's brand new from some online mega chain—we're not allowed to get used books in here. It's called *The Bird King* by G. Willow Wilson. The first line is *"Hassan was deep in prayer."*

There's no return address or note. Shafiq tells me neither he nor Khadija sent it. And it wouldn't occur to Abu. It might be Ashlee or Mrs. Michaels, but I doubt it.

Which leaves one person.

But I don't dare to hope.

I want to read the book in a day, but I take my time with it. October is easing into November and the cold makes everyone ill-tempered. The book is an escape to another time, another life. I savor it over three weeks, and just as I begin to mourn the fact that it's almost finished, another book arrives.

This one is called *A Monster Calls* by Patrick Ness. I crack it open to the first page. *"The monster shows up just after midnight. As they do."* I finish it in a day because it's short and beautiful. Then I re-read it. Ama would have loved it.

If I were at home, I would have bawled while reading the end of *A Monster Calls*. But I've had to learn to control my face here. My body. So I read it with dry eyes. Still, I don't stop thinking about it for two weeks—when the next book comes. *West with the Night* by Beryl Markham. I've just cracked it open and read the first line— *"How is it possible to bring order out of memory?"*—when the CO enters the group cell.

"Time to move," he says to me. "Get your stuff."

If the CO slapped cuffs on me right now, they'd slip right off, I'm so nervous. People in here have told horror stories of old cellmates: guys who wake up screaming in the middle of the night; guys who want to kill you; guys who talk constantly.

I follow the CO down a long hallway. A few of the inmates who have become not friends, exactly, but friendly, nod as I pass. All of them are Muslim, because the one thing movies get right about jail is that people stick with their own.

I say a prayer Ama taught me in my head, enunciating each word and trying to find the power in it. But I abandon it halfway through. Prayer didn't help Ama. Why would it help me?

Some days in here are like this. No matter what I tell myself, I feel like a failure. My abu is fighting his battle alone, because of me. My ama lost the thing she poured her soul into, because of me. The girl I loved—still love—has moved on. The thoughts circle and repeat, an evil refrain.

I can't escape my own head.

When the CO finally stops outside a cell, I make sure my RKF is in place before stepping inside.

Only to find my new cellmate standing up in surprise, smiling.

"Ah shit," he says. "I guess they got you, kid."

I struggle to remember where I've met him. Then I see the tattoo on his arm. *Ecclesiastes 1:14.*

"Santiago," I say. "Right?"

"You remembered," he says. "Guess you didn't remember what I said about the cops, though."

The CO locks the door with a thud. I laugh. "Yeah." I unpack my books. "I should have listened to you. I'm Salahudin. Sal."

"'Sal'? No way." He gets back in his bunk. "You make people call you by your name. If they can say Santiago, Alexander, Demetrius, and"—he holds his arm up—"Ecclesiastes, they can say Salahudin."

"My mom used to say that."

"Smart lady."

The anger I'm so used to flares in my mind. "I don't know about that." I eye his tattoo. "I meant to look that up."

"It's from the Bible," Santiago says. *"I have seen all the things that are done under the sun; all of them are meaningless, a chasing after the wind."*

"That sounds grim."

Santiago shrugs. "Most religious books are, right? Doom and hellfire and all that. But this stuck with me. My dad was a minister. He'd say the whole Book of Ecclesiastes was about how we put so much value into material things—possessions or places. Shit that isn't permanent. But to have meaning in your life, you have to find it in something greater."

"Like if you don't have God, what's the point?"

"Except I'm not actually religious," Santiago says. "I'm agnostic. You ever listen to Johnny Cash?"

I smile, thinking of Noor, and nod.

"He's got a song he sang with U2," Santiago says. "Old as hell.

Older than you! It's called 'The Wanderer.' It's a postapocalyptic thing. Anyway, it was based on Ecclesiastes. All about this guy looking for meaning in everything and not finding it—"

Santiago keeps talking, but my mind has slowed, stopped, fixated on what he said first. "The Wanderer." Of all the songs he could have mentioned, what are the chances that he would mention that one?

I think of Noor the morning Ama died, with "The Wanderer" spilling from her headphones.

Listening to it together at the funeral.

Her asking me if I remembered the song when I told her how much money I needed for the motel.

Seeing the tattoo on Santiago, months ago.

And somehow miraculously finding him again, only for him to tell me the one thing I desperately needed to hear. The thing Noor was trying to tell me. The thing Ama was trying to tell me.

Each moment joins the next, a murmuration of starlings exploding out of the rafters of my mind and into the heavens, moving as one, revealing a greater purpose.

"There's more to life than the things in front of you," Santiago says, and now, finally, I listen. "Sometimes we hold on to things we shouldn't. People. Places. Emotions. We try to control all of it, when what we should be doing is trusting in something bigger."

"'If we are lost, God is like water, finding the unknowable path when we cannot,'" I mutter.

"Who said that?" Santiago asks.

I smile. "A smart lady."

That night, I consider my anger at Ama, and how long I've held on to it. Rage can fuel you. But grief gnaws at you slow, a termite nibbling at your soul until you're a whisper of what you used to be.

I didn't want to face the grief. I still don't. But I think I have to try.

I start to write. I write to escape. I write to find that greater meaning Santiago spoke of. And I write to understand. To forgive. Snippets first, then sentences and paragraphs and pages.

The sky over Lahore was purple as a gossip's tongue the day my mother told me I would wed . . .

The fortune teller beckoned me to sit across a rickety wooden table and took my hands . . .

"The Clouds' Rest," I whispered to him. "We'll call it the Clouds' Rest Inn Motel."

I mine my brain for everything I know about Ama, everything Abu told me, every anecdote she shared, and weave it together to conjure up the things she didn't share. I tell her story—my story— Abu's story. Our story. Day after day. Week after week. Month after month.

But as I get to the end of that story, as I find the words to finally speak of Ama's death, of her last word—*forgive*—I realize something.

The story isn't over quite yet.

CHAPTER 63

Noor

I don't talk about Salahudin. For weeks I'm angry. Angry at what he put me through. Angry at how he managed to destroy his own life. My anger is fresh and cold and pale. Some days, I think I'll carry it forever.

I tell myself that Salahudin Malik and I are done.

But I've never been great at staying angry. My memory eats at the edges of it. His rage at Chachu, like the guy in Okkervil River's "Black," wanting nothing more than to destroy the man who hurt me. How he looked at me when I laughed. The strange, wonderful club I had with him and Misbah Auntie.

One day at the dining hall, "With or Without You" by U2 comes on, tinny and distant. It was never my favorite U2 song because, like, pick a side. Do you want to be with her or not?

But now I get it.

Soon, the anger fades. Faster than I think it will. Questions replace it. Is he sleeping okay? Is he bored in prison? Is he safe? Has he changed? Does he think about me?

That's when I start sending him books.

It's also when I start to imagine him beside me. Walking with me through the Los Angeles sunshine on the way to work study or my Organic Chem class. Whispering to me as I write my first

English essay and during my first rock concert with Neelum.

He's beside me through Christmas break with Khadija and Shafiq, though they never bring him up. He studies with me under the shadow of Royce Hall in the spring, and keeps me company through the summer, during my internship at a lab on campus.

When Khadija tells me that Chachu has been arrested on domestic violence charges after hitting Brooke, Salahudin's holding my hands, telling me it's okay that I'm crying and don't know why. The next day, he's there as I walk into UCLA's counseling center, as I make my first appointment with a therapist.

And when I learn my uncle doesn't get jail time—only probation and anger management—it's Salahudin who takes me to a kickboxing class, and urges me on as I take out my anger on a bag.

But I don't write to the real Salahudin. He doesn't write me. I don't visit. He doesn't call.

You're done with him. He's done with you.

I think about the terrible things I said to him the day he told me I got into UCLA. I think about how it's not just me who has to forgive him, but he who needs to forgive me.

I meet boys who like me. Who I like back. I go to dinners, coffee dates, movies. It's never enough to make me forget him.

One night deep into sophomore year, I drop into bed with one of Neelum's playlists blasting. "Turn" by the Wombats comes on. It's about a guy who doesn't know what he wants in a relationship. He just knows he misses the other person in it. The song starts out sort of sly and then shifts, hitting a crescendo. The singer wants his lost love back, come what may.

Somewhere between the first listen and the tenth, I realize that

I don't want to be with any other boy. I never did. The only person I want is Salahudin. The only arms I want holding me are his. The only lips I want on mine are his. The only voice I want to hear close to my ear is his.

Salahudin's body is the one I want to explore. His laugh the one I want to share.

But you're done with him.

Right?

CHAPTER 64

Salahudin

Juniper's graveyard is quiet and empty, but somehow not creepy. The groundskeeper sees me and asks me if I need help finding someone.

But I know where she is. Where she's been. Waiting.

Her stone gleams in the winter sunshine, the area around it free of weeds and scrub. A single sunflower, still bright, sits atop the grass. Abu comes twice a week. He told me when he drove me home from jail a few days ago. Today, I asked him to let me visit alone.

MISBAH MALIK

MOTHER. WIFE. FRIEND.

WE BELONG TO GOD

AND TO GOD WE SHALL RETURN.

I sit at the foot of her grave and recite every prayer she taught me and a few I learned in prison. Then I take out the thermos I brought with me, and the mugs, and I pour us each a cup of tea.

Her tea steams beside her headstone, and I sip my own slowly. The warmth of the mug, the smell of cardamom, reminds me of her hands reaching for mine, always so careful, so gentle. I close my eyes and let myself remember.

"Forgive me, Ama. I took too long," I finally say. "There's a lot to catch up on."

When I'd had a bad day or week, when I was lost or just sad for the reasons I didn't understand, Ama knew. She'd sit on my bed with her tea, or perch on a stool in the kitchen. "Bol," she'd say. *Speak.*

So even though I am certain that somewhere, she already knows, I tell her everything, from the day she passed away to yesterday, when I sat down for the first time with a psychologist who Dr. Ellis recommended.

My teacup is empty by the time I'm done, and the mountainous horizon fades to a blaze of desert scarlet, like someone's scattered poppies across the sky. The wind rises, still chilly. I forgot my jacket. I should go.

"I'll be back," I promise Ama. "With Abu. He's doing good, Ama. He even started working again. You'd be proud of him."

I'm closing up the thermos and getting to my feet when I feel someone behind me.

"I—I have a song I've been saving for today." Noor's voice is hoarse, almost a whisper. "Do you want to hear?"

I nod, but don't turn, because I'm afraid that, like a dream, she'll disappear the second I look closely. I feel her breath, light on my neck, and then the cool plastic of an earbud.

A guitar strums, a man sings, and it's not a Noor song, and it's not a Salahudin song, either. It's an us song. About brightness and beginnings and love and hope and everything else I used to think I didn't deserve.

She comes around in front of me now, hair flying in a dark cloud around her face. Her hand is soft against my skin, and she brushes tears away. I do the same for her and we lean forward, forehead to forehead, breathing each other in.

"Forgive me?" I whisper.

"Always," she says. "Forgive me?"

"Depends," I say, "on whether you'll stop making fun of my jokes."

"Ugh. You didn't learn any wit in prison?"

"Don't you mean in . . . the *puni*tentiary?"

She laughs, high and beautiful, and then she's kissing me, and I'm kissing her, and there's no monsters lurking, no pain, no anger. Just the euphoria of reunion, of rediscovery. The sense that anything is possible because despite everything, we are here, together, with each other. We survived.

When we finally break apart, I pull a piece of paper from my pocket.

"I've got something I've wanted to show you," I say. "Do you remember that day at Imam Shafiq's, when you found out about UCLA?"

Noor closes her eyes, pained. "I'm so sorry—"

"No," I say. "Don't apologize. It's just, you told me about Ama's last word. Prison is boring as shit, so I was thinking about it a lot. Wondering if you maybe misunderstood her. And . . . well—here."

I hand her the paper, dated a few months earlier, and watch as she reads.

Dear Salahudin,

Thank you for your letter. I had worried that when I came to visit you, I upset you.

To answer your question, on the day that your childhood came up, your mother had actually come to speak to me about her concerns about another young person, whom she was worried was being abused. This was when she was quite ill. She was in deep distress about the situation and wished to take action. However, her illness progressed rapidly afterward.

She was a good woman, your mother. I miss her.

With best regards,
Ellen Ellis

Noor shakes her head. "I—I don't understand—"

"Ama knew Riaz was hurting you, Noor." I put my hands to her cheeks. "But she didn't have time to do anything about it. It was eating at her. Do you see? When she was dying, she wasn't telling you to forgive. She was asking you for forgiveness."

CHAPTER **65**

Misbah

In this, an endless whiteness, I feel my son. I feel Salahudin. He is a heavy presence, weighed down by regret. But then he begins to speak to me. His voice is deeper now, thoughtful and measured. A bit like his father's—but tempered by an undercurrent of calm. As if there is a tall, strong oak at his core, anchoring him to the earth.

My son speaks, and my own spirit trills as he unburdens his. A mother carries her child's innocence in her memory. No matter who they become. We carry our hopes and dreams for them and such things are woven into our souls as God is woven into the fibers of this earth.

My son is alone for a time.

And then he is not.

As he is a steady oak, Noor Riaz is a breeze, warm and powerful and gentle, come to weave her song with his.

But I cringe away from her, and the whiteness brightens. I did not help her. I did not save her. I could not set it right.

As soon as the thought forms, I feel her love for me, the love of a daughter. Pure and kind as a desert morning, steady as the beat of a dholak. I feel her forgiveness.

Oh, my children. My little ones. I have such dreams for you both. The world is right, finally. For here, in this sweet, deep night, I see now that you were always two halves of a whole, two hands interlaced, two voices raised to a melody sung in time.

Bear witness, then, to the beauty of each other's lives. Bear witness and burn bright as one.

The white around me dims, a gentle embrace. My baba, his dark eyes kind, steps out of the blue. He offers a hand.

"Come now, little butterfly," he says. "Time to sleep."

—30—

ACKNOWLEDGMENTS

My deepest appreciation to:

SLM, for friendship on a lonely playground long ago.

Mama and Daddy, who clawed out a life from the dust of a barren place, and made it beautiful.

Kashi, for knowing.

Mer, for more than I could ever express. Boon, for the music that lights the way.

Alexandra Machinist, who said, "Write it."

Lauren DeStefano, who got me to the finish line.

At Penguin, Jen Loja, Jen Klonsky, Ruta Rimas, Casey McIntyre, Shanta Newlin, Felicity Vallance, and Carmela Iaria, a dream team I am thankful for every day.

My squad of brown radness: Samira Ahmed, Aisha Saeed, and Sajidah Ali. My second family: Nicola Yoon, Abigail Wen, Renée Ahdieh, and Adam Silvera. My sisters in faith: Tala Abbasi, Heelah Saleem, Lilly Tahir, Haina Karim, Nyla Ibrahim, Sana Malik, Zuha Warraich, Tahereh Mafi, and Somaiya Daud. My dear friends: Marie Lu, Leigh Bardugo, and Victoria Aveyard.

YAC, taken too soon.

The lawyers, doctors, and police officers who patiently answered my questions: Ben Azar, Dr. Monika Goyal, Dr. Scott Gremillion, Dr. Ajit Mahapatra, Cpt. Saul Jaeger, and the MVPD. Michael Shepard and Sonia de Assis, for helping me understand the history and meaning of Ecclesiastes. Daniel José Older for the chat about EMTs and Narcan. Michael Phillips, for answering an email from an old student about a play we read more than twenty years ago. English teachers really are the best.

The many others who consented to interviews but who did not wish to be named. Thank you.

Every artist whose music was mentioned in this book, especially the Smashing Pumpkins for "Bullet with Butterfly Wings," Benjamin Frances Leftwich for "Look Ma!," Anna Leone for "Once," U2 and Johnny Cash for "The Wanderer," the Game for "My Life," Radiohead for "Street Spirit (Fade Out)," Masuma Anwar for "Tainu Ghul Gayaan," the Wombats for "Turn," the Decemberists for "The Beginning Song," and Florence and the Machine for "Shake It Out."

My final thanks, as ever, to Ash-Shaheed, who bears witness to all things.

If you or anyone you know needs help, please contact the organizations below.

The National Domestic Violence Hotline
1-800-799-SAFE (1-800-799-7233)
thehotline.org

National Child Abuse Hotline/Childhelp
1-800-4-A-CHILD (1-800-422-4453)
childhelp.org

National Sexual Assault Hotline
1-800-656-HOPE (1-800-656-4673)
rainn.org

National Network for Immigrant and Refugee Rights
1-510-465-1984
nnirr.org

Children's Defense Fund
1-202-628-8787
childrensdefense.org

Women of Color Network
1-844-962-6462
wocninc.org